NOW

A NOVEL ABOUT
BEING & BECOMING

BY

Stan I.S. Law

INHOUSEPRESS, MONTREAL, CANADA

Cover design and layout by
Bozena Happach

This book is a work of fiction.
Names, characters, titles, places and incidents are either the products of
the author's imagination or are used fictitiously.

Library and Archives Canada Cataloguing in Publication

Law, Stan I. S.
Now : a novel about being & becoming / by Stan I.S. Law.

ISBN 978-0-9780267-7-6

I. Title.

PS8623.A92N68 2010   jC813'.6   C2010-903012-5

Published by
INHOUSEPRESS
http://www.inhousepress.ca

For my Ruth,
Bozena

Content

Part One

LIMBO

"O Baba, the splendour of Maya is deceptive.
The blind man has forgotten the Name.
He is in limbo, neither here nor there."

Sri Guru Granth Sahib

1

The Accident

Ascreech of brakes, a dull thud, then silence.
The lights go out. My car's and the lamppost's. Then my
own. For a moment I'm completely disoriented, then I
begin to see an ocean of stars. Must be lying on my back.
'Why no pain?' I wonder. The other half of my brain answers:
'Post-traumatic shock.' Only I am not in shock at all. I actually
enjoy looking at stars. *Twinkle, twinkle, little star...*

Damn! They'll ruin it all!

The oscillating lights of the ambulance follow the wailing
sirens.

Wheee... wheee... wheee...

Why can't they switch the blasted things off? *The stars are
losing their brightness.* They've arrived, haven't they? God, how
people like noise. Both audio and visual. Noise. Big noise. My
head is splitting. People are running up and down, adding to the
confusion. They're going frantic. All I can see are their shadows
silhouetted against the glaring lights of the cars above me.

"In the ditch! Look in the ditch, George. There's no one in the
car. Not that anyone would have survived it. Lamppost one, Honda
nil."

Not funny. I am just beginning to hurt all over. Then searing
pain hits me right between the eyes. That's where my nose used to
be. I decide to get out and let them do their work. I can also see

better from outside. Everything is sharper, more distinct. And you should see the colours! Even the light from the streetlamps is split into an array of prismatic shades, like sharp rainbows cutting the night air. And speaking of air... it never smelled so good, and so rich in textures. Like summer and autumn and spring all rolled into one. Isn't it winter, out there?

There sure are a lot of vehicles around. An ambulance, two squad cars with at least four cops, and a dozen other vehicles. They must belong to reporters, or just the curious. Others are still coming—they come out of the night to feed on human misery—the usual accident gazers, maybe even some ambulance chasers. You know, young lawyers looking for a case and some money from the insurance. Or from anyone.

Two cops are slapping their holsters. I wonder if they'll draw their guns and do some target practice the way they do on TV down south, in LA, or somewhere. Or spray everyone with pepper spray. They're good at that, lately. Or zap them with their zappers. Or tasers, or something.

It's amazing how fast a crowd can gather, even on the outskirts of town. One moment it's a quiet country lane, well, almost, and the next a veritable country fair. Everyone's talking, gesticulating, pushing to get as close as they can to the scene of the accident.

"Please stay back," a girl says. Her voice is youthful, but it carries authority. "Now, back!" she repeats unnecessarily. People already took a step back, their necks still stretched out like hungry geese. Maybe she's not used to men obeying her.

"Hey, easy!"

That's me. How come I couldn't hear my own voice? I mean with my ears? For a moment I must have inadvertently slipped back into my body. They pulled me, my body, out of the ditch as if they were in a hurry. I wasn't. For as long as I didn't feel any pain, I didn't care if I was in a ditch or in the ambulance. I hope they didn't forget any of my body parts—you know: legs, arms... I seem all disjointed.

All those people...

"Move back, please," says the girl's partner. He backs up his request with a gentle tap on his holster. I wish policemen wouldn't do that. Anyway, the crowd that gathered takes another step back. There must be some thirty or forty people already. Still gawking.

Hey, maybe I'm important? Ha, ha! We all think we are important, but it only shows when we smash into a lamppost. Or slide into a ditch. Nobody wants to be a Nobody. Somebody or not, the pandemonium they make is unbearable.

"I knew this would happen! I knew it!"

"It was only a question of time!" An elderly woman nods her agreement. I wonder what she's doing this far out, at this time of the night, on a night like this. Shouldn't she be at home putting her grandchildren to bed?

"With all the taxes we're paying, they could do a better job." Everybody's a wise guy. Or a wise girl. Woman.

Why do people make such a fuss? Accidents happen all the time. In nature they're called mutations. If it weren't for mutations, there would be no evolution. Only, right now, I seem to be rapidly devolving. My head hurts and I feel woozy. Christ, it hurts. And then it doesn't. In an instant it goes away. The pain, I mean. It doesn't hurt at all. I feel great. Light as a feather. Wow! This is fun!

I see them moving me on the stretcher. Yep! I'm all there. Bloody, twisted, but all there. I wonder why I feel so protective of my body. Ex-body? This, too, is wonderful. They are moving me like a sack of potatoes and I don't feel anything. No pain, not even discomfort. In fact...

In fact, I don't feel anything besides lightness. Except for a feeling of *laissez faire*. A 'let things be' attitude. As if nothing much mattered. From the owner of a vicious headache, I instantly became a bystander. An observer. I seem to be floating about, oh, I don't know, some distance above the crime scene. Only this isn't a crime scene. Except for the cops. They still haven't shot anyone. That's a change. There are now three squad cars. All spinning their violet lights. Only they don't hurt my eyes anymore. I don't care what they spin.

I watch dispassionately as the medics place my body on a portable stretcher and cart it off to an ambulance. Two guys in yellow jerseys outside pushing, two more inside pulling the

stretcher in. I wonder why they bother. As I was saying, I don't
hurt at all. In fact, I feel just fine.

Wheee, wheee, wheee...

The ambulance takes off amid gyrating lights. Good riddance.
Too late I realize that my body is gone. What am I supposed to do
now? I have half-a-mind to speak to the cops and ask them where
they are taking me. My body, I mean. Surely, I have a right to
know? But they seem busy. The tapes are out; they are measuring
the skid marks. Others are snapping pictures with flashlights
galore. Still other officers in blue are taking notes; one is speaking
into a cell phone. She's quite cute, that one. Must be new on the
force. Doesn't look more than eighteen or so. Then I remember
Ruth. Watch it, boy, I tell myself. And anyway, there's not much
you can do without a body. That makes me laugh. Ruth at home, a
cute babe practically all over me, actually all under me, and I have
no body. In fact, she doesn't even know I am here.

That's when it hits me. I'm dead. I'm bloody dead. For crying
out loud, shouldn't somebody say something? A psalm, or sprinkle
some holy water on me? I know I was not a regular churchgoer, but
come on... A bit of Christian charity wouldn't hurt? Forgive and
forget? I think forget is the easy part. Then it strikes me. Do dead
people go to church?

I am dead and nobody knows it. I suppose they all think I'm
still in that body they drove away.

And then it hits me again. Poor Ruth. Poor, darling, little Ruth.
She'll cry. And she did tell me not to take that second Scotch. Poor
Ruth.

For a while I just continue floating around, watching them
puttering about the scene of the accident. There seems to be an
order in their madness. They check everything—I mean absolutely
everything. They photograph the Honda from all sides. Not
difficult since it's lying on its roof. They already know what the top
looks like.

"It's a blow-out. The guy was lucky he didn't hit oncoming
traffic!"

Funny. "I am dead! How lucky can you get?" I snort at them. Somehow no one seems to hear me. "I said, I am dead," I repeat louder. "DEAD!"

"It must have been that pothole up the road. It must have happened right there."

"The same one that woman hit earlier this week. I suppose it's getting larger."

"They'll repair it come springtime. In the meantime it will keep us busy."

I take a deep breath. I mean, figuratively speaking. So it wasn't the Scotch.

"He wasn't even driving that fast," the girl says. "I sure hope he'll pull through," she adds, but there is no conviction in her voice. I don't blame her. I wonder if there is any way I could tell them that I am here and not in my body. I tap the girl's shoulder.

The girl shivers. "It's getting cold, George. I think we might as well pack it in."

"Yes, Corporal. Right away."

So the pixy made corporal already. Maybe she only looks that young. Young and cute.

I watch as the cops methodically wind up the investigation. For them, of course, this is just routine. Come early, take measurements, make notes, go back, file a report. Happens everyday. To someone, somewhere. Only, it never happened to me. I've never been dead before. Not even once. Gradually the thrill seekers are also dispersing. Thinning down. Thirty is down to twenty. I must say the accident must have looked spectacular. While I, I mean my body, ended up in the ditch, the car flew right over it and landed among some trees. That's why it took them so long. Only I don't really know how long is long. I see things happening, sequentially, but I do not have any feeling of the passage of time. Just for fun I think of the moment I hit the pothole. If I had something to shudder, I would shudder it right now. Clear as daylight, I see my right front wheel dipping into a hole and then slamming into the oncoming sharp rim of the godforsaken crater. The tire literally explodes. I mean really explodes, right there before my eyes. Like a slo-mo replay. I watch the car swerve into a lamppost, turn a somersault and end up in the bushes. Halfway there I fall out of the door, which opened on impact with the lamppost. I must have forgotten to wear my seatbelt.

"Ruth will never forgive me…"

I must have been stupid. Or it could have been that second Scotch, after all. Mom and Dad will be worried. Mom always worries, just in case. 'I'm afraid…' is her favourite beginning of every sentence. *Façon de parler*, of course, but still, if words are things, as Ruth says, then she has plenty to worry about. Dad is strong; he'll take care of her and her worries. He always did. As for Clara, Ruth's mother, she won't help Ruth much. She's good at increasing sales of all the paper tissue manufacturers. Goes through a dozen boxes a week. I think she really likes crying. At least she does it quietly.

That leaves Ruth. As I said, she'll never forgive me. Poor Ruth.

And then, incongruously, I hope that they, the cops, may not have noticed. Surely, the young corporal girl would have said something. 'Tsk, tsk, no safety-belt,' or something like that. Perhaps the strap got torn out? Instantly the picture shifts. My vision reaches out to the car careening through the air. I was right. Well, almost. I see the belt tight across my shoulder. My body, as it catapults through the open door, is still firmly attached to the car seat, belt and all. Together we almost clear the ditch. Not quite, though. The strap must have gotten loose only on impact as my body hit the ground. Frozen, but still softer than the lamppost, I suppose. I find it vaguely amusing how I can reach back in time and look at things. I wonder if it would also work the other way. Forward. I try peeking into tomorrow. No luck. In fact, I feel rather silly trying it. Perhaps my will or my heart wasn't in it. I try again. Nil. No tomorrow. Maybe dead people don't have any tomorrows. Maybe we have only the past. Time will show, except that time got all twisted up. At least as far as the past is concerned. There is a great deal to learn about being dead.

For some reason, not having a future makes me feel sad. I always had a future. Good or bad, but something to hope for. To look forward to. Anything…

Or something to avoid?

But if I am dead, then what did the corporal girl mean by 'I hope he pulls through'? Isn't that what she'd said? Something like that. I am playing with the idea of going back in time to confirm, but I'm pretty sure. 'I hope he'll pull through.' Yes, that's it. But if she was right, I, I mean, my body, is not dead. Then who the devil am I?

Sorry, I didn't mean that part about the devil.

I know. I must be unconscious and this is just my dream. You can do funny things with time, in a dream. I did, lots of times. Not that I could actually control it—time, I mean—but, well, it was sort of more flexible. Sometimes whole years had passed in an instant. Or at least weeks, or months. This must be it. I am knocked out cold, sleeping on that stretcher on the way to the hospital. Wheee, wheee... I can still hear the siren. Either that, or I am playing games in my subconscious. Perhaps one can only do that when one's body is knocked out. I am sure I'll find out sooner or later. If I were dead, I would have gone through a tunnel, seen a bright light or... or something like that. I read stuff about such things. Quite interesting. They call it a near-death experience. And what I am doing now has been referred to as OBE. No, that's not the Order of the British Empire, though had I struck an inconvenient royalty... never mind. It stands for an Out-of-Body Experience. Boy, is it ever. Only not quite the way it was described. One is supposed to be able to go through walls and other solid objects. As far as I know, I haven't gone through anything. And I don't really see my body. I know when I am standing, or sitting, but it is more like a state of mind than actually feeling some solid object supporting me from below.

I look around. Everybody is gone. Almost. The last stragglers are starting their engines. The show is over. My first and last starring role. Maybe I'm dead after all. Otherwise I would have some sort of a body. An astral body, they called it, I think. I wish I'd paid more attention when I read up on all that stuff. The problem is I never really took it that seriously. Metaphysics was never my strong subject. I like things I can touch and feel. Like Ruth. God, she's so good to touch. I wish I could tell her I'm all right. I mean, not in the old sense, but still, all right. I can see, and think, and I don't hurt.

Yeah. I like things I can touch and feel and enjoy. A good game of golf followed by a few Black Labels in the clubhouse was more my line. The rest of the time it was strictly office. Nine to five. Or six, or seven, or much later if we had a new proposal to make. In case you're wondering, I am, oops, I *was* an architect. Big projects, mostly multimillion-dollar variety. My firm specializes in commercial buildings. Office buildings, hotels, hospitals. Commercial stuff. My partners had contacts, especially Jacques; I had talent. Seriously. My dear buddies (we also played golf together) couldn't design a building without winning a lemon. That's an official recognition of the worst building in town. But they sure were good at getting clients. Old-boy network. The right schools, the right university, the right time. Their parents knew each other. They sold themselves—I sold my designs. Suited me fine, even if their names came first on the letterhead. Well, Beaulieu's did, anyway. Frank came last, but that was only to get the right-sounding abbreviation. Like a radio station, or TV. Not that it matters, anyway.

I stick around waiting to see what will happen next. The cops are gone; soon oncoming cars don't even slow down to see what the fracas was about. Just some broken glass on the pavement. The lamppost is gone—the light, I mean—but the shards pick up the light from the oncoming cars like a handful or two of diamonds strewn across the surface. Rather nice, if you had time to look.

When all is near nice and quiet, some bright yellow flashing lights come up the road. A garage truck pulls to a stop right next to me. A long crane swivels out and reaches over the ditch. Two guys get out and attach some thick chains to the wreck of my Honda. That's sort of bad luck. We only had the car for just over a year. Too new to wreck. Too young to die. Do cars have a heaven?

Then the derrick lifts my dear Accord and swings her over the ditch as if she were feather-light. That's what Dad did. Does. He always calls cars 'her'. Like a ship. English, or British, I suppose. He emigrated when very young. Some things stuck with him. My Honda swings a little, to and fro, hovers for a minute over the truck's platform, and then comes down with a clank and a screech.

"*Easy!*" I shout.

I forget they can't hear me. And, frankly, they can't do my Honda any more harm. She's dead all right. I'm no mechanic, but I'll bet my bottom dollar she's beyond repair. At best they'll recycle her parts. Like mine. When they're sure that I'm dead, they'll just recycle me. They call it a funeral, but, let's face it, our bodies get recycled. You get buried, you get eaten by worms, the worms defecate you underground, the tree roots pick up the nutrients, they grow leaves, we make compost from leaves, feed our vegetables, eat the vegetables... In a way, we are all cannibals. Everyone is. Recycled cannibals.

What am I doing here?

If this is heaven, you can keep it. It's dark. The cars don't even slow down anymore. I am the past. The accident is in the past. My presence is disembodied, lonely, lonesome and ignorant. What am I supposed to be doing now? There is only now. I have no future, at least none that I can see. And past? When I look at it, it's also now. Funny that. I spend a few moments peeking at the accident again. Various stages of it. It was a nice car, the Accord.

What am I supposed to do with myself? Don't dead people go somewhere? That's what the priest said. Up or down, he'd said. Up to heaven or down to hell. Unless you were in Australia, I suppose. There it must be the other way around. Wasn't there also a Purgatory? They'd never explained it to my satisfaction. As I said, I'm not much at metaphysics. Or is it theology? I try to think back. Then I remember my time travel. At least, I think of it as such. Whatever I think of, it becomes my present. Becomes now. Or it feels like it. It is as if I were there and then.

Purgatory. I see the word spelled out in front of my eyes. I must have read it somewhere. *A place of temporal punishment for those who are not entirely free from venial fault, or have not fully atoned for their sins.* I blink and the inscription goes away.

Entirely free from venial fault...

That's nuts. Venial sin is like slipping on a banana peel. It's just a slight error in judgment. It's like having a second dessert when you're five pounds overweight. There are, give or take, six billion people on earth. When they die, Purgatory will be filled to the brim. God being infinitely good would never send anyone to hell; my mother always said that. She is a really good Catholic, but she, too, has her limits. That leaves Heaven and Purgatory. And I don't believe anyone had ever *not* had a second helping of ice cream. Given a choice, of course. Ruth wouldn't let me have it but, well, I am—I was—a bit more than five pounds over. That leaves Purgatory. Population six billion plus, all the guys and gals that ever lived, I suppose. What with time, this side of the great divide, being sort of funny, it could pretty well last forever. Christ! That's a long time...

I am beginning to understand why the universe is such a large place. Not bad. I've only been dead a few minutes and I've already learned something. Infinity to go. The Eternal Now. Thank God we're immortal. There's so much to see...

On the other hand, I am going to miss the future.

And Ruth.

Mostly just Ruth.

There is another screech of brakes, and a thud. No, I'm not reliving my accident of moments ago. My Honda is gone. I raise myself a little to see better. About ten feet above the ground. Just in time, too, or they would have run into me. The driver ignored the little red flare the cops left behind, warning drivers about the pothole. I see the car taking off in absurdly slow motion, spend timeless moments in the air, and then, with an unholy grinding noise, wrapping itself around the hapless lamppost. What's left of it. The oscillating lights, ambulance, squad cars, flashing photographers follow. A sort of déjà vu. A replay in real-time. Like a movie you really don't want to see, but you paid for your ticket and are stuck in your seat. This time the cops barricade the right side of the road and leave a dozen red flares. We learn. We learn slowly, but we learn. *Homo sapiens.* Still on the slow side.

Poor sap. I guess he must have someone waiting for him to get there. Wife? Mother? Worse—children. I can hear it now: 'Mommy, when is Dad coming home? When, Mommy?' I see his wife glancing at her watch, nervously. She must be getting worried by now. Not that I have any feeling for the passage of time. But she must be getting worried. Unless the guy was single, of course. I wonder how many mothers and wives are waiting for their husbands to get home tonight. Waiting and waiting. As I am now. Only I have no idea what I am waiting for.

It's getting grey now. The wee hours. I wonder why I don't feel any cold. Of course, I don't have a body. That must be it. I have no idea where I am. Not really.

I can't help smiling. Poor sap. He must have had that second Scotch. The driver, I mean. Maybe a third? I half expected to see whoever drove that car emerging from his body, oozing out in a long nightdress. Sort of as I did. Nothing happened.

Poor lamppost.

**

2

A World Apart

Peace at last. I look around, just making sure. Yes, my body is definitely missing. There is a guy sitting on the other side of the ditch, looking at me. I come down and assume a sitting position myself. Floating is OK, but it seems unnatural. Especially when someone is looking at you.

"Hi?" It seems the right thing to say.

I still have no idea where I am. I mean, this is not real. I did smash my head through the windshield. At least I think I did. Hard. Or could I have forgotten? I seem to be neither here nor there.

The guy smiles. There is something awfully familiar about him. We must have met.

He must be the guy from the other car, a Ford Mustang, I think, which got wrapped around that lamppost. My lamppost. Must have been a young fellow. People my age don't drive Mustangs, do they? Too sporty. He looks unscathed, like me. Only, frankly, I can't tell his age. He also keeps smiling as if we really have met before. I take his smile as a yes.

I search my memory. I met many people in my time, mostly clients. There were also Ruth's friends, their husbands, wives, cousins. An unholy bunch. Just adults. We never had children. First it was too early, then, as it turned out, too late. We could have gone for artificial insemination, but Ruth didn't like the idea. If God wanted us to have children, we would have had them, she told me, a number of times. Not if we waited till you were over forty, my love, I could have said, but I kept my thoughts to myself. Of course, by the time she turned forty, I was on the wrong side of fifty. Maybe she was right. Maybe there is such a thing as destiny. Or divine benevolence.

Thinking of Ruth brings me home. I can actually hear snippets of my conversation with her just before I left to drop off the plans.

"You really shouldn't be driving, darling." There is concern in her eyes. "It's much too slippery. They say there is more freezing rain coming."

"I'll be all right. Aren't I always? I have little choice, darling, I promised I would drop in and deliver the plans to Frank." Frank Drake is my partner. Was. Everything for me is was. Except for the present. Doesn't make much sense, does it? Frank was leaving with the plans early the following day to present them in Quebec City. I had another design to work on.

"But you had two Scotches. Shouldn't you at least wait a while?"

She was right. She very nearly always was. You could say she is my better half. Much better. She is wise, I'm impulsive, which makes me impatient. Thank God we have copies of the plans in the office. They are bound to send someone, once they hear about my mishap. Some mishap!

I allow myself a mental shrug and get back to the man in the ditch. By some quirk of fate he's dressed exactly as I am. Black polo sweater, grey corduroy pants, Adidas, and a khaki parka to keep warm. Amazing how I can see the colours, even in relative darkness.

I can't find the man anywhere in my memory. It is as though he just came out of nowhere. Or it could even be nowhen. Whatever that is. I mean, you couldn't put any age on him.

"I'm sure we met somewhere?" I say, forming it into a question.

"Let's walk," he says, getting up.

Again I become aware that my head doesn't hurt. What a wonderful feeling. Or, really, an absence of feeling. A thought crosses my mind. Are feelings really necessary? I turn to the man beside me. I suddenly realize that he's the only one that can actually see me. Since, you know, since the accident.

Even his voice sounds familiar.

"You from the other car?" I ask, just to start a conversation.

"No."

"No?"

"No."

Well, that sounds pretty final. I wonder where the other guy went to. The guy from the other car. I also wonder where the stranger wants to take me.

"Where?" I ask.

"It doesn't matter," he says. "Away from here," he adds, as an afterthought.

The road ahead seems straight and narrow. The white lines on each side merge with the line down the middle somewhere far, far away, sucked into a single point on the horizon. For no reason I remember my schooling. Once you get past Euclidean geometry, two lines merge in infinity. Einstein, I think. I wonder what lay beyond it. Not infinity. Beyond that point.

"Let's find out," the man says. He seems quite relaxed.

I observe the man without actually staring at him. He's almost exactly my height, my age, my colouring. If it weren't for the colour of his eyes and a strange posture that seems halfway between an athletic youth and a man many years my senior, he could be my twin brother. Even as I stare at him, part of me realizes that I see him as though he were real. I mean not dead, like me, only flesh and blood. The next moment I become aware of my own body. It is not exactly solid, but the contours are clearly discernible. It is as though I were made of dust that whirled in countless gyrations around some common axis. I am made up of tiny stars, tiny foci of light that are in constant, minute motion. For a moment I cannot take my eyes away from my hand, which I hold, in awe, in front of my eyes. I presume I must have eyes, by now. It's a strange thing, being dead. You keep discovering new things, even about yourself.

The stranger rises and walks ahead.

For a while he follows the street, then veers to the right, across the fields, thinly covered with snow. Or thickly. We don't exactly walk on it. We both seem to move about a foot above it, at about walking pace.

"A shortcut," he explains.

With the first rays of sun, the weather seems to be improving. No more sleet and freezing rain. In fact, it's quite comfortable. Again, I become aware of incredible lightness. I'm reminded of a book I had read: *The Incredible Lightness of Being*. I don't remember the book, but I love the title. Incredible lightness. That's exactly how I feel. It's as if an enormous stone had fallen off my back. I feel like flying. We walk.

I have no sensation of the passage of time. When the sun rises to about three feet above the horizon, the man stops. For some reason we both walked in silence. Perhaps he also has things to work out.

"That's it," he says.

I look at him, then around. There is nothing to see. Just more of the same. "What is?" I ask, doing my best to keep irritation out of my voice.

"This is where the two lines meet," he says, the same surreptitious smile playing about his lips.

"But there is nothing new here," I protest.

"Of course not. This is the future."

This is the future? What the devil was the man talking about?

"It's not created yet. I mean, it's all there, but it's not arranged in a sequential order. It's as if it weren't there at all."

I wish he would wipe that smile from his face. On the other hand, I cannot help being curious. I am determined not to sound stupid. OK. Not *too* stupid. But I have to ask.

"Who are you?"

"When you enter true reality, there is only such time as you require to make it real. It is relative. Einstein told you that some years ago." For some reason he chooses to ignore my question.

"You a physicist? I mean a scientist?"

"I am," he replies, his smile getting broader. "You will learn soon enough. If I tell you now, you will not believe me."

Well, thanks for nothing. I wish the man didn't look so familiar. I feel as if I were making a *faux pas* by not recognizing him.

"I am John Clarkson," I extend my hand. Might as well be civil about it. It's not as if I were surrounded by a bunch of friends.

"I know," the man replies, ignoring my proffered hand. He manages to make it look accidental. "We met a long time ago." There is that infernal smile again. He seems to find my predicament highly amusing. Practically hilarious. I am sure he doesn't laugh outright just to spare my feelings. And he makes it sound as if it were my fault that I don't remember his name. "It will come to you," he adds, as though my inability to recognize him were of no consequence. "It will come," he assures me, this time his voice sounding more kindly. "It takes a while…"

What takes a while? The recognition? Don't I have enough to learn out here in this Purgatory, or whatever this is, without having to play games?

Up ahead a rabbit is running across the road. A car is approaching it at high speed. I hold my breath. They are on collision course. The rabbit stops in mid-step instead of accelerating. The car passes, missing the rabbit by inches. Our furry friend is all right. He, or she, continues on his or her way. Probably to make more rabbits. The first thought that comes to me is: 'Time is relative.' Relative to what? Different for the car and different for the rabbit?

I glance at the stranger. He hasn't moved. It is as though he, too, had stopped. In time, I mean. As I did, over at the site of the accident. Perhaps he even moved back to stop the rabbit. I shrug my shoulders. I am glad I can. I'm glad I have shoulders.

"Let's walk," he says again.

After a while we come across a knoll with maybe a dozen trees. The maples are denuded, but the pines and the firs make a nice point of reference in relatively flat, snow-covered fields. I have no idea where we are. After all, the man said we'd gone past infinity. Wherever that is, and whatever that means, for that matter.

He lowers himself to a quasi-reclining position, about a foot above the frozen ground. I follow his example. I touch the ground to make sure. I don't feel it. But, somehow, I know it really is frozen. So, at least, this can't be hell. Unless it really can freeze over.

"We were walking across the Sahara desert. You and I. Step in step. We'd run out of water. We caught a sand snake and drank its blood. We survived the thirst."

"We?"

"But we died of snake poison an hour later. Remember? Well, almost." The smile never leaves his face, but his tone is serious.

"I don't remember what I had for breakfast yesterday," I reply, watching his face. I no longer care if he thinks me rude for staring. He is exactly the sort of guy you would meet in a dream. Fairly taciturn, enigmatic, with that *je ne sais quoi* attitude. If the guy is playing a game, I'm not having any of it. Enough is enough. Any moment I'm going to wake up and my near-doppelgänger is going to disappear.

I decide to give him one more chance.

"Are we in Purgatory?" I ask, watching his face intently.

"What do you think?" he counters, returning the stare.

"Are we playing games?"

"Not at all. But whatever you think, is likely to materialize. You must be careful with your thoughts here."

I could accept that. After all, the same was true back when I was alive. Or awake. Whatever. "And where exactly is here?" I pursue my line. I am now determined to beat him at his own game.

"But don't you see, John. That precisely is the problem. You have to decide."

I'm about to get up and go, or at least glide away, when he raises one hand.

"I don't mean to offend you. But here, as everywhere, we create our own reality. We make our own hell and our own heaven. Or Purgatory, for that matter. I am not trying to be funny, but whether you knew it or not, down there on earth you were doing exactly the same. Creating the world you lived in."

"Why do you say, 'down there'?" I ask.

"Convenience. Heaven up, hell down, Purgatory—you choose."

"More or less as in the Church. The Catholic Church."

Now I know I am dead. For the last twenty years I haven't
been near a Catholic, or any other, church. Yet now, for no reason,
I start expounding Catholic notions to a total stranger. What's even
more surprising is that the concepts that have been etched on my
mind in my youth, the concepts incontrovertibly connected with
religious upbringing, seem to hover on the edge of my awareness.

"They have some convenient ideas. The fact remains you
make your bed and you have to sleep in it. Even if it is a foot above
the ground."

"How come we float?" This last must have been his idea of a
sense of humour. Obviously, it exists on this side also. It seems,
ghosts or not, life goes on.

That laugh again. Only I don't find it sarcastic any more.
Perhaps it never was. "Look at yourself," his eyes give me a once-
over. "You are almost transparent. Lighter than air."

That makes sense. I am transparent the way light is
transparent. You can see where it goes, but you can't touch it. Like
a ray of sunshine going through a bit of dust. At last he said
something that made sense even to me. As for that thing about
creating your own reality, I'd heard about it before. Ruth had
always said it. There was a standing joke between us. 'Be careful
what you draw on your plans, darling,' she'd say, 'they are likely to
build it.' In a way, that was the same philosophy. Ruth knew so
much more about such things than I. Funny how her knowledge
seems to be seeping down to me. I mean now — now that I am sort-
of dead. There are brief moments when I can actually hear her
voice. From the past, I mean. As though she were standing right
next to me. When I wake up I am going to dig into this
metaphysical business. Better late than never.

The man before me stretches out on his back as if he were
watching the gathering clouds. He doesn't seem to mind floating on
air in the middle of nowhere. In fact, he doesn't seem worried by
anything at all. There is a palpable peace about him. A sort of
'wisdom of the ages'. It is as if he'd been there and done it. Done it
all. Yet, at the same time, there is a certain curiosity about him we
usually associate with youth. Like asking me what I think about
this or that.

I watch him from the corner of my eye. About six-foot one, fairly broad-shouldered; athletic is the word that comes to mind. High forehead, a permanent grin on his mouth and, what is more unnerving, in his eyes. He and I could be friends, in other circumstances. I wonder why he refuses to tell me his name.

"It's time you stepped out on your own," he says, his eyes never leaving the clouds. "You have to, sooner or later," he adds. Did I detect sadness in his voice?

"Just where exactly do you expect me to go?" I ask. After all, we are in the middle of nowhere and I have no idea where nowhere is. And it was he who brought me here.

"End of the road, where the two parallel lines meet, remember?"

Something tells me that the stranger is playing games again. First with that road to nowhere, or infinity, then with his name, and now this. I thought we were through with the games, once we died. Or woke up—whichever is more appropriate. And anyway, is he reading my thoughts?

"You will go wherever you are pulled the most. It's the law of attraction. To start with, we react. Then we accept, finally we become proactive. That's when the fun starts. Then you can go anywhere. Anywhere at all."

Now that made it perfectly clear!

"Now that makes it perfectly clear," I say, my tone none too polite.

"Yeah, I'm sorry. I heard you the first time. Anyway, try to relax; take one thing at a time. Or one experience, or realization, at a time," he almost snorts. "We have all the time in the world," he adds, something close to a sardonic twist on his lips. "All the time in the world," he repeats, this time looking straight at me as if he saw me for the first time. Actually, I think he is looking for some reaction from me. Well, amigo, not yet.

This isn't getting me anywhere. For some reason, unexpectedly, I feel the need to know what happened to my body. For all I know I, or some part of me, is still in it, fighting for its life. Do bodies have a life of their own? Ruth once said that there was a thing called *nephesh*, that's Hebrew for animal soul. 'It's more like your subconscious,' she'd said. 'The Immortal Soul is El.

Read your Bible,' she admonished. I never did. For a moment I
wonder if the stranger would know.

"Do you..."

I am alone. There is no one on the knoll, no one floating on a
cushion of air. I am in the middle of nowhere, with clouds
gathering overhead. This also looks like the middle of winter and
there is no one to tell me where the devil I am. I am not amused. I
suppose I could call him, but I don't even know his name. Hey,
you, whoever you are, just doesn't sound right. Anyway, he'd
probably ignore me. It's not as if he had volunteered much
information.

I am beginning to feel sorry for myself. It wasn't my fault that
the City Authorities did not repair the potholes. As someone had
said, we sure pay enough taxes. They must all go into their
pensions, I suppose. Or worse, into their Christmas parties. To hell
with them. To hell with potholes, with cars, with driving, with the
police, ambulances, sirens, spinning lights. To hell with every
bloody one of them. All I wanted was to deliver the plans I'd
prepared to my partners. To keep my promise. I'd spent three hours
looking them over just to make sure they were ready for the
presentation. I must say, the boys and girls in the office had done a
really good job. The plans were neat, the shadows on the elevations
were cast just right, the colour coding easy to read. Perfect, as
usual. Another job well done, another contract coming up. It would
pay for that cottage Ruth had her eye on by the lake. It would...

And now? All's screwed up. All thanks to one bloody pothole.
And the bloody unions who refused to work on weekends. To hell
with all of them.

For a moment I see an image of the stranger shaking his head.
Then, nothing again. Only his words reverberate in my ears. I must
have done that trick of going back in time. I hear him, clear as a
bell. 'We make our hell and our heaven.' Or Purgatory, I add
myself. Isn't this what I am doing right now? Am I not creating a
reality in which I have no peace, no serenity? A reaction to a reality
over which I have absolutely no influence. It's like crying over
spilled milk, regardless of who spilled it and where. I find myself

smiling the way the stranger did. A sort of wise-sardonic all-knowing smile. Not that I know much, but I think I've just learned my first lesson. Don't get bothered by things over which you have no influence. Do what you can, and leave the rest to take its course. Or something like that. I've only been dead a short while. Or unconscious.

I wonder what they've done with my body?

I don't think I can influence the answer to this question, but curiosity persists. I know they took my body, with wailing sirens, to the hospital. This implies that my body must have had some signs of life. It had to be the heartbeat. I don't think they carry electroencephalograms on ambulances. I know what they are. I designed two hospitals. They measure brain waves. No waves, no life. Simple. Anyway, there was no time to make a graph. If there were faint signs, they had to hurry. Hence the racket they made.

This makes me feel better. On the other hand, I left things unfinished on this side. Who was that man who took me to the end of time? He practically called it that. 'There is nothing more,' he'd said. 'It's the future.' Not written yet. But he also hinted that it already exists in some form. All jumbled up, he'd implied. There is so much to learn. Whoever thought up the expression, 'Let them rest in peace,' didn't have any idea what he was talking about. There seems to be far more to learn this side than on the other, the one we call life.

The clouds are gathering in that unpleasant shade of bluish-grey. It probably means more snow. Snow or freezing rain. Or it could be just a reflection of my dark thoughts. I wonder how rain would affect my translucent body. Would it go right through me? Would it hurt? The next instant I remember that I have no pain. None, of any sort. In fact, I don't actually feel any part of me. It's as if I were asleep...

Or dead.

But if dead people don't feel anything, then what's the big deal about hell? You can fry all the oil you like, but no one would feel any pain. On the other hand, nor would there be any pleasure. At least not physical or sensual pleasure. The Moslem would be sorely disappointed. Especially those who blew themselves to smithereens. Fancy that. Make yourself into a bomb and then look at seventy-two virgins, but not be able to feel them. I'll stick to Ruth. At least I would, given a choice. She was, she is, all body. Warm, pliable, comforting body. The only thing missing is my own, and I didn't even blow myself up.

It's not fair.

I close my eyes and try to imagine my body as it was before the accident. In a way, I resembled the stranger. Same silhouette, similar physique, just, sort of, younger? Not that he was old. In fact, Ruth would go for a guy like that. My contours but better brains. More knowledgeable.

My mind is wandering. Images of the accident are floating before my eyes. Not just images. It's a first-class, three-dimensional audio-visual. Maybe the universe is recording everything on a universal digital recorder and then, when you're dead, you can replay it. This would account for life events flashing before your eyes. And for the Last Judgment.

I can picture the Judge sitting on a high dais, his finger poised threateningly over the replay button. "On (date and time inserted) you did, willfully, have a second helping of ice cream. How plead you?"

"But, your Lordship, I only..."

"The defendant will answer yes or no."

"But..."

You couldn't argue with a digital recorder. You would have to take what was coming to you. On the other hand, what was coming? I already know that I don't feel anything. So what could they do to me? And anyway, who are 'they'? I've been floating here for, I don't know, half of eternity for all I know, and I haven't seen a single person.

"Sure I had a second helping!" I announce out loud. If it hadn't been for Ruth, I'd have had a third.

If that was blasphemy... So how come a lightning doesn't strike me? The clouds are dark enough. Then I remember. We must create our own hell and our own heaven. So what's God going to do? Ride herd and just watch? I couldn't quite picture God as a voyeur. What with that long beard, the old worn face taken directly from the Sistine Chapel—and just watch?

Those images just don't work up here. Down here... never mind. They just don't work.

I have to find out what's happening with my body. If I am still alive, I am wasting my time trying to understand mysteries of the universe. Time enough when I'm dead.

My thoughts—or is it desires—bring me back to the scene of the accident. The knoll just disappeared; the day turned into night, and the road is dark and unfriendly. I move back a little. The garage truck, the stragglers, the cops and photographers... I am on a fast rewind. Funny how it works so smoothly. I don't even have to press the button.

Then I see the ambulance taking off. The sirens wailing, it speeds along semi-deserted streets. I half-expect it to skid into one of the oncoming cars. Or hit the curb. Wouldn't that be funny? I would die twice. In the next image it is stopping under a canopy. Someone has the decency to switch off the siren, but the spinning lights are still spinning. The back door opens and two guys jump down, one of them holding an IV on a long metal stick. They lower the stretcher, the wheels automatically opening below to make it into a gurney. A corpse is lying inert on top of the narrow platform. That's me. The other, physical me. I'm already covered with a white sheet. Maybe I died on the way to the hospital? I look up. *Lakeshore Hospital* is spelled out over the entrance. Next I notice that my head is not covered. My eyes are closed, my face covered in blood. Judging by the movement of the white sheet, the corpse is hardly breathing, perhaps not breathing at all. A corpse shouldn't, should it? The two guys who brought me here return to the ambulance. They start the engine and pull out. The moment they clear the hospital gates, the siren starts wailing. It must be a busy night. Two other guys grab hold of the stretcher and pull/push me towards the self-opening door. I'm inside. I wonder if I'm going to make it.

This is no fun at all.

***

3

Hospital

I wish they wouldn't make such a fuss. Placing my body on the stretcher is not going to do me much good if they shake it to within an inch of its life. 'Easy,' I whisper. 'Easy does it.' No one is paying any attention. They all seem in a hurry.

"Easy!" I raise my voice. Still no effect.

I look down at my body. From what little I can see, not a bad body as such. I tried to take good care of it. Not that I exercised that much—no time—but I didn't abuse it with any excesses. Well, not much. Perhaps a little sleep deprivation, but business is business. It took me nine months to make it. My body, I mean. Well... I had a lot of help. A few million years of it. Not that time matters that much. In the year minus a million or two, the experience would have been different. Like that time when I fell into a smouldering abyss. If the dino hadn't broken my fall, I would have been a goner. How do I know that? Funny how snippets of my past flash before my eyes. Is that what they mean happens just before you die? If so, then I am not dead yet.

I shake my head.

The dino is still there. That's right, a dino. A dinosaur. I have to watch my thoughts. The replay seems to be on automatic. Still, it's better than being one. My God! I think I am one. A dinosaur. I'm back there. Here? A very long-necked creature is looking at me with suspicion. Or it could be maternal love. How do I know? Actually it is more like 230 million years back. No humans around. None. I feel rather stupid having to talk to my own tail. It seems miles away. It very nearly is. I try to shake the image away. It's as if it were yesterday. Maybe it was. As I said, time doesn't matter much. I blink it away.

They move me, I mean my body, to the OR. I wonder why they are so preoccupied with the body until I remember I'm human now. Still, I can always make another one. Even monkeys do it. And birds, fish—you name it. We all make new bodies, crawl inside and pretend we are it. Or they. Sometimes it's fun. At other times it can give you a mighty headache. Like now. Thank God it's not my headache any more. It belongs to the body.

"On three. One, two…"

Two guys and one nurse lift my body and move it to yet another stretcher. I can smell the sterilizing vapours rising from the floor mixed with the sweat of the nurses who lift my body. I never realized medicine is so physically demanding. I thought it was all brains and gadgetry. Then I stop. How come I can smell if I can't feel any pain? Some senses work, some don't. This reality is confusing. What if it were a painful aroma? Would I still smell it? It wasn't. Unpleasant, but not actually painful. It is relatively indifferent, though I wouldn't swap it for the smell of the pines on the knoll.

Two other nurses are running around as if they had no idea what to do.

"I think he's slipping…"

I was slipping on the black ice, young lady. That's how I smashed into the lamppost. They can't hear me. I try to speak louder.

"We are losing him…"

There is some sort of instrument showing a green line going 'blip, blip, blip…' followed by a zig-zag line on a screen. Running around stops when a man in a green coat walks into the screened cubicle. This is not the OR. It must be the antechamber. A sort of waiting area to die. The new guy alone doesn't seem to be in a hurry. There is an air of quiet confidence about him.

"Two cc's of…" Something I can't pronounce.

They give the body an injection directly into the heart. In seconds the zig-zag stabilizes and the blips become more regular. The nurses who wheeled me in wipe their foreheads. The younger nurse sits down and lets out a lungful of air. I can hardly believe

my eyes. These people actually care what happens to that body. I
mean my body. Perhaps more than I do.

"Call me if there is a change in rhythms," the young green-
clad doctor announces and, without another word, moves to the
door. A curtain, actually; there is no door. "Any change," he adds
over his shoulder.

There is a murmured confirmation of his order. These people
are tired. As the doctor draws aside the curtain to the corridor, I
hear muted sounds of the ambulance siren. Another one. Not that
the curtain blocked any sound, but my attention automatically
covered a broader area. At least I think that's what happened. I'm
new to this.

One nurse remains at my bedside, the others move out.
Probably to wheel in another pothole beneficiary. Screw the city
management. Won't they ever learn? Ever? Maybe it had been
easier being a dinosaur millions of years ago than being one now,
in the City Hall.

I turn my attention to my body. There is no blood that I can
see except on the bandages that surround my head, seemingly on all
sides. My eyes are slits, air has access to my nostrils from a gap
under my nose; another slot has a tube coming out of my mouth.
The IV is attached to my left arm, the side opposite to all the
electronic equipment. I am covered by a freshly laundered sheet,
two crisp creases running the length of my body. It's all very clean
and proper. Hygienic, I suppose? I don't dare to peek under the
sheet. It could be just a pile of broken bones.

The whole place smells of antiseptic.

I hear movement outside. The curtain opens and Ruth comes
in. Her face is covered by a mask, but she still looks beautiful. I
know that mask. She only wears it when she needs to control her
emotions. She really does look good. A short fur coat (nylon—she
wouldn't wear another animal) stops at her knees, exposing two
perfect calves and ankles. I cannot see her eyes peering from under
her hat, but I know she's looking worried. Who wouldn't be?

She walks slowly to the foot of the bed, even as the sole nurse
gets up and puts her hand on Ruth's arm.

"He's stable now, Mrs…"

"Clarkson." She doesn't say any more. Then, "Can he hear me?"

"No, Mrs. Clarkson. I'm afraid he's resting now."

I bloody can!

"He's asleep?"

The nurse glances at the EEG. The alpha rhythms are completely replaced by theta waves, which are associated with sleep. How do I know this? Bits of knowledge keep popping up in my head. I know. I don't have a head, but they keep popping up anyway. The nurse presses a button on the console.

"I'm afraid you have to leave now, Mrs. Clarkson." The nurse keeps being afraid. Afraid of this, afraid of that. Or just afraid. Maybe all nurses are afraid. Maybe I would be, in their circumstances. I've never been responsible for somebody else's life.

The nurse gently but firmly moves Ruth bodily out of the cubicle. At the same time Dr. Morton walks in, two other men right behind him. The nurse rolls back the blanket and the sheet. My right arm and both legs are immobilized by heavy bandages. I've no idea if they are broken. My right knee is dark blue, matching my left thigh. There's also a wide swathe of elastic bandages around my chest. Must be the ribs.

Christ! Am I glad I'm not in that body!

Nobody seems to care. They all scan the electronics and the doctor gives depositions in a quiet, precise voice.

I move outside to be with Ruth. Not that she'd know it, of course. I feel as if the two of us became one body, one mind. Aren't we all one? Ruth pulls out her Rosary and her lips start moving. I haven't seen her use the Rosary for years. Many years. She'd said something about vain repetitions; "...use not vain repetitions, as the heathen do: for they think that they shall be heard for their much speaking," she'd said. Funny how I can remember that... Anyway, it's no big deal; people always talk too much.

Poor Ruth.

We are all one, I try to tell her. We are all one... you'll never be alone. Never. I try to will my words into her mind. She's a great believer in the Teaching. I and my father are one, I whisper. I am the light and the resurrection...

I have no idea why I am saying these things. I was always baffled by this particular Christian maxim. I and my father... I was born in silence. In outer darkness. There was no light in my mother's womb. Warm, cozy, but no light. Except for minute electrical discharges. Something to do with the electrochemical system my mother's body employed to communicate with itself. Trillions of reactions per second. Like being in the middle of a galactic cloud. Now, how would I know that?

Ruth wipes a tear on her cheek. I wish, God how I wish, I could tell her that I'm all right. By now I know she can't hear me. I say it anyway. "I-am-all-right." I scan the words. Perhaps she can feel my presence.

I also wish they wouldn't make so much noise here. I always hated extraneous hullabaloo. People are running up and down the corridor, stretchers are rolling, six or seven are lined up against the wall. There are people on them. Live people. Waiting their turn to die? Or have they all put their head through the windshield? Ruth was right. I shouldn't have driven so soon after my second Scotch. On the other hand, if it was meant to be...?

"We are losing him..."

The voice behind me is youthful, nervous. Almost out of place. It is the young nurse. Or she could be an intern on her first emergency room stint. Must be scary. Yesterday she was sitting in a classroom. It was all theory. Today...

Three more people run into the room. More hullabaloo.

"Clear!"

A couple of horse's hoofs kick me in the chest. I shift back to the bed. My body jumps as if I were trying to get out. I already am out. No, I am not. Let me out...

"Easy!" I scream as loud as I can.

"Clear!"

"Shit! Not so hard! You crazy?"

It's that bloody horse again. I wish they wouldn't treat sick people this way. And they shouldn't scream so loud. There are sick people here. Hey, how come they can't hear me?

"Clear!"

Thump!

That's it. I'm going. I've had enough. I can't. Something tugs me and straps me inside the body. I hurt all over. My lungs are about to explode. Then, in infinitely slow motion, darkness comes from all sides. Warm, embracing, wondrous darkness. I am back in my mother's womb. It is soft and cozy. And then all is quiet.

I hear voices again.

"His heart is all right, Mrs. Clarkson. He is breathing weakly but regularly. It's just… I'm afraid he slipped into a coma."

"So would you, laddie, if a horse kicked you in the chest that many times. So would you!" It's like talking to myself.

Ruth doesn't say anything. I try to console her with my presence. It doesn't work. Then she repeats, "Coma?" It's a question mark.

"There is nothing you can do, Mrs. Clarkson. All we can do now is wait."

"How long," she asks after a little while. She looks relaxed, but I know better. There's a tiny vibration in her left cheek, just under the eye. Her calmness could explode any second.

"We don't know, Mrs. Clarkson. We never know in such cases. It was the original shock. I'm afraid it was quite severe. A concussion. We must give his body a chance to heal itself."

Ruth nods, still looking at the white blanket covering my body. She can't see my face for all the bandages. I must look awful to her. Poor Ruth.

"Get some rest, Mrs. Clarkson. We'll call you if there is any change."

"Just what is a coma, Doctor…"

"Morton. Dr. Morton. It is caused by seve… by a head injury, a brain infection, or a damage resulting from a lack of oxygen for too long. Or an overdose…"

"I didn't ask what causes coma. I asked what *is* coma, Doctor."

Good old Ruth. She's in charge now. In control. I know coma comes from the Greek word *koma*, meaning deep sleep, but I suspect there is a big difference between deep sleep and my body being in a coma. I just sense it. I wouldn't be here otherwise, would I?

"Well, Mrs. Clarkson," Dr. Morton glances at his wrist watch, "it is a profound state of unconsciousness. We stabilized your husband's vital signs. His blood pressure, breathing and temperature. He's also getting dextrose. That's a glucose solution, Mrs. Clarkson, naloxone and Thiamine—that is the B vitamin. And oxygen, of course. We are monitoring his EEG patterns. That's electroencephalograph, Mrs..."

"You don't know, Doctor." This is not a question.

"I'm afraid a comatose patient cannot be awakened. He doesn't respond normally to pain or light. He also does not have sleep-wake cycles, nor does he exhibit any voluntary action..."

"You don't know, Doctor." Ruth's voice is normal, if a little resigned.

"I beg your pardon, Mrs. ah..."

"Clarkson. I am the patient's wife, Dr. ah-Morton. You have described for me a series of symptoms, and methods of treatment, not the condition itself. It seems that you are not quite sure what it is that you are treating." Ruth speaks in a matter-of-fact voice she would use to tell me that she'd run out of eggs for breakfast. "You could also add that patients in a coma do not always lie still and quiet. Contrary to popular belief, comatose patients may talk, walk and perform other functions that may or may not appear to be conscious but are not."

Doctor's face assumes a distinct shade of pink. He wipes his forehead with his sleeve and looks at the nurses for help.

"Thank you, Doctor." Ruth's words are hardly above a whisper.

"Would you step this way, Mrs. Clarkson?" The male nurse takes a step towards Ruth, sees her eyes, and takes two steps back.

Good for you, Babe!

What a pity no one can hear me. I may not be exhibiting much life in my physical body, but I'm as frisky as ever without it.

"This is a very technical matter, Mrs. Clarkson." The doctor begins again, then raises his hands, makes a few half-hearted circles as though clearing the air, and drops them limply by his sides. "We don't know, Mrs. Clarkson. We only know that the patient may or may not enter a vegetative state, and he may or may not recover. I am very sorry, Mrs. Clarkson."

Shit! I was hoping to find out myself. Now I'll just continue as a vegetable while I try to find out what the devil I am doing here. Ruth's face registers a cynical smile. I doubt she could have found out much more. She turns on her heel and walks towards the curtain. As she passes by me, I will her a mental kiss. There she turns once more. Her face is wearing a mask again. That's my Ruth. When things were tough in the office, some project fell through or we got a poor write-up in the press for overrunning a budget, she was a tower of strength. I wonder where she got it from. I've often wondered about it before. She is one of two children, was good in school, got an MA in history of art, and has been teaching it ever since at college level. Twice a year she goes abroad; rejuvenation trips, she calls them. I know she spends her time visiting not just old museums but all the galleries where *le dernier cri* in art is shown. Paris, Rome, London, even Moscow and Leningrad. She pays for her trips with the fees she gets for extracurricular lectures she gives on her return. She is fluent in French and Italian, with a smattering of Spanish, German and, yes, even Russian. She is a very, very bright person. I often wondered what she saw in me.

Ah… if only she could cook…

Compared to her, I am, at least I was, a loner. I'm happiest in my office, poring over plans, solving problems, coming up with interesting ways of wrapping my buildings with good, exciting façades. Firmness, commodity and delight are my motto. Ruth approves most of my work although, on occasion, she would pass a comment that I could never ignore. Though I would seldom admit it, at least not immediately, she was invariably right. She had, sorry, she *has* that inimitable, innate sense of proportion which also took her to the very top as an art critic. Let me tell you, I am one lucky guy.

And now? It seems that now I am on my own. No more Ruth, no army of assistants, young and eager architects, post-graduate interns striving to come up with a solution that would please me. All alone. Except for the stranger. I almost forgot about him. I wonder if I'll find him again.

I am ready to wander back to the site of the accident—that place has a magic pull on me—when I hear the doctor giving instructions to the nurses. Since it concerns my body, I listen in. I catch the last segment of it.

"...electrolyte abnormalities. Also renal dialysis to remove toxins and maintain normal electrolyte balance in the kidneys. We'll start with the cocktail. The usual thiamin, glucose and naloxene. Also schedule him for a CT scan. We may need surgery."

I think he told Ruth he'd already done some of that.

Still, as far as I'm concerned, he might as well have been talking Greek. I shrug my invisible shoulders. Then I remember the maxim: *Don't let things you cannot influence get to you.* On the other hand, I wish they would leave my body alone. Surgery? If I had my druthers, I would slip into my body and walk away before I'd allow a neurosurgeon to drill holes in my head. That's all I need. Someone poking around inside my head after they admitted they have no idea what coma is. I am glad Ruth isn't here. She would probably blow her top.

For some reason I float around the ward. Actually I walk, but I have no sensation of my feet touching the floor. In a way, it's rather nice. I still jump out of the way when someone is coming the other way. I wonder what would happen if I didn't.

Each bed is occupied with someone who's probably in as much trouble as I am. I hear gasps of pain, retching. I smell blood, as if I were a vampire dying of thirst. There seems to be blood everywhere, some of it, hopefully, still inside the patients. There are mostly women, one or two men, standing in the corridor, leaning against the walls. Some are crying, others try to keep the children quiet.

"Mommy, Mommy, is Daddy all right?"

"Daddy, when is Mommy coming home?"

"Mommy, Daddy... Mommy... Daddy...?"

Who needs hell? This place is as bad as any I can imagine. I suddenly realize that I have no idea what time it is. Did I visit the hospital the day of the accident? How quickly was Ruth notified? Did she come at once? She was at home when I left for the office. I mean for Frank's place. That was about 7:30 p.m. But which day? For that matter, which day is it now? I glance at my wrist. It may surprise you, but ghosts, or whatever I am, don't carry watches showing dates. At the far end of the corridor there is a window. It's dark outside. It could be the night of the accident, or it could be the next day. Ruth wouldn't wait any longer to visit me. She wouldn't wait any time at all, but I smashed up the only car we have. Had. Ruth is very keen on ecology. Global warming and all that. She must have taken a taxi. Poor Ruth. No car and no husband.

I am at the scene of the accident. They're just pulling my car out of the ditch, or from that clump of trees just on the other side. Time is playing tricks on me. It doesn't seem to follow any rules here. This side of sanity. I wish I could curl up and die. Too late. This makes me laugh. The dead don't die, I tell myself. Does anyone? I mean does anyone really die? Ever? If this is heaven or hell, or that godforsaken place they call Purgatory, then how am I supposed to get out of it?

They got my car, or what's left of it, on the truck. They will soon leave. I know. I am watching a replay, compliments of the infernal universal recorder. I don't think I like it here. Things are sort of impersonal. Even the guy who is going to smash himself later this night won't be here to keep me company. I wonder what happened to him. Maybe he went to Bardo. That Buddhist place.

"It's a Tibetan word," Ruth had said. She knows all there is to know about such things. Or places. "It means 'intermediate state'." Apparently there are a number of Bardos, six in all; some of them may even be enjoyed while still alive. "That's the Bardo of Meditation," Ruth told me, although I have no idea why she thought I ought to know that. Anyway, as I said, she knows an awful lot about such things. As for the 'intermediate state', isn't this where I am right now?

My mind wanders to the hapless pothole ex-driver, who made use of the same lamppost I did. He may have invented a reality that's invisible. Or maybe he really did die, and doesn't know it, while I am just filling time until that vegetable in my bed recovers. Or dies.

Poor Ruth…

I wonder if I can see her, I mean at home, while I'm in this condition. She's one tough lady; I am sure she'll pull through. I chuckle. That is what the police pixy said about me. Seems like ages ago. I think it was still daylight when Ruth left the hospital. Here, I'm surrounded by darkness. If it's daytime, wherever Ruth is, I'm sure she's giving her lecture as if nothing had happened. If I am watching a replay, what is her 'real time' now? I mean her 'now', not mine. For me, everything is now. She will not allow her personal problems to reflect badly on the work she is doing. It isn't her students' fault that the City fails to repair potholes on weekends. Or that I was so punctilious about the delivery of my plans. Or tried to be. As if they were really important. Life goes on. No one is indispensable—it's just that some of us are a little more indispensable than others. At times. Everything on earth is 'at times'. Sometimes you are important and sometimes you are not worth a dime. Not in the grand scheme of things. I'm sure the universe will find a suitable replacement for anyone, to do any job. Any job at all.

There is a grand scheme of things, isn't there?

I try to concentrate on her face. Her slightly sallow complexion, the delicately arched eyebrows, the slightly curved nose, so elegant; her thoughtful eyes, filled with images of great works of art, past and future, as if time didn't matter. In a way, it didn't matter to her. Art is timeless, she told me.

"It is the gift of gods," she assured me on many occasions. "Art is the result of a perfect blend of order and harmony. And love. Don't ever forget love. That is where beauty comes from. That is where it is born. People talk about suffering giving birth to art. What nonsense. Art is the act of overcoming pain, of overcoming suffering. Art gives you release, freedom. Yes, and serenity. It puts you in touch with that within you that makes you immortal."

I remember it word for word. It's the recorder again. If I can hear her, why can't I see her?

Maybe she's right about that part that makes you immortal. I'm not sure I qualify on the art angle, but I certainly have problems dying. Or at least, making my death permanent. Even my body seems to be just taking a rest. If only she knew…

Nothing happens. I try to see her sitting, walking, or even sleeping. All I see is the slim pine directly in front of me, gently swaying, just barely, in a practically non-existent wind. How come I can't feel its caress? She would enjoy being here. She would compare the view to some of her favourite van der Neers, or Berchems, de Valenciennes... So many others. Richards, La Farge, such forlorn, desolate landscapes. She knew them all. She *knows* them all. She still is. It is I who am gone. Forever?

I miss her. God, how I miss her. I'd gladly give up all my bodies just to hold hers in my arms. Just once. Just once more. Just for a moment... Only I can't feel anything. I wouldn't feel her touch, her arms, her lips.

Maybe this is hell after all.

***

4

Back on the Knoll

"So we met before?"

I have to get back to that. His previous answers were quite unsatisfactory. If we have met before, I want to know exactly where and when. For some reason I find myself back on the knoll, floating on a cushion of air. Under the pine, directly in front of me, is the stranger, looking at me as if nothing had happened. Some cool character, that stranger. I wonder if anything could get him out of kilter.

I find his apparent familiarity with me annoying. At the same time, not that there is anything but 'now' here, I find it embarrassing to stare at him, as if my curiosity were somehow offensive, or as though I were peeking into aspects of him that are very private yet, simultaneously, familiar. At the same time, deep inside me, there is a nagging notion that if I understand who or what he is, I shall learn a great deal about myself.

There is that smile again. It makes me wonder if he takes any of this seriously.

I search my memory.

A car accident. I am thrown clear off the road. A screech of brakes, then silence. The silence of outer space. Not that I ever heard outer space. You cannot hear silence. Funny how all those science-fiction films fill space with sound effects. Not so. God resides in absolute silence. In nowhere. In never. Beyond time, space, beyond vibrations. How do I know this? Even beyond music, though that last is probably my, I mean His, first manifestation.

"Are you dead?" I have to ask. We may have met when we were both alive. Way back when, but I would have remembered.

This time he does laugh. As I already mentioned, his body is much more real than mine. If you met him on the street, you would assume he was very much alive. He opens his mouth, shakes his head, and then laughs again. Long and hard.

"You asked me that so many times," he says, still practically doubling over. Then he takes hold of himself. "Are you?"

"I asked first," I say. I hate that he plays these games.

"That's true. But it is you who wants to know the answer."

This guy is probably as stubborn as I've been known to be. To have been. Or, just maybe, we take our traits over to the other side. Other side of *what*, still remains to be answered.

"My body is in a coma at the Lakeshore Hospital in…" I am not sure where the darn hospital is.

"Point Claire," he finishes for me.

"That's right. How the devil do you know? Are you following me?"

"Sort of. In a way, I am looking after you."

"You my Guardian Angel, or something?"

This gets him going again. If he really were on a real hammock between those two pines, he would have tumbled over. His titter seems to last interminably. At last he relaxes.

"Or something," he answers with a straight face.

"Or something what?"

"Just 'or something'." He swings his legs to the ground facing me. "Look, John, if I told you I was a ghost, would that make you feel better? Or waiting to become your ghost, after you lose your body permanently, would that score any points? It's as good as a Guardian Angel, but that depends on what you mean by this concept. Different religions made up different stories about divine intervention. Or divine protection, for that matter. What's yours?"

"Are you asking because you want to know, or because you want to have a good laugh?"

"I am asking because you have to decide what you want to believe in. Whatever works for you. It really doesn't matter who or what I am, or might be. You are the decider."

"Decider of what?" He's not going to shape me into a mental image of the former president of the USA. He'd been a 'decider'.

He'd said so. I am no more than a seeker. I am also in deep blue waters without a straw to grab at.

"When you were young, you read a book by Carl Jung. Remember?" The universal recorder spins on its axis. "He wrote: 'Individual is the only reality.' What do you think of his statement?"

For a moment the book he mentioned shimmers before my eyes. The title is *Man and His Symbols*, and it is yellow with age. Strange how the recorder works.

The flashback comes complete with my study, my favourite chair at my desk, and even a fresh flute of flowers on my desk. I can even smell them; they are as beautiful as they are tiny. Lilies of the Valley. My father loved them, and now I do. Anyway, Carl G. Jung contributed a single article, *Approaching the Unconscious,* to this collection of well-known dabblers in the human sub- or even unconscious. In the human psyche. The recorder scans the pages. There it is. 'The Individual is the only reality.' All this seems to have happened in a single instant. Except for the aroma. This lingers on.

"Yes," I admit; for some reason I am slightly embarrassed. "I remember."

"Well?"

Evidently my friend—at some point I began to regard the stranger as my friend rather than a lackadaisical incarnation of the devil—does not believe in doing the thinking for me. I am back where I started, only about twenty years older than I was when I read the book. And I only read it because Ruth refused to discuss the unconscious until I read at least the Jung article. Evidently, Jung did not make the requisite impression on me. I don't remember what Ruth's reaction was at the time.

We are back. "Well?" he repeats, this time stressing the interrogative nature of the question.

"I don't know..." As I say, I really do feel lost in the field of metaphysics. I would rather discuss buildings, construction, suitable sites for development or even the weather. Or, right now, the picturesque nature of the *paysage* surrounding us. Or, frankly, anything else. Yet I know with incontestable certainty that my friend won't let go. I asked the question and now I am stuck trying to figure out the answer. After all, until very recently I was a reasonably successful architect, not a third-rate philosopher.

What's-his-name is watching me from the corner of his eye. It seems that he enjoys seeing me squirm.

"Whatever I accept as reality is real to me," I volunteer after a pregnant pause.

He keeps staring at me. I try again. "So whatever I imagine, must have some sort of influence on the reality as I perceive it?"

"Some sort of influence?" There is almost a snigger in his tone of voice. "That was true back then. Now? Now we live in the present. Haven't you noticed? You cannot imagine something that you would like to be or appear out of nothing. You must accept that it exists. That it is yours to explore. If you don't do that, it cannot appear to be part of what you are."

That's pushing it too far. "Are you suggesting that what I see is part of me?"

"Part of your mind. Part of your perception. Part of what is in the here and now."

Now that will take a very detailed dissection. I see the knoll, the knoll is part of me, therefore I am part of the knoll, therefore the knoll is here and now. Does this make any sense?

"But each time I open my eyes, I see something different." I am nowhere near convinced.

"Yet someone else, looking at the seemingly identical things, sees things you do not see, and vice-versa. We can only see what our perception creates, and perception is an instrument of our mind."

If I ever wake up from this coma thing, I am definitely going to dig into metaphysics, philosophy and maybe even some Jung and his colleagues. How come I never thought of those things? Too busy, I suppose. Too busy and too tied up in the realities limited to my profession. And to Ruth, of course. At least she had some broader interests that made up, in part, for my ignorance. I certainly hope so. Otherwise I couldn't even begin to understand what my friend is talking about.

And this, once again, brings my office to the forefront of my mind. What the devil happened to the plans I was going to deliver to my partners? They must have gotten all mangled up. Fred and

Jacques will have kittens. They were supposed to present my
proposal the day following my accident. That was... I have no idea
when that was. I've lost all sensation of time. If I don't do
something, BCD Architects will be in serious trouble. That's
Beaulieu, Clarkson and Drake. An acronym people don't forget.
BCD. Good, eh? Just the A is missing.

Anyway, we were counting on that contract. The budget was
$65 million. That's no shack for a firm our size, and only the sixth
multimillion-dollar project since we formed our partnership. I
wonder if Ruth has been in touch with them. I wonder so many
things. Drake, that's Frank, can take over the design. He's not
much at conceptualizing but has a good, a very good eye for detail.
The job won't suffer. And Jacques Beaulieu will take care of the
business end. That's what he does best. In this day and age, if you
don't specialize you get left behind. Too much competition? There
is no room for a Leonardo da Vinci any more. It makes me laugh.
Architect, engineer, painter, sculptor, scientist, mathematician,
anatomist, inventor, botanist, musician, writer... did I miss
anything? Ah yes, and a long beard like God the Father Himself.

"I like that," he says out of the blue. My friend swings on his
hammock, looking pleased.

"You like what?"

"Your calling me your friend," he says, smiling. Only now do
I realize that his smile was missing when we began talking in
earnest about the nature of being. At least, I think that was what we
were talking about. Nature of being and reality. Somehow it sounds
pompous when equivocated in as many words. Yet talking about it
with my Friend seems perfectly natural. I'm beginning to capitalize
the word 'Friend' in my mind, as though that were his name. Like
George. Or my George. Also, it seems, I don't have anything else
to do. Maybe all this happened just for this reason. To get me on
the right track.

"Everything has a reason. It cannot be otherwise," Friend
offers, his eyes now drifting to the sky. The threatening clouds
dispersed long ago. Or it could already have been another day. I
really have no way of knowing.

"Are you reading my thoughts?" I ask, trying to read his facial
expression.

"What makes you think they are your thoughts?"

"That's silly. I was thinking them."

"What if I was thinking them and you were just reading them from my mind?"

Back home, on earth—I mean, when I was still in one piece—this would be called walking around in circles and getting absolutely nowhere. I refuse to pursue this sort of nonsense.

"So up here," I make a gesture with my hand encircling the knoll, "cause and effect still hold sway?" It is a statement as much as a question.

"Of course. Only the cause is differently defined here than," he smiles broadly, his finger pointing downwards, "down there."

I have a grave suspicion that Friend is patronizing me. Not that I don't deserve it, but I don't like it, anyway. Nobody does. I was never much good at taking bullshit from anyone. Not that people who knew me tried it very often, my being six-one and a hundred kilos. That's a lot of kilos saying 'no bullshit, please.' Still, I am a little surprised that my personality didn't change up here. I was hoping that I would be, well, a sort of 'higher' being. Perhaps 'better' is a better word. More humble? Saintly? Have some ennobling traits? None of this applies if we are on the way to hell, of course.

"Now you are patronizing yourself," my Friend puts in.

It is my turn to smile. And anyway, why should we be any different here from how we were there? I am beginning to think that things are exactly the same, only more so. Everything is more intense. More powerful. We may be endowed with some abilities we didn't have before, but not to the degree that it would change our viewpoint. We would just have a much higher, or more acute, perception of reality.

"And then some..." This time there is only a broad grin accompanying my first pat on the back. I must be on the right track. For some reason, I am pleased as Punch. And then some, I add in my thoughts. My Friend continues to grin but keeps any comments to himself.

For a while we recline on a cushion of air, looking at the sky. After some indeterminate time, I begin to discern stars in broad daylight. They are not as bright, of course, but they certainly are distinct from one another. As I peer harder, the blue sky recedes and the firmament surges forward. It makes me think of the velocity of light. Space is filled with such splendour as I never imagined possible. The photos made by the Hubble telescope pale in comparison. All of them. I recognize some constellations. Auriga, Taurus, Orion... The Gemini twins—Castor and Pollux—holding hands... Again I am mystified how I know these things? I never studied astronomy. Nor astrology, for that matter. Not that I can remember.

But what makes these images different is that all those constellations are three-dimensional. Yet, as though by magic, my mind links the component stars with no difficulty. The images are no longer flat, as on a photograph, but spanning light-years.

"Christ!"

I cannot help myself. The next instant I feel a pang of sorrow. How Ruth would have appreciated such beauty. She'd probably be willing to wrap our Honda around a lamppost herself if she knew what was in store. My second notion is that anyone who is an atheist is a congenital moron. I, more or less, count myself among them. Both—atheist and, as of now, moron.

This is flabbergasting... Thousands of light-years?

I don't move. I don't have to. I'm not just looking at the stars, I am among them. It is they that are moving away from me, yet, strangely, not losing their brightness. And the colours... You should see the colours!

Down there, in the real world, stars are pinpoints of silvery-golden light. Here, the palette used by my principal interior designer would not suffice to describe the half of them. And not just colours but shades and sizes...

The word splendour repeatedly comes to mind until I can no longer sustain my awe. I blink and the stars come to life. They quintuple in size, then start spinning, and display a diversity of shades and nuances that the Great Masters would give their life for.

"W-w-hat on earth w-w-was that," I stammer. I'd never stammered in my life.

I glance at my friend. At Friend. At my Friend—there, that's settled! He just floats there as if he had no idea of what I am talking about. That original grin is back on his face. I repeat the question, this time without stammering.

"This is what happens when you peek into my thoughts," he says. "It's going to rain tonight," he adds.

"It's bloody what?"

"It's going to..."

"I heard you the first time. What do you mean I peeked into your thoughts?"

He lets that float for a while. Finally he turns and looks a little uncomfortable. "I think we'd better move under cover."

"What do you mean I peeked..."

"All in good time. You coming?"

"Where, to the moon? And anyway, what's wrong with a bit of rain? Will I feel it?"

"No, but it interferes with your concentration. It's beautiful if all you want to think about is the rain. Is that what you want to do?" He glances at me, that infernal smirk now full-blown across his lips. "I didn't think so. Come."

We are sitting in a park, flooded with sunshine. When I say sitting, I mean we both manifest a sitting position, this time an inch or two above the grass. I cannot actually feel the air, but know it's warm. Or, perhaps, I'm just reading his thoughts.

Suddenly I am baffled again. "Did we move?" I ask. I'm almost afraid to hear the answer.

"What do you think?"

"Please, don't play games again." My Friend can be most exasperating.

But I know. The warm clime, the park, the sunshine is no more distant than the stars, the galaxies I'd just visited in quick order. They all exist in my head. Or, better still, in my mind. I don't put much stock in bodily parts anymore.

"Now you do it," he says, ignoring my previous question.

"Do what?"

Actually I already know. It's a request. He wants me to take him for a spin around the moon. The man is crazy, a magician, or some sort of an angel. I just don't get why he reminds me so much of somebody. If I could only place him in my past...

"Well?"

It's the 'Well?' game again. "I can't control my dreams," I say.

"Dreams?" There is sadness in his voice. "Why do you reject the evidence of things seen?"

"The evidence of things *not* seen," I correct. I also went to school.

"Yeah... the substance of things hoped for, the evidence of things not seen. Hebrew eleven-one. But you've seen it. You don't need that faith any more. All you need is to have faith in the evidence of things seen." The stranger, Friend or otherwise, sounds strangely persuasive, and just a little annoying. He also begins to sound like a know-it-all, and like a priest Ruth introduced me to some time ago, to boot.

"Sorry, John. I didn't mean to preach." He actually contrives to sound contrite.

"It's OK. I didn't mean to bite your head off."

This reminds me of my head in the Lakeshore Hospital. For a moment the dully lit corridors, the smell of antiseptic, the white-and green-clad bodies pass me on both sides. I only just manage to dismiss the vision of myself lying in bed, all bandaged up, waiting to die.

"There, that's how it's done." Friend manages to sound excited.

"What's done?"

"Didn't you almost transfer to the hospital just now?" Rhetorical question. I'm sure he knows the answer.

"Yes..." This comes out as a protracted 'yeeeeess?'

"You must have total commitment. Exclude all other thoughts. You must accept what is..."

For once he seems to be running out of words. Then he sighs deeply. I am beginning to get an inkling of what he is driving at. It is like creating a building. If I didn't pay total attention, the damn thing would fall down. Or leak, or lose panes of glass under negative wind pressure, or the bricks would come loose from tiebacks… it took total commitment and dismissal of all other mental and physical interference. Yes, total commitment.

"I like your initials," he starts, apparently on a new tack.

"J.C.?"

"Jesus Christ. No one believed him, either. But he never 'almost' cured someone, nor improved someone's sight just a little, nor, for that matter, made someone half-alive. His cures were total, absolute, uncompromising. It's like being a little pregnant. It can't be done."

Total commitment. It's as though the previous condition didn't exist anymore. You're either sick or healthy. Either dead or alive. Except that I am neither.

My Friend sighs again.

"We never die," he says. "There is no death," he adds, hardly above a whisper. "We change realities—in one you are dead, in the other alive. Sometimes one can be in both. It's rare."

"So I'll recover?"

My own future—or present, for that matter—is still foremost in my mind. Images of Ruth once more flood my mind. This time I can almost see her. I feel her presence, close, ephemeral, transient. A whiff of her perfume touches my nose. The same instant I get scared. What I mean is, I don't want to scare her away. I have to learn this thing about reality the stranger is talking about. Did it have something to do with the biblical Jesus?

No answer. Apparently I have to work out some things on my own. I begin to hope that I would not recover too soon. If I could only understand what he is talking about, I could make those stars visible to Ruth. The name Jesus returns to me with renewed force. I always thought that he'd created a religion which, frankly, judging by the various sects, didn't quite grab me. What did my Friend mean—that he is…

"What you did, back then, with the stars… can people do the same in their, you know, in their physical bodies?" I ask. I am really thinking aloud.

"You do it all the time. It is only a question of degree."

I mull that over. "Why does our mind reject new concepts?" I ask instead. When my Friend doesn't answer, I continue myself.

"We create the reality we live in. But we put up barriers. We impose limitations on ourselves. Is that it?"

"Ye are gods..." I hear his thoughts reverberating in my head. Easy for you to say.

R uth shrugged. For a moment she could swear she felt my presence. It was as if I stood over her shoulder, as if I almost embraced her, and then I was gone. She didn't believe in ghosts or apparitions. Not that she'd seen anything. She just felt it. Ghosts, for those who believe in them, are said to be cold, forbidding and scary. This was warm, kind, and somehow filled with longing. I sensed all that just by looking at her.

The next moment it was gone.

"Perhaps I should pray more," she muses, a melancholy look in her eyes.

This was the first time I actually overheard her thoughts. I felt deeply ashamed. I had no intention to spy on her. Quickly I put distance between us.

Her parents had been very religious. In a way, still are. Not necessarily in the deepest sense of the word, but they are both conscientious, practicing Catholics. While she lived at home, before she met me, she attended Holy Mass every Sunday as well as on all the Holidays of Obligation. It was a way of life. Her parents didn't question any of the Church's teachings. They lived on faith or, as she later discovered, on habit.

Since Ruth's father died, her mother, Clara, grew even more attached to what she believed was the only true faith. This lack of tolerance did nothing for Ruth's allegiance.

She'd drifted a long way since those days. Her God metamorphosed into a non-religious deity. He, or She, became the God of beauty, or the Creative Force that inspires humanity to reach ever higher, beyond themselves. She liked to quote Captain James T. Kirk. 'To boldly go where no man had gone before.' Only she didn't mean to some physical destinations. She thought that the greatest undiscovered land lay within her. Within each one of us—if we'd only allow it to come forth. To unfold.

Then she met me.

Practically from the day we met, she saw what total commitment I had for my profession. I would forego sleep, eating, even holidays, to get the job done. And to do it as well as I humanly could. She said she'd never seen such dedication. Not in her parents, not among her friends. While on occasion she apparently felt pangs of jealousy for my ability to concentrate, yet, simultaneously, this very commitment had attracted her to me. I taught her, by example, that one cannot serve two gods.

Soon she went back to McGill University to get her Ph.D., in fine arts. *Summa cum laude*. They didn't award *egregia cum laude* at McGill. They still don't, but her own professor had told her that if others before her got 'with highest praise', then she deserved 'with outstanding praise', as though highest were not high enough. There were champagne, speeches and press releases. I told her that I would build her a temple.

"Minerva has nothing on you," I affirmed, raising my sparkling flute.

It was the highest academic achievement anyone in her family had ever had. Yet for her, almost to her own surprise, it was just the beginning. While she might sound like a paragon of virtue, it should be mentioned that she had absolutely no patience with mediocrity. She didn't expect you to be a genius, but if she detected a smidgen of a divine spark flickering somewhere within your heart or mind, she would turn into an intolerant monster determined to awaken you from your stupor.

We live downtown, both for convenience and for the proximity to my office and Ruth's interests. Montreal is not exactly a Mecca of art, ancient or modern. But she thought that both New York and even Chicago were on her doorstep. She thought nothing of getting up at 4 a.m. to see an exhibition at the Museum of Modern Art, or the Guggenheim, and be back in time for her afternoon lectures.

Lecture tours and academic invitations followed. After a few years, she settled down to teaching—History of Art at college level. There were higher academic places of learning, but she wanted younger, unspoiled minds. Minds and eyes.

"When they know too much of the wrong things, it is so very difficult to un-teach them. I need fresh, hungry, curious minds. Minds I can spur into independence of thought. To let them flourish in their own garden, not follow some established fashion or fad."

She did that. Soon some of her students began to make names for themselves. They were always original, but not for the sake of originality. The uniqueness of their art flowed from their own individuality. This trait was as important to her as was the fact that her students became her lifelong friends. Our house, condo, was always open to them, day and night. She often joked that she had to go on a tour to get some rest. In this sense she and I were a perfect match. We were both unabashed workaholics.

Over the years, we both lost most of our previous social contacts. We gained, instead, dozens of dedicated friends. They became practically our children. All thanks to Ruth.

And now, these last few days, I know that she would gladly give up all this to have me back at her side. Even for a moment. There had been months during which we'd both been so busy that we hardly saw each other. But there was always a strange, unbreakable bond between us. A bond defined by a word so often abused, even bastardized, on TV and in other mass media. The word was love.

And now, here I was. At her shoulder.

I saw that, for the second day, she couldn't concentrate on her work. It's not fair to my students, she told herself. I must let nature take its course. I must have faith. I must, she repeated, her lips pressed tight in an unaccustomed thin line. I must...

And then I saw her eyes. "I must hold him again, even for a short blissful moment," they said. "I must..."

***

5

Early Years

Way out, all the way to the horizon, the surface is as
smooth as a mirror designed to reflect the wisps of
clouds making their lazy way towards the land. Just
wisps. Scattered over a vast area. Some of them pick up the rays of
sunshine, making them quite three-dimensional. One actually
shows a faint rainbow. No wonder so many artists paint seascapes.
They really are glorious. As the clouds get closer, they become
magnified, swelling into more vertical forms. Over time, a slight
swell develops on the lustrous surface of the ocean. There seems to
be a connection. The closer to the shore, the richer the cumulus
clouds, the more boisterous the swell. And then a breaker takes off
on its own and charges at the sand, leaving the clouds far behind.
The wave grows, increasing in height and volume before my eyes.
Finally, with a sense of fatality, the once lustrous sea crashes into
the shore.

"Take that!" it seems to say. "There is plenty more where this
came from."

All to no avail. By the time the fulminating water reaches dry
sand, its anger is already spent. It is but a frustrated ripple, its
convoluted fury long spent on the way from afar.

I'm playing in the sand. The waves continue to perform their Sisyphean dance. To and fro. Quick, quick, slow. Quick to roll up the shore, slow to retreat. *Ad infinitum.* Or at least since time was born. Or for as long as I am here. Is there a difference? Perhaps Zen Buddhists would know. They would make a köan out of it. None of this is accessible to rational understanding. Not rational as I understood the word.

"Johnny!"

Did any of this exist before I came ashore? Like the rest of the animal kingdom, did we not all emerge from the primordial soup that now delights our sense of grandeur? The ocean and the mountains: two symbols of eternity on earth. Just symbols. They don't really exist. At least, not according to my friend. To Friend. According to him, they only came into being when I saw them in my mind's eye. Let there be light. Let there be oceans and mountains. Let there be me. According to him, that last came first.

I am, he said. And so are you. The rest? You decide.

"Jooohnnie, don't go in so deep!"

Hogwash? Some days ago I would have said so. Today, some forty years ago, I can't argue. I just can't absorb it so fast. I'm reminded of the Greek philosopher Democritus of Abdera, some two and half millennia ago, 'Nothing exists except atoms and empty space; everything else is opinion.' It sounds like something Friend would say. He probably did. For all I know, he knew Democritus. He seems to know just about everything else. Thank God time is so flexible. Yesterday I was on my way to sixty, today I am around ten. A cute lad, at that. I see myself from within and without. It's a funny feeling. Not at all like looking at other people or other things. Only I am not he. He only exists in my mind. Like the clouds and the ocean. As in a dream.

I find it amusing to look at my tiny feet.

"Johnny, come back here at once. Now!"

The 'now' sounds pretty final. It took me a while to realize that my mother was calling me. It takes me even longer to accept that I am the cute lad playing in the sand, then in the water, then in the oncoming waves.

"They say there is an undertow today." She sounds worried. Of course, mothers always worry. Doesn't she know that I'm immortal? Doesn't she know that the mortal part of me is lying in a coma, way back, on shore, safely tucked in a hospital bed?

"I'm coming, Mother!"

I always call Mom mother. Ever since I can remember. Mommy is for little kids. I am big. I am probably also a bit of a nuisance. I always venture into areas that spell danger. I like to explore. Too deep in the water, too high on the mountain. Too close to the edge of steel girders when supervising construction. That last comes later. I guess, I always felt that I cannot die before my time. Even now, I seem to have problems dying. I mean now, in the hospital.

Joan and Elaine, my sisters, are playing in the sand. Joan is my senior by three years, Elaine's just a baby. I think of most children who are younger than I as babies. Elaine is three. She was named after my mother's sister, who married a French Canadian. Elaine grew up into a most beautiful woman. In these early days I resented her. I mean, having a younger sister. I thought I deserved a brother, to balance the odds. No luck.

On top of that, my father seems completely enamoured with Elaine. She's the proverbial apple of his eye. Of both eyes. I might as well not have been born. Now, when I am just beginning to see reality, I realize that those early years gave me the sense of independence necessary to become a partner in a leading architectural practice. Perhaps even to wrap my Honda around the lamppost and survive. That's assuming I'm still alive. I probably wouldn't see any of this if I'd never been in a coma.

I wonder what brought me here and now. To the shore, I mean. I am quite happy hanging out with Friend. Then, seemingly for no reason, I find myself in a ten-year-old body. It must have something to do with how the subconscious works. Or it could even be the unconscious.

From afar, I notice the expression in my mother's eyes and go ashore. I suspect she means business. I usually try to do as my mother tells me. I sit down on the sand and start throwing small seashells at my sisters.

"Johnny?"

My mother wants to know why I use my sisters for target practice. There is no one else within reach, I want to tell her but keep my observation to myself. I stop.

A crowd begins to gather about three hundred yards down the beach. Before my mother can stop me, I race down to see what's going on. Like an oversized lizard, I slither my way along the sand, between people's legs, to get to the front line of the circle of gawkers. Three men are carrying a man out of the water. He looks unconscious. They turn him on his stomach and try to press water out of his lungs. There are two or three slurps, and then they turn him over again, hold his nose to breathe air into his mouth. I think that's disgusting. Anyway, it doesn't seem to work. By then an ambulance is parked on the street and two men with a stretcher run down to pick up the man the other guys fished out of the water. Running on soft sand is funny. They look like circus clowns, or something. Only they are not smiling. I have no idea if the man they want to pick up is dead or alive. This is the first time I have witnessed the death of a human being. A possible death. It poses a question for which, to this day, I cannot find an answer.

"You see, Johnny, there really is an undertow," Mother says when I get back. By now the speaker announces, again, the dangers of the currents.

"Mother," I ask, ignoring her belated admonition, "where do people go when they die?"

"Don't be silly, Johnny. They go to heaven, of course. Unless they were very bad."

"How bad, Mother?"

"Never mind, dear. Never mind. I am sure that man, if he doesn't recover, will go straight to heaven."

Somehow I find my mother's answer distinctly unsatisfying. Then and now. The ambulance starts its wailing and, with lights flashing, takes off. It's a strange *déjà vu* in reverse. It is as if I saw a piece of the future. Friend said this couldn't be done. I realize that my own image of the flashing lights and the attendant wailing is already in my future's past. Does this make sense? Moments later I find myself sitting on the side of a ditch, next to a lamppost that looks the worse for wear. The ambulance is just taking off.

"Bye-bye, Johnny..." I wave goodbye. "So long," I correct myself. I wonder if his name was Johnny. Aren't we all one?

It is dark and lonely. Since that time on the beach, mother nearly died of complications trying to give birth to my brother. He didn't make it. It may be why, to an extent, I've always been just a little preoccupied with death. I keep wondering if my brother made it to heaven. He couldn't have sinned yet. I blink myself back to the seashore.

"Where do they really go, Mother," I repeat. Mother doesn't answer this time, either.

I smile at the thought of Friend knowing all the answers. I really miss him. But only for a moment. He is right where I left him. At the knoll. Smiling.

I am beginning to like that smile.

"What did you learn?" he asks. That's my Friend. No preambles, no 'how are you?' Straight to the point. Also, he never seems to grow tired of hanging on an invisible hammock between those two pines. Or it could be that he takes wild spins through the galaxy while waiting for my return. I would like to ask him why he bothers to wait for me, but I'm sure he would answer with another question.

"That people make much more fuss over the dead than over the living." And then I ask him pointblank: "Tell me. Do you think that I am preoccupied with death?" I half expect a 'what do you think'. I am spared.

"Not at all, John." His smile gets broader. "I would argue there is ample evidence that you are quite extraordinarily preoccupied with life. Don't you agree?"

I am beginning to really like my Friend. What he said definitely rings true. At my first contact with a drowning man I had had no concern at all about his possible death. My only interest lay in 'what now?' What happens after you get out of your body. There must have been something in me, even at the age of ten, that made me regard my own body only as a temporary abode. A place of in-between. In-between what, I had no idea. Like Bardo? And behold, here I am, four decades later, still trying to solve the puzzle.

"You mentioned that we create realities. Is this what Christ did? Did he just substitute one reality for another?" I bet he knows the answer.

"What do you think?"

There we go again. I should know better than to ask him for an opinion. Democritus saw to that. But, I must say, it seems that way. Jesus could not have denied the laws of the universe by accelerating the healing process, or restoring life while denying the laws that *this* reality has determined. Einstein insisted that God does not play dice with the universe. But are we not free to perceive it as we want to? What is beautiful to me may be ugly to someone else. This applies to everything. What's more, each and every opinion is just as valid for each and every person. You cannot say who is right. Eye of the beholder, and all that. And if God is beauty, as Ruth claims, then even God would be perceived by everyone in His or Her peculiar way. To become a Christian one must, therefore, agree with the reality as Jesus saw it. I mean as Christ sees it. Otherwise, one just does lip service to his teaching. And it very much seems to me that Jesus found a way to adapt reality to his perceptions, without breaking any of the universal laws.

"Can one do that?"

By now I all but assume that Friend can read my thoughts all the time. It is too late to withdraw the question. Serves me right, I have to smile.

"What do you think?"

We both laugh. I am awfully glad that one can laugh in this, whatever it is that I am in. Purgatory? If any major religion makes any sense, then this is the more likely, if not the most appropriate locus for my present circumstances. Between heaven and hell, in a state of suspension. Isn't this what coma is? I'll never forget that extra portion of ice cream. Anyway, it seems I got a good handle on how Jesus performed his miracles. The next question is how to acquire the skill myself. After all, a number of saints did it also. And some not so saintly people, or even members of other faiths altogether. There was a time when I had been taught that only Catholics go to heaven. I concluded, then, that heaven must be a very dull place.

I am bending over my desk, poring over a pile of documents. On top is the program I received late last night in the office. My secretary stayed after hours to put together for me all the documents, plans, maps, and bylaws I would need to prepare my preliminary sketches. Gracie is a wonderful girl. Woman. She has a girl of her own.

The time is seven in the morning. I can hear Ruth taking her shower. I like to analyze the basic program requirements on my own, in the seclusion of my study, at home. In the office there are too many telephones, too many questions from an army of assistants. It got so bad—or good, depending on your point of view—that I had to produce the preliminary design on my own, my staff being kept busy on all the on-going projects. They will give me a hand drawing out the presentation drawings, the model and the perspectives, of course; but they have to know what to draw out. It's just as well that I love my work. It's like solving a three-dimensional puzzle with the element of time, scheduling, by-laws, legal constraints, climate, budget and client's idiosyncrasies thrown in for good measure. And don't forget firmness, commodity and delight. I don't dare. Ruth would never speak to me again. In fact, from the visual point of view, she's my best critic.

I have to fit 800 rooms into a footprint which can accommodate about 25 of them, side by side. Per floor, that is. That comes to at least 30-32 floors, plus all the public spaces, restaurants, lounges, cafeterias, bars. Ballroom and the meeting rooms will have to go underground. And we'll need a large space for the lobby. An atrium, if possible. Plus parking, of course.

I check for height limitations, setback requirements, the aspect and the prospect from the site, prevailing winds, soil and subsoil conditions, existing structures, availability of services: water, gas, oil, electricity, telephone, sewage. Then I look at city plans to assess the road network, traffic patterns, proximity of public services, transport. We would add up to 1000 cars on the existing network at peak hours.

Finally I study the buildings around the site. Their height, quality, materials used, orientation and anything else that might catch my eye. Preliminary analyses take me about two hours. On the way to the office I'll take a cab to the future construction site, just to get the feel of it. By nine I try to be in the office to be available to my staff. They seem to work much better with me around. I don't push them, but I do express interest in their work. Our work. I couldn't do any of the major projects without them.

"Darling..."

Ruth tells me that breakfast is ready. She's in a great mood. She's always in a good mood, but this week there is something extra. We went dancing last Saturday, and ever since she seems to be walking on clouds. Cloud nine, to be precise. I'd already set the percolator going, but she sets out the table. We use the low one, in the sitting room. It's more relaxing, and we have a glorious view all the way across the St. Lawrence River. We never talk business at breakfast—neither hers nor mine. The most we allow ourselves to discuss are the ideas we woke up with. Some time ago we both realized, almost simultaneously, that the best ideas come during the night, when we are fast asleep.

"Funny, that," she tells me when we draw similar conclusions on the flow of creative currents, "the Hebrews knew that some three thousand years ago. Actually, more like three and a half."

I know better than to interrupt when she is searching for the right words to share an idea with me. I'd learned more about myself from Ruth than I ever could by self-analysis. And as far as reaching the same conclusions, well, it was she who actually reached it, and I who agreed. But with conviction. It was the day I got the hotel project.

I smile encouragement.

"In the first chapter of Genesis, there is a fascinating piece of instruction. We recognize the day as time between sunrise and sunset. The Hebrew did the opposite. The Hebrew day started at sunset. In order for an Idea to take root, we must *not* try to think about it but... sleep! The greatest ideas anyone ever had did not take seed in the scientists' labs, but at night. We are reminded here about the true source of ideas, and the true 'developer' of such. The nearest we get to participate is through our unconscious. So much for our egos!"

This is typical of Ruth. She would sip coffee, chew on a piece of toast and make statements that, over the next few days, completely inverted the way I worked.

"As a matter of fact, the first chapter of Genesis deals exclusively with the creative process. The birth of the world is only used as an illustration, an example. What really matters is the birth of an idea."

I am chewing on that day while lying down, again, back on the knoll. I do a lot of that lately. I suddenly realize that I don't eat. I neither eat nor drink. But I go through an awful lot of knowledge. Of accumulated facts. Perhaps they keep me going?

I regard the Stranger, my Friend, with renewed respect. Isn't this what he keeps telling me? Everything is an idea. It lives in our mind. It's already there.

I am still in awe of that breakfast Ruth and I had that day. An ordinary day, like any other. Except that Ruth was there. I remember going to my study, folding my papers, and not looking at them till the following morning. Then, also at seven in the morning, I sketched out the basic form that the hotel would take. Without Ruth it would have taken a week. At least. And chances are, the solution wouldn't have been half as good. I'd decided, there and then, to take her dancing more often. For a while I did.

I think Friend is beginning to understand why I keep going back to Ruth. She is part of me. The part of my life I miss the most.

I am back in the condo. Again we are on the terrace, enjoying a pre-dinner drink. It must be a few days after Ruth's statement about creativity.

She returns to the same subject. Only this time she is more direct.

"*In the beginning God created the heaven and the earth,*" she announces out of the blue.

"I dare say He did," I say, studying her face over the rim of my glass. The ice in my Scotch is picking up the dying rays of the setting sun. I had a good day. Thanks at least in part to Ruth, the client had accepted my preliminary schematics. "Or She did, as the case may be," I add, raising my glass. She ignores me.

"Note two important factors, John. One, God is always at the beginning of everything; and two, in order for anything to become manifest, we need to initiate the concept of duality. Heaven and Earth. In heaven, every idea is only in its potential state."

"I'll drink to that," I mutter. Ruth sounds as though she is thinking aloud. Her eyes dreamy, her drink untouched on the side table. Only then do I notice that she is holding a small, leather-bound Bible in her left hand.

"And the earth was without form, and void; and darkness was upon the face of the deep. And the spirit of God moved upon the waters."

This time she reads out the verse. Her index finger is holding the right page. "Obviously, the earth was without form; it wasn't there! It was only in its *potential* form. It was an idea!" she concludes triumphantly, italicizing the word 'potential' with two fingers. This time she reaches out for her drink. The ice cubes won't last much longer.

She takes a minute sip and raises the Bible to her lap. I wonder if I am in for a long tirade on a subject which doesn't hold particular interest to me. Not creativity as such, but biblical pronouncements on the subject. A sip later Ruth announces, *"And God said, Let there be light; and there was light."*

I think it best to remain quiet.

"Light, John, in the Bible, stands for knowledge. It's a well-established symbol. An illuminated person is a knowledgeable person. To put ideas into concrete form, we need knowledge."

I recall studying volumes of documents my secretary amassed for me, before I could even think of putting pencil to paper. Knowledge, lots of knowledge. Maybe there is something to that stuff in the Bible. I take another sip myself, just to play it safe, in case I start taking all she says seriously. But I do start listening more closely. The problem is that just looking at Ruth, particularly in the evening twilight, is deeply distracting.

Ruth continues through the remaining verses of the first chapter of Genesis. My mind is beginning to wander. If Ruth is right, then all knowledge already exists in its potential form. Creativity is limited to bringing out to the conscious awareness that which heretofore has been hidden within.

Mozart wrote complete compositions—sonatas, concertos and symphonies—without the need to make a single correction on his manuscripts. He saw or heard them complete, whole. All he had to do was to 'bring them out', dispose the notes neatly on music-paper, and hope that performers would do them justice. Great sculptors have been known to say that the work of art is already extant within the stone, within the block of marble. They just have to remove the redundant pieces of material. The poets hear, or rather feel, the poems before they write them down. It is not the process of writing that is creative; it is the process of listening.

I imagine Ruth paraphrasing the biblical statement, 'Blessed are they who have eyes to see and know how to listen!' She probably already did, when I wasn't paying attention.

It is self-evident that the biblical attitude demands of us a great deal of humility. I suspect Ruth has that. Innate humility. She glorifies other people's creation even if we are not really the creators, although we partake in the creative act. We are instruments through which the creative process manifests itself in our physical, mental and emotional environment.

I am looking at the white field, still barely covered with a delicate blanket of snow. The taller twigs, even yellow, dry stems of grass, still protrude in irregular clumps through the snow. There is peace here. Winter is the time of peace. Of reconciliation. The rest of the year it's dog eat dog. Now, nature sleeps. Even as I do, somewhere in a small room in a suburban hospital on the western outskirts of Montreal Island. *Ile de Montréal.* My personal oasis suspended in the infinity of space.

I also feel at peace with the world. I am grateful to my Friend for allowing me to reach back in time and listen to Ruth's voice. And to see her in the evening light of the setting sun. She's at her most beautiful then. She is always at her most beautiful.

I miss her touch.

I wonder if my Friend continues to fill my mind with knowledge. He'll probably claim that it's already there, mixed in a haphazard way among the one hundred billion neurons within a structure nature took five billion years to construct. He'll tell me that all I must do is to become aware of it. To arrange the components in a sequential order. The way time does. He'll tell me that the potential is within me. Within all of us?

I feel a stirring across the knoll. It is like a whirling of air I'd seen, many times, over tarmac on a hot summer's day. And then I hear his voice.

"What do you think?" he says. And we both start laughing.

***

6

Ruth

She tried praying. It always worked in the past. It was so easy when she was a child. God was a fatherly figure, old, benevolent, somewhat like Uncle Jim. Jim also had a long white beard. It was flowing and curly on the ends. It was also so long he didn't have to wear a tie. She once wondered, as a child, if that was why God grew such a long beard.

Ah, yes, it was so easy then.

Now? Now God had changed so substantially that it was difficult for her to address Him directly. Still, without prayers she felt lost. What else could she do? There was no one to lean on. Except Dad. He died when she was quite young, in her late teens. She remembered him as always being nice, always being supportive. For years he was—and remained to this day—her official contact in heaven. She didn't pray to him, of course; but she knew, with unshakeable confidence, that Dad would press the right buttons, up there, in the never-never land, where angels and departed dads held great sway. Usually, it worked. If it didn't—she knew with equal confidence—she must have been asking for the wrong thing, or at the wrong time, and her prayers would be heard as soon as it was at all possible. It was a nice arrangement.

"Thank you, Dad," she would always add. "I know you will do what's right for me." That was how most of her prayers would end.

And she prayed for almost everything. From wanting to meet me, to my becoming successful. I know—she told me. When we met, I was just a junior assistant. A good one, I like to think, but still junior. Young architects who aspire to become designers have to wait their turn. They must prove themselves. Young, aspiring architects all think they can design, but, she knew, it isn't so. *'Many are called but few are chosen,'* she liked to quote. She often quoted the Bible. To her, the Bible could be applied to all walks of life. Sometimes, surprisingly so. Since losing her father, she leaned on the Bible a lot. Mother wasn't much help. She was too busy feeling sorry for herself. Mother also prayed, but, from what Ruth observed, she prayed in the old-fashioned way. Always asking for something. Ruth preferred to give thanks.

"Lord, thank you for hearing my prayers. Thank you for John, for my work, for my students, for our condo, our wealth, for the view from our balcony..." It was a long list. "I know you will do what's right for me."

A win-win situation.

Ruth thanked the Almighty in great detail for the health He gave John and herself, for her students discovering their true potential. For the right weather on holidays. It's not that she spent her life on her knees. Far from it. Nor was she a regular churchgoer like her mother. But the faith she developed as a child served her to keep her on an even keel, to give her strength in moments when pressures were seemingly too heavy for her shoulders. In time she learned to rely on her own strength, but those early years were always there to lean on when necessary.

Until now, Ruth was very content with her life. The ever-changing rotation of her students compensated most adequately for the lack of her own children. She never resented fate, or God, for not giving her her own family. Her students were more than enough—indeed, often overwhelming—and she learned to channel her own creative juices through them, for their good.

Sometimes she felt guilty for not praying for Canadian soldiers fighting overseas. The Canadian government felt it expedient to meet the American president's implied obligations. The Americans started wars and then expected friendly nations to fight them. Ruth felt strongly against killing under any circumstances. To her, killing in war was no different from murder in a dark street corner in Montreal or New York. Murder is murder, she said, many a time. The Pentagon had a different name for it: collateral damage.

"What a pity that they seem to specialize in damaging tens of thousands of women and children," she told me, her eyes expressing a strange mixture of anger and compassion.

Ruth has strong views on taking other people's lives. She once told me that we are all murderers. "We don't bother to vote to kick murderers out of office. They murder in our name." I had a good idea whom she was talking about.

I know many Americans who are as much against the wars as she is.

As for her mom? She had Ruth late in her life, and although now a lady advanced in years, she still shows from where Ruth inherited her beauty. Her delicate features seem reminiscent of some old portraits, those gravitating towards the gothic period of Madonnas, which later artists preferred to portray as plump ladies disposed towards man's insatiable pleasures.

Her mom, Clara, always was, and remains to this day, a bundle of goodness. Aren't all moms? It's just that, all too often, she finds her consolation, almost pleasure, in covering herself with tears. Clara cries when she's happy; she cries when she's sad. She cannot sit through a TV sitcom without going through a box of tissues. This predilection may be helping her, but it does nothing for Ruth, who has to keep a keen eye out for when it may be necessary to cheer her mother up, or just pass the next box of tissues. The one advantage is that Ruth has little time left to dwell on her own woes. Especially now that I am of no use to her at all. It was a great relief when Ruth's mother moved out to live with my parents. Ruth missed her mother, but not her constant tears. Luckily, until now, Ruth had few problems to distract her from her work, or even from her mother's insatiable need for additional tissues.

Actually, even before the accident, Ruth had only one woe. Myself. Peeking gently into her mind, it seems that I was, that I had been, the main source of her deepest pleasure, but also of her distress. I was never good at looking after myself. As energetic as I surely was, I would never think of buying myself a new shirt, let alone a new suit or a pair of shoes.

"But, darling, I had these for years," was my favourite argument for not discarding them.

"My sentiments precisely, John. After all, you are representing your firm, not just yourself," she would counter. There were moments when I hated that she was right.

"But they are sooo comfortable."

I strongly suspect that most men are as I was. These last few days, they change my sheets twice a week, though I have no idea if I am even wearing any pajamas. Now that I think about it, it's amazing how little interest my old, broken-down body has for me. While it continues to hover at the edge of my awareness, I have no desire to see it, touch it, or be near it. Yet I seem to have a peripheral if morbid interest in its condition, as a man might have towards a prison in which he'd spent some fifty years for crimes he didn't commit.

What I really meant by my previous comment was that superficialities did not detract from nor in any way interfere with my total immersion in my passion. Design. With all her personal commitments, Ruth would still find time to take me by the hand, drag me to a shoe store and willy-nilly force me to buy at least two pairs to make up for the rarity of such occasions.

The same was true of my business suits. I admit that I was happiest working in a pair of old overalls. Clean but threadbare. I always kept a clean shirt and a jacket in my office, in case an important client dropped in. My theory was that what was good enough for Churchill was good enough for me. Winston Churchill had been known to carry out most of his prime-ministerial duties in an old boiler suit. Ruth would never admit to me that, even in my overalls, I looked more handsome, yes, even more dashing, than any man she'd ever met. Or at least than Winston Churchill.

Unfortunately or otherwise, Ruth's assessment of my masculine traits was not shared by most women I knew. If it was, they remained uncommonly silent about it. Their loss.

As you can see, modesty is my second nature.

Anyway, on top of that, Ruth considered me to be so very much alive. According to her, I was a living dynamo. I admit I tried everything, and I liked to constantly explore new ideas. People who don't make mistakes are people who never try anything new, was my motto. She agreed. She thought that some people went through life in a half-dormant condition.

"They move like snails, think even slower," she told me, more than once.

So she identified me with a bundle of unrestrained energy. She often said that I reminded her of a little boy. "You seldom walk, darling, you jog." In a way it was true. I did everything fast. Yet, according to Ruth, my concentration was such that I always did a thorough job. By the nature of my profession, I always paid attention to details. I had to.

"I always hold," I told her, "that architecture is only as good as the details."

Ruth reminded me of that when I paid no attention to my clothing. "Why can't you think of yourself as a piece of architecture?" She remembered most of my sayings.

Details regarding my work, never my own person. Yet in all this seemingly haphazard behaviour, she admitted that I never once forgot about her birthday, our anniversary, and, in earlier years, the day of her patron saint, which Catholics liked to celebrate as an occasion. What she didn't admit—and what I assume, nevertheless, to be adamantly true—is that if there was one passion that overrode my love of designing, it was, is, and always will be, herself. Deep down I think she knew it. Likewise, whatever art exhibition, lecture, display, or VIP trip, pulled her away from me, it was never stronger than the love I knew she felt for me. It was the kind of love that kept us close even when we were miles apart. Distance did not matter. In the middle of the night she would awaken seconds before the telephone rang—when I was calling to tell her that I had just gotten back from a meeting in a different time zone. We were one, inseparable, happy. Till now.

Now I watch her as she sits in my study, looking at photographs of my projects filling most of the west wall. On the left is my desk and, facing it against the east wall, my drawing board. Though I did most of my work on a computer, I still felt the need for a soft-lead pencil for initial sketches.

"Till now," she repeats my own thoughts. "Till now."

The day after the accident, Ruth made a concentrated effort to have my body moved to a downtown hospital. She'd made arrangements at the General, virtually a short walk from our condo. She wanted to be able to drop in on me at odd times, whenever she found a minute or two in her own, often taxing, schedule. Not that she wouldn't cancel her engagements to see me. The way I am now, I have no concept of time. I am lost in some strange country to which she has no access. God knows she tried. She prayed, read masses of material on the subject till the early hours, researched the whole of the Internet and even paid a visit to a psychic.

To her great disappointment, the physicians strongly advised against moving me.

"Coma is a very fragile condition, Mrs. Clarkson," they told her. "We don't really fully understand it. And in such cases we practice the old adage, *Primum non nocere.*"

She knew the expression. First do no harm. In her own way she understood it well. She saw a dozen wonderful paintings of Old Masters literally ruined by inept restorers. *Primum non nocere*, she would say herself, when asked her opinion about removing the grime of the ages from the darkened-with-age masterpieces. And she is recognized as a foremost expert.

I, or at least my body, remained at Lakeshore Hospital and Ruth reduced her sleeping hours to five per night. She visited me twice daily—usually, morning and night. She would arrive at the hospital while the staff doctors were taking a bunch of eager interns and residents on morning rounds. She would step aside and let them examine my body. After a week or two, she and they would nod to each other like old friends, respecting each other's privacy. They had to concentrate on every word uttered by the senior member of the staff. She had to listen in case I uttered a single word.

Up to the day she received the official police report of the accident, she was a little angry. It helped to balance her consternation. She was blaming herself for not insisting that I delay the delivery of my plans until next morning, or, at the very least, for not going with me to keep me company. I did have, she remembered, those two Scotches.

When she read the report, she breathed a deep sigh of relief. There was no guilt attached to either of us. The City was the only guilty party. The mega-size pothole had not been attended for two days—Saturday and Sunday. There was no evidence that I could have avoided the hazard without coming face to face with oncoming traffic. None of this made me feel any better, but she gazed at my still bandaged, lacerated, sleeping face as though asking for forgiveness.

"I've told Dad about you. He'll know what to do," she whispered into my ear. "You will see…" If she had only turned, she would have been face to face with me. My invisible, insubstantial face.

She continued to clutch on to the foundations of her faith. The accident had made a gaping hole in it. It shouldn't have happened, she reasoned. John had been doing what was right. One shouldn't be punished for doing what is right. Her God, at least in part, was still a god that meted out punishments and rewards. I suspect this is true of most Catholics. Even ex-Catholics. Even though she told me herself that Jesus said that his Father judges no man, old traditions seldom die. In spite of her knowledge, this philosophy served her well, until this time. She always managed to reconcile adversities with her personal, inimitable form of logic. Not now. Now was different. It just wasn't right.

> There is evidence that the air from the right front tire escaped in a single burst, making it impossible to control the vehicle even at normal speed. There is no evidence that any fault can be attached to the driver. Therefore, no demerit points will be filed against his driving license.

This paragraph concluded the police report. She re-read it three times. There was a sketch attached, showing the position of the pothole, the vehicle after the accident, and the offending lamppost. Well, thank heaven for that, she mused. No demerit points! John can drive right on. The moment he regains consciousness. Provided he's still alive. Now I can rest, she told herself. She couldn't keep sarcasm away even from her thoughts. No apology, not a word that they are sorry. Are they not part of the City Administration? Is no one to blame?

The lectures she delivered with punctilious preparation gave her strength. She arrived in MacDonald College early and was in the lecture theatre before her students arrived. She set up the projector, lowered the screen, and inserted the disc into the mega-size LCD high-definition equipment. Some time ago, she had been offered to produce her own TV series. She had refused. For now, she didn't want to dilute her academic priorities. Perhaps later, she told them. When I am older, less active.

On the third day after the accident, she returned home at the regular time. She had rented a car; taxis were too expensive and she had no time to wait for the unreliable bus service. She drove it directly to Pointe Claire, intending to do some mundane shopping on her way back. There was no change in my condition. I was stable, the nurse told her.

"It can last for weeks," she added sadly.

Or years, Ruth knew. On day one she researched the Internet for all the facts about coma. There were lots of words, opinions, but not many facts. As Dr. Morton had said, they didn't know much.

On her return, the moment she opened the door of our apartment, she was overwhelmed by a powerful aroma. Moments later she saw them. The condo was filled to overflowing with flowers. They were standing on both kitchen counters in a number of vases, the sink held about six bunches. She took off her coat and peeked into the powder room. There, too, the wash-basin acted as repository for a bunch of bouquets, all ends submerged in water. She was glad the janitor hadn't used the toilet in like manner. There was also a cleaning bucket, probably supplied by the super, filled with flowers to overflowing. It was on the floor, directly on her path to the living room.

On the dining table, to the right of the passageway, she found a scribbled note.

Sorry Mrs C but me and my Missus didnt know were else to puttem in water. They all came in abaut for oclock and almost all at once.

It was signed *George Super.*

About four o'clock. Half an hour after she gave her last lecture. They probably thought I would go straight home. Ruth was well aware that she was liked by her students. After all, a number of them remained her friends long after they completed the course she was giving. But this was something else. This was a sign of a deeper caring. Even of love. The vast majority of her students didn't suffer from excessive affluence. Perhaps abundance of talent, but hardly money. Artists are seldom rich, at least not while still alive. Art may well be the only profession in which one is worth more dead than alive. Yet here, her students had spent their hard-earned money to fill her life with flowers.

She reached out for the first bouquet to put it in a proper vase. She held it at arm's length, then drew it towards her, inhaling its fragrance. Red carnations—hardly cheap this time of the year. For a brief moment she stood very still, then she leaned her back against the kitchen counter. Quite involuntarily, her chest rocked with a series of convulsions. Then, just as spontaneously, tears came in great abundance. They were mixed with sobs and grimaces of joy in equal measure.

"I love you, too. I love every one of you. I really do…"

She didn't sleep very well that night. She kept telling me how much she loved me. And then she said the same to everyone of her students. And then to every other person she could think of. I know I spent the whole night watching over her. Like a guardian angel. Only I couldn't help her. I didn't know how. This was the last night in the foreseeable future that joy won the battle over sorrow in her heart. The last night that she was reasonably happy. What followed wasn't nice at all. The next day came anger. Anger and rebellion against the world, against whoever determines her fate.

I'm in the condo again. I choose a time when I know Ruth is at the College, in the middle of giving her lectures. I cannot control the dates, but I am getting fairly good at recognizing the times of day. Day or night, for that matter. Not that it matters. I can switch them at will.

Till now, I was more or less following Ruth's every move, like an invisible dog on an invisible leash. I find it too taxing. She has no idea I am there. I inhale all her emotions. It is exhausting. Did you know that ghosts can get exhausted? I can.

Now I am afraid to come here when Ruth is home. I already see her in the hospital, every time she visits, but at home it's different. It is one thing to see her give melancholy glances at my inert body, quite another to have her close, in an environment where but a few days ago I held her in my arms, where we shared the same bed, close, together...

I might do something I have no control over. Some time ago Ruth read stories about poltergeists and other extrasensory phenomena that weren't very nice. At least not for those on the living side of the equation. I always thought of them as products of an overactive imagination, both Ruth's and the writer's. Now? Now I am not about to become a ghost-prankster, or expose Ruth to the danger of some sort of possession. I am darn new to being 'dead', or half-dead, and I am learning each day new rules that control this reality. Until I master them, I shall keep my icy fingers from her spine. And frankly, Friend is not that much help.

I move about—remembering. I assume that the better I refresh my memory, the easier it will be to find my way here in the future. I remember that this reality has no control over the future, but, well, I want to be prepared for all eventualities. Friend says that it isn't necessary. That every fragment of my past exists in the present. That it is only a question of attention. I smile and concentrate on the knoll.

"Learn the trick and hey, presto, you are here," he says, the sardonic smile never leaving his face. I blink the knoll away. This is weird.

My study is exactly as I'd left it. Even my pencils lie sharpened, ready to sketch another idea. I always sharpen them after I finish work. That way, when an idea comes, I don't have to wait for it to dissipate into thin air while I am sharpening them. My assistants use felt pens, but I find them too final. Too committing. At the beginning I need freedom.

There is a knock on the door. Next a key is inserted and the super comes in with a bunch of flowers. Actually it is a bunch of bunches. There must be a dozen of them. He's followed by the overflowing Mrs. Super. They put their bunches in the kitchen sink, peek into the living room—curiosity, I presume—and leave, snapping our lock shut. I float over to read the notes.

A lover? Shouldn't he wait for my body to get cold?

There are none. Just bouquets without any notes attached. Either it is an extremely secret lover, or somebody died.

It takes me a while to realize that it might well be me. I haven't been to the Lakeshore since this morning, and for all I know my body is kaput. Would I know it? Would Friend?

The key again. More flowers. This time they fill the powder-room sink. A bucket comes next. Right in the middle of the passage. That does it. I am dead. Quite dead. I don't want to play this game anymore. I may not feel any pain, but there is such a thing as anguish, as loneliness, as sorrow of never holding Ruth in my arms again. I wish ghosts could cry. Mother says that crying helps. Clara specializes in it. It releases the tension, they both claim. I never realized that real suffering has little to do with physical pain. Maybe there is a hell, after all.

And then I remember. The universal replay.

I just finished my work, my drink is waiting for me on the terrace. I do fast forward. After twenty-four years of marriage, I still get a kick out of watching her undress. For whatever reason, she does it slowly, perhaps deliberately trying to entice my attention. She doesn't have to try hard. I roll over the bed and help her out of her trousers. She always wears them to work. There is a standing joke between us that when she retires she'll start dressing like a woman. Tonight, she is all woman. For me, she always was. She always will be. I cut the replay. It's too hard.

This isn't real.

I am back in the present. At least, I think it's the present. My timing is still bad. I can't tell my past from the present. I panic. I replay back this last scene from the beginning. Then again and again. God, how I love this woman.

Again, in the present.

I hear the click of the key in the lock. I picture the knoll. It works. I am out of my condo just as the door swings open. Friend is smiling. I think he has a dirty mind.

***

7

I am Nothing

I *am not.*
I am nothing.
I am nowhere.
I am nowhen
Which I am—am I?
I am the nucleus of awareness. I have no points of reference.
How do I know that I am? I am infinite potential of everything,
everywhere, at all times. Only there is no time.
   I am everything, everywhere, everywhen in my potential form.
Only I have no form.
   I am everything everywhere that ever was, is or will be. Only
there is no everywhere. I am nowhere. There is no space.
   I reach out to infinity. Only there is no motion. I am infinity. I
am everywhere and nowhere.
   I just am.
   I am aware of being and nothing else.
   I am and I am not. This is unsatisfactory. I must manifest my
being. Prove to myself that I am.

I shut off my perceptions. I am my mind. I am the vortex of
my creative potential.
   My Friend is grinning. He looks at me as one regarding a child
who is given a new toy, and he is glad that the lad finds the toy
pleasing. The observer and the observed. My emotions, such as I
have, are whirling unrestrained, precluding any logical explanation
of what is happening. It all takes place now. Here and now. I
haven't moved from my invisible perch, a perch I'd also created in

my mind. This is not at all like being alive. It is even farther from being dead. Not that I'd know it. For a while there, nowhere, I experienced an awareness of non-being. How can nothing experience itself? I shut off the senses that I am aware of. I tell myself that I know that I am, therefore I must be.

My Friend is staring at me. His eyes draw me in with indomitable force.

I am aware of a new stirring within me. Yet it is neither within me nor without me. I perceive thoughts gathering from all parts of me, a movement... vibration? Time comes into being. Time gives birth to the future. Now I have room to expand my thoughts. There is no past yet, just future. Future that is void yet unfolding in my eternal present.

I wasn't and now I am. I am that I am.

I am a blaze of light. I am that I am. I am the light, I am awareness of myself. I reach out to limits of infinity. I fill future with my presence.

For a moment I escape the grandeur of what is happening. I cannot embrace that which is infinite with my thought. I feel like a drunk on Friday night.

I AM   I AM   I AM   I AM

I hear atonal vibration so fine as to permeate infinity with aliquot harmonics. It holds, sustains and glorifies the essence of my being.

I am reverberates in limitless glory of my consciousness
I am the birth, the sustenance, and the fulfillment
I am forever the essence of the infinite potential
I am life that is yet to come into being
I am the power of my own awareness
I am the source of all knowledge
I am that I am and I am no other

I am suspended on my trusty hammock in the middle of an expanding darkness. I am the points of light that give my presence a sense of reality. My Friend is gone. I am alone. I sense endless parts of me vibrating in strange unison. I smile as infinite aspects of me swell into harmonics. I am music; I am the music of the universe not yet born.

I swing between two pines in the center of the universe.

Ghosts don't sweat. Less so, become covered with sweat. Yet my body, such as it is, has sheen, as though covered with droplets of dew... nay, with particles of light. No. It's more than that. I sit in the light. The light is me. I am the light. Someone already said that. I know: Sai Baba. An Indian saint. Something happened out there, out when, that I am yet to understand. One day I shall. In the future that is not yet born.

Slowly the pines dissolve...

Again I watch time stretching to infinity. Gradually past comes into being, but I place no limits on the future. I dream of all that I am in time yet to come. I am all that is, that I ever shall be. In the eons of time. In the infinity of space. Vibration becomes a function of time that will become motion. Angular momentum, forever connecting parts of me to me with immutable attraction. No parts of me shall ever be apart. I shall remain as one.

I am that I am.

I am the dust from which galaxies will be formed. I am the concept of stars that ensue from my desire to create life in the image of me. I seed my universe with the ideas of my potential children, all living, all dreaming, all yearning to see themselves as reflections of me.

I am that I am.

I wave eons away. I am one in the many. I assemble parts of me from the dust I draw from the hearts of stars. How did they come into being? I endow parts of me with diverse identities. I give them joy and teach them the essence of attraction. The essence of love. I teach them that I am one and there is none other.

They grow and evolve.

More eons whirl past my awareness—mere fragments of eternity. I inhale my own essence; then, a strange fragrance of an enchanted orchard fills my esoteric senses.

"Tell me more," Radha whispers, gazing at the young prince.

The cowherd in princely attire sets his flute aside. His voice sounds like music imbued with wisdom...

I am the taste of water, the light of the sun and the moon.
I am the sound in ether and the ability in man. I am the

original fragrance of the earth, and I am the light in fire.
I am the original seed of all existence, the intelligence of
the intelligent, and the prowess of all powerful men.

Radha rests her head against Krishna's knees. She gazes at his
face, luminous in the setting sun. I hold my breath not to lose the
wondrous vision. By some miracle they both seem so very familiar
to me. Have I walked this orchard before? Surely, I don't deserve
to witness such beauty...
      "Tell me more," she whispers. "Please tell me more..."
      This time Krishna's flute sings the arcane verses; the words
form directly in my mind. Strange magic engulfs all who listen...

I am the strength of the strong, devoid of passion and
desire. I am the Self, seated in the hearts of all creatures.
I am the beginning, the middle, and the end of all beings.
I am ever detached, seated as though neutral. I am the
source of everything; from Me the entire creation flows.
I am seated in everyone's heart, and from Me come
remembrance, knowledge and forgetfulness.

And forgetfulness... Why have I forgotten so much? Surely
my Friend is right. We have but one life—life that is eternal? Even
as Krishna and his beloved Radha. Will they not live forever
amongst us?

A gust of hot wind touches my face even as a new image fills
my vision. A young man, perhaps in his early thirties, sits on a flat
rock. His back straight, his blue eyes intense. They seem to
embrace the landscape all the way to the horizon. A gentle smile
lights up his face. The land falls away towards a stream,
meandering through a patch of green in the surrounding desert. A
dozen men dispose themselves all around him, waiting for him to
speak. Then the young man rises. A strange light emanates from
his face. He speaks slowly, as though making sure his words
remain etched in the listeners' minds. And beyond...

I am the light of the world. I am the door: by me if any

*man enter in, he shall be saved and shall go in and out
and find pasture. I am the resurrection, I am the way,
and the truth, and the life.*

Who is this man? Who am I? Is there an answer hidden in
those words just for me? For all of us? The image shimmers,
wavers like the air rising over the nearby desert, then dissolves as I
open my eyes... I hate empty words which people perpetrate as
trite quotations, but these words strike an echo in my mind. I've
heard these words before. So long ago...

Before me I see an old man. A long, pale-blue robe covers his
gaunt body. In front it is swept back, showing traditional clothing
of a medieval philosopher. He sits on his haunches. A simple man.
His head is adorned with a turban as was worn, in those days, in
Persia. His eyes are closed, a long, white beard touching his meager
chest.

"The Roman," people whisper. "He's going to speak..."

There is a protracted gasp from the group, which in seconds
has gathered around the ancient, as if in great expectation.

I am standing among the crowd, holding my own breath. I'd
never given his teaching much thought. In fact, I'd given it no
thought at all. Why am I chosen to hear his words? Yet here I am,
my head, my mind brimming with learning that I never made my
own while alive. I seem to know this man. This is the great
Mawlana Jalal-ad-Din Muhammad Balkhi, known later only as
Rumi, the Roman. A poet, a Muslim philosopher, a theologian.

It's all coming back to me...

They call him Roman because he lived most of his life in
Anatolia, part of the Roman Empire. But his kingdom was also not
of this world. Surely, I also lived there at that time?

As silence envelops the crowd, the ancient speaks.

*I am where My servant thinks of Me. Every servant has
an image of Me; whatever image my servant forms of
Me, there I will be. I am the servant of My servant's
image of Me. Be careful then, My servants, and purify,
attune, and expand your thoughts about Me, for they are
My House.*

My mind is spinning. So much knowledge had been available to me all my life. Yet I'd learned nothing. Not one word of wisdom that now flows into me by some inexplicable grace. My eyes search for my Friend. He must have dipped his fingers in this magic. I am alone, except for the people gathered around Rumi.

What wondrous mysteries are mine to witness?

The next fragment of eternity finds me suspended in the middle of nowhere. The heart of the universe? Time fluctuates along the matrix of the universe still forming. Where am I? Even more so, when am I? But most of all, I'm still searching for my true nature. For the essence of my being. And what of my children to come?

I am the Way-Guide, the Supreme Mind, the thoughts of Atum the One-God. I am with you—always and everywhere. To the sinful and vicious, I may appear to be evil. But to the good—beneficent am I.

The man who speaks these words is a head taller than I, yet I detect my presence within him. I am adorned like an Egyptian priest. I'd just initiated two acolytes to the Secret Order of Hermes. The rest of my mind is lingering on the lost wisdom of the Pharaohs. Will it survive the ages? Will I?

A slight man, his snow-white beard reaching to his waist, smiles, waves to me and utters the words like an echo of a forgotten melody:

Heaven's Tao has no particular affection... there is no partiality of love... it is always on the side of the good man...

Ah, yes, I know this man. I've known him for ages. They call him Lao Tzu, the Old Master. He spoke of universal benevolence in such simple terms. For some reason my Ruth invades my mind.

I look upon my children with love. They have their being only in my mind, but for me they are alive already. They are growing ready for their becoming. And even as I think of them populating my universe, I search my mind for guidance for them. It is in that transient instant I hear his words for the very first time. He's standing right next to me.

A lamp am I to you that perceive me. A mirror am I to you that know me.

"Thank you, John," I whisper, hoping for more of his wisdom. In spite of my abject ignorance, I recognize the voice of John, later known for his Apocryphal Acts. I have no idea how I know this. Yet he says nothing more. He just smiles. A slow, contented, understanding smile. Just before his image dissolves into the ethers, his face strikes me as familiar. For an ephemeral moment I am convinced I recognize that smile.

The Stranger is swaying gently to and fro on his cushion of air, as if rocked by a cosmic wind. He seems suspended beyond time. Doesn't he ever get tired? He looks at me, questions in his eyes. They are shining with an unusual light, even for him. If he can read my thoughts, why is he waiting for me to talk? Then I see it. He can read my thoughts, but not control what I think. For some reason this realization gives me pleasure. Remnants of my ego?

"Well?" His favourite question. It always seems to come back to what I know. What I've learned. Why am I so important?

"Did you do that?" I am thinking of the visions, the concepts that span the universe of my mind for the last few billion years. Billions? I try to pierce through his seeming indifference. I cannot. It's not that I can't read his thoughts; it is more like hitting an ocean of vacuity. A vacuous universe waiting to be populated with my thoughts. Till now, I was convinced it was the other way around.

"Before, there was no time. Eternity was just eternity. Immeasurable," he says slowly.

"And now we can measure it?"

"Of course not, but people continue to try. They need a beginning and an end. It is in their nature. The nature of duality. But..." His voice trails off.

"But...?" It is my turn to prompt him.

"Now you know that it isn't necessary."

"I thought it is *not* in our nature. Aren't we endowed with some latent, potential traits, you know...?"

"Of divinity? If we were left to find our own way at the rate the universe is evolving from first principles, we wouldn't achieve self-awareness for another hundred or two hundred billion years. Hence, duality."

"I thought that's something to do with good and evil."

This time he laughs outright. "Yes," he says, at last. "That's another of our quaint quirky traits. No, it accelerates the process."

"What, good and evil?"

"No, John, the concept of duality. The cause and effect. Also the concept of pain, of suffering, of Satan, hell, Beelzebub..."

His eyes turn into great pools of swirling atoms. For a moment I resist, then I feel drawn into them as though into the vortex of a gargantuan black hole. I recall the phrase... *connecting me to me, with inseparable, adamant attraction...* we're going back, back...

The rest comes in fragments, snippets I can hear just in parts. I recognize the voice of James, my friend of yore. Yet he speaks for his Master...

I am he who was within me... I am the beloved... I am the righteous one.
I am the process of becoming...
I am the silence that is incomprehensible... I am the one before whom you have been ashamed. I am strength and I am fear.
Never have I suffered in any way, nor have I been distressed.
I am the one whom they call Life...
I am the one whom you have hidden from. I am sinless. I am the one who alone exists.

"There is no room here, John, for good and evil, except by our ignorance and forgetfulness. Evil has no existence, no substance, by itself. It is an absence, rather than a presence. Leave it alone and it dissipates into the primordial darkness."

"I am the one who alone exists..." The words still reverberate in my mind. Is this where Jung got his idea of reality? I've learned so much, yet my mind is humming with a million questions. Why have I wasted so much of my life? I hardly hear my Friend speak.

I emerge from the black hole unscathed. His words reach me as I adjust my senses to the here-and-now. "There is no evil..." I repeat, my intonation hovering between a question and hopeful affirmation.

"No, John. There is but Single Source."

This I do remember. From before the world was, I am. From before time was, I am. From before... "No, my dear Friend. There is no room, for even in my creati..." I pull short of completing the sentence. My portentous presumptions astound me. Suddenly I am afraid. Afraid? I am scared out of my wits!

Friend looks at me with a dash of pity.

"It takes time," he says. "Even eternal now is composed of infinite segments of infinity. It takes time..."

He sounds less and less vacuous. For the first time since I first saw him sitting on the edge of the dark, damp, cold ditch at the side of the road, I hear, I see, I feel genuine compassion. It washes over me in waves of emotions quite unknown to me. They are impersonal. Undemanding. Asking nothing in return. He really is a Friend. A Friend such as I'd never had before.

"Thank you, Friend," is all I can muster. "I really think..."

His knowing smile stops me. For a moment I forget he can read my thoughts.

Even as I express my gratitude, the phrase I heard minutes or perhaps ages ago, the phrase I heard in a peculiar dream-state, hovers, again, persistently, on the edge of my awareness: *A lamp am I to you that perceive me. A mirror am I to you that know me.* I still don't like quotations, just for their sake, but this one intrigues me. What a strange thing to say. What a strange world this is. Not at all like the other side.

I am back at the Lakeshore Hospital. I no longer notice the green and white tunics floating by me along the corridor. I don't even notice the smell of antiseptic. I wonder, instead, why I always find myself inside the corridor, and not directly in my room. In John's room. My room. I suppose it's a force of habit. Or it could be that I am holding back, reticent to find out if I am still alive. Apparently, here, in my new reality, we also form routines. That's too bad. Habits become traditions, and traditions limit our freedom. They hold us back from moving forward.

How do I know this? I always liked traditions...

My body is lying motionless. There doesn't appear to be any change. That's as it should be. Otherwise, I would not be in a coma. I would just be asleep. They'd removed some of the bandages from my face. I am delighted that I still have a nose. Broken, blue stretching all the way to my right cheekbone, twisted, but it's still there. On my face.

At least, I haven't died, as the flowers in the condo had implied. I am vaguely amused that I didn't bilocate or transfer to the hospital to check straightaway the moment I saw them at the condo. Have I lost interest in life and death? I am reminded of Mark Twain: 'We go to heaven for the climate, hell for the company.' I think he meant for companionship. It must be lonely up there. Of course, according to my Friend, there is no such place as heaven and hell. There is not even such a thing as death. I don't think my Friend actually said so, but that's how I took his meandering answers.

I'm vaguely interested how the rest of my body is doing. I'd hate to slip into it, inadvertently. I might remain trapped inside it, contorted in chronic pain of some sort for years on end. I'll wait. Forever—if need be. Time is such an elusive concept.

I look at the clock on the wall. It's 4:30. It's still light outside. Must be the afternoon. I decide to wait for Ruth. Seeing her in the condo is more than I can handle. Seeing her here is less demanding of me. Usually there are other people around; and I know this sounds strange, but my body lying right there, in front of both of us, has the effect on me as if a third person were present. I know that's ludicrous, but there it is. It's either that or it would be like having sexual desires right in front of a corpse. Half-corpse. Your choice. It's hard to believe, but in spite of all I've seen and heard since the accident, I still share all my dilapidated body's memories.

Call me a kinky ghost, but not that kinky.

As Ruth is not here yet, I take a quick tour of other rooms. I transfer to one floor up. There seems to be an awful lot of suffering on this floor. Wasn't it Buddha who said that life is suffering? Funny how I know things now that I never knew when alive. I never had any interest in Buddha's teachings, and now I'm quoting him. Life—or death, for that matter—is full of mysteries.

Anyway, pain, here, is equally distributed throughout the floor. Like an equal-opportunity employer. It affects everybody. Not just their bodies, but their minds and emotions. I can feel it in the air. My Friend must be from another galaxy. He is, of course. Another world. But then I recall what Ruth told me once. She was reading—I could run the recorder and make sure—I think it was the Gnostic Acts of John. She read: 'Learn how to suffer and you shall not be able to suffer again.'

There I go again: quoting people I'd never heard of while walking this valley of tears. I must sound like a wise guy. I wonder if it's my Friend who keeps feeding me these thoughts.

John's statement almost captures, in a single aphorism, the Four Noble Truths of Buddhism. Why don't they teach us that? I mean teach them—I already don't suffer. Wouldn't just about all the patients in this and every other hospital benefit from such knowledge? Buddhists, Gnostics and everybody else. As would all Christians, though some seem to love suffering so. Yes, and Jews and Moslems. No more pain. Surely, truth is universal? It doesn't belong to any one religion. Of course, the physicians wouldn't make the money they are making; but, after all, aren't they overworked, anyway?

"Please, please, Nurse, give me another... it's been hours..."

She is begging for her next injection of morphine. I peek into the nurse's mind. The woman had one less than an hour ago. From what I see, cancer patients would be excellent subjects for learning the Buddhist truth.

"We must wait for Dr. Prentis to come. He'll be along any time now..." she lies.

It is a lie of kindness. It gives the woman hope. Dr. Prentis, the resident oncologist, won't be making his rounds for another two hours. Poor woman. I bet she would love to join me in my comatose state. Let's face it. I am actually having fun. More so, every day. Poor Mrs. Smith. Mrs. Brown. Mrs. Jones. Poor all the men with prostate cancer. Even the stupid smokers who lined their lungs with tar. Poor... there are so many of them. The terminal cancer patients are virtually nameless. Just numbers. Soon they will be statistics.

A strange thought crosses my mind. If Jesus of Nazareth came to visit the Lakeshore, would he heal all these people? Would the patients have sufficient faith to accept his healing power? Would they accept the change in reality? And... and would they contract the same disease soon, again, by not changing their ways? "Go and sin no more?" He must have been kidding.

I shift back to the floor below. I don't go there. I accept myself in my room, and I am here. There is no travel involved. I am there—I am here. Neither time nor space is involved. Not even movement. Just reality. As when Jesus was healing. You are sick—you are whole. Just a change in reality. I wonder if we'll ever learn from his example. It seems so easy—for me. Of course, I have a Friend. And I am dead. Almost.

I can hear them walking down the corridor. A bunch of them. I hate it when others come. I mean, I am very much taken by their concern, but what I really want is just to watch Ruth. And, if I'm lucky, to hear her voice. God, how I love that voice. If she sang in opera, she would sound like Alison Metternich. Or Maria Olszewska. I heard her in *Lohengrin*. A magnificent mezzo-contralto. Pretty, too.

In a way, I suppose I just wallow in self-pity. But seeing Ruth caring for that lug in that bed makes me warm inside. Or something like that. Ghosts don't feel warm or cold. They don't feel, but they see and smell and hear, and do funny things with space and time and velocity. As for Ruth, well, it is as though a warm glow washed over me. She is that good. Really. My Ruth.

I can't face the rest of my family right now. They are so terribly parochial. We all are. Were. We think our tiny consciousness is the centre of the universe. I think Aristotle started it all, and then the Catholic Church picked up the idea. Or maybe the Church was the first? The concept expanded to become the geocentric view of the world. Ask Galileo. It wasn't funny. It's changing slowly. Traditions slow them down. In a way they had the right idea but the wrong interpretation. We *are* the center of the universe. Our private, personal universe. Our consciousness, our awareness, is just like the center of operations.

They should listen to Paul. I die daily, he'd said. He was willing to accept completely new realities each day. He healed the sick, walked through walls. Ruth is a bit like that. I don't mean she heals and walks through walls, but she is not set in her ways. Each day, when I wake up, it's like being next to a new woman. Her gorgeous wrapping is the same, but she generates fresh views, fresh opinions, fresh ideas. As if she made them up while sleeping. Now, I know that she actually does that. Her unconscious never stops, it's just that she doesn't put clamps on hers just because the ideas might contradict her previous viewpoint. She would feel so good here. Where I am. So very at home. I don't hold on to anything. Not even to my body. Nor to the place I'm in. Not even to my understanding of things. These grow exponentially. Like the dust clouds and the galaxies. Like the expanding universe itself.

Ruth is so alive. In constant becoming.

Here's my mother, tissue in hand. That's it. I am gone.

I am energy. I am sitting on air, facing my Friend. I have no mass. Do I have mass as a ghost? Unlikely. I'd be affected by the space-time continuum. I'm not. Ergo, no mass. If I am a body of light, even dim light, then, though photons have no mass, they do exhibit properties of both waves and particles. Not that this makes me feel any better. Now I am countless squiggly minute pieces of lint in desperate search of a melody.

"You are energy," my Friend repeats. He's not here, but I can hear him. And then I am alone again. Not even his voice reaches me here. I am surrounded by absolute, impenetrable darkness.

Blackness extends with equal density in all directions. I am surprised I can see me. In fact I can't. I don't have eyes. Just tiny pieces of lint. If anyone blew at me, I would fly in all directions. Like dandelions at the end of a hot summer—miniature galaxies in their own right. Only, I suspect, I consist of infinitely smaller components and an infinitely larger whole. Somehow I retain awareness of my being, regardless of the ridiculous substance of which I am made. Ridiculous and spanning the whole universe. At least, I think I do. There seems to be nothing beyond me.

It is either the beginning or the end of the world. Perhaps Brahma is still sleeping a dreamless sleep. Or is about to wake up. I am still an endless ocean of squiggly, vibrating bits of thread. Actually, I don't know if my component parts are large or small—there is no comparison. I only know they, or I, are omnipresent. Anyway, I am aware of them. I know they are me. I have no perception where I begin or end. I am endless, like the universe. Infinity is my middle name. Except that there is no universe. I am just an ocean of unfulfilled energy.

All of me is vibrating. I feel the need for harmony. For order and harmony. Surely this would be an expression of beauty? I am beauty in search of an expression. I decide to examine myself more closely. I must do so by direct perception. Not by the use of senses, but by accepting what I am and experiencing my present form. That's right. Direct perception. The yogis can do that. They become the object of their contemplation. Only I already am. I do it in reverse order. I became the object, and now I try to experience my own nature. Does this make sense?

"Frieeeend!"

There is no way he can hear me. He'd know what to do. I am surprised that I can still think in terms of words. Or, perhaps, I am just imagining I can. Perhaps this is a trick that my Friend is playing on me. That's it! I am supposed to learn something. Only what? I have a strong suspicion that if I don't, he'll repeat the exercise again and again. Like my piano teacher—way back when. Or eons ahead in the future.

I can no longer say that I am nothing. Myriads upon myriads upon myriads of bits of string are not nothing. Even if they don't really have any dimensions. Not three, anyway. Two at most. Not much, but still, not nothing. But why? Is this how the universe began? Whatever happened to the Big Bang? Was the universe just an omnipresent soup of bits of vibrating energy?

I don't want to be here. I don't want to have my being as an omnipresent soup. I know that's from which the biological life emerged on Earth—primordial soup—but the whole universe? No way. It's too dull, too uniform. I may be vibrating, but otherwise I am completely static. I make a great effort of will, and some strings begin to vibrate at different frequencies. I am fascinated. I try again. Soon a wondrous symphony fills the totality of my reality. The totality of me. I remember the words of a great scientist, Dr. Leon Lederman. Way, way into the future. Can you remember the future? I can. The future is my present, just like this is. Eons from now Dr. Lederman will say that God may turn out to be a beautiful melody.

Is this what I was intended to learn?

I am back at the knoll, suspended between heaven and earth, unsure of what I am. I had been given glimpses of the mystery of being, even of its glory, but I neither feel nor understand any of them. Those mysteries seem to belong in a different reality where I am but a visitor. A stranger in a strange land. I am not even sure of my purpose, of what I want to be. I'm neither alive, as I was when I held Ruth in my arms, nor am I in a state of being, with becoming insidiously stirring within me. Insidiously, because I have no knowledge of my direction—not when I'm suspended between two pines in an indeterminate hinterland. I am neither hot nor cold. Neither dead nor alive. I neither feel nor am I without feeling.

I am in a state of suspension, neither here nor there.

I am nowhere.

I am nothing.

I am not.

***

8

The Rosary

Hail Mary, full of grace, the Lord is with thee, thy kingdom come, thy will be done…
    Just who is riding herd over our will? Whatever happened to free will? Why are they praying? Don't they believe in divine benevolence? I always did, and look where it got me. There I am, lying on my back, not showing any overt signs of life. But praying?

Divine benevolence. It's simple. Everything always happens for my good. Perhaps, for my ultimate good. It beats the dickens out of worrying about tomorrow. Of course, if you act like an idiot, you get treated like an idiot.

…*and the fruit of her womb, Jesus.*

The Buddhists and the Hindus have their mantras, we have the Rosary. Droning, repetitious sets of words.

Aummmmm…

Ruth sighs. She must have left home in a hurry. She's wearing the same suit she wears to give her lectures. This one and three others. In rotation. Simple, clean-cut. Nice. I like it. There is nothing I don't like about Ruth. Except when she starts praying in public. I hate that. She ought to know better. At least her face seems relaxed. She's a good actress, my Ruth.

I'm sure she finds kneeling hard. Ever since that double somersault she performed skiing on Mount Tremblant. She was as close to the other side, to the side I am on now, as she ever will be. Anyway, hard vinyl tiles are not designed for kneeling. Walking at best, or rolling stretchers to the emergency rooms. Nor are church pews, for that matter—I mean, designed for kneeling—though the Catholics deny this. They think that suffering is good: it purifies the soul. Sure. Tell that to a mother holding a starving child. They also say that Christ suffered so that we wouldn't have to. Illogical? On the other hand, I am told they introduced upholstery on their *prie-dieux* to save their faithfuls' knees. How about their souls? Can you upholster your soul, or character or whatever, to save your body? Trust me, if you could, I wouldn't be lying here.

I detect a certain tension in me, bordering on anger. I have no idea why. I didn't even know ghosts, or whatever I am, can get angry. There's an awful lot I don't know about the here-and-now.

I look around.

My body continues to lie motionless, just as I saw it the last time. My face is partially unwrapped. On top I'm still wearing a white turban. I could impersonate an Arab in any desert. Or is it an oil field? The rest of my face begins to resemble the one I wore when alive. The blue patches have turned yellow; my nose looks like a nose. Almost. But the room is different. They moved me to a private one. It seems I got here by being drawn, pulled, or somehow attracted to my body, not to the room as such. Thank heaven for insurance. If it weren't for my firm, I would be lying in a public ward, cell phones flashing and beeping all over, and my whole family making a public spectacle of themselves.

Actually, my body shows signs of life. Indirectly. There is a little green light on the bedside table going blip, blip, blip... *ad nauseam*, you might say. Only... if I am in that body on that bed, then who am I?

Next to Ruth, my mother sits on the edge of the chair, as if making an effort to be uncomfortable. Dear mother. Her face is showing the strain of seeing me in such a dire condition. Usually dressed to a tee, she seems to have left home in a hurry. A light coat, inappropriate for this time of year, open in front but still dressed over her shoulders. She kept it on to keep her warm. People her age need warmth, and they don't overheat the hospital rooms. The wide-brimmed hat she's wearing at an equally inappropriate coquettish angle is more suitable to an Easter Parade than a hospital visit. Kerchief in hand, she murmurs the Rosary in unison with my cousins. Ruth must be doing this for my mother. She's a deep believer, but not in praying in public.

"You're coming over to the dark side," I told her after we watched a video of *Star Wars* some time ago. We were probably the only people in Canada who did not see the movie when it first came out. We'd rented the video to cheer ourselves up. Just that morning we had received a card about the passing of a dear friend.

"Why would you say that, Lord Vader?" she bowed low before me.

"You don't pray any more." I never saw her on her knees.

"When thou prayest, enter into thy closet and... pray to thy Father in secret," she quoted Matthew from memory. I don't think she would go through these Rosary rites on her own. It must have taken wild horses, or, well... or her mother.

There is also Ruth's mother, Clara; my father, George; and two of my cousins, Doris and Brenda—both good Catholics. Clara always elegant, my father in his double-breasted suit, probably the one he wore to our wedding. The rest of Dad hasn't changed, either, these last twenty years. Even when staying at home, he always wears a tie. Old habits linger on and on and... As for my cousins, the less said about them the better. We don't really get along, they and I. Lack of common interest? Not that I know what their interests are, except for their coifs. No kidding! You should see their hair! But they are good at praying. Faces drawn, a vertical crease between their tightly closed eyes. Oh, yes... they are good at praying.

Not at all like me. Dear cousins. I have a strong suspicion that they are keeping their fingers crossed in case I left them something in my will. I might get back into my body just to spite them.

The only people missing are Joan and Elaine, my sisters, who are happily married in the United States. I'm sure Ruth told them that there was nothing they could do.

Clara is always correct. Also, she tends to be *plus catholique que le pape*. I bet she can still recite the Holy Mass in Latin. And then some. Funny that. I am beginning to talk like a youngster. Perhaps I am. Perhaps, on this side, I am no more than a babe-in-arms. I have the whole universe to explore, the whole eternity. No matter—we'll see. Or at least I shall, I hope.

Ruth and the cousins are kneeling down. Mother and Dad and Clara are sitting on chairs imported from the sitting area in the waiting hall. The chairs can only just fit in at the foot of the bed. My room is little more than a large cubicle for long-term patients. But it does have a door, not just a curtain. It is pale green, bland, sterile, insipid, flat, prosaic, and... did I say bland? And the fluorescent light is positively hideous. There is a small incandescent lamp on my bedside table, tucked behind the electronic stuff. That's in case I want to read, I suppose. Ha, ha. I suppose the room's good for dying in. But there is a bunch of flowers on a twin bedside table, on the other side of the bed. I wonder who brought them. Probably Clara. She's always correct, remember? No one can be sorry to leave such surroundings. Believe me. I am an architect.

I was an...

One other thing. They substituted an eiderdown displaying nice autumn colours for the ever-present white blanket. It goes well with the flowers. Together they contrive to make the room look almost habitable. And there is a telephone next to the flowers. In case I want to call my office?

They don't know it, but my extended family are all making a frightful noise with their unspoken pleas. I mean their thoughts. I don't mean I peek into their minds—they just keep muttering. To me it's like talking aloud. I can't even tell them apart. They are reciting the Rosary, but their minds are wandering all over the place. Subliminal chatter, they call it. 'They' being people who study such things.

Make him healthy again, please God. Make him wake up. Do I have enough milk at home? Make him talk again (sometimes I sooo wish he'd shut up!)...
Holy Mary Mother of God...

We had that part, already. And anyway, if she's the mother of God, then who is her mother?

That last wasn't nice, but the question always bothered me. As for my cousins, if they want to pray for me, that's fine, but they should switch off their blabbering minds first. Now that I am just beginning to pick up other people's thought waves, I am also beginning to realize what the stranger, my Friend, has to put up with. If my mind generates as much subliminal clutter as the members of this little congregation do, then no wonder he needs time off. When I'm far away, he can get some rest. Maybe that's why, in eastern cultures or religions, they teach meditation. A sort of switching off of the jabber.

Yak, yak, yak...

The scourge of humanity! Whatever happened to 'Silence is golden'?

I had a friend, a client actually, who said that noise is the curse of the twentieth century. It's not any better now. Even that which passes for music, these days, doesn't stray far from noise. The screaming banshees on each TV program are ample evidence of that. They scream at the beginning, at the end, and as often as possible in-between. Mostly girl teens, but their mothers are rapidly joining them. It is so bad that Ruth and I stopped listening to TV altogether.

And now this. The Rosary.

Weren't they supposed to contemplate on the mysteries of whatever? Mother told me, years ago, that Rosary is like a mantra. You don't think about the words, you just repeat them, round and round, to enter into a lethargic state.

"It helps you contemplate the mysteries," she'd said.

What mysteries? She never told me. And further, most people I know already are lethargic. However, the Church is obsessed with mysteries. If only we resolved to observe the world with open minds, surely the haze would slowly dissolve.

Our father, which art in heaven...

My mind drifts to my schooldays. From elementary school onwards. I don't transfer, I just think about it, as if I were still alive. I mean awake—although that's also inaccurate, since our subconscious doesn't switch off when we sleep. Anyway, for some fifteen years I've been inundated with mysteries. The mystery of the Holy Trinity, the mystery of the Virgin Birth, the mystery of the Incarnation, the mystery of Transubstantiation, the mystery of Immaculate Conception, Transfiguration, Ascension, Assumption, Resurrection, the mystery of Original Sin, the mystery of

Infallibility, the mystery of the Seven Sacraments, the whatever-I-can't-understand mystery. Could it be that long before the introduction of Papal Infallibility, during the first eighteen centuries of hierarchical conformity, there might, just might have been some basic teachings misinterpreted at the outset and then religiously built into a conservative tradition? Some time ago I had discussed it with Ruth.

"The Gnostics thought so," she'd said, "and were unceremoniously destroyed by Bishop Irenaeus, who was never proclaimed infallible. I gather his zeal had been misguided, as were other fervours manifested in the Crusades, Inquisitions, and other deviations from the teachings of Christ."

She knew. She was into that sort of thing. I'd become a lost sheep long ago. Or perhaps, I just got fed up with being a sheep. Poor Ruth. She is still immersed in at least some of those mysteries. Not that I understand much more.

Let me tell you, if only anyone would listen, *I* am a mystery. I am a living mystery. You don't believe me? Try my lamppost for size. Get yourselves knocked into a coma. Then we'll talk mysteries.

Mysteries? Ha!

And now this. My whole family praying to someone or something they can neither see, hear, touch or understand, for I don't know what. My recovery? I am not sick. For my return to their valley of tears? Why, what have I done to deserve it? I have a good mind not to wake up at all. At least I wouldn't, if it weren't for Ruth. I wonder if I could take her with me. Of course, I would still need my Friend to show her the universe.

Hallowed be Thy name…

Ruth glances at her watch.

"Get up," I whisper in her ear. "Get up and sit on the bed."

She gets up and sits on the bed. I've done it! I can communicate with her. I whisper "I love you." Only she doesn't react. She rubs her knees with both hands. The Rosary her mother gave her is lying on the bed, at my feet. God, how I wish I could tell her I'm all right. She doesn't deserve any of this.

"I am all right!" I try her other ear.

Thy kingdom come…

Kingdom? They have no idea what they are praying for. If their prayers were answered, they would never believe it. A kingdom that stretches from one end of infinity to the other. Only infinity has no ends. Perhaps this is the only mystery. Who knows what there was before the universe came into being? A Black Hole? But there was no space, no time. Hence, no Black Hole. How about omnipresent Black Holes, so black they were invisible? Outside time and space. Then, when they exploded, all at once, time and space were created.

Why not?

My Friend took me to my beginning. Sort of. Perhaps I just woke up from a trillion-year slumber? They think that of Brahma. They may be a lot closer to the truth than we are. There is no time, hence there is no beginning. Mutually exclusive.

A nurse comes in. Prim and proper. Quite cute, actually.

"Sorry," she whispers, so as not to disturb anyone.

She's used to family gatherings, bending their knees in supplication. She tends to rely more on medicine. Chemicals and suchlike. She has witnessed too many unanswered prayers. She slides between the chairs, hurdles over the outstretched calves of my cousins, and finally reaches the bedside table. She checks the electronics, the IV, peeks under my eyelids, pats the pillows, smiles weakly and goes out.

...give us this day our daily bread...

A nice prayer, Our Father. Ruth told me that it should be written in the affirmative tense. Our Father, Thy Kingdom *has* come, Thy will *is* done on earth as in heaven. Thou *givest* us daily our daily bread... And so on. Surely, if it's daily, then we are getting it every day. Why ask for it? Give thanks instead, as Ruth does. We don't begin to appreciate the blessings we receive. And, of course, His will *is* done. How can you oppose the Almighty? The whole universe is a manifestation of His will. Of His benevolence. Of the Creative Spirit. How could it be otherwise?

I'll have to ask Friend about this. "What do you think?" he'll answer. But I'll ask anyway.

Mother blows her nose. Ruth reaches over the footboard of my bed and pats Mother's knee.

"It's all right, Mother," she says. "It's all right."

Mother smiles and wipes another tear rolling down her left cheek. Sometimes I think she weeps only to attract attention to herself. Or else, she really is that emotional. Perhaps all mothers are like that. Perhaps Clara would also cry all the time if Ruth were here, instead of me. Hey, how about if both of us were in one bed?

Ah, forget it.

I can't take much more of this prayer business. I am in and out of my room three times. The first two times I go back to the knoll and start all over again. It's not easy. You can't just imagine you are going somewhere. You really must find yourself already there, and then it happens. It takes practice. I wonder how many times Jesus missed the boat before he learned to change reality. He must have.

Finding the knoll is becoming easier. The stranger is there every time. Almost. Friend. My Friend. I wonder if he hangs out there just to give me a point of reference. The first few times I had been drawn to the scene of the accident. Now, the knoll is my base of operations. It's where I hang out to work things out in my head. I mean my mind. I don't really have a head. You know what I mean. Although there is still that morbid attraction to my body, of course. Or is it of curse?

Each time I ask my Friend, again and again, what I should call him.

"Just call me your friend," he says. Again and again.

"It feels awkward," I confess each time.

His final response makes things worse. "How do you address your reflection in the mirror?" he asks. He's not smiling.

"I don't talk to myself in the mirror," I reply haughtily. He's beginning to get on my nerves.

The next moment I'm standing at home, in my condo, in front of my mirror, having an animated discussion with myself. I am discussing how to best present a project I worked on the previous three months. It was an important but complex design, and I suspected the presentation would be neither smooth nor easy. I assumed different voices, changed stances, waved my arms pointing to imaginary drawings on an imaginary board behind me.

"So as you see, gentlemen..." there followed a tirade advocating my solution. When I finished, I glanced once more at my reflection as if asking for approval. I got a wink and a smile.

"But I didn't talk to him," I insist.

The stranger looks at me with something that can only be regarded as paternal indulgence.

"I thought your presentation was first class," he says.

"...ah, thanks," is all I can manage.

I return to my room at the wrong time. They are just starting the Rosary. Five decades to go. Their minds are not yet tired. There is a bit less uncoordinated chatter. Mother decides on the Joyful Mysteries. For those who don't know, the Joyful Mysteries, the subjects you are supposed to contemplate while reciting the Hail Marys, consist of The Annunciation of Gabriel to Mary, The Visitation of Mary to Elizabeth, The Birth of Jesus, The Presentation of Jesus in the Temple, and finally The Finding of Jesus in the Temple. That should be joyful enough for anyone except for Ruth's mother, who is already reaching for a box of tissues. Clara and my mother are really good at waterworks. I know I won't last the whole cycle. And, as I said, I don't really like mysteries. That is why I am trying to solve them. One by one. The mystery that bothers me the most right now is why I can't arrive at the right place at the right time. It's already better, but, contrary to my previous existence, I'm obviously not paying sufficient attention to detail.

Dad starts the Apostles' Creed in a firm if slightly tired voice.

I believe in God, the Father Almighty, Creator of Heaven and earth...

My knowledge of the Apostles' Creed is limited. I split.

"Christ's descent into hell is not to be found in earlier manuscripts," Ruth says, sipping tonic fortified with but a smidgen of Gin. Her legs are dangling over the edge of the balcony through the spaces between the verticals.

Darn good legs, I must add. I had to escape the Rosary. Too monotonous for my taste. A blink and here I am. We are sitting on the terrace of our 27th floor condo on the corner of Sherbrooke and Guy. It was a brand-new building when we moved in. The view is fantastic. In winter, when the cold snaps moisture out of the air, with a decent pair of binoculars we can see Adirondacks. Dark shapes capped with white hats. At this height we can hardly hear the traffic below. The air is balmy and the view compensates for the lack of greenery on our tiny terrace, though many would recognize twelve by eight feet as quite substantial for downtown. Ruth is discussing her favourite subject: religions. After all, they were the underlying source of a vast preponderance of art. The various churches were, some still are, the original patrons of painters, sculptors and architects throughout history. Much more so than their laic counterparts—the laic nobility. I do my best to look interested.

"Yes, darling. More ice?" She ignores me.

"The idea was probably an interpolation from the fables of Bacchus and Hercules and adopted as an article of Christian faith. A similar comment would apply to the myth of the resurrection of Osiris, Adonis, Bacchus, and other sun-gods in pagan religions. Strangely enough, the credo being recited in the Catholic mass in Vatican states, '*Et expecto resurrectionem mortuorum.*'" Her two curved fingers frame the Latin words with inverted commas. "That is to say, it affirms the resurrection of the dead, not of the body. Since Jesus called dead those not yet spiritually awakened, I wonder why this distortion of a bodily resurrection was allowed to entangle the faithful. On purpose? And why isn't it yet rectified?"

"I really couldn't say, darling." Let alone understand all that she was saying.

And in Jesus Christ his only Son, our Lord...

They are still at it. My father continues to recite the Creed from memory. My thoughts drift back to the terrace. Just my thoughts—I remain watching Ruth at my bedside. There was a time when I could do it. Recite the Credo from memory. Things change. We grow up. Perhaps I've become too mental. Too intellectual? I satisfy my emotional needs with the creative process of architecture. And with Ruth, of course. Yes, mostly Ruth. Although she's more like an integral part of me. To me the Credo contains about a dozen words of history and the rest is myth. Pure and simple. Even the Church couldn't agree what should be in it.

One billion people still believe in those myths. They are a powerful emotional drug. The opium of the masses? Once absorbed into the psyche, it is extremely difficult to revert to a rational stance. Why must religions assume that God is illogical? For some reason the recorder presents another statement for my edification. I see a cross of blazing light. For an instant it blinds me, and then I see the writing. *I have suffered none of the things...* I remember this statement. Ruth cited it to me years ago. How come I remember it now? I never paid much attention when she talked about such things. The quote is from a vision of John. Saint John, I shouldn't wonder. Why am I thinking about it right now?

...the resurrection of the body; and the life everlasting.

Ah, yes, the Credo...

Dad finishes the Creed and leans back in his chair. He is no longer a young man. He was over thirty when he sired me. And I am no spring chicken myself. Going back to the Creed, I have serious reservations about the body. On the other hand, I am pretty sure about everlasting life. Otherwise, what would I be doing here?

I concentrate on Ruth. She, too, is looking even more tired. I seem to be the only one who doesn't suffer because of the stupid pothole. I wonder if the City people know what unpleasant *karma* they are accumulating by not doing their job better. I suppose there really is *karma*. I must have done something good in my life to have earned that accident. I could have waited another million years to be shown what my Friend already showed me since that fortuitous accident.

Was it fortuitous as in lucky? Many wouldn't think so. I do.

Ruth is looking tired but handles it well. Her upper eyelids droop a shade lower than usual. Not that she has drooping eyelids. Far from it. I realize that she is not here for her own sake. Not even mine, for that matter. She knows that both Mother and Dad, and Clara, and even my cousins, need her strength. Not that my cousins are particularly enamoured with me—I'd been too busy to give them much time—but they probably think that if it happened to me,

it could happen to them. They are covering their bases. 'I'll pray
for you now, if you pray for me later.' You should be so lucky! A
long life is not a reward. It's the punishment for not learning your
lessons faster. Or for not discharging your negative *karma*. But if
so, why can't I be with Ruth? She's the only one I would like to
share my present experience with. I would share the universe with
her. God knows it's big enough for the two of us.

   Poor Ruth. I wouldn't hurt her for the world. Not her. With
her here, the universe would be a more joyful place. She would
teach me about the beauty of the stars, the galaxies. We would
dance a tango among the galactic winds of the Crab nebula. We
would straddle the comet's tail and count the shooting stars. We
would...

   They are running out of Hail Marys.

   It's the last mystery. The Finding of Jesus in the Temple. The
place is huge. I smile and quickly stop. The smell is disgusting. I
am standing at the back of the temple and watch the activities.
They, too, are a mystery to me. Then I see him. A short lad, about
twelve or thirteen, a mop of curly hair like a reddish-golden halo,
stars shining in his eyes. He must have seen all the galaxies... I
keep my distance. He is talking to some very serious-looking guys
with long beards. I am too far back to hear him. Anyway, there is a
racket going on at the back. Some people are wheeling and dealing
goats, chickens and some other goods. This accounts for the smell.
Don't those people ever wash? Or it could be the goats and the
chickens. It's a regular marketplace. I wonder what the lad is
saying. How can people make so much noise in a place of worship?

   None of my business.

   I am back in my room. I didn't find anything particularly
joyful about the scene I witnessed, but, of course, his parents, Mary
and Joseph, haven't found him yet. I suppose all parents would be
glad to find their lost child. Wherever it was. But I cannot see how
one can contemplate such an event for the duration of a decade.
Ten Hail Marys take time. Not that I ever measured how long.
Anyway, I don't care about time anymore.

   Poor Ruth. Even though she's sitting now, her knees must be
giving her hell. It's not just her eyes that look tired. I really think

she misses me. I mean, really. Not like the times when she goes on a tour, or I travel on business. Then, too, we are apart. We are, and we're not. There is that intangible knowledge that we are never really separate. That, in an inexplicable way, we are one. Darling Ruth. I wonder why she imagines that God will hear her prayers better if she's in a supplicant position. Or was, before she sat down. If God is everywhere, He's also within us. Within our hearts and minds. And if He's also in our bodies, then why make things so uncomfortable for Him?

I can't stand looking at her subjecting herself to pain on my account. I much prefer when she sits back and shares with me her passion for art. Paintings, sculpture and, yes, even architecture. That's how we met. She was a slim girl, her hair in a long ponytail, her waist so tiny she reminded me of a precious hourglass. She was as fragile as the objects of art we were both studying. I, a freshly baked architect; she, in her first year of the History of Art.

But what really attracted me to her was her implicit innocence. Also, her total commitment to her chosen studies. When she looked at a painting, her face grew serene, her eyes dreamy, as if she stood by the artist, watching him paint. I could even detect a certain inexplicable humility in her gaze—as though being made privy to a fragment of some sacred scrolls. A moment later, her enchantment would turn to an effusion of passion, though still tempered by respect that all great art commands. Then she would remind me of Sister Wendy Beckett, that elusive Carmelite nun whose love for beauty inspired thousands of youths to peruse higher aims in their lives.

From that day on, Ruth became my muse, my inspiration. I realized only later, or admitted to myself, that on the day we met at the Museum of Fine Arts, in Montreal, I fell madly in love with her. Under her influence, I began to learn that there is more to life than advancing from one day to another. When absorbing art of the immortal artists, she made time stop in its tracks.

Under her tutelage I experienced my first state of being.

***

Part Two

BEING

*"The Universe has as many different centers
as there are living beings in it."*

Alexander Solzhenitsyn
(Nobel Prize for Literature 1970)

9

Flashes

I think I am going to get it for keeps. I think I am dying. Till now, under my Friend's guidance, I managed to visit some segments of my life, which held pertinent answers to my problems of today. I strongly suspect this is Friend's way of telling me that all the answers lie within me, if I only care to look. Imagine. All knowledge dormant within us, waiting, ready, available, and we're too lazy to dig inside our own mind to get it out. Sounds pretty stupid to me. And I'm not the first to think so. To paraphrase Albert Einstein, the universe may or may not be infinite, but human stupidity is.

Not really funny, that. At fifty-five, I don't feel particularly clever. On the other hand, I don't consider myself particularly stupid. Does anyone? Maybe that's the problem. We can only compare ourselves to each other. No big deal. Anyway, I suspect that the other trips I'd experienced were just by way of encouragement. They worked. Since I found myself in a state bordering on depression a number of times, I experienced what I can only describe as euphoria. And until this moment, I was truly enjoying myself.

That's right. Until now.

I wish my Friend would tell me if I am, or am not, going to die. I don't mean sometime in the future, but soon. As a direct consequence of the accident. The reason I want to know is that I am beginning to get flashes—as in life flashing before my eyes. I've always been told that this is what happens just before you die. Still no tunnel of light, but the flashes are unnerving.

I hope Ruth doesn't sense anything. She's so perceptive. She can tell things about me that I don't even know myself. Surely, I can't leave her behind. This is not a question. Aren't we one?

I wonder what will happen. Shall I spread myself across timeless eons of space, like a faint, evanescent veil spanning light-years, carried on the ethereal wings of angels? Shall I brighten the Universe, momentarily, on a transient pyre of a timely nova, only to shrink to a dark dwarf star, or even to an invisible, forgotten Black Hole? Or shall I become integrated into the matrix of the universe—melt into an infinite number of vibrating bits of string? Or, is it possible, just possible, that the Universe, or God Himself, will allow me to retain some tenuous semblance of I AM, of individuality, of personal identity?

Am I really immortal?

I also fear that should I die, Ruth would never forgive me. Once, we'd made a pact. We swore that, whatever the future holds for either of us, we shall meet it together. At the time I had no idea that the future extends to infinity; but now that I know, I must have her share it. Infinity without her is my concept of hell. Hell by exclusion. I always thought of myself as being a loner, but this didn't mean without Ruth. Ruth is as much a part of me as breathing in and breathing out. You can't do one without the other. I'd already experienced being nothing. This would be far worse. This would be like the absence of hope to ever become anything. Anything at all. Aren't we supposed to have faith, hope and charity? Ruth always said so.

"And the greatest of them is charity," she said, cuddling under my arm.

Charity, or love, by any other name... But how can you hold on to either if you lose hope?

Why isn't my Friend here when I need him?

I hear a baby crying. I am covered with something wet and sticky. I am cold. Terribly cold. Why did she push me out? I don't want to be born. Not yet. I am not ready. Now I know. It's me that's crying.

Whaaah… I am not ready… whaaaah…

They ignore me. All of them. They are huge, much bigger than I am. They are scary. They pour more wet stuff over me and cover me with something soft, but not as soft as before. Why are they blinding my eyes? It's too bright here. Much too bright. I close my eyes. I am asleep. That's better. I am back inside. And at last it's dark. Again. It's warm and cozy.

No, I am not. Whaaah…

I shake my head. I must find a way to communicate with Ruth. She said there are ways. Some sort of ESP. Extra-sensory perception. People tried it in the past. I just don't remember if they succeeded. I must speak to her. Tell her it's not my fault. Tell her that I'm willing to wait for her. As long as it takes. What would she do without me? Meet someone? No. Never. She ought to, of course. But she wouldn't. Not my Ruth. She wouldn't do this to me. I must get her here, to join me. Here. We would dart through the universe together. We would sail on the solar wind. We would spin on the carousel of Saturn. We would… we would do a million and one things together. She would teach me. Or Friend would teach both of us. Time and space would be ours to explore. We would have eternity to share.

"Sit up straight, Johnny…"

I am sitting at the second desk on the right, in the second row. Right next to the window. I tend to sit sideways to see what is going on outside. I am curious what's happening out there. I've always been curious. And I already know the alphabet. I knew the alphabet when I was four. My older sister told me that even babies know it. I had to learn it. I am no baby. I don't know why other children didn't learn it faster. Before school. At home. Perhaps their parents can't read? No. Everybody can read. So why shouldn't

I look through the window? I shall learn to fly and soar in the sky. The way those birds do. I shall soar higher and higher...

"Johnny, I won't warn you again..."

I hate her. She is bossing everyone. One day I'll be bigger than she is and I'll tell her how to sit. She won't like it, either. Well, that's just too bad.

Why can't she let me be?

I am soaring among the clouds. I have to smile. Do all dreams always come true? Or do we have to die first? I can't be dead yet. Only my early years flash before my eyes. If I'm flying now, then Friend must be back. I'll ask him. Flying is wonderful. It takes no effort. You just spread your arms and shoot up in the air. As in a dream. I can see tiny figures of people below me. They all seem to be in a hurry. I wonder why. They have all the time in the world. Don't they know they are immortal? There is no need to hurry. And if they are immortal, then I am, also. Good old Friend. What would I do without him? Get miserable, I suppose.

Can a dream I once had be a flash?

I wonder how old my Friend really is. He looks a bit like me, but you cannot put an age on him. I don't think he is aging. He just is.

I feel the gentle touch of cotton-wool clouds caressing me on all sides. That's strange. Until this moment I couldn't feel any external stimuli. I hear Friend snorting. I can't see him, but I know he's here. Right next to me. Is he always so close?

"What do you think?" I can almost hear him asking.

Actually I can, only inside my head. My mind. So what about this sensual experience? Of course... I decide. I feel what I want to feel. It's up to me. All is up to me. Always. I create my reality. But wasn't it here before I came? This reality, I mean?

"What do you think?"

Thanks for nothing, Friend.

I hate this noise. It's droning like a dentist's drill, only louder. It fills my ears all the way to the inside of my head. I hate it, I hate it, I hate it!

"I hate it, Mother!"

She reaches over, undoes my strap, puts her arm around me and drags me onto her lap. I'm a bit embarrassed. I'm already five-and-a-half. Almost six. I am sitting in my own seat. At least I was till Mother reached out for me. I only let her because she's sitting by the window. A small oblong window looking out to the sky. I can almost feel the clouds outside. I've never flown in an airplane before, but it's not so bad. If you ignore the noise, that is. I reach out to touch the clouds. There is that plastic stopping me. I imagine it isn't there. For a moment it works. I can feel its puffy softness. Then the effect is gone. Mother said, later, that it was my imagination. It wasn't. I really did touch the clouds. One day I shall fly among them. I shall dive into them the way I dive into a pool. Or onto the soft, bouncy mattress in Mom's bedroom when Dad's not looking. I'll practice at home.

The plane disappears and I am flying on my own. I love flying.

Oh, hi, Friend...?

I must see Ruth. She might know about my condition in the hospital. I don't know what time it is, but it is still light. I wonder if I can read Dr. Morton's mind. That would tell me something about my body. About the medical condition of my body. I could do this right now, only I don't know how to ask him any questions. He might be thinking about a dozen other patients. Or about what he had for supper last night. There must be a way.

If only my Friend would help...

If I stand by Dr. Morton's shoulder forever, or be there during the rounds, I could then read his mind. Or he might even give instructions to the nurses, or the interns, or...

Actually, they don't bring interns or residents to my bedside. Not any more. There's only so much you can learn about a vegetable. That's what a vegetative state is. A vegetable. Like being a cabbage. Or maybe a six-foot bush on its side. The simile does not please me. Not that I don't like cabbage or bushes, but, well, it's not very flattering.

Guess what I've been today. That's right. For a moment there, I was a cabbage. All green and leafy, and wrapped up in myself.

Then a tiny worm tickled me. Just a little. I must tell you, it was fun.

I am lying on my stomach, floating, barely moving my fins. My mask is a bit tight, but I wanted to make sure no water could get in. I spat on the inside of the mask and then rinsed it, just as Dad told me. It was worth it. It's not fogging up at all. Now my attention is completely absorbed by the world beneath me. The colours, the sheer diversity of life grabs me and refuses to let me go. I am literally in a different world.

I love the snow. I love skiing. I love skating. But this is out of this world. It's my first time in the Caribbean. Dad promised that if I did well in my exams, he'd take me to Jamaica. He kept his word. He always does. I've learned that from Dad. Never make promises you can't keep, he'd said. He repeats it quite often. *Never*, he stresses the word.

We are in Runaway Bay, Jamaica, halfway between Montego Bay and Ocho Rios. Every second year a hurricane, or a powerful storm, tears away the beach, and pulls it into the ocean. It leaves behind a fresh bottom of the ancient coral, freshly populated by hungry fish and a veritable plantation of sea urchins. They are also called sea eggs, though I have no idea why. They are black and spiky, and they hurt like hell if you let one of their spikes prick your skin. You can't really bathe here, but it's a glorious place for floating flat on your stomach with a mask and a pair of fins.

I can't possibly describe what I see. Wait till I tell Mom. She's afraid to go out snorkeling. She's afraid of many things. I can hear her now.

"I'm afraid it might rain tomorrow."

"I'm afraid we shall be late."

"I'm afraid we shall oversleep."

This last she said on the eve of our departure for Jamaica. We took the seven o'clock plane. By two in the afternoon I was snorkeling. For the last three days Mom was afraid we wouldn't make it to the airport on time. Mom's always afraid of something. But most of all she's afraid of water.

"If God wanted us to swim, he would have given us fins instead of legs," she repeats, each time Dad attempts to drag her toward the sea.

In the end she succumbs. Knee-deep. Dad swims like a fish. So do I, thanks to Dad. And now I am also looking at fish. Good old Dad!

Beneath me, I see fish of all shapes, sizes, and bright, opalescent colours. That's what Dad had called it—like Mom's brooch made of an opal, he'd said. Some fish are striped and as thin as paper. Well, almost. Little yellow and black lines run diagonally across their slim bodies. Others show off their blue and green accents, probably just for fun. Some, to be different, are long and wiry, with speckled skins, more like snakes I'd seen out in the country, back home, than fish in the water. Or maybe they are snakes?

And then there are the corals…

First there are lots of star corals. They dominate the fairly shallow water. Further down their cousins look fuzzy—they look like giant fingers reaching out to the sky. Are they asking for help? Or just trying to attract attention?

"Hey, Mister, look at me!"

Then, deeper still, I see the famous brain coral. It's scary. It looks as if Dr. Frankenstein had tried to create a new generation of giants. They really do look like brains of giants, with their bodies still deep in the sand below. Yet further down, cavern-like holes open up, with sand still trapped at the bottom. The water is so pure that the sand reflects the sunlight, giving the tapering branches growing on its sides an eerie, back-lighted look. In this light they look almost fragile…

A flap of my fins brings me over lettuce leaves growing in great abundance. No kidding! Corals that look like lettuce leaves. I could take some for Mother, though she would never believe me. Only Dad said, 'Look, but don't touch. Remember, son, don't touch.' I was in such a hurry to try out my snorkeling equipment that I didn't even ask why.

I flip my flippers again. See, Mother? God gave me fins. Actually it was Dad, but he's as close as I can get to God, right now. My body shoots forward almost by itself. It's so easy.

I see a starfish, masses of tiny fish, the sea urchins I already mentioned, and a dozen or two of other forms of life I cannot even name. If my mouth weren't shut firmly around the breathing tube, it would hang open. No kidding.

It's getting darker. Just a little. I'm wondering if a cloud has sneaked in front of the sun. The caverns seem to grow deeper. Below a particularly deep and wide vertical cavern, there is a veritable forest of enormous sea eggs. The image looks like a photo negative of a night-sky, the firmament littered with evil, black, exploding stars. Black Holes? These really are black!

And then it happens.

Below me there is nothing. Just bottomless, forbidding darkness. Nothing to give me any idea of the depth below me. For a moment I panic, then blow in my breathing tube and count to three. Only I don't know which way to swim. The darkness below me is so intense, it is drawing me ever closer. It's pulling me down. I am afraid to lift my head above the water to see in which direction to swim. I cannot take my eyes from the impenetrable darkness. And then, for no reason, I understand, and fear leaves me. I feel a great sense of peace. I feel suspended in the middle of the universe, in the heart of nothingness. I feel that if I blink, stars will come into being. I may be just a boy, but right now I feel a surge of power I'd never felt before...

"How did you like it, John?" He looks and sounds almost anxious. "Well?" he repeats. I don't think I would recognize him if he didn't say, 'Well', and soon after, 'What do you think?' I'm sure that's coming.

My Friend looks at me with what I can only describe as admiration in his eyes. His position hasn't changed, as indeed, neither has mine. Someone is playing tricks on me. Both with the matrix of time and the propensities of space. And water. This is the first time I had a flash involving water.

"Am I dying?" I ask instead.

"Why do you ask?" he counters.

That's silly. I know he can read my thoughts. A lot better than I can read his.

"S-sorry," he mutters, "I thought it best…" He almost stammers. "Are you sure you don't know?"

I give it a moment or two and shrug inwardly. "If I think I am dying, then I probably shall…" I mutter. "But surely, there are outside circumstances that are beyond my control. They can turn off my oxygen, cut off my IV, cut my throat…"

"In which reality?" he interrupts me.

"Why, there. In the hospital, of course." Sometimes he asks the most inane questions.

"Do you consider that reality controls this one?"

This gets me stumped. I never thought of that. I never thought of any reality having sway over another. The idea of God crosses my mind. If there is heaven, and God resides therein, then wouldn't God's own reality be superior to all others? Then another strange thought strikes me like lightning from a clear blue sky. In all that I've seen and/or experienced since I left my physical body, I saw no sign of heaven, let alone God. Not even a mention of a Superior Being riding herd over everybody and everything else.

"Are you sure?"

"Methinks my Friend is being facetious. I rather think I would have noticed, had I met God, don't you think?" I counter.

"I don't mean that. Haven't you met anyone who was, as you call it, riding herd over everything?"

For some strange reason the image that floats in front of me is that of an infinite ocean of submicroscopic lengths of string that change vibrations at the beckoning of my will.

"That w-w-was just a, ah, an image…" I say, suddenly very unsure of my ground.

"And what is this?"

"This?"

"This. You and I reclining on invisible hammocks between two pines in the middle of a wintry field, in the middle of nowhere."

"This is j-j-just an image?" I suddenly find great difficulty in expressing myself. "We? You and I?"

"You just said that your body is in the hospital, somewhere in the real world."

This didn't come out right. Surely the concrete world is real. Isn't it? The buildings I designed are real. They stand up, last for years, people work in them. My home is real. My car... before I wrapped it around the lamppost and flung it over the ditch, was real. Ruth is real.

"Ruth is real!" I say triumphantly.

"And you are not?" My Friend sounds coy. "And what about your memories? What about your joys and sorrows? What about your love for...?"

For Ruth. My love for Ruth is more real than all the things I named. Compared to my love for her, the physical world is little more than a pale backdrop, stage design scenery for my life with her.

For a while I try to listen to the birds having an argument on the upper branches of a fir on the west side of the knoll. They are arguing over something. Perhaps they are discussing the reality of a grain of grass one of them had picked up. Food can be very precious in the middle of winter. Very real to a hungry bird. Are we here, I mean in the here and now, in a reality limited to three dimensions, constrained by the flexible proclivities of time, confined to a physical body that can fly through neither space nor time, which is practically static, like this pine in front of me? What if we can be lugged across an ocean in a sardine can? What if we can glide on four wheels propelled by a gas engine? What of the solar system, of the galaxy, of the trillion galaxies beyond...

We are a race of gadgeteers who have lost their purpose. Who have lost their way. Isn't that what the Bible said? Sheep that lost their way? Ruth would know. She knows so much. She gives my life on earth reality. She makes it real. I may like to design, to ski and swim, to flex my muscles, but it is she who makes me feel alive.

"We create flashes to find meaning in our lives," I say. "We search for what, if anything, we have learned and that we can take back home with us."

"Back home," my Friend repeats slowly. "I like that. I like that a lot."

"They are acts of desperation. Those flashes, I mean. We cannot reconcile ourselves that we lived a life that has been wasted.

And the benevolence of the universe, in its infinite wisdom, in its infinite compassion, shows us that it isn't so. That we have learned *something*. That we had glimpses of true reality, which we can enrich with our presence."

"Why are you so leery of using the word 'God'?" Friend seems to be looking at me with renewed interest.

"Because I don't know what it means," I answer, looking away from him. I know he won't accept my answer.

I like playing in the sand. I can build things with it. Mountains and valleys and castles. Only Joan gets in the way. She always wants to do something else. She says she can because she's older. I begin looking forward to being older. I'll just push everybody away and play anywhere I like. I tell her that. She laughs.

"There will always be someone older than you, stupid," is her kind way of enlightening me.

So that wouldn't work.

"What if I am bigger?" I ask, not at all hurt by her turn of phrase.

Usually, she is quite nice to me. After a short argument, my father convinced my mother to let me go to the beach with her. My parents wanted to take us with them. It went like this. Joan convinced Dad that the sea is calm, and anyway, we didn't have to go in the water and there is a lifeguard, anyway. Then Dad convinced Mother. Otherwise I would have had to stay in the hotel. There is TV, but I have TV at home. Here I got sand. There are advantages to having an older sister.

I move a few feet away and start another castle. After all, there is enough sand. Soon Joan comes over, sits on her haunches and watches me. I am pretty good at building castles.

After a little while she asks shyly, "Can I help?"

I told you. Usually she's pretty nice.

When our parents get back, I have a question ready. "How many grains of sand are there, Mother?"

"Ask your father," she replies. "Your dad's a mathematician. You should always ask an expert in the field."

That makes sense. I imagine thousands and thousands of mathematicians on thousands and thousands of beaches counting grains of sand. I think there must be an awful lot of mathematicians.

By the time Dad comes down to the beach, I had almost forgotten my question. But then I look along the sand stretching all the way to the horizon, and I remember.

"I don't know, son, an awful lot. They don't teach numbers that big in school." Then Dad smiles, looks up at the blue sky and says, "But Carl Sagan says that the total number of stars in the universe is greater than all the grains of sand on all the beaches of the planet Earth. Does that help?"

I remember to look up at the sky the following night. And the night after. I resolve that when I am big, bigger than Joan, I'll start counting the stars. All of them.

The sky overhead is littered with stars. We are both looking up, as we usually do when we talk. My Friend never seems to sleep. Come to think of it, nor do I. But I sure dream a lot; only my dreams translate into reality. It's like thinking in three dimensions. Sometimes more. I don't mind having flashes anymore. I don't associate them with death, the way I used to. I am thinking of the memory flash I just had—of the grains of sand on the beach. I don't bother to ask Friend. I know what his answer would be. Another question.

"You know, Friend, I never really stopped counting, or trying to make any sense of it. I still have no idea. Each time I think I am getting close, the universe seems to expand and I, more or less, have to start from scratch. I start with counting the galaxies and go on from there. The last time I reached a figure of fifty thousand billion billion. A billion billion has eighteen zeros. And that you have to multiply by fifty thousand. Only by now, the figure is probably too small again."

I glance at my Friend. He only smiles.

"Keep counting," he says. But I know he's kidding. I don't have to read his mind. I can hear it in his voice. Nevertheless, for an instant we find ourselves surrounded by stars on all sides. Above and below. All around. And then I hear his laughter.

"Does this help?" he asks.

I know what would help. Not with counting the stars but with serenity, which seems to be missing in my heart of late. I mean now. Or since the moment I realized that Ruth is not satisfied with her fate. That she is getting angry. At me? At God? Perhaps just at her fate. Perhaps I would be able to count the stars better if her anger didn't disturb my peace of mind. It does. More and more often. I no longer live in the present. No longer am I suspended in a state of bliss. In the bliss of carefree being. I seem to be worried about the future. About Ruth's future. She deserves better.

***

10

Dying

Once again Ruth came to see my body. I mean, to see me. I hover right next to her, like an invisible shadow, trying to cheer her up by projecting good, positive thoughts. I have no idea if this has any effect on her, but I must try. I am better at reading thoughts than at emanating them. My Friend can do it both ways with equal facility; I'm just a beginner. By reading—or actually overhearing—thoughts, I learned about today's meeting. I 'heard' what's in Dr. Morton's mind. Ruth has to decide if they should disconnect my IV or let me continue to pretend that I'm still alive. Dr. Morton is not very hopeful.

"It's been three months, Mrs. Clarkson. Three long months. We are doing all we can."

Dr. Morton is not his usual immaculate self. His white coat, usually spotless and pressed to perfection, shows signs that he's been working today, long before Ruth arrived. His eyes also show fatigue. I peek into his mind. He was on call last night, and the night wasn't easy. One man had fallen off a roof. Just two stories, but he'd landed on his head and... lived to tell the story. He might even walk again. His head saved his legs. There had been seventeen more ambulance cases in all, nine of them admissions. Mostly car accidents, three cardiac arrests, one unsuccessful murder, one brutal rape.

All in a night's work.

Usually, when Dr. Morton is on call, he remains at home and offers consultation only by telephone. Last night it was just too much. The two residents and three interns were swamped. They needed physical help. As Dr. Morton lives nearby, he'd decided to return to the hospital. I never realized what a gamut of human depravity physicians are exposed to. Even a cursory scan of his mind reveals that years of experience have not eliminated the stress that human folly had placed on him. People may be stupid, irresponsible, but they are still human. There seems to be some sort of a bond between us. No matter how many people we murder in territorial wars, or just in search of oil or gold or any rare commodity, in some way we still seem to care for each other. In my profession I did not really have much opportunity to experience this feeling of allegiance, of belonging. I may have mentioned, I'm essentially a loner. Now, I am truly alone... in the whole, wide world.

On the other hand, I really don't know why some physicians work so hard while others do precious little. Only yesterday, while waiting for Ruth, I was floating around the wards when I heard amorous or lewd—depending on your taste—sounds emerging from a linen cupboard. I hardly needed to pass through the wall to confirm my suspicions. I am not a voyeur, but I did peek, anyway. For one second, your time. There were two couples there, in a state of near hysteria. A veritable *ménage à quatre*. One resident, one intern, and two nurses. One of them ugly. They didn't look tired at all.

And now Dr. Morton stands in front of Ruth, his arms raised in a gesture of hopelessness. He looks so miserable, I feel sorry for the guy. Almost. As I said, I can read his mind.

"I'm sorry, Mrs. Clarkson," he adds, his voice sounding like an afterthought. Or just resigned. Human depravity still takes its toll on him, and I don't mean the *ménage*. It is all the ongoing suffering—to death he's inured.

So that's it. It's out in the open. They need the hospital bed. There's a shortage of hospital beds throughout Canada. Certainly in Québec. Maybe the world? I suspect there are just too many of us, humans. *Homo sapiens.* It's getting so bad there is a waiting list if you want to die in a hospital.

"Sorry, Madam, you can't die today. We're all booked up. We can book you a bed for December, next year."

This is only half funny. It's too close to the truth.

Perhaps that's why people live longer. No beds. After all, nobody wants to die on a street, as I almost did. There's been a shortage of hospital beds for as long as I can remember. The last ten years I haven't even seen a doctor. Nor has Ruth, except for her knee. And that was a good six or seven years ago. All these years Ruth and I have been paying the highest taxes in North America to get a half-decent medical service. No such luck. The politicians' pensions and salaries went up, the hospital beds went down. If you need an operation for a bad knee, you have to fly to India. Or at least to Mexico. Or pay through the nose in the States. If there is such a thing as *karma*, and Ruth says there is, then I feel almost sorry for them—both the politicians and the members of the medical profession. They are creating a future for themselves that I wouldn't wish on my worst enemy. Just as well I have no enemies. Not that I know of. But I am prepared to correct this omission if they pull the plug on me. I am not ready to lose sight of Ruth, and I have no idea what would happen to me once my body goes kaput. I must have Ruth. She is my life.

"There is nothing we can do, Mrs. Clarkson. We just do not have the knowledge."

He can't actually say what's on his mind. I know. This is I, peeking again. Liar. Coward. Go on, I dare you. Say what you really think, Doctor: *"We can't pull the plug, Mrs. Clarkson, we are not allowed. Regulations. But you can—you are the next of kin."*

The Federal Government introduced this law to ease the pressure on Medicare. As the population aged, more and more hospital beds were taken up by the old and the infirm, often the incurable. Geriatric wards displaced in numbers the obstetrical wards. Age before beauty, they joked. Simultaneously, medicine advanced sufficiently to keep the decrepit bodies almost indefinitely. The parliament passed the proposal with only ten opposing votes. They, too, had to protect their own pensions. So go on, Dr. Morton, are you going to advise Ruth of her rights? *"Kill him. Go on, kill him, you might as well..."*

Poor Morton, I would hate to be in his skin. No. Of course he didn't think that. This is me being bitter and twisted. Maybe I'm just getting tired of being a ghost, or whatever I am.

OK. These were not all exactly his thoughts, but the effect is the same. It's just that he'll never say those words. He would have to add that they are making more money out of people requiring operations, complex treatments and suchlike, rather than just occupying precious beds with their useless carcasses. *"It's all about the money, Mrs... what's your name?"* I swear to you, for a moment he actually forgot Ruth's name. After seeing her almost daily for three months. Never mind. He did have a sleepless night, but to forget Ruth? Perhaps I am biased.

He really looks like a nice guy, this Dr. Morton. Perhaps I'm just making things up.

"It's the bedsores, Mrs. Clarkson. They are bound to appear in due course..."

So that's the way he's going to play it. Smart. It's his concern for the patient. No carcass—no bedsores.

"And there's nothing you can do about the bedsores, Dr. Morton?" This is the first time Ruth has spoken. She sounds as if she had no idea what the good Dr. Morton was driving at. Perhaps she is giving him enough rope to hang himself. Or hoping he'll hit a pothole or a lamppost. She's a very smart girl, my Ruth. But I can see the slight narrowing of her eyes. So small I am sure no one can possibly notice. I know this is a sign of anger. Now, I've never been on the receiving end of her temper, but there are stories about some inept restorers of old paintings who refuse to come within a mile of her. She can be tough when she wants to be. Very tough.

"We could use him for body parts, Mrs. Clarkson. Other than the coma, he looks in excellent shape..."

Now there's a thought. He'd probably think that if he weren't so tired. Kill off all patients who are 'otherwise' healthy, to heal those who are otherwise sick. Think of the money we could make that way, Mrs. Clarkson. Body parts are in great demand. There is a long waiting list. We could chop him up into little pieces and even

sell parts of him to other hospitals. Maybe even ship them to
Ontario or British Columbia. They have lots of money there...

So I *am* bitter and twisted. This is my contribution to the
greedy Medicare system. Of course, he didn't think that last tirade,
either. I told you before. Deep down inside, he's a nice fellow.
Ignorant, but nice. I mean about the coma. Isn't everybody?

Ruth remains silent while Dr. Morton looks progressively more
uncomfortable. Who knows? Maybe he had to say those things. I
mean, the things he actually did say. Maybe he is required to say
them by some hospital regulations. Or even Provincial Government
regulations. They don't tell the citizens, us simple folk, everything.
We just pay for everything. Do I sound sour? Well, too bad. After
all, this is my body. Mine! Useless as it is. I had a lot of fun in this
body. Even with Ruth...

On the other hand, if I am getting bitter—I see Ruth is getting
angry. I have too much respect for her to actually invade her
thoughts. Well, I do, but I'm trying to avoid it. Sometimes I can't
help it. At least I stopped doing so continually after those first few
days. I was really lost then. Remember? It would be like peeking at
her without her permission. Like being a vegetable Peeping Tom. I
mean *veritable*. Except for sometimes. Sometimes I can't resist it.
Sue me.

"I shall take it under advisement, Dr. Morton."

Her voice is as sweet as honey. Now *that* is dangerous. Ruth is
a very, almost extraordinarily, honest person. She never minces
words. Life's too short, she'd told me. So when she pours honey on
open wounds, you'd better look out.

Dr. Morton either senses something, or he is too busy. Probably
both. Or maybe he just wants to go home and get some sleep.
Without another word he bows slightly and leaves the room. So
there we are again, the unhappy *ménage à trois*. That's right.
Another *ménage*. Ruth, me and my body. A very unsatisfactory
combination. Ruth sits down and seems to go into a trance. For a
while, she remains completely motionless. Very, very gently I
probe her mind. Not invading it, just sort of seeing if I can overhear
anything. It's quite dark in there. Dark and almost empty. Then
there is a single thought that pushes out the darkness. The thought
is quite clear. It seems to rotate as though on an automatic replay. *If*

you have to go, I am going with you. If you have to go, I am going with you. If you have to go, I am going with you. If you have to go...

I pull my hooks back and shift to the knoll. I can almost feel the coolness of the air. She is too young to die. And too beautiful. And... oh Ruth, please don't do that. I'll wait for you. I'll wait for you for all eternity. Please don't die...

M y Friend is nowhere to be seen. This never happened before. I feel lonely and dejected. Some kind of heaven I created for myself. How dare he tell me that I create my reality? What did I have to do with Dr. Morton's words—or thoughts, for that matter? Did I create that reality? I may have helped it along with some slightly unfriendly commentary, but he'd started it. He told Ruth about the bedsores. I know they can treat them. I read all that stuff in the back of Dr. Morton's mind. He's got a storehouse of information there. Tons and tons of facts and figures.

Bedsores are also called *decubitus* ulcers, pressure ulcers, or pressure sores. I couldn't quite understand what I read in his mind, but apparently Dr. Morton thinks that I have a predisposition for them to develop. Something to do with dermal circulation of blood. The epidermis has no blood vessels, but just below, anyway... I seem to have some weakness there. The ulcers develop on skin covering when a weight-bearing part of the body is squeezed between the bone and the bed. Or another body part. They can be painful and can actually be life-threatening.

"Don't give me that crap, Dr. Moron. I don't care about the pain bit. My body doesn't feel a thing, remember?"

As for life-threatening, I'm already in that condition. A coma is threatening my life. Anyway, you have to die of something. Oops... that's what I am trying to avoid right now. For Ruth's sake.

I shift back to Morton's mind. To my surprise, I don't have to be near him to do so. It seems that human mind is omnipresent. I have to dig deep—65% of elderly people hospitalized with broken hips develop bedsores. Treatment of bedsores amounts to $2,900 per person.

"I suppose that's chicken feed to you, Doctor?"

Why am I so nasty to this guy? He didn't dig that pothole, did he? Just as well he can't hear me.

There are dozens of treatments. You start with relieving the pressure. You treat possible infection with antibiotics. There are special dressings, drying agents, lotions, ointments which should be applied to the wound in a thin film three or four times a day... OK, so there is some work involved. But you don't have to do it, Doc. Nurses can do it all. So what's the big deal?

There is also zinc and vitamins A, C, E, and B complex that help to repair the injury. Also...

This is boring. His head is so full of facts that I'm sure he'll never have a chance to use them all. Quite a smart fellow, this Dr. Morton. Perhaps I've misjudged him. If only he weren't quite so greedy. Is he greedy? I must learn to control my temper. Till now, I didn't know ghosts could have tempers.

On the other hand, Ruth did offer to die. If I could let her slip into a coma and get her a bed next to mine, we could romp the universe together. Wouldn't that be fun? I wonder if she'd also have a Friend. He, or she, would teach her. Or, more likely, she'd already know. She studied such things. Metaphysics, philosophy—on top of Fine Arts. There is only one problem. With the exception of my Friend, I never met, saw or even sensed anyone's presence in the inner world. I am my present reality. They, those others, must all be there, but I can't see them. Perhaps Friend could teach me to see people on the other side. They must be there. Even if I couldn't see any dead people, assuming they all are in a different reality, there must be thousands of people, worldwide, who are comatose. I should have bumped into at least one of them in my meanderings.

Well? Shouldn't I have?

I know. "What do you think?"

The question is, how do I put my attention on someone who is not in the physical world. It must be a whole new ballgame. Or it could be that you have to die first. I mean really die. Get divorced from your body.

Nevertheless, I make a firm commitment to keep my eyes open. To attune my new senses, such as they are, to discern the presence of other ghosts. Or light bodies. Ever assuming that any such beings are here, where I am. Should I succeed, they might be able to help me in my endeavours to save Ruth from herself.

It seems that I am in that strange state where, or wherein, I have an awareness of what is happening, but am completely unable to influence anything. At least, not in the physical world. I am also in, but not of, the reality I am in. It is as if I have completely lost my ability to become and instead I remain uninvolved. As if I have engaged my gears in neutral and, no matter how hard I press on the accelerator, the pedal has no effect on the velocity of the car. Even my own body—regardless whether I think of the one that gives me my present expression or the one in the hospital—I have no effect on it, either. I am in a state of abeyance. In a state of suspended animation. I just am.

The experiences I had since the accident in no way deny this premise. On closer examination, it appears that they, those experiences, are all drawn out of what already happened in the physical reality. If there are other realities, then I am still to discover them. For now, I am destined to be an observer, an inactive bystander. If I am to experience any motion, or any creative activity, then I am confined to doing so as a replay of events that had already taken place. The future, the bringing out of new experience into the matrix of life, is not in my terms of reference.

In spite of all this, I am determined to contact Ruth. I must tell her not only that my attempts to affect or change reality are beyond my ability, but that I am in no way suffering and in no way is my life, such as it is, in danger. And I must do so before she learns to hate her own destiny, before she loses her faith in the benevolent omnipresence that, until my accident, filled her life with joy, serenity, and great success.

I must find a way to give her a sign, or at least to delay any foolish notions she might foster with regard to her own future. She, at least, is not in neutral, and at present her life seems to be accelerating into quite the wrong direction.

I wonder what's happening in my office. I've spent a great many years there. A joyful, creative life. Somehow, I don't have the courage to just visit there. I am sure it would be another thing I would begin to miss. More so than I do already, not that I think about it that much. Rather than shifting my attention to the seventeenth floor of the CIBC Building on the corner of Peel and René Lévesque, I saunter into my partner's mind. Distances, as you know, don't matter to me. I choose Frank Drake. It is with him that I work most closely. Correction, I used to work. We were on the same wavelength. Also, he's a really nice man. Whenever I need help with anything, he volunteers.

Frank is sitting at his desk writing some notes. I peek over his shoulder. Actually, and surprisingly, through his eyes. Now here's a new experience! There is a heading on the top of his notebook underlined twice. *Must do today.* I presume he means tomorrow, in the office. I skim over his notes. I don't like what I see. About half of his chores are things I would have done, had I been there. I never passed the buck to anybody. Not even on holidays. I would advance my work sufficiently for it to roll, for a little while, under its own momentum. But not this. These are fundamental decisions. Things you cannot postpone, delay or even delegate. Except, this time, I did.

Sorry, Frank. I really didn't mean it. Really...

You know, Frank? If you only stepped outside the box, you would be a great designer. You have the taste, the imagination. What's missing? The *je ne sais quoi*? No, Frank, *je sais quoi*. What you need is guts. You must venture where no man has been before. At least, no architect. Don't give me a tribute to eclectic configurations borrowed from big names in architecture. You must always work from first principles. Remember Vitruvius? *Firmitas, utilitas* and *venustas.* Firmness, commodity and delight. These three, but the greatest of them is delight. Like with love, Frank. Like with love.

Funny how I slip into French when I think of work. That's Québec, I guess. Actually, French and Latin.

Be careful, Frank. You really have a talent, only it's hidden under layers of rules and regulations, under protocol, tradition, restraints, feasibility studies, and a great deal more. Step outside the box, Frank. Soon, you might have to.

I am out of here.

Jacques Beaulieu is the senior partner. He looks the part. Average height, high forehead, grey hair combed straight back, and piercing brown-greenish eyes. Always immaculately dressed. Handsome. He looks his part. It had been Jacques who actually formed the firm and took Frank and me on as partners. Jacques had all the contacts, I (blush, blush) the talent, and Frank was the workhorse. The three functions basically divided into administration, design and execution. I did the design. All three functions are equally important, but without Jacques, BCD Architects wouldn't exist. You need to have clients. No matter how good you are, there is nothing to design without a client needing a project. Likewise, Frank would have nothing to 'execute', to prepare the documentation for construction, if I did not provide a design solution. Actually, that last is not quite true. Frankly, most architects can produce designs. It's just that they are despicably lousy. Horrid. Disgusting. Look around you. Walk down any street. About one building in a thousand has any architectural merit.

I rest my case.

Right now, Jacques is sitting in a deep leather chair, perfectly poised, a drink in hand, listening to light opera. *Die Fledermaus*, I believe. An operetta. Frivolous, but in good taste. I can hear his wife moving in the kitchen. The maid is setting the table for six. Probably prospective clients. That's what Jacques does. His life revolves around meetings and ingratiating himself to prospective clients. I would hate doing that. For him, this is fun.

I rev forward.

Six people are sitting around the table. Jacques is, of course, at the head, showing excellent teeth he got last year to two semi-clad ladies. Two elderly gentlemen flank his wife, Janette, at the other end. Both, ladies and gentlemen, look rich. Old money. Somehow you can always tell.

It's not that I'm a snob. If anything, I'm an inverted one. I like shocking people. Not Jacques. He believes in *chaque chose à sa place*. Sort of, to each his own. Too restrictive for me. Jacques is always correct. As was his grandfather. As are his guests. *Bon chance, Jacques.* I must make myself even scarcer than I already am. I split.

It's just as well that I am dying. At least, according to Dr. Strangelove-Morton. Or is it Moreau-Morton? You'll have to find yourself a new designer, Jacques. Better luck next time. Perhaps he will do for you only neo-classical designs. As they used to be. All in impeccable taste. Fluted, tall columns in the front, with Corinthian capitals. Or at least Ionic ones like those shrimp your maid just served. I'm sure you'll like that. Bye, Jacques.

And then it strikes me. I haven't eaten since the accident. I really am a ghost.

I am floating around like a square peg in a round hole.

Mother will miss me the most. Dad will help her. Clara? Clara will still have Ruth. And Ruth? I don't want to talk about her. I suppose even now Mother remembers me the way I used to be. The way I was when I visited Ruth that time we danced all those Argentinean tangos. Did I tell you about it? My sense of time is all mixed up. All things really do happen at once. It's up to us to sort them out. Up to me.

"Hi, Mother, it's me."

She's sitting in her favourite chair, looking out into the garden. All I can see is her grey hair pinned up into an old-fashioned bun. It turned so very white. Like Dad's. Like the snow still piled on the north side of the fence. Her hands rest on the armrests, as though she is ready to rise and go. Go where? She'd only get lost. She did twice, these last few months. Now, Dad locks her in.

She's all alone. I guess Dad and Clara went shopping. She doesn't seem to mind being alone. She has her memories. She's also probably looking for spring to come and bring new life. Or just new zest for life? It's really the same thing. Perhaps she already sees, in her mind's eye, the buds on the ends of twigs and branches ready to burst with new vitality. Or she might be thinking of the times that we'd spent together, when she was young and beautiful.

She really was. Dad was crazy about her. Like those days in Florida or Jamaica. Those times on the beach...

Ah, yes, the cycle of life. There is a time to be born and there is a time to die. Outside this precious cycle, there is no time.

I wonder if it's really my turn.

I think Mother's fading memory is really a blessing. She can concentrate on all the wonderful moments in her life. Going further and further back. Perhaps this is the way it should be. We are born running forward, at break-neck speed. Children never walk, do they? They jog or run or hop, but they don't walk. They are anxious not to miss anything in this new experience of transient becoming. They soon become teenagers, then young men and women, then mothers and fathers, then successful businessmen and elegant ladies... attending elegant dinner parties. With shrimp appetizers, served on patrician English Bone China, on pristine silken tablecloths, in houses fronted with Ionic columns. Their whole life is an ongoing stream of becoming.

With my mother, it's the other way around. It is as if she were retracing her steps, carefully, one year at a time, rediscovering once again the various stages she went through. What a marvelous arrangement. If she only knew how lucky she is. If she only knew how grateful she ought to be to her God. Or to nature. Or to whoever is responsible for the sense of becoming.

But she'll still miss me.

Children shouldn't die before their parents. It doesn't seem fair. Not because they don't deserve to die, or haven't lived long enough. Just for the sake of their mothers.

***

11

I am a Galaxy

I condense time and watch bursts of energy when parts of me explode in gargantuan panache. I gather the heavier elements and pull them in rarefied clouds to new locations and then nudge them to initiate their motion, their angular momentum. I wrap them around the centre of my being. Soon parts of me condense into new vortices, new gaseous giants, only to condense still further into new stars. I leave some matter behind to create new planets. They are my children. Rough, crudely hewn, uninhibited children. Gradually they will stabilize in their orbits, settle down around the suns, and start the wondrous, unimaginably complex process of becoming. After billions of years, parts of my self-awareness will invade some of those planets. Parts like me. Just like me. Then they, my embodiments, will create their own, new galaxies. New cousins, whole families of marvels, joyful, resplendent in their glory, galaxies that populate the universe.

I have to smile.

When I stretch out my arms, I span one hundred thousand light years. I don't mean when I unwind my arms, but just as I sit in the middle, at the heart of my being, and reach out with my thoughts to the limits of my awareness. Ahh... the heart of my being... One day some will call it a Black Hole. A sphere beyond understanding—where the laws of physics no longer hold sway. A place where only gods can tread, can hold their vigil. Where neither time nor space has any meaning, where the process of becoming is suspended in a state of blissful being.

At right angles to my rotation, I am just one thousand light years across. By galactic standards, I am slim. Unobtrusive. Elegant. I could have been a globular galaxy instead. I'd chosen to become a spiral structure. I love the shapes of seashells I will have seen in the ocean. I find it strange that my awareness of me is always defined by the mode of expression I assume. Yet all of me is present in all modes of my expression. I am the universe; I am also a grain of sand. Yet I am neither of these. I sit apart and I observe my becoming from within. I cannot be divided, sectioned off, or perceived only in part. Yet I am what my expression thinks of me.

To some, observing me from afar, I seem immutable, frozen in time, almost static. In truth, I pulsate with life. I am vibrant.

Now, I'm not nearly as large as I am in some of my other embodiments. If fact, compared to the universe, I am tiny. A mere virus invading the matrix of eternity. Seen from some light years away, I am a mere speck of dust, shimmering in the sky. A shiny, slightly dim, speck of dust.

Here, my name is the Milky Way.

I look around me. I have my becoming in one hundred billion stars—give or take a few million. That's a tiny number compared to the cells I enliven in my human body.

As a man of six feet, I have some one hundred *trillion* cells at my disposal. That's like a thousand Milky Ways. A thousand galaxies. As man, I am much more advanced in my mode of becoming. I enjoy much greater self-awareness, exhibit greater diversity of choice. I wonder what mode of existence I shall assume tomorrow. Or, for that matter, what I have been until yesterday. It is hard to tell. I have neither tomorrow, not yesterday. I am aware only of the present. The eternal Now.

I am what I am.

Each now is a different now. I am like St. Paul. I don't mean as holy, but I also die daily. Whatever I was yesterday I am no more.

There are infinite ways of looking at myself. In the present, I am always the same; the unchangeable, static state of being. Yet I have an infinite number of modes of becoming. Being is definitely motionless. Like Spirit. Static. It is omnipresent—no need to move anywhere. Quiescent. Inert. In a way, I am the observer. I am the observer within each indivisible part of me. I don't do anything but contemplate the nature of my being, from which ensues my becoming — an infinite diversity of forms. The act of becoming is transient. It is also fascinating. That is what life is. A state of transient becoming. Even as I regard myself, I become aware of another of my attributes. All the states of becoming already exist in me in their potential form. Some also exist as actual experienced states. I could call them my past, but that would not be true, either. They are as much in my present as any other mode of becoming. They all coexist. Rather like people on earth. Each different yet each an inseparable part of the human experience.

I am what I am.

I shrug my *ennui*. I initiate motion.

I am sitting, inert, in my hammock. My Friend seems preoccupied. Apparently he, too, is watching something. Observing with all his attention. Something new?

I feel a deep sense of satisfaction. If I am to remain neutral in relation to the future, then at least I shall experience the many states intended to be available to me. Perhaps by observing the past, I shall learn the key to unlock the future. Not only my own, but also, and especially, that of Ruth.

I am not sure yet, but I have strong suspicions that I am right. There are consequences to regarding time as an illusion. I wonder when people on Earth will learn that. They think that they reincarnate in an endless procession along the paths delineated by Kronos. Ruth read a great deal about it. I wonder what whetted her appetite. They say that everything has its purpose. She'd said that many religions accept reincarnation as a fact of life. The cycle of life. The Awa Gavan. Hinduism, Jainism, Buddhism, Sikhism, Taoism as well as later religions. They all preach it. As did the early Christians. The Sethians as well as the Gnostics all believed in the cycle of rebirth. There had been many others. The Upanishads explain the process in detail. It applies to humans, animals and plants, equally.

How do I know all this? It must have been Ruth. Perhaps I did listen, after all, when she talked.

"They all taught it. As did Socrates, Pythagoras and Plato," Her eyes are shining. I love gazing at her when she's excited.

"Fancy that..." I murmur. I have no desire to interrupt her.

"You know, darling, this is fascinating. The Hindus claim that we are reborn because it is our desire. We want to live again. Fancy that..." she repeats my comment.

I am sitting opposite my wife, across our low coffee table.

"Fancy that," I mumble again like an echo. I am lost in her beauty. The gentle curve of her neck, her hair flowing onto her slender shoulders, smooth as silk, beguiling, inviting, designed to be touched, caressed, admired... I feel some sort of comment is expected of me. After all, for Ruth these are weighty matters.

"It is only after a great many reincarnations that we become dissatisfied with the limitations our physical body imposes on us..." she continues at length. I should have listened. Actually, only now do I know that I did—that I did listen. My subconscious records even when my mind wanders. Sometimes, I just pretended not to. Was it a form of escape? Escape from commitment to my inner self? My true potential?

"Fanc... Yes, dear." I have to finish reading the specifications by tomorrow.

"Thank you, dear. Had you said 'fancy that' just once more, I would have kicked you. Hard."

I welcome the pines and the solitude of the knoll. Where was I? Ah, yes, the sequential reincarnations. Suddenly I find my knoll unsatisfying. Limiting?

I shift my attention. I am in the heart of my home. My galaxy.

Another escape? I am...

...not so. All reincarnations are simultaneous. Even as mine are. After all, I cannot be set apart from my creation. I am one. I am the source of all experiences. The beginning and the end of each form of expression. I am the birth, the life and the death of all the stars. Yet in all of them I have my becoming.

My invisible shoulders shudder involuntarily. I realize that at this moment I am the worst and the best that I ever was. Had been.

I am all those things, all those forms, means of expression. Gandhi and Hitler. St-Francis and Genghis Khan. An eagle soaring the blue wonder and a vicious virus eating at my own body. I am also the vast ocean and a paltry grain of sand. All these things, those people, simultaneously. Now. My mind refuses to accept it. All that I am aware of, at this moment, rejects such a proposition. Rebels against it. And yet...

I am also as my component parts perceive me.

My present form was born in a wandering cloud of dust. I consisted of an infinite number of parts. Then the vibrations of my elements induced in my body an angular momentum. I began to rotate about the heart of my being—about my static, eternal, immovable present residing at the very centre of me. All my parts pay obeisance to my essence. Yet I am equally present in all aspects of me. I am.

My head is spinning. I tumble back to my knoll. I have to steady myself, impose limits on my perceptions. My true nature is more than I can bear. Is that really my nature? My authentic nature? Or is this but a dream? That's right. I am in a coma. I am unconscious. The neurons are playing tricks on my mind. I cannot tell the difference between a dream and a nightmare. Only this isn't night. It is both day and night; it is a dream that continues. I escape it momentarily, only to awaken in its continuum. Is this my new existence? Sequential dreams that will not let me escape? Perhaps I've gone mad. I am losing all sense of reality. Is this how madness insinuates itself into a human soul? And why are there such strange, such varied degrees of my somnambular adventures?

Perhaps I am not ready. Perhaps I am not ready to look into the universal mirror. I need to be human, to be ordinary. To be just me, John Clarkson, MRAIC, OAQ, Architect. Ruth's husband. That's enough for now. I still have so much to learn in my profession. So much to learn, so much to do... Institutions for the insane—asylums—are full of people who think of themselves as Napoleons, or Josephines, or even saints or saviours. I want to be just me. Just John Clarkson. At least, for now.

W e are walking down St-Catherine. As usual, Ruth is looking spectacular. A short fur coat with a puffy white trim of fur at her cuffs and knees matches her hat. I'm sure she could make a fortune as a model in a number of Parisian or New York journals. Her right arm is firmly anchored under my left elbow, her gloved hand holding on to me for dear life. It is slippery, and she insists on wearing high heels. We had some freezing rain this morning, and now the sidewalks feel like a skating rink.

I am both inside and outside my body. We took this walk some years ago. For both of me—it is now.

We have to fight our way through the crowds that are milling in and out of shops, doing their last-minute Christmas shopping. Thank God there is but little snow this year, or we would be sloshing around in galoshes. Snow is great in the countryside, but in town it's but a wet slurry of salt and dirt.

Ruth and I already bought our presents for each other and only need one or two items for my sisters. They'd both decided to join us, with their husbands, in Montreal for the Holidays. Apparently their own children deserted them, preferring a sailing trip in the Virgin Islands. Not that I blame them, though I know both Joan and Elaine feel a bit hurt. They show a brave face, but this is the first time they will not have their children around their Christmas tree. My parents and Ruth's mother are in Florida. They've been snowbirds for years. Come November they pile up their favourite books and off they go. All three of them. They'd bought a condo in Singer Island, West Palm Beach. It took all their savings, lumped together, to make it. The prices were astronomical. As are most things, these days. For them, sharing a condo is ideal. They can help each other. And it's only a two-day drive to avoid the snow for three or four months.

"We need warmth for our old bones," they announce in unison every year.

Luckily, our condo association has guestrooms. Ruth booked two extra rooms well in advance. Our guests spend most of their time with us, but there is that blessed moment, each night, when they retire to their own quarters. Don't get me wrong. I like my sisters. I also like their husbands. We both do. But Ruth and I love our solitude even more.

For now, we are free. My sisters and their spouses decided to go shopping on their own.

"We want to surprise you," all four declared. They seem to speak a lot in unison.

By the time we pass Peel, it is already turning dark. It's past four o'clock. In Montreal, nights come early in December. As does the cold. Still, Christmas is only once a year. We want to look at the decorations along McGill College Avenue. It is our version of the Champs-Élysées. A tiny version, but Montreal is a tiny city compared to Paris.

As we reach the corner, the view takes my breath away. That and the gust of wind from the mountain. By now, it must be minus ten or fifteen, Celsius. With the wind-chill factor, it feels like minus twenty. But the view is still fantastic. To our right, the trees are salted with tiny white bulbs that terminate on an enormous Christmas tree, installed on the top of the Place Ville-Marie terrace. It dominates the raised square all the way to Dorchester. Actually, they changed the street name to Boulevard René Lévesque, but most of us old-timers continue to refer to it as Dorchester. It was named in 1844 in honour of Guy Carleton, 1st Baron Dorchester, then Governor of Quebec, and later Governor General of Canada. He meant a great deal more to most of us than naming it after a short, balding, chain-smoking man, who tried to break up Canada against our will.

Not that it matters that much. They're both dead, in a way.

But it is only when Ruth and I turn west, and face Mount Royal, that we become speechless. At the very top of the mountain, there is the usual illuminated cross. It was there for as long as I can remember.

A great deal happened since Jacques Cartier scaled the mountain in 1535. He named it in honour of his king. Hence Mount *Royal*. The village of Hochelaga has grown into a metropolis that, in 1967, hosted one of the most exciting Expos the world had ever known. For those few days, Montreal was the centre of the world. A city of lights. Like Paris. Yet its name had been formally applied only in the 18th Century. Before that it was called Ville-Marie.

Hence the cross. Its first version had been erected by Paul Chomedey in gratitude for having his prayers heard. When the Virgin Mary averted a disastrous flood, he'd made a vow to her, and kept it. In 1643, he installed the first cross.

The present version rises over 31 meters from the crown of the mountain. Its fiber-optic lights can change colour at will. In April 2005, they shone with purple light to mark the death of Pope John Paul II. Today, in the crisp dry air, they are sparkling white. Like stars.

Yet, glorious as it is, this is not what stopped us in our tracks. Stretching all the way to Sherbrooke Street, there's an ocean of tiny white bulbs. Cluster after cluster of shining pinpoints shimmer in the cold air that seems to make them brighter. The wind moves them as though spinning about their axes, millions and millions of stars trapped forever around their galactic centre atop the mountain. By some optical trick of perspective, an illusion, the pinpoints of all the galaxies seem connected to the cross on the mountain. A long procession of lights paying reverence to the source of All Light.

In ancient times, the Dutch would call it the Vronelden Straet, the Woman's Path, a procession of chosen maidens, their sparkling veils of intricate lacework streaming behind them. Perhaps they all led to the altar at which Paul Chomedey prayed to the Virgin Mary.

Ruth is the first to react.

"John, am I seeing things? This is the Via Lactis... I've seen it in my dreams."

"I've seen you in my dreams, darling, many times."

"But look..."

And it was then, as we walked toward the mountain, that she told me all about the Vronelden Straet, and many other mysterious things. We both forgot about the presents we set out to buy for my sisters. We also forgot about the cold, about the biting wind. How can one think of such mundane things when one walks, arm in arm, along the starlit path to heaven?

For nine weeks they met to say the Rosary. Nine weeks. A novena. Mother insisted. She flew back from Florida the day after the accident. Ruth didn't want to hurt her feelings. She looked after Mother herself, at the condo.

Mother and my cousins are fairly orthodox. That's another name for Catholic Fundamentalists. I feel Ruth cannot quite pray any more. Not in public. Not by vain repetition of words that are meaningless to her. More so every day. After two weeks, Ruth persuaded Mother to return to Florida to rejoin Dad and Ruth's mother. My cousins continued praying. They are here right now. So is Ruth. Before my mother's departure, Dr. Morton assured her that there was absolutely nothing she could do here, and that her son, me, was not in any immediate danger.

"These things can drag for months and months, Mrs. Clarkson," he assured Mother. Ruth begged the doctor to tell her that. She simply has no strength to look after Mother right now, she explained. Dr. Morton understood. His own mother was about the same age.

Mother resisted—Ruth insisted. She drove her to the airport and put her on the plane to West Palm Beach. Dad would pick her up. Finally Ruth breathed easier. For a while Mother called daily, to inquire about my state of health. This was better than driving her to the Lakeshore Hospital, day after day. And then back. And then reassuring her. After some weeks, Mother forgot the details. I was in hospital, Dad reminded her, but not every day. There was no point worrying her.

The cousins continue praying. The Rosary. On and on...

Father, let Thy will be done. But if you choose to take him away from me, then please, take me as well.

I didn't enter her mind. I swear. In fact, I tried hard not to listen. But her plea was a scream that I couldn't help hearing. My Ruth. My Ruth would give up her life for me.

My Ruth.

I am twenty-six light-years away from where I was an instant ago. That's assuming that I observed my body from the very centre of the galaxy. I don't know how I know this. At least I didn't till I noticed Friend grinning from ear to ear. If I were made of light, I would not be able to travel that fast. Perhaps that is why I must always assume a body that is already there.

"Well done, John."

This is my Friend who seems to be following my exploits with increased interest. It feels as if he were actually waiting for my return. Sooner or later I shall find out who he really is.

So the knowledge really is within me. Perhaps, in time, I shall learn to gain access to it, even without my Friend taunting me. Actually, he doesn't really taunt me, but he forces me to keep trying the new, the unknown. He's like a bundle of curiosity, only he makes me do all the research. Not that I mind, really.

In fact... this is a dream come true.

There is something very unfair in all this. Yesterday, or in a previous reality, I was fairly miserable seeing Ruth going through the pangs of decision-making. Not that I ever doubted her conclusions. I also felt that we are one. Yet here, this side of the great divide, there is such splendour that it feeds my insatiable desire to continue my exploration.

"Is there any limit to the experience of becoming?" I have to ask.

"What do..."

"...I think? I think there isn't. If there is no time, then there is no limit. And furthermore, if I remember right, I can only explore the past, and I am not yet sure if the past has a beginning. What do you think?"

"Good try, my friend. Good try!" There is that laughter again.

"Qui ne risque rien, n'a rien," I respond. After all, he did it to me many times; and furthermore, if he can read my mind, then I assume he can also speak French. "No, I do not believe the past can have a beginning if there is no time. But this is not the primary reason. I believe that there is no past. I have grave reservations if the future really exists, either. From the point of view of being, I am fairly sure that only present exists."

My Friend takes a long time opening his mouth. I take his silence as encouragement. "The main thing is that once I eliminate time from the equation, I can travel light-years within a blink of an eye. I am no longer limited to 300,000 kilometers per second."

He is looking at me, his eyes getting wider.

"And finally, with the elimination of time, I am omnipresent." I hope I didn't go too far this time. Ha, ha! This 'time' again! The word is still convenient for sequential activities.

My Friend shakes his head.

"You know, John, we met like this a few million times. Today is the first time you voiced this conclusion. You made a giant step today." Then he smiles, sighs and smiles again. "Of course, as you say, there is only today, right?"

"Are you asking me?"

"You are my only source of knowledge, John."

"B-b-but I thought..."

"Yes, I know. You thought it was the other way round."

I am sitting in the very centre of light. I am also its source. I am the light. I am filled with silence. I am aware only of my own being. I am in repose.

I am the heart of the Milky Way. They know me by many names. I draw all my becoming towards me. I reach out and hold on to my children, in infinite diversity of all my forms. They cannot see me, but they experience my attraction. I am the light, yet they cannot see me. This is the mystery of my becoming.

I rejoice in the vicissitudes of my expression. I multiply the infinite parts of me that all might experience my splendour. In time, in eons of realization, I shall absorb them into my being, again, even while I remain immobile, at rest, serene in the heart of each galaxy. For I am omnipresent. I am beyond time. I am the knowledge that emanates from me. When they learn of my nature, I shall spew them out again to continue on their infinite journey. I shall create space and time and seed it with my presence.

I have neither beginning nor do I have an end. I am.

I am that I am.

Not so. I am back at the knoll. I am fooling myself. As I already concluded, I can only examine what is already there, or here, but I cannot affect the future. My creative acts are mere echoes of what I have already accomplished. I remain in a state of being. Imagine being a god and being totally helpless. Talk about irony!

I am past trying to get anything out of my Friend. For all I know, he is no more powerful than I am. Perhaps he, too, is just an observer, waiting his turn to learn enough to escape this stagnant existence. Not stagnant in the real sense—he and I can both travel in all directions but one—yet, regardless of what we replay from our past, I now feel that I, the real I, am; the essence of my being remains static. I doubt I even have a potential existence. Just my past.

I am beginning to have vague thoughts of why God decided to create man. Of course, He didn't start with man. He must have started way back when there was nothing. No space, no time, no life. Nothing. Not even energy, as we know it. God is not a thing, hence Nothing best describes Him. Or Her or It, of course. As for fashioning us after His own nature, well, I think our forefathers just added that bit to bloat their egos. They've tried to de-bloat it ever since by calling each other sinners. Not one of them would agree to be described as Nothing. No matter how benevolent, how omniscient, how omnipotent. We, humans, even in the condition I am in now, demand, we need to be, Something. With a capital S. Or Somebody.

Not what I am now.

I've worn the mantle of the early Universe. My mind was immersed in conclusions drawn by mystics of all times defining the nature of Being. Or, at the very least, of our ability to understand what the nature of Being must be so as to explain what is. What IS. To explain reality. I've examined our galaxy; I've dwelt for timeless eons in the heart of a Black Hole. The ocean of light, inaccessible to anyone, that seems to lie in the incipient nature of my own being. Not that it makes any sense. The nearest I can speculate on the nature of light is that it is the essence of knowledge. All knowledge. It is the Knowingness Itself that abides in the heart of everything; inexhaustible, eternally inaccessible, seemingly dormant, yet there to be discovered. Like the apple of the Garden of Eden. A divine temptation. As for the rest, I remain nothing. Even now.

I wonder what happened to Friend?

People try to define the enormousness of the universe. Einstein speculated that it might be infinite. He wasn't sure. Some scientists try to measure it by multiplying how old we think it is by the speed of light. This would give it a diameter of some 20 billion light-years. We already know this is nonsense. What we see may only be a small part of the physical universe. Later astrophysicists limited the universe to at least 93 billion light-years across. According to others, the universe began at a single point, some 13.7 billion years ago, and kept expanding ever since. This is backed up by the Big Bang theory. Others have a humbler view. They allow a latitude for the universal girth to fall somewhere between 15 and 20 billion years. There is also the expanding universe theory. There are other theories, including those defined by the Kabbala. Why not? Everyone else had a go. And frankly, who cares? Who cares if we are off by a billion or two? I would still hit that pothole. I would still be hanging right now on my invisible hammock in the middle of nowhere. We, humans, always need a beginning and the attendant end—of everything. Haven't I already said that? Our minds are not constructed to think outside the confines of time.

Perhaps this is why I am here.

Whatever happened to the Stranger? Is he no longer my Friend?

I am swinging on my hammock like a Foucault pendulum. Do not worry. I will not stop the Earth in her rotations. I don't carry any weight. I do not matter. Perhaps I never did. Regardless of how much I learn, were I alive, the rest of eternity would still lie before me. For the taking. For the creating. But not now. For now I don't matter. I am as close to Nothing as I can get.

Perhaps I am close to Divinity?

***

12

Who Are You?

The knoll is my new home. If God abides in heaven, then I abide in the knoll. I may be helpless to affect my environment, but at least here I am allowed to think freely. Whoever pulls my strings gives me that much.

There are no changes here. The white field remains as white as the day I got here. A few pines, a fir or two, and a half-dozen trees denuded of their summer glory are my world. Even the sky seems frozen outside the confines of time. Or the other way around. It is free of the ravages of both time and climate. There is a strange stillness here. Not even extraneous thoughts invade my domain. Other people's thoughts. With my Friend absent, I am truly alone. Even when a gentle breeze touches the tops of the slim, elegant pines, it is probably the product of my desire to break down the monotony. Extracted from the past. To create an illusion of movement. Is this place also an illusion?

Why also? Isn't all else an illusion? Seriously, is physical reality anything other than illusion? Or any reality? What I used to see with my physical eyes was essentially empty space that separates the electrons from their nuclei. Now, do you believe me?

Only silence acknowledges my questions.

I like it here. When on my illusory hammock, I become aware of my state of being. I do not really learn anything new. Not here. I abide in the stillness of winter. It is as though I, too, were hibernating. I rest between seasons of great discovery. Seasons of growth, of learning. Here, I just am.

He's back. For all I know, he is always here. Probably he just decides to remain invisible. He is like that. He does his coming and his going in private. And in utter silence. Most of the time he also just is. Like my mirror. Like the moon, feeding on reflected light.

"Where were you?" I ask.

I try to keep my voice normal, though I'm slightly annoyed. I scold myself for taking him for granted. On the other hand, there is no one else. Perhaps man is not made to be completely alone. We are herd animals. We live in packs, groups. Like bacteria, we believe that strength lies in numbers. Also like bacteria, we tend to destroy the environment which supports us. We don't really care about the future, about our progeny. We destroy nature that feeds us, that sustains us.

On the other hand, we claim that we had been created to reflect our Creator's glorious attributes. We do not extend this assertion to anyone else. To no other species. After all, aren't we immortal? Unless this also is but an illusion. Perhaps our need to create reality is contagious, like a disease. Don't we all do it? Is this why we create illusions?

"I didn't want to distract you. You had some interesting thoughts."

Of course. He was peeking.

I pretend annoyance, but I don't think he believes me. I strongly suspect that he knows me to be glad that he is here, always, even if invisible. Just to keep me company. My thoughts drift back to my original query. He is the one that is always here, visible or not, at my beckoning, yet seldom answers any of my questions directly. Is he also no more than a figment of my imagination? I cannot accept it. I have ample evidence of his vast knowledge.

My Friend and I had this discussion many times before. I insist on trying to determine his real nature. Not just his appearance, his erudition, his peculiar abilities, but also the fact that, even if indirectly, he seems to follow me to the ends of the universe. He seems endowed with enormous powers.

"Who are you, really?" I ask. I am determined not to let him wiggle out, again, before I'm satisfied. "It's not as if I am going to run around and tell everybody."

From the corner of my eye, I see him smiling. Nevertheless, this time I will not be swayed by his glib questions. After all, I have time. Infinity of time, if such exists at all.

On previous occasions we both came close to unraveling my nagging mystery. I don't know why I have to know his identity, but I do. I never liked unresolved riddles. In architecture any such can prove a danger to the occupants of my buildings. I must put an end to this one.

For a moment I am distracted. My mind spans centuries to a similar conversation. Only this was in reverse. *Who do men say that I am? And they answered, John the Baptist, some said Elias, still others said one of the prophets...* Why is it that he who posed this question refused to identify himself for who he really was? Only when Peter guessed right, did he no longer deny it. Is this what I must do? Guess right before my Friend will admit who he really is? Is this a game played to stimulate my mind?

"I am whatever you seek of me. I can be neither more nor less. It is my nature to guide you. To show you the way. But this will change soon," he adds.

At some moment in my becoming, Ruth read me some verses from a Sufi poet, Jalaludin Rumi. This sounds like something taken from her collection. Dear Ruth, I hope she's bearing up under all this.

Looking at it from a different angle, my Friend sounds like a parent who loves his child yet feels the need for it—in this case for me—to wean away, to stand up on my own feet. There is a contradiction in this stance, as if he had two functions. One pushing, one pulling away. As if he regretted leaving me alone to face the cruel exigencies of the world in my own way. This is peculiar, because I think I already do. I think I am standing, and flying, and traversing eons of time on my own. Aren't I?

"Yes, John. Yes, you are," the sadness remains. But also, there's pride. Pride at my progress?

"Then what is your function?"

"I think you already know."

The old smile returns. I am a child, again, who has been given a puzzle to solve. A bright child who is getting close to the answer. "You as much as said it but seconds ago," he adds, on seeing my blank stare.

"You are quoting time to me?"

"It is always convenient for sequential progression. In fact, it is its only function."

I can relate to that. Time might not really exist, but sequential order is an imperative of logical progression. I cannot do without it. I try to review what had been said so far.

"Not just said, John."

"I have to review my thoughts also?"

"For me they are no different, whether you vocalize them or not."

I already know that every thought that my mind generates has a purpose. I review the stream that preceded the present. I have it. It seems so simple. Watching my Friend's expression, I know I am right. It was Ruth who gave me the answer. It is always Ruth.

"A lamp am I to you that perceive me. A mirror am I to you that know me," I quote unabashedly.

Friend smiles. I don't blame him. So do I. Since Ruth learned about Sister Wendy's being a Carmelite nun, her interest in Carmelites swelled. Next she began to study the lives of saints associated with the Order. She came across the writings attributed to Saint John of the Cross, somehow connected to the Carmelites. Sliding her finger along all the Saint Johns, she came across the Apocryphal Acts, also attributed to, though to a different, John. And there it was. The quotation.

"Things happen that way, John. All things have a purpose." My Friend sounds amused.

"Are you trying to tell me that Ruth took up art, to meet Sister Wendy, to drift into John of the Cross, to find the Apocryphal Acts?"

"Not at all, John. The Acts of John date back to the 2nd century Christian collection. Saint John of the Cross graced the dualistic reality around the 15th century. He was not only a major Spanish mystic and poet, but renowned for his cooperation with Saint Teresa of Avila in the reformation of the Carmelite Order. Hence

Ruth's connection. Along the way he taught Ruth a great deal about detachment."

"How do you know all this?" I am flabbergasted. He seems to know more about Ruth than I do. His next answer confuses me still further.

"I was there. Don't you remember?"

I fail to see how his being there is supposed to help my memory. I am on the verge of spinning my universal recorder to bear witness to his words, but I know that if I let Friend go, I might never get him to speak so freely about himself. Or about Ruth, for that matter. Also, somehow, I know that my Friend is quite incapable of making up stories.

Friend spreads his arms as though seeking guidance.

"John," he says after a while, "think outside the box. Have you not remembered a great deal since the accident?"

"I remembered…?" I know I learned a great deal. I remembered hardly anything.

"No, John. You remembered."

A series of events flashed across the screen of my mind. I experienced those fragments of my early years, of course. There were also some dear moments that Ruth and I'd spent together. Precious moments. I wish I could make them last longer. But further back? Is he talking about my previous reincarnations?

"You forgot already? All reincarnations are simultaneous."

I did come to this conclusion some time ago, only it did not really make sense. Except for one thing—there is no time. That is why they must be simultaneous. Contemporaneous. They happen at once, and then we arrange them in an order so as to make sense out of them. I think I am beginning to get it.

"OK. That's one. And what is the other factor?"

He's like a father teaching his backward child the ABCs of reality. "Give me a hint?" I ask. My head is about to explode.

"Remember Jung?"

How could I forget him? Ruth had pushed his papers in front of my nose. "In-di-vi-du-al is the on-ly re-ali-ty." She had scanned every syllable. There is a tiny pinpoint of light spinning in the darker nooks of my mind. It vibrates with a life of its own, then bursts into a blinding nova moments later.

"Individual is the only reality. You are me..." I say slowly, disbelieving my own voice. "You are me," I repeat louder as the thought begins to anchor itself in my feeble awareness. "You are my Friend?"

He allows this concept to take hold for a while, then smiles and nods for me to continue.

"You are the sum total of what I have become so far. No one knows the future. It is up to me to unfold it." Only I can't. I seem frozen in the stillness of being.

"You must accept what you are before you can continue becoming," I hear his thoughts. It is ludicrous to keep talking. In a way, it now feels as though I am talking to myself. "Have I reached a point of no return?"

"Not exactly," he butts into my own mind's perambulations. For a moment I forget about the friendship and resent my other self's telling me anything. After all, he is but an image of me.

"I exist only in your mind."

There we go again. So by being angry at him, I am only angry at myself. And then I remember. "Isn't this what you say about all reality?"

"And you still doubt it?"

My Friend has not lost his smile. I'm glad at least one of us enjoys being proven a congenital moron.

"I seem to be the one who shows you the way. I am nothing of the sort. But I do show you the truth. In this sense I am your enabler. But when you come to face me, I am no more than your mirror, a mere reflection of you."

I see Ruth. She's curled up on the settee, her legs tucked in under her long skirt. She's being a woman today. Not a teacher, professor of the history of art, but woman. My woman. She looks like a beautiful girl and a mature woman rolled into one. I really have no idea how she does it. She seems to be all things to me across the vastness of time. She never changes, yet she's always fresh, always new. She is also an inexhaustible fount of stimulating ideas.

"Let me be your mirror," she says. "A mirror of a lesser god."

I seem to import into our discussion the knowledge I acquired in my last discussion with my Friend. This, of course, is impossible. Or... it would be possible if time didn't exist. If I can import ideas back in time. Also, my Friend does claim that all knowledge is already within me. If I accept this premise, then there is nothing peculiar about any of this. Yet the 'replay' is in the here and now of way back when...

Somehow I am still in the state of being.

From what I've learned, mirror, in the Apocryphal Acts of John, refers to the divine spark within us which, in the initial stages of our unfoldment, acts as a guide. Later, a stage which my Friend seems to imply that I've reached, when we grow more cognizant of our true character, it becomes a mirror of our true self. Of what we *really* are. The observer and the observed become one. Paradoxically, my Friend implies that one can only reach one's ultimate potential in infinity.

The day before this discussion, which I revisited thanks to my trusty universal recorder, Ruth and I went to the movies. We saw a film called *Children of a Lesser God*. I think she is referring, somehow, to that film, although I don't quite see the connection.

"You never tell me that you are fully aware of my obvious faults," she says, her head cocked at an inquisitive angle.

"Your faults, darling? You are jesting, my love."

She continues ignoring my interruption. "Our nature disposes us to be aware of our own shortcomings only when exemplified in another person. In marriage, this predisposition to see our own weaknesses in others is tempered by love. We see the apparent or imagined foibles in our beloved but, due to our emotional commitment, we endeavour to rise above them. We might both see that we do not live up to our self-imposed standards, but we tend to forgive and forget when we miss the mark."

As usual, at the time, I hadn't been paying sufficient attention. I am glad that this 'flash-back' brings me up to the present, so to speak. As for her faults? That's nonsense. She must be referring to mine. I can only rarely see my own faults reflected in some of what she does, or usually says.

"Seldom, if ever, are we aware that we discern almost exclusively our own weaknesses reflected in the personified mirror we have chosen to spend our life with."

"Bingo!"

"What, darling?"

"I was just thinking that. If there is anything at all that ever gets my gander, it's when I see you acting the way I would. Does this make any sense?"

"If you saw my faults more often…"

"I would be more aware of my own?"

"Bingo—I believe that's the right expression?"

"But why are you calling us children of a lesser god?"

"I was only alluding to the movie we saw last night, darling. You are definitely a very large son of a very large god."

Well, I was. In a flimsy way, I still am. Or what's left of me. I should look in on my bones. For all I know, they might well be mending. After all, shouldn't a god look after even his lesser children?

I no longer feel shock when my awareness shifts from one scenery, or reality, to another. Actually, I am constantly in just one reality. It is my attention that shifts, nothing more. I know that now, but it was not an easy concept to accept. Especially, to accept it emotionally. Each time I experience scenes from my past, they come with all the visual, aural, and sensual accoutrements. Even the smell permeates the room or the place my attention visits. Moments ago (I know it is simultaneous, but it is easier to make myself understood if I employ the concept of time), I could smell the Arpege Ruth likes so much. Eau Arpege, by Lanvin. Ruth finds the perfume too powerful. Nevertheless, here, only its memory lingers on. The scent is gone. As is Ruth.

"You get the idea, John?" My Friend, if I can continue to call him that, seems quite unaware that for a time my mind was wandering.

"Am I supposed to look for my faults in you?" I couldn't keep a little sarcasm out of my tone of voice.

"Aren't you?"

"There, always asking questions, instead of employing the infinity of your mind to find the answer. But I am under the impression that *you* do it. Not I."

This time, time stretches. I don't care if it really doesn't exist.

I am experiencing a sequential procession of silent moments of eternity linked to an unpleasant odour of stupidity. After all our discussions, which can also be portrayed as a cathartic search of my own mind, I still find it hard to accept that he is me. How do I know that it is not the other way around? How do I know that I am no more than a figment of *his* imagination? He certainly seems real enough. In fact, more so than I. A lot more solid, so to speak.

"It's because your body is made up only of the past you remember. I am the sum total of your memories."

Still reading my thoughts! It's practically as if I were talking to myself. I turn my head to face him. There is a big grin on my Friend's face. The next moment I realize that I am also grinning. After all, having an animated discussion with myself is a bit on the funny side. Or insane. I prefer funny.

"You mean my conscious and subconscious memories?"

"And cellular, and sub-cellular, and molecular, and atomic, and sub-atomic…"

"I get the idea. You really remember when you were an entity consisting just of whirling atoms?"

"I made them whirl. Actually you did. When I say I, it's just a figure of speech."

"And the universe, when it was no more than an endless ocean of squiggly little pieces of lint?"

"Why not? You did."

I let that sink in. There is something extremely reassuring about having a friend. A Friend with a capital F. It's like having a Guardian Angel, after all. He never forgets, he's always at your shoulder, he, as far as I can see, is immortal. Certainly not subject to the ravages of time and/or erosion. I find that I am also getting used to his presence. In whatever form.

"Are you my soul?"

"I could ask you what do you think, only it's too late for that. I know that you know that I know exactly what you think. To make your thoughts more orderly, I am what is called an animal soul, though it has nothing to do with any animal. That is the sum total of all your memories portrayed in a shape and form that reflects your present appearance. This includes not just your human form, or forms. But you already know that also."

"That's a lot of memories…"

"That is why you still, if I may say so, need me. Any particular embodiment, no matter how wonderful, cannot contain the totality of conscious experience. Not even if you managed to limit your memories to the last fifteen or twenty billion years. Also, it would probably drive you insane. It would be like portraying, on stage, the parts from Hamlet, Othello, Sir Toby Belch and all the female parts, particularly Viola and Desdemona, simultaneously. Now multiply that by a few trillion roles from other plays, or from life itself. Although, to give credit where credit is due, I think you've done justice to each one of your Shakespearean roles."

I wince. I think I just experienced all Shakespearean plays flashing before my eyes at the speed of light. Probably faster. It feels as though I'd written them all myself; then edited, proofread and performed all the parts. He's right. Funny that. The truth is supposed to set us free. Me? It just drives me a little crazy.

"And what about, you know, the immortal part...?" I try again.

My Friend looks at me with eyes that are again filled with disbelief. "You are asking me?"

I feel as though I had asked my mirror if I looked good, only a million times more silly. I find myself trying to control my thoughts so as not to offend my Friend. I am acutely aware that my thoughts are all privy to him, even those that do not necessarily reach my own awareness. Maybe that is why the analogy of a guardian angel seems to be apt. I am sure that in time I shall get used to it, but the very idea that I no longer have any privacy is unnerving.

Another flash shows me the thoughts I had as a little boy. All boys have 'dirty' thoughts. Lewd thoughts, or desires. It's part of the hormonal process of growing up. Mine appear to have been particularly imaginative. I'm desperately trying to dismiss them from my mind before my Friend takes part in the replay.

I am the one before whom you have been ashamed.

The words join the images. I've heard them before. If I understand them correctly, I have been ashamed before myself? It seems that way. Then other phrases spill into my awareness. I didn't understand them when I first heard them. I didn't understand any of them. *I am he who was within me. I am the one whom you have hidden from. I am sinless. I am the one who alone exists...*

Now I have to make up my mind. Either I am sinless, or I alone exist. There is still so much to learn. So very much…

There are many other phrases, quotations, sayings, axioms, adages, all clamoring to get into my awareness. Thank God there is no time.

I try to stop thinking. I place my attention on the field around me. On the twigs maintaining their brave stance, holding their proud, empty heads above the thin layer of white powder. I am glad there is not much wind in this field. It would be too hard on them. I never thought of them as life before. I do now. All is life. Without life there is just potential. There would be no movement, no becoming. There would be only stillness and the past. Like my present reality.

I glance at my Friend. He looks like a regular neighbourhood ghost. Then I look at myself. I am likewise wearing a flowing off-white robe with some pant-like tubes protruding below it. Now that I think about it, I would probably be welcomed at any Moslem gathering in Saudi Arabia, or even at The House of Bush. Perhaps they are all ghosts? Just for fun I think myself wearing a regular suit. The moment my thoughts form, I am wearing it. A glance at my Friend confirms my suspicions. He really is my mirror, in more ways than one. I decide to play a little trick on my Friend. I don't 'change' but I think of myself in a flamboyant Madame Pompadour wig. True enough, my Friend looks like a cross between an effeminate sissy and a blond Elvis Presley. I try hard not to laugh. A moment later he's changing back to 'normal'. After that, I let him be. After all, he is my Friend.

"Are there other modes of being that I can experience from my past?" I ask.

I know the answer. A countless number. I must simply place my attention on them. My Friend will do the rest. How I wish I could take Ruth with me. Perhaps she has her own Friend. Her own guardian angel. Perhaps we all do. Even Mother. I say *even* because she's so set in her religious ways. I am sure they hold her back. Someone once said that traditions are just bad habits repeated *ad nauseam*. Fundamentalists are like that. They stopped in their becoming. As I did. And my sisters. And Ruth's dad before he died. I wonder where he is?

"Is there heaven and hell?" I ask instead. We've been through this before.

"What do you think?" my Friend replies.

At least he's no longer a stranger. I've known him from the beginning of time. Perhaps, in a way, I gave him life. His sense of being. Even becoming. Isn't that what life is? A sense of becoming? After all, we are one, my Friend and I. Inseparable. Aren't we?

"What do you...?

And we both start laughing. Did you ever hear a ghost laugh? It would sound better in an old English castle. Preferably one with lots of spider webs and creaky staircases and echoes reverberating in vast, empty chambers. Yes, two ghosts laughing there would be almost acceptable. Otherwise, you should avoid it. It's not pretty.

***

13

I am the Solar System

D r. Morton goes through the motions of performing his duty. I am really getting quite used to him. Slim, about five-eight or nine, he tries a little too hard to dominate his staff. His elevator shoes don't help much. Anyway, he doesn't have to wear them. Most of the junior staff happen to be barely average height and, regardless of his physical appearance, or stature, he is already well respected by his colleagues. As for the nurses, I noticed that Nurse Joan is not the only one who rubs her behind provocatively against him whenever she has a chance. I suppose they want to advance their careers.

Dr. Morton may also be suffering from a slight complex on account of having lost most of his hair prematurely. Nevertheless, with the gold-framed spectacles he strikes quite an imposing figure. The word 'professor' comes to mind. He would be more impressive in a well-pressed suit rather than the white coat he insists on wearing. Not all senior staff members do so. For most of them the proverbial stethoscope draped around their necks seems to suffice. Or, the absence of a white coat may have something to do with status, or seniority. I don't really care.

He comes in regularly at eight-thirty. Always punctual. In my room he checks the instrumentation, assigns the next battery of drugs. He checks my back and hips, making sure that the bedsores are kept to a minimum. Next he issues instructions to minimize my discomfort. It takes him all of five minutes. There is little he has to do himself. The nurses already know the procedures. The routine, really. They perform the same functions, round and round, to keep my body in a reasonable condition. To keep me alive.

Of course, I don't really know how long a time elapsed since my accident. Traversing the 'non-existent' time in both directions tends to confuse me.

"Don't you find it peculiar how well he looks, Nurse Jones?" he remarks, peeking under my eyelids. Poor Joan. Evidently the good doctor prefers the more formal form of address.

Miss Jones, the senior nurse, thinks Dr. Morton is god. Or almost god. She does her best to look attractive whenever he is due for his rounds. After all, Dr. Morton is single, and still young enough to get involved. She knows he is neither married nor burdened from previous dalliances. She doesn't give him more than forty-five. Plus-minus. With luck it could be minus. Nurse Jones is thirty-one. With luck, Dr. Morton could be her second husband.

As for my looks, the nearest I can describe myself is that I make a good facsimile of an Egyptian mummy. King Tut or one of his noble colleagues. While the colourful hues have left my face, the rest of my body remains wrapped up in all sorts of bandages. I suspect it may have something to do with bedsores. Not that I have so many, but as a preventive measure. I'm surprised how little I care.

I don't dare to peek under my own eyelids. I might inadvertently slip inside my body and come out of the coma. I feel about my body as if it were a prison from which, but for the will of the gods and a convenient pothole, I became liberated. In fact, I continue to feel a certain undefined distaste for my physical counterpart. In spite of my six-foot-one, it still seems small, restrictive, with limited senses that hardly scratch the reality outside its confines. Oh, I know that, compared to other members of the animal kingdom, my body has a complex brain capable of translating the perceptions of my mind into a series of visions that give a semblance of reality. In a way, my brain acts as an imperfect mirror for my mind.

Very imperfect.

On the other hand, there is a certain feeling of latent power resting in my prostrate carcass. OK, in my prostrate body. It is the centre of a tiny universe, a nucleus, around which lives of other people revolve. Like the ancient concepts of our Solar System. Aristotelian? From my inert centre, I body, I John Clarkson, influence their activities. I sit at rest and they move about me in predetermined orbits. They pay obeisance to me. To my body. To Earth that remains ever at rest, surrounded by her children.

Early, just after dawn, the cleaners perform their duties with mops and brushes. They are in my outer orbit. They take care of the outer rim of my tiny macrocosm. Actually, microcosm. They keep their distance, well aware of their secondary importance. Yet, in a way, they are just as vital. Even the few visitors I receive would leave my world in a state of abundant decay. If it weren't for them, the cleaners, my other visitors would be knee-deep in the offal of their own skin.

I wonder where Ruth is. She's never late...

"**D**o you know, darling," Ruth is looking down at the pink toes adorning her feet, "that we walk in our own biological waste?" She's wearing light sandals with neither socks nor stockings. My mind shifts to the present of some months ago. Not that I can be sure exactly when.

Interesting how memories are grouped together. Not sequentially, but more like in files pertaining to the same, or at least similar, subject. I've just been thinking about offal, the biological waste.

We are walking along one of those narrow winding paths that crisscross Mount Royal Park, at often perilously contorted inclinations. Some are really steep, snaking between large boulders and sharp rocks. Nevertheless, we love leaving the main, wide, gravelled road and wandering off the beaten track. Here we are closer to nature or, as Ruth calls it, closer to our origins. Also, she's quite capable of finding beauty in the most unexpected places. A bent branch of a withering tree, or a gnarled root protruding underfoot, would cause her to stop, ponder, and share her admiration. My geometry is mostly rectilinear, hers free and flamboyant. Exactly like nature's. Left to myself, I would merely trip over the apparent works of art and swear at the groundskeepers for not preparing the footpath with greater care.

"I was under the impression that it is soil, dear." I glance at the stuff under our feet.

"I don't mean now, John, at home!" She gives me a look I would reserve for a wayward child.

"Of course," I agree.

Sometimes it is better to let Ruth expound on her thoughts, reserving one's comments for later. On this occasion, however, my innocent acquiescence elicits another dirty look. Then she evidently decides to ignore my ignorance.

"When we walk indoors, darling," another of those glances, "we shed around one and a half million dead skin flakes every hour. We recognize them as dust on our floors. But, not to worry. A veritable army of insatiable mites spends its entire existence eating up bits and pieces of our dead, dried-up fragments of skin. Epidermal delight. The more we shed, the more they eat... and multiply. Our loss is their gain. They save us from eventual drowning in the dead cells of our own bodies. I suppose they are a little like domestic help in some illustrious residences of our social elite..."

...or the cleaning staff in the Lakeshore Hospital. I mean the offal sucked up by the powerful nozzles of the cleaning staff...

No, the cleaning staff do not have nozzles. They carry them at the end of long tubes connected to a vacuum system. I am back in my Lakeshore room, hovering in the corner, to stay out of the way of the nurses. It is a very strange feeling when someone walks right through you. It happened to me once, and I thought it would be the end of me. Ever since, I jump out of the way, often submerging or immersing myself into a wall behind me, just to avoid human contact. There is something about coming in contact with a human body that is distinctly repugnant. Or not repugnant, perhaps, but extremely odious and certainly unnerving. It is a bit like touching a live wire, only there is no pain, just repulsion. It could be that human bodies generate some sort of energy that is perceptible to ghosts such as I am, even if I can't understand it. I avoid physical contact with people ever since the time that a nurse backed into me with a tray of washing paraphernalia. As I said, it's strange, though there is nothing physical about me. It is even stranger that I still associate life with the physical body.

Nevertheless, I regard the cleaning staff with new respect. For a moment I feel they deprive poor mites of their epidermal delight. On second thought, I am sure there are other universes where mites can enjoy more nourishment. Movie theatres, churches, synagogues, and other locations, where humans congregate in great numbers.

Whatever happened to Ruth?

The cleaning staff in my hospital is made up of solemn men and women who go about their business with quiet dignity and efficiency. Just as well that I don't have many visitors. As I mentioned, only Ruth visits me daily. In addition to my cousins and their biweekly Rosaries, each of my office partners put in their appearance twice, and my faithful secretary, Gracie, brought me flowers on three occasions. Surely she must know that I cannot appreciate them? Actually, it just so happens, I do! This 'I-am' appreciates them, not that 'I-am'. Perhaps, Gracie knows something nobody else does?

How come she still isn't here?

I would love to have Ruth on my side of the great divide. I suppose I should spell it with capital G and D. On the other hand, I would hate to sate my desires by having her drown in other people's offal. I find the idea most disagreeable. I think I am beginning to mix up my realities.

If only Ruth would come…

Dear Ruth. I shift my attention to our condo. There, she continues to enlighten me on matters of hygiene. It must have been about two years ago when my cousin, Brenda, was sick and the hospital ancillary staff went on strike. It lasted two days. They had been classified as providing 'essential services' and ordered back to work. Funny, we often have to wait months to see a physician. Evidently the doctors are not essential to our wellbeing.

The cleaning stuff went back, grumbling. Their case went to arbitration.

"...a single bacterium can divide and conquer at an exponential rate. In a mere eight hours, it can merrily reproduce into one billion bacteria. That's right, one billion!" Ruth repeats, to make sure I get the idea. "All in a day's work."

I'm back, waiting for Ruth to arrive in the here and now. I have 'time' on my hands. Ha, ha. Funny how we create figures of speech. Anything for a laugh. I peek at length into Dr. Morton's mind. I'm no longer embarrassed about being a Peeping Tom. After all, I have a right to know what my attending physician thinks of my condition. It's not as if I could ask him a question, is it?

His mind is a veritable storehouse of, what seems to me, completely useless bits of information. Also, the info seems to be thoroughly jumbled up. I learn that we live in relative harmony with some hundred thousand billion microbes. We are permanent hosts to this churning congregation. Without them, according to Dr. Morton, we would die. That is to say, our biological functions would cease. Another misnomer.

I can't say I like that. We are at the mercy of vermin. Furthermore, we also seem to be hosts to hosts of viruses—pieces of genetic material surrounded by protein. And prions—bits of protein which, contrary to bacteria, viruses, and protozoa, do not even need DNA to divide and multiply.

If I had a stomach for it, I would vomit.

And then there are the parasites. According to Dr. Morton, parasites are responsible for more deaths than any other organism. Hence the bedsores. He doesn't like them a bit. It is abundantly clear, at least to me, that my life, the life of my body, is much more dependent on the cleaning staff than on nurses and even doctors. Thank heaven for the little men. And women. It's a strange world my body lives in. Surely, I am better off here. Aren't I?

"What do you think?"

Aw, shut up!

On the other hand, I'm beginning to see why I find my physical body so disgusting.

My horizons are shrinking. I no longer have my being as the incipient universe. I recognize my boundaries, accept my limitations. I am much smaller and unsure of my function. Surely, I am not becoming?

I look around me. No. My outer counterparts are spinning, but I remain static. Inert. Immobile. I am still in a state of being.

I sit in great repose at the centre of my world — only my viewpoint has changed. I am surrounded by my children, sons and daughters, that came into being by an act of my will. I hold them around me by my benevolence in concentric orbits. I hold them all in my sphere of influence. They are not all equally close to me. The nearest is my Moon; then Mercury followed by Venus and the Sun moving about me in concentric circles. Further out there are Mars and Jupiter and Saturn. Only later do I come to observe that a great many stars also surround me at great distances; but mostly they, too, are at rest. Like me. Like the Earth that is my heart, the centre of my perceptions. Farther out, my influence is limited to vague awareness.

My planets also have children paying them obeisance. They move about them in epicycles, always orderly, always in the same direction.

Yes, I do sit in supreme repose. I sense the echoes of Buddha. I am contented with my reality. I am proud of the order and harmony that surround me. I am proud of my world. I perceive it as beauty.

I was right. I must have witnessed the Aristotelian universe. Or, perhaps, Ptolemaic. Not that I really know the difference. Something to do with epicycles on epicycles. I recall a lecture at the Montreal Planetarium on Rue St-Jacques. Next, I presume, I shall become a flat world. If I am allowed to move, I am bound to fall over its edge.

This never happened before. Really. Ruth is never late, not without calling.

How much greater the experience than the illusion created by the hospital? Both must be expressions of reality that my mind had created. Yet there is a fundamental difference. The planets orbiting me, orbiting the Earth, are subject to indomitable law. They have no power to veer off to a new path, a new orbit, to come closer or drift farther away from my being. The centrifugal and centripetal forces must remain in perfect balance. In hospital, all the satellites that surround me also seem to hold to their own circuitous orbits. It is almost as if they had the power to act under their own cognizance. Their own free will. Almost.

Ruth is really late today. I don't mind waiting. Something must have happened. Her car must have broken down, or she couldn't get a taxi, or an unscheduled lecture popped up. There is no reason for her to call, of course. It's not as if that body, down there, would raise objections. Still... Actually, this really is strange. The hospital is the only place where I experience a semblance of the passage of time. Perhaps I'm so close to my physical body that some of its nature rubs off on me. I feel like rubbing spirit. Get it? Rubbing alcohol? Spirit?

Never mind. To the best of my knowledge, ghosts are not required to have a sense of humour.

My mind takes me back to the hospital orbits. If the cleaning staff represent spheres of the outer celestial bodies, then nurses and other attending staff, such as masseurs, must perform the function of nearer planets.

I know that I can withdraw my attention and re-enter the hospital reality to coincide with Ruth's arrival. Yet, though I would never admit it to my Friend, I feel a peculiar need to act as if I were a part of the world of my body. Perhaps it keeps me in touch with Ruth. I miss her. I continue to miss her more than I can say. I do my best not to keep going back in time, her time, to relive an evening or a morning coffee with her. I tried attending her lectures. I couldn't. I never attended her lectures in my life. I can only visit my own past. You cannot cheat here. No more than a cow can fly. I do my best, but I fail. It should be possible. After all, I have my being in the present. I see her here, in the hospital, don't I? Something is not kosher. I also see her daily in my past, just short glimpses—glimpses of joy. I know it is phony, like a well-worn movie, but it is better than nothing. If you only knew her...

Nurses go in and out, an intern looks in, studies the electronics for a little while, sniffs and sniggers, and goes out without a word. The nurse comes back, sits down as though taking a rest. Actually, she does look tired.

"Yes, I'll tell Dr. Morton. Yes, of course. The moment he arrives. Thank you." She takes a deep breath.

Ghosts don't get shivers. They might give shivers, but they cannot shiver themselves. Let me tell you. I shivered.

The nurse replaces the receiver, glances at her watch, then compares her time with a large clock on the wall. She shakes her head in disbelief and leaves the room. I catch on too late to read her mind. By the time I gather my wits, she is gone. I completely forgot that I can read thoughts at a distance. For some reason, I am becoming a nervous wreck. And, as with the shivers, I don't even have nerves.

Friend!!!

The nurse is back, together with Dr. Morton.

"There is nothing we can do until she's back in circulation. Those things happen. Stress, I suppose," the Doctor murmurs.

The nurse nods. "Poor blighter…" She is thinking of me.

I dig deeper. Surprisingly, her mind is more orderly than Dr. Morton's. Less knowledge, I suppose. I can read it easily. Ruth had a heart attack, presumably induced by stress. She had been taken to the General Hospital, downtown. My reality collapses. I am in the corridor of the department of cardiology at Montreal General. I'd been there before when Dad had a check-up. I listen for Ruth's voice, for any fragment of thought that might point me in the right direction. Nothing. She's nowhere to be seen. I mean, I can't see her anywhere. How stupid of me. I still my thoughts and picture Ruth in my mind. I am in her room. She is lying on the bed, wearing a hospital gown. She seems to be sleeping. I see her regular heart beat. She's all right. She seems to be? A little pale, but even her make-up is properly applied. Not that she wears much. Her eyes and a dab of lipstick. Why are there no doctors here? Why aren't they looking after her?

Relax, John, I tell myself. You are not doing any good by these histrionics. I look around. There are flowers in her room. Already?

Must be her students. She must have been brought here from the
College. But... she doesn't give lectures in the morning. Good
God! She's here from yesterday. She must have collapsed
yesterday while delivering her lecture. But she saw me last night.
That was after school. What is going on?

I'm really no good at this time business.

A nurse comes in. She lifts Ruth's hand and takes her pulse.
She's counting, multiplying... she's satisfied. Ruth wakes up.

"What's happened...?"

She remembers, takes the nurse's hand, glances at her watch.
"How long have I been here, Nurse..." she looks at her tag,
"...Brown?"

"You just take it easy, Mrs. Clarkson. We are taking good care
of you." Nurse Brown sounds reassuring, as she ought to be. This is
not what Ruth wants to know.

Tell her, I yell; tell her, I yell, forgetting that no one can hear
me.

"Let me rephrase it, Nurse Brown. I want you to tell me how
long I've been here." Ruth's voice is as liquid as honey. That's
dangerous when coming from Ruth. Nurse Brown gets the
message.

"Just since last night. You collapsed at a party students gave in
your honour last night. They brought you all these flowers, Mrs.
Clarkson. Do you like them?"

"Last night?" Ruth repeats, unbelief in her voice.

"Yes, Mrs. Clarkson. The ambulance brought you here at..."
Nurse Brown glances at the report card hanging at the foot of
Ruth's bed, "...twenty-oh-seven."

It all comes back to her. For the first time since the early days,
I read, quite unabashedly, Ruth's mind. It was Ruth's birthday
yesterday. My God, is it the end of March already? Three months
since the pothole. Three months and a bit. It must be March 27
today. How time flies when there is no time. Ruth must have gotten
quite emotional. It was the first time she and I weren't together for
her birthday. She must have been lonely. Very lonely. Good old
students. They must have found out about her birthday. They knew
of my condition. They must have tried to make it up to her.

There is the vaguest smile on Ruth's lips. I withdraw. Suddenly her thoughts seem private. Is she thinking of me? Please... let it be so. If she doesn't, who will? I might as well be dead. She seldom leaves my thoughts. Yet, somehow, I forgot about yesterday. How could I?

She blows out the candles in a single breath. In a way it's a pity. She always looks lovely, but by candlelight every woman looks her best. There must be something about live fire. I've already put Piazzolla's Argentinean tangos on the disc player. What else? Tangos, candlelight and a beautiful woman. Memories are made of this.

We both dress for dinner. Her slim shoulders look beguiling. Her hair, pinned on the top of her head, is crowned with a tiny diamond tiara. She's my princess. Now and always.

"And many, many more, darling," I raise my champagne flute.

We do this every year. We tell everyone that we are leaving town, switch off the telephone, and order a dinner from the Ritz. It comes complete with chilled Moët & Chandon *brute*, and a birthday cake. And, of course, a first-class waiter. We can never finish it, it's too large. The cake, not the waiter.

After dinner the waiter collects the plates, clears the table and moves the champagne and the cake to the coffee table. Then he discreetly withdraws. We dance, nibble on the cake and sip champagne. I hope the night will never end.

Piazzolla takes us through the seasons: *Verano porteño, Otoño porteño, Inverno porteño* and finally *Primavera porteña.* Seasons in Buenos Aires. We always play them in that order. Ruth's birthday announces that spring is nigh. Even in Canada. The tangos play round and round and round. We dance and we sip and we hold each other as on that day we met. Yesterday? A million years ago? Time stopped the day I met her. It still remains frozen. Except for the seasons in Buenos Aires.

Mi Buenos Aires querido...

Ruth is all right. She really is. She sits up and wants to get up.

"We mustn't get up yet, Mrs. Clarkson," the nurse is up in arms.

For a moment I expect her to push Ruth back on the pillows. I wouldn't advise that. Paradoxically, I scan the nurse's demeanor. She's OK. She cares. I wish nurses would occasionally change the colour of their uniform. They look like clean robots. At least her little cap is cute. As for this 'we' business...

"But why?" Ruth sounds surprised.

"Dr. McKinley will be here any moment, Mrs. Clarkson. He asked me to make sure that you take adequate rest." The nurse sounds slightly desperate.

I know the protocol. I also read her mind. Unless there's an emergency, the good doctor will be here, on his rounds, at four in the afternoon. He'd already been here this morning. Ruth had been sedated. I glance at the nurse's watch. It is only eleven-thirty. She'll never last till four.

"Would you take these, Mrs. Clarkson?" The question is rhetorical.

Suddenly Ruth looks tired. "B-b-but I must see my husband, he's..."

"We know, Mrs. Clarkson. We notified Dr. Morton at the Lakeshore. They will call us if there is any change."

This seems to take the remaining wind out of Ruth's sails. Suddenly she is compliant, almost obedient. Her mouth opens without uttering a word. She takes two green pills from the nurse, washes them down with a paper cup of water, and leans back against her pillows. Her eyelids seem to drop under their own weight. She might as well be in a coma!

Sorry, I didn't mean that. I am frantic.

"We will let you know, Mrs. Clarkson," the nurse whispers again. This time her tone is full of kindness. They are good people, these nurses.

I can't take my eyes off my wife. Would she be the same on the other side? When I first realized that she might be coming over to my side, I had very mixed feelings. Actually, they were not feelings. It sounds callous, but it was more like my observing my own thoughts. There was a part of me rejoicing that we might be together again. Then again, I don't really know what happens to other people. Other people who die. After all, I am not really dead. And if Ruth were to die, I might never see her again. Why didn't my Friend tell me if there really is heaven and, you know, the other place?

According to him, I already know all that he knows. What I cannot always do is to reach deep enough to recall some of the stuff imbedded in my subconscious. He can, even if he doesn't really admit it. Or is it I who refuse to admit it? Why, even in a state of coma, must I impose limitations on myself?

I'll have to wait for her. As long as it takes. I cannot leave this reality without sharing it first with Ruth. She would teach me to discover beauty in all the universes I stumbled into. The beauty of stars, dust clouds, nebulas, galaxies of all shapes and sizes. We would ride on the solar wind of an exploding nova, even supernova. We would spread our wings...

It's a mind-boggling universe. I read somewhere that if you start travelling in your car at 55 miles per hour, it would take 520,000 centuries to reach the nearest star. That's fifty-two million years. I can do it in the blink of an eye. Less than that. How can I not show it to Ruth? She'd never forgive me.

Suddenly an idea strikes me out of the blue. The ambulance brought Ruth here at 8:07 last night. A qualified physician must have admitted her. I shift back in the sequence of events. I see two green-coated men carrying a stretcher. It's not Ruth. I try again. On the third attempt I score an ace.

"Easy now," one man says. "Lift your end a bit, George."

They carry Ruth to the emergency. A young woman walks fast towards her. She does whatever young residents do when faced with a heart attack. She calls a senior physician. I read her mind.

...cardiac arrest... cardiopulmonary resuscitation, emergency cardiovascular care... trauma, yes, trauma... focus, focus, focus... support of airway, breathing, circulation...

The young woman appears to be panicking. The senior doctor arrives and calmly gives dispositions. Within minutes he moves to another patient. There is a queue along the corridor. Ruth was lucky. She arrived during a relative lull.

"You're all right, darling. You're all right..." I whisper. Who knows. Perhaps she can hear me.

I hang around until they wheel Ruth to her own room. Fancy that, in this day and age, her own room? Then I remember. My office has medical insurance. For all I know, she has her own, also. We never discussed sickness. Only health. Until now. And now it's too late. We can't discuss anything. I am scared. I still don't know what happens to people when they die. I must play it safe.

"Ruth, come back, I say. Come back."

I needn't worry. I mustn't worry. Be positive. By now Ruth is fast asleep. The good doctor gave her something to make her relax even further. To diminish the tension which caused the attack. She's all right. Somehow, I know she is. Don't ask me how I know. And then I remember. I'll see her tomorrow. Tomorrow is already my past. Thank God for time. Sleep well, my darling. Sleep well.

***

14

I am a Tree

I am useless. I might as well be one of those trees. Ruth is in a hospital, my body likewise, while I am swinging on a hammock. There ought to be a purpose in life in every reality. It finally dawns on me that I really am not alive. I am in a state of stagnation. I am, but I am not becoming. I have the power to examine the past, things and activities that, according to my Friend, I already know. A sort of glorified navel-gazing. Within that which already was, I am a supreme being. A god wielding absolute power, like an exalted Peeping Tom. Provided I watch, but don't touch. An emperor without an empire. Without becoming there is no life.

To experience even a semblance of life, I have to relive something that already served its purpose. Something that should have been long-dead and buried. Mostly, it is. Only I bring it back to the present. That's what life is. The present. Always on the verge of a precipice. Always conquering. Always about to disappear into the past. Life itself is balanced, precariously, on the edge of order and chaos. An exercise in suspended states of complexity. And then?

Coma?

Well, I am conquering no more, and my knowledge is in a supreme state of turmoil. I am also a supreme example of pseudo life. An imitation. Like a three-dimensional movie with all sensual effects kicked in. I'm sure humanity will soon reach the stage of technological evolution that will make this possible. Make my present reality accessible to mere mortals. Immortals? We're good at gadgets. They'll send a guy or two into a comatose state, examine their brainwaves, and they will bring out our, or is it their, past. That will be their definition of progress. By then, I shall be long gone and buried. Or burned, to make sure I do not pollute this world with my remains. Sorry, not this world. That world. Your world. I don't have a world anymore. I have samples. Like the weather in England or Vancouver. Just samples.

At least there are no more Rosaries.

With Ruth away, there is no one who would bother. Not that she did, frankly. I watched her closely. Her faith had undergone a great metamorphosis. She stopped believing in benign benevolence. I must tell her that she's wrong. That I am neither suffering nor even paying for any of my sins. Anyway, it's an old adage that we are punished for our sins We're not. We are not punished *for* them, only by them. They're punishment enough.

For once my two cousins are of some use. Doris and Brenda, always together, inseparable, act as a go-between. They come and see my body, say a prayer, speak to the nurse and report to Ruth. It's already the second time they have come to see me on their own. If I can read their minds well enough, Ruth can go home in a day or two, but only if she promises to take a week off from work. On the other hand, time means nothing to me.

"You are overworked, over-stressed, you don't sleep enough, you eat irregularly, you worry too much, you lack faith in medical expertise and, judging from your own words, you don't exercise enough, Mrs. Clarkson. No one can live like that and not get a heart attack."

This is Dr. McKinley. I hear the nurse trying to stifle a giggle. Apparently this is the longest speech the doctor has ever made. He actually did sound frustrated. He's very different from Dr. Morton. Younger, radiates confidence, quite openly giving the glad eye to the prettier nurses. Whereas Dr. Morton's life is medicine, Dr.

McKinley is much more of a regular guy. His profession is medicine, provided it doesn't interfere with his life. Tall, as tall as Dr. Morton would like to be, seemingly always suntanned, slim, piercing blue eyes that immediately engage whomever he meets. On top of that he's elegant in an offhand way—an easy, unobtrusive way. He'd probably be a success at whatever he did. He's very young to be holding a senior position at the General.

I got all this on my preliminary scan. I'm getting very good at peeking. Or scanning—a more sophisticated way of spying, I suppose. I can even arrange the pertinent facts in an orderly fashion, not like some months ago.

So Ruth is in bad shape?

Well, at least we don't smoke, I muse aloud. You've guessed it. No one can hear me. Whatever happened to ghosts that make funny noises? Rap, rap, rap... I hit the wall repeatedly. My hand goes right through it.

Ruth lowers her eyes. I could swear she's actually blushing.

"I promise to be good, Doctor, really I do." Now she sounds like a twelve-year-old who was late to school. Surely, she's not falling for this guy? Come on! You're old enough to be his mother!

"I certainly hope you take what I said seriously, Mrs. Clarkson. This is not a laughing matter. Some people are not as lucky as you were. There may be strokes, gastrointestinal and other complications." Apparently my Ruth failed to pull the wool over Dr. McKinley's eyes.

"Keep Mrs. Clarkson in bed another day, Nurse Brown. Call me if she gives you any trouble."

I've never seen such surprise in Ruth's eyes. We have been married for twenty-odd years, and I never spoke to her in those terms. The surprising thing is that Dr. McKinley is probably right. She both does and doesn't do all those things. She doesn't walk the treadmill, but she does walk to and from the College. She doesn't sleep long enough, but she's very good at catching catnaps. As for lack of faith in medical expertise, well, he only has the government to blame. With waiting periods stretching to infinity, it had to rub off on the profession as a whole.

So you tried to play him for a sucker, Babe? 'I'll be good if you let me go, Doctor'? Bye, darling, see you soon. At least now I have reasonable confidence that she's in good hands, as long as he keeps his hands to himself. Good for you, Doc!

I have a sudden need to discuss Ruth's condition, and her very being, with my Friend. I hope he'll not play the 'What do you think?' game. It's frustrating.

Once more I am in complete darkness. I find myself either in outer space or in the murky depths of the Caribbean Sea. I feel my way around, slowly, tentatively. There is resistance, and my movement is impeded by all sorts of elements that are foreign to me. It is as though I were sharing my reality with other substances that are in a state of stasis. Perhaps waiting for their turn to take part in the act of becoming. As I am.

Strangely enough, my present nature is such that I, too, am immobile. I reach out deeper and deeper. The deeper I reach, the more rigid I become. Yet there, in outer darkness, I find what I am seeking. Moisture. I absorb it with gratitude. Now I remember. I am responsible for supplying nutrients to the rest of my body. Most of my work is around a yard or so below the surface; but here, at my very centre, I have to dig deeper. My efforts are rewarded. I know that I shall survive, as will the rest of my embodiment.

I feel a great thirst directly above me. It is my trunk. I also keep it stable, straight and proud. I am vaguely aware of its calling. I feed it water from the very tips of my many pronged fingers. Water with all the attendant nutrients. Each part of me below is responsible for different parts of me up above.

I live in a world of duality. Part of me is in eternal darkness, the other part benefits from the light and warmth that comes, periodically, to touch my many fractalled components. Up there I am busy with my other work. I convert sunlight into elements vital for survival. I am well aware of the essential function I perform. All biological embodiments depend on me. Without me, the galaxy I live in would wither. Without me, the world around me would never survive. I am the alpha and the omega. The beginning and the end of all life.

For now I am resting. Soon my arms will spring new surfaces to absorb sunlight. I shall be fully alive then. I shall go through the cycle of becoming. But not yet. For now I'm still in repose. Almost. I enjoy my state of being.

There is light again.

I look at the denuded maple in front of me with new respect. For a fraction of eternity, I experienced the process of photosynthesis and all the ancillary processes that accompany my main function. The tree's main function. The maple is leafless now, but soon it will be bursting with life. How I envy this maple. I still feel deeply divided between utter darkness and the blinding sun. Only the sun is not really blinding. Together with the maple it supplies my body, the body waiting in the hospital, with oxygen. I feel a great sense of gratitude. Of belonging. In a way, we are one.

We are all one. We are one, and there is no time. The mystery of the universe.

Also, it seems there is always a reason for everything. Cause and effect rule supreme. In the East, people refer to it as *karma*. It is unavoidable, impending, meting out both punishment and reward. You don't need an Old Man with a carrot and a stick. It's all built into the system. The truth is that it is we, our own selves, who mete out the momentum towards a state of balance. If we destroy all trees, our bodies will die, whatever our concept of life. Whatever gods govern the infinite source of all realities, we are the supreme rulers of those to which we are made privy. Gods create laws. We obey them. Or pay the piper. 'Human beings, vegetables, or cosmic dust, we all dance to a mysterious tune, intoned in the distance by an invisible piper.' Einstein. Imagine. A physicist, mathematician, scientist, talking like a poet. Whenever Ruth shares her sayings with me, her eyes grow misty as though she were listening to the author actually saying them. Ruth lives in a strange reality. In some ways, one close to where I am now.

How I wish she were here.

We find our expression in our vision which, like the universe, is no more than a persistent, yet still transient mirage. The universe is subject to the ravages of time and our imagination. We all see it differently. To some it expands; to me, right now, it's in a shrinking mode. Perhaps one day I shall become aware that I am no more. Like the universe before the Big Bang. And life, out there, in the 'real' world, is another illusion. I only became aware of life when I stepped outside it. When I left my body behind.

And since I have stepped out, I've been observing, absorbing, and consolidating my knowledge.

I learned that in many realities I'd already experienced, I did not require a 'body'. Not as we understand it. Not a body the medical profession, indeed most religious fraternities, refer to as life. Nor any construct that physically defines and limits my sphere of influence. Life is change. Continuous becoming. I? I am no more than an observer. Static, immobile, like the tree. Less so. I do not provide nourishment to anyone. Though I wish I could. At least to Ruth...

"You really miss her, don't you?..."

My Friend is back.

"As if you didn't know," I say brusquely, but I'm glad he's back. Sometimes I think I might not ever see him again. I think I know what his true nature is; but, surely, we all need our mirrors to tell us the truth. Especially now that Ruth isn't here. There. Mirrors cannot lie, either.

"No man is an island..." It's my Friend's turn to muse aloud. Either that. or I can finally read his thoughts.

"John Donne, seventeenth-century English author. Clever. Doesn't quite jibe with Carl Jung's 'Individual is the only reality,' does it?" I know a thing or two, also.

"You sure? It's only a question of perspective. Now, you continually miss your wife. You are not self-sufficient. Inadequate. She's intricately woven into the fabric of your immediate past. You even observe her present."

"What's your point?"

"In the creative, the becoming mode of your being, you are the only reality. Ruth is what you imagine her to be. Both pluses and minuses."

"Ruth has no minuses." He really ought to know this by now.

"My point precisely. You create a reality in which your wife fulfils your yearning for perfection. Even her faults you deem to be merely reflections of your own inadequacies."

"But we do argue, and often we don't agree," I say defensively. "You're implying that I make Ruth into some sort of goody-goody person. That would be unreal."

"Nevertheless, when you do argue, your arguments are confined to cerebral polemics. You do not allow your emotions to muddy the intellectual waters. All the same, it allows you to escape your own responsibility."

"For what?"

"For perfection." My Friend presents me with a perfect poker face. I can only assume that I look the way he does. In my case it only means that I am completely lost.

"Just whose perfection are you talking about this time?"

"Yours, of course."

"You are joking, *of course*." I stress the last two words with just a mite of sarcasm.

"No, John. Remember, the only way to be a master is to act like one. And, as you already know, *I am what my servant thinks of me*. Remember?"

"Aren't you confusing things? I am the servant, not the master."

"Then, my Friend, enlighten me. Just who is your master? And don't forget Carl Jung."

He has an annoying habit of confusing me each time we speak about the essence of being. I am still not ready to accept that I am the only reality. It's just too much, even if I do admire Jung almost as much as Ruth does.

On the other hand, there was some truth in what my Friend had to say. Ruth and I did discuss many things; we didn't really argue. My Friend responds immediately to my unspoken thoughts.

"You'll note, John," he resumes, "that such a relationship as you have with your wife is only possible between people who enjoy individual passion for their particular professions. You both get rid of your frustrations outside the confines of your home. In such a case, your home can, and does, become a haven in the turbulent waters of your emotional lives."

This was the longest tirade my Friend had ever offered me. Although his thesis does not tally with Ruth's idea of the children of the lesser god, he sounds convincing. It may be true that I idealize Ruth, but, surely, isn't she pretty perfect?

"You are making it sound as though she doesn't exist in her own right." I say out loud. Bit silly considering his telepathic abilities.

"Does anyone? Do I? Yet you find me a useful mirror."

"That would be an extremely lonely world, wouldn't it?"

"What, with you being the only occupier, so to speak? Of course it would be, and it isn't. You populate your realities in any way you see fit."

I don't know. There are moments when I would rather be a tree.

Ruth is diagnosed with arrhythmia—a disorder of the regular rhythmic heartbeat. Such is fairly common. In the United States there are more than two million people living normal lives with atrial fibrillation. It can occur in a healthy heart and be of minimal consequence.

"You understand, Mrs. Clarkson, we would like to keep you here for another day or two for observation," Dr. McKinley says, placing his stethoscope back around his neck. He'd just listened to her heartbeat.

It could be just me, but he sounds a little embarrassed. Judging by the whirlwind of his thoughts, I very much suspect that he feels he should have detected symptoms of arrhythmia the moment Ruth arrived at the General. There is a relatively wide range of a normal heartbeat, anything between 60 and 100 beats per minute. Nevertheless the electrical impulses causing abnormal heart rhythms are easily discernible on an electrocardiogram, which had been conducted on Ruth almost immediately after her admittance. Some arrhythmias are so brief that the overall heart rate isn't greatly affected. This must have been the case with Ruth. A repeated graph, however, showed the rhythm to be slightly erratic.

I am jumping from Nurse Brown to Dr. McKinley to gather this information. In both minds I detect embarrassment rather than worry. Detecting emotions is very different from reading thoughts.

One has to gather them from a number of sources, including external expression, heartbeat and even from temperature variables. A little like a polygraph machine, only more precise. I seem to be doing it automatically. Like seeing or hearing.

Ruth's arrhythmia tends towards palpitations. Dr. McKinley thinks that if they do not subside, he'll treat them with electrical shock, and maintain the regular heartbeat with medication.

That's as much as I can get on this visit.

Once again, I am torn between wanting Ruth to join me, and fear that her destination may be different from mine. In spite of what my Friend is implying, I simply cannot accept that I am the creator of the reality in which she finds herself.

"Of course you are not," I hear inside my head. "You are in a state of being. You are playing the waiting game, remember?"

So he is here. He did say that he'd never leave me. But I didn't quite realize that he is not just my mirror but also my shadow.

"Do you also follow me when I go back in time?"

I just couldn't bear his being there when Ruth and I, well, when I assume that Ruth and I are alone.

My Friend doesn't answer. He would probably say, 'What do you think,' and leave it at that.

"It seems that Ruth is not in any real danger," he says instead. In a strange way I am grateful that he did not answer my previous question. At least I can pretend to fool myself.

"Thanks," I tell him. "Thanks, my Friend."

I do what I never imagined I would. I visit my own supine self with untoward intentions. Doris and Brenda are there, again, regular as clockwork. Without being able to watch Ruth bringing me up to date, I have no choice but to peek into their minds. For some reason I find the idea vaguely repugnant. Still, I have little choice. To my embarrassment I realize that I hardly know my cousins.

I suppose my lack of enthusiasm for my cousins began on the day they arrived in Canada. Not only had I brought them in from Dorval Airport, not only had I rented for them a half-decent apartment and paid for the first and the last month of the lease, but

I never heard a thank-you from either of them. Nor have I had any
offer to reimburse me for my financial outlay. Perhaps they both
think that exploiting one's, even distant, family is part of the game
of life. Well, call me a miser, but I still have no desire to change
our relationship of mutual ignorance, though I do want to know
what's going on with my parents and Ruth's mother in Florida. (At
first I found it hard to believe that my parents would go off to
Florida when I, their beloved son, was so incapacitated. Still, it's a
three-hour flight. Like coming from East Montreal to Point Claire
during the rush hour.) For some reason, it never crossed my mind
to zip over to Florida and find out for myself. As I keep repeating,
I'm new at this game. Also, my cousins might know something else
that I might not even think of concerning Ruth. Not that I can do
much with such knowledge but, well, curiosity may have killed the
cat, but there is no word about a tree.

My two cousins have just finished saying a prayer for me,
well... 'over my body'. I wasn't there; not really. How nice. I
never imagined that they would care enough to do so on their own,
when no one was watching. As if in response to my thoughts, a
nurse comes is. It's not Joan.

"My name ees Nurse Francine," she says, with a strong French
accent.

Now this is how a nurse should look. Young, fresh, cute, blond,
slim, smiling... did I say cute? It is the sort of nurse all wives pray
their husbands will never see in a hospital. Unless their husbands
are in a coma, I suppose.

"Could you tell us how is Mr. Clarkson?" Doris asks without
any preambles. She sounds as though she were giving the nurse a
business interview.

"We feel zat Meester Clarkson eez doing very well...
considering," she adds after a little pause.

"Yes?"

"Well, Mees..." Doris continues to stare at her. "...considering
ee's not in zee very best of physical condition."

"I am Mr. Clarkson's cousin," Doris adds as an afterthought.
"Just what condition is he in, Nurse Francine?"

"Eet ees zee usual busy-executive syndrome, Mees Cousine,"
the nurse says with a straight face. She doesn't look like the type

that would allow Doris, or anyone else, to pull the wool over her eyes. "Too much work, not enough exercise, not enough sleep, rushed meals, and even breezing exclusively zee downtown air. I am sure you know what I mean." Each short phrase ends up on an up swing.

Take away the accent and it's as if I were listening to Dr. McKinley enumerating Ruth's peccadilloes. So I've been naughty. Naughty but happy. We both were, Ruth and I. It was never our intention to live forever, but to live, fully, until we died. Still, I make a mental note that if we both come out of the present, at least partially self-induced, condition, I will suggest buying a place in the country. For the air, if not for the exercise.

It's a funny thing. We are both mature adults, both happy and successful in our professions, yet both Ruth and I lead unbalanced lives. Does one ever reach a stage when one can stop learning and just live to the fullest?

What do you think?

No, I don't see him, but I hear him gallivanting freely in my mind. By now I know that the answers lie within me, probably within all of us. If there is a Friend looking over our shoulder, carrying the wisdom of the ages ever ready at our disposal, then none of us have any excuse for acting like juvenile delinquents. Or worse.

Nurse Francine glances over Doris's stick figure with only slightly concealed disdain. Her eyes are saying, 'Eef anyone needs exercise eet ees you, Mees Cousine.' I know. In my mind she still speaks with that delightful accent. I like Nurse Francine. In fact, I conclude that I like all nurses. I make another mental note to visit hospitals more often.

Doris doesn't bat an eye, but Brenda gives the nurse a dirty look. You don't know what a dirty look is until you see Brenda give one. Ouch! Still, they did both pray over my body. I mean over me... Whatever.

I wonder how the Catholics picture their prayers being heard. I presume, when they ask God to heal someone's body, they are asking the Almighty to rearrange some three to six trillion electrochemical reactions per second to accommodate their request. It's not as if they believed that the physical world is just a manifestation of an inner reality. I wonder if they consider that there may be a reason for the dis-ease, which in the vast preponderance of cases is but a temporary adjustment of the functioning of the cellular structure of one's body. Perhaps to adjust it to fresh external conditions, or to cope better with emotional stress... but invariably it is a short, transient period during which we can learn an awful lot about the doing right and the doing wrong. Ultimately, we must end up in that field Rumi's talking about. Or on Buddha's Middle Path.

On the other hand, I strongly suspect that Friend has little interest in my physical body for the simple reason that it, too, is so transient. That's right. It's not the spirit or ghost that is ephemeral, it is the body. It goes—the spirit continues. On still another hand, the physical body is instrumental in aiding us in the experience of advancement. That's exactly what I am missing now. I need people, even Doris and Brenda, to learn something which otherwise would be inaccessible to me. We need our bodies, no matter how temporary, weak, and restrictive or abused they are. Abused, mostly, by ourselves. By our stupidity. As long as we don't take them for something they are not. They are a means, not an end in themselves.

Not even if we look like a stick insect.

That's not fair. Doris has done me a favour. I'd learned something that, if it hadn't been for her, and Ruth's absence, and my accident, I would probably never have known. Now I can only hope that neither of my dear cousins mentions the decrepit condition of my earthly abode, my body, to Ruth. That wouldn't help much in my dear wife's recovery. On the other hand, I have no idea how I can possibly dissuade them from blabbing it all to Ruth. I could try wrapping a white sheet over me and attempt to scare the living daylights out of them, but I strongly suspect the sheet would fall right through me.

I'll just have to grin and bear it. Perhaps I should have been nicer to my cousins before it became too late. Not that it would have been easy. I still have to decide how Doris and Brenda reacted to the news of my dilapidated physical state. I follow them down the dull corridor, trying to ignore the overpowering smell of the deodorant mixed with sterilizing solutions. I never suspected ghosts

were so sensitive to unpleasant smells. Well, we live and learn. Or
in my case... never mind. Three doors down the corridor, I know
why. The man inside is suffering from something that must be
chronic diarrhea. I need a gas mask.

I catch up with my cousins in the main hall. It's hard to believe
that the maintenance people had managed to make even this area
look pale, dull, insipid and boring. Certainly uninviting. I'd seen
army mess halls looking cozier.

Still, I am lucky. My cousins stop for a coffee. They will chat.
If not, I'm going to peek in, no matter what I find there. In their
minds, I mean. My Friend never told me it's a no-no, but I feel a
sort of natural aversion. I already said that, but it needs stressing.
You must either like the person, or the people you spy on must be
completely neutral to you. My cousins are neither.

"He's going to die?"

This is Brenda. She passes judgment on my life with a sweet
lethal, I mean little, smile. She actually said it out loud. Has the
woman no shame?

"He's stronger than you think," Doris mutters. For a sales-
person of an investment company she does a lot of muttering.
Maybe that way she doesn't get blamed quite so often for the
advice she sells.

"It will all go to Ruth," Brenda says between sips of coffee. I
actually saw her take four lumps of sugar. Ain't she sweet?

"You mustn't talk like that," Doris remonstrates, but her voice
carries no conviction.

"Unless Ruth goes, too," Brenda's voice assumes an angelic,
dreamy quality. Her smile would melt icebergs in hell.

"They do have a nice condo."

Keep your hands off our condo, I mutter to myself. I forget if
we ever invited them over. Of course we did. Some years ago. We
are still waiting for reciprocation. We were lucky. It never came.

"I remember the view," Brenda's voice is still dreamy.

I wonder how my Friend would react to an act of willful
murder. After all, according to him, there is no such thing as death.
Perhaps there should be. Right here I have two prime candidates.
For a moment I forget that I need my cousins to act as go-betweens.
As emissaries between heaven and hell. I am beginning to dislike

my state of being. Perhaps I should forsake the countless universes I still haven't seen and slip back into my overworked, unexercised, insufficiently rested and badly nourished body. I could get it into shape and then murder my cousins. Wouldn't that be fun? I could die another day.

***

15

I am an Insect

I am bothered by a theoretical question which, I feel, has something to do with my present condition. Not that I know exactly what my present condition is. I also have no idea why it bothers me, but I must ask my Friend how many incarnations there are? And of these, how many in a human form?

An infinite number.

I think that was he. Or it could be just an echo in my head. If I heard that many voices in my head in the other reality, I would be placed in a nice padded cell, and the key would be dropped in the middle of the Atlantic. I can just see a distinguished psychiatrist tapping his polished mahogany desk, adjusting his gold-rimmed pince-nez, and asking me, 'And just what were you today, Mr. Clarkson?' 'A tree, Doctor.' 'And may I ask why?' 'Well, Doctor, I was tired of being the solar system—you understand, don't you? All this going round and round and...'

The way my Friend puts things, he seems to imply that I am all people now living, as well as all who ever lived. Not to mention an infinite number of evolutionary systems in various stages of development. This would explain why I haven't met anyone in my various realities. Not memories but realities. I already am everyone, but the field of meeting my doppelgänger is limited by the law of quantum mechanics. It is theoretically possible—all things are—though, practically, the probability is zero. Except for my Friend, of course. But he is not really me. Or, I am the consciousness of his becoming. Only right now, I am not becoming.

And to tell the truth, I'm not sure what I'm talking about. These concepts don't make much sense in the dualistic reality, do they?

Right now, I'm an observer. I observe matter in its universal manifestations—galaxies, stars... I observe the flow of energy, trees, even insects. But other than visiting the dualistic world of my physical body, I meet no man. No human being.

Could it be that my Friend is right? Think about it.

I travel along a path. Let's call it evolution. We already established that the process is called becoming. Better still, life. I come upon a fork. I turn left and undergo a mutation that sets me back. I withdraw and in the same instant take the right fork. Here I prosper. I advance to the next evolutionary step. The previous step is erased from my memory. If I died, I am not aware of it. There is an infinite number of steps. Or reincarnations. I don't reincarnate into a baby but into whatever I was the instant I was whisked away. I am not saying that there are no babies. They are born and they prosper. Only some, however, become *alive*. The physical cycle of birth and death is only a means, not an end. All things physical are just illusory. I am not a physical entity with a soul. I am a soul, which temporarily occupies a physical body. Whatever soul might be. Perhaps consciousness is a better word. Whatever body it occupies. It doesn't really matter. The bodies are not really alive. They are no more than reflections of the true reality. They perform their biological functions as prescribed by universal laws. We are alive within them. Not the same thing. Some two thousand years ago, Jesus of Nazareth referred to some, perhaps most, people as dead. The walking dead? 'Let the dead bury the dead,' he'd said. You are not. Come with me, he might have added. What a magnificent manifestation of life He is. With a capital H. Always will be.

A baby is endowed with *nephesh*. An animal soul. A god in waiting, but not in fact. A glorious potential within a single biological construct. To be a god is a conscious act. It doesn't come with the territory. It's not automatic. Many are called, few are chosen. Few choose to become gods.

This way I can never experience my own death. The moment I make a fundamental error, I am whisked away and set on the right path. I think this is what Ruth calls universal benevolence. Darwin diluted the same concept into the law of natural selection. We are predisposed to do the right thing. A sort of universal morality. When we don't, we are erased from the NOW. From the eternal reality of the present moment. From the only reality that evolves.

Otherwise, if we identify with that which is transient, all that we leave behind are shadows fading into the eternal matrix of the universe. Shadows I can visit, but I cannot evolve within them. They are no longer NOW. Only the here and now is life. All else is an illusion. As is death.

Gloriously, universal laws also evolve. They do not repeat past mistakes. Only we do. On occasion.

I am the universe.

I am the solar system.

I am an insect.

I am impressed! This is just in my mind, but it's definitely my Friend.

"I thought you were gone forever," I remind him dryly.

I am always with you. It cannot be otherwise.

"But you told me that you don't really exist," I remind him again.

Do you? Do you really exist in your present form?

I couldn't answer that. I am beginning to think that I have no form. That I merely assume various quasi forms, or shapes, in order to manifest what I think life is. To manifest becoming. Evolution. Or it could be just my ego.

"You are the conscious I," Friend says. First I see his smile, then the rest of his face becomes visible.

"That makes you my subconscious?"

"Close enough."

"So what of God?"

"What do you think?"

"So we're back to that game?"

"It's not a game. It matters. In fact, it is vital."

"I am whatever my servant thinks of me," I blurt out. This is a quotation I'd heard before.

"Rumi." Friend smiles. "You have great knowledge within you," my Friend mutters a little sadly. It sounds as if I had had something and lost it.

"But I am right, aren't I?" This is a question as much as a statement.

"Yes. It reaffirms who you are."

"And I have no form?" Same again.

"And you have no form."

"How do you know?"

"Because you know."

That makes sense. At least it is consistent. I am what my servant thinks of me. All that an insect ever was, I am. It is an integral part of me. The insect and I are one. How many times have I been reincarnated as an insect before I entered a more complex organism? That's easy. Once. But I used a countless number of insect bodies to accomplish my learning process. Then I looked up and became more than an insect. But the insect remains within me.

It all comes back to me. I am flung back in time to my realization that I was, that I am, nothing. Only nothing has a different meaning now. It means that I am not limited to being a thing. Not an object. What then? The conundrum fills my mind to the exclusion of all other thoughts.

I am where My servant thinks of Me. Every servant has an image of Me; whatever image my servant forms of Me, there I will be. I am the servant of My servant's image of Me.

I am whatever image my servant forms of me. I am a tree. I am a virus. I am an insect, a bird, an eagle...

And then a stern warning:

Be careful then, My servants, and purify, attune, and expand your thoughts about Me, for they are My House.

For countless generations, man has created images of God in his own image. Masters and minions alike. We assign our strengths and our foibles to that image. To our divine image. To our idea of perfection. And we serve that image, filled with our iniquity. Purify, attune and expand your thoughts about Me. Is this what I am doing? Is this why I am here? Was that pothole the greatest blessing in my life?

They are My House. Where I dwell. In all the universes—in a paltry grain of sand. I am neither the universe nor a wondrous atom. My house is your thoughts. I am a state of consciousness. Eternal, unchanging.

I am as much an insect as I am a king of kings.

Yet I am neither.

I AM.

R uth is still resting. She looks beautiful in her state of repose. In a way, right now she, too, is outside the confines of time. She just is. Her pale complexion is offset by the whiteness of the pillow. Her hair cascades in gentle waves, as though arranged by the Old Masters she loves so much. Even her lips hold a promise hidden by a gentle smile. I would give up eternity to kiss those lips again. Can I really just slip into my body and hold her in my arms? Give up eternity, the wonders of the eternal universe, endless oceans of germinating stars…

Just for one kiss.

"There is no change?"

Nurse Brown shakes her head. "No, Mrs. Clarkson, not yet. These things take time. Don't let it get to you."

I hardly noticed that Ruth had opened her eyes.

The nurse called the Lakeshore just before bringing Ruth her evening meal. I've come to visit Ruth. I grew tired of spending time staring at my shell at the Lakeshore. Not that my body is all alone. For some reason, my two cousins have taken a renewed interest in me. Before the accident, we saw each other regularly at least once or twice a year. Now? Within days I saw them on five occasions saying the Rosary at my bedside. They must be trying to impress somebody. Only… whom? Perhaps they are counting on

the nurses to talk. Gossip. To whom? My parents, on their return?
Ruth, after she recovers?

I can't be bothered to read their thoughts. I don't want to be
disappointed. They look so sad. Maybe they are sorry I'm still
almost alive?

Sorry.

Perhaps all spinsters look sad. These are pushing forty-five
(they both admit to middle-thirties), a forced, or possibly a frozen
smile on their glossy lips, their eyes made up heavily to hide the
onset of lines. Tiny little wrinkles that seem to come as much from
laughter as they do from aging. My cousins don't laugh all that
much. Perhaps they have little to laugh about. At least both, Doris
and Brenda, appear to enjoy playing with their hair. Doris carries
her rich reddish-brown locks pinned up in a complex superstructure
reminiscent of aristocracy from a bygone era. Being a bit too tall,
or too skinny for her height, she shouldn't really choose to add to it
with her elaborate, pointed coiffure. Both cousins also dress well.
Doris prefers a well-cut suit—she probably needs it for her job. In
England, she was the local guru in matters pertaining to the stock
market. In Grimsby there was not much competition. Here she is a
reasonably successful investment adviser, at least according to
Brenda. I often wondered how come, if she advises so many people
how to make piles of money, she doesn't seem to have made much
for herself, or even enough to pay her debts.

Funny, in 'real' life I'd already forgotten about that… only the
distaste lingered on. Still, she's like a morbidly obese doctor giving
people advice on a slimming diet. I wouldn't recommend her
financial know-how to anyone.

Brenda is her exact opposite. Quite short, with a decisive,
energetic step. She probably needs it, to keep up with her… her
what? Cousin? Sister? It seems unbelievable, but I'd never learned
what precisely is their relationship. Perhaps I just couldn't have
been bothered. I just didn't care. They were family—of sorts.
Distant family. Anyway, whatever it may be, Brenda is blond,
seemingly natural; she allows her hair to swoop down to her
shoulders, with just an artful curvy upswing at the bottom—a
gesture of confidence perhaps better suited to a woman half her
age. She is still pretty, but, apparently, not quite as pretty as she

thinks she is. According to Ruth, she turned down proposals from at least half-a-dozen men. There is a certain pride in her posture, which I, were I single, wouldn't find unattractive. If it weren't for her eyes. There is something biting, or sour, in the way she looks at me. I don't mean now. Before, you know, before the accident. And talking of insects... Even as I see her whispering the Rosary, Doris must have evolved from a praying mantis. As for Brenda? My other cousin would surely qualify as a scorpion. Together a rather deadly combination. Just for fun, I enter the body of a praying mantis.

I am hungry. I am absolutely starving. Yet, simultaneously, I am consumed by an overwhelming desire to procreate. To procreate and to eat. Simultaneously. I mean now, immediately. My reproductive body is my whole universe. I am complete.

It took me a split second to get inside her. It took me a lot less to get out. Even as I entered her spindly body, I sensed that she was voracious. Ravenous. Insatiable. And, in an odd way... sexy. For the second time in my new existence I wish I could shudder.

Perhaps not surprisingly, as my cousins live together, Brenda is the housewife, while Doris is the breadwinner. Just as well that Brenda seems to be the decisive one. Were it left to Doris, they would probably have to sustain themselves on a diet of flies and aphids or, as Doris is definitely of a larger species, on small frogs and lizards—as well as, on special occasions, snakes and succulent rodents.

I'm so glad I don't eat anymore.

Perhaps they nurture more than a liking for each other. Ruth had once suggested that they might well be lesbians. "Why else would they always look so well dressed, made up and cared for if it weren't for each other?"

I had no answer to that one.

Actually, they were both unlucky. They immigrated to Canada from a small town on the North Sea, in Northern England, at an age when making new friends already did not come naturally. On their application for an immigrant visa, they'd stated that they were both political refugees; that they were leaving Great Britain in protest against British involvement in American Wars. Canada is known for her peacekeeping missions, they'd both said.

"We want to contribute," they wrote and underlined the statement on their landed emigrant application forms.

They never did.

Strange as they were, I found their British accent with north-country overtones quite amusing, even though they did not fully appreciate my own 'colonial' slant. They actually used this word. Colonial!

"It must have been simply years since you left the Old Mother Country, dear cousin," Brenda once told me.

It so happens I was born and bred in Canada, as was my mother. My father came over when very young. Doris and Brenda are very distant cousins. They were even more distant in Grimsby, but Notre Dame de Grâce, the semi-English enclave in Montreal, has to do. We choose our friends—not our kinfolk. When they first came to Canada, more than a decade ago, I picked them up at the airport and drove them to their temporary apartment. Flat, they called it. They still live there. I suspect, the poor women had been told that there is always a shortage of beautiful women in this man's country. Well, this may be true among the lumberjacks in the Northern Territories, less so in the elegant restaurants of Montreal.

As I'd previously done at the Lakeshore, I try to visit Ruth when someone else is present; at meal times, or during morning and evening rounds. This gives me at least three visits per day. I learned only later—not that time has any meaning here—that throughout Ruth's stay in the hospital, there was an endless procession of well-wishers dropping in on her. Just seconds, minutes at most, at a time. Students, members of the staff, people I'd never heard about. No wonder her room looked and smelled like a flower shop.

In addition, Nurse Brown seems to be always there. She's nice and gives an impression of being competent. Busy as she must be, she always stops for a minute or two just to chat. She diverts Ruth from murky thoughts, probably about me, and chats for a few minutes about nothing in particular. I discovered, quite by accident, that she'd been to some of Ruth's lectures. Judging by her adoring gaze, she seems to worship my wife. As, apparently, do countless others. She also gives Ruth detailed reports on the weather, provides her with the latest gossip about Federal-Provincial one-upmanship games, and generally helps Ruth pass the time. I let them be. It hurts too much to see Ruth and not to touch her. I thought I was beyond the long talons of pain in this limbo existence. Believe me, not so.

Tomorrow they are sending Ruth home. This is the first time since the accident that I am made privy to something that is going to happen in the future. Of course, I might well be dead by then, but somehow I feel that some universal law has been broken.

"Not so," my Friend assures me later that day. "It is you who cannot affect the future. You cannot create a cause that will leave its mark in the present. There is nothing to stop you from witnessing it."

"That's probably the most convoluted sentence you have said since I first saw you."

"Thank you," he agrees, nodding his head with a perfectly straight face.

"I see you even inherited my sense of humour!" I just can't be angry at my mirror anymore.

"I meant to add, to be a conscious cause..."

"I think I know what you mean."

So, as of tomorrow, I am back to seeing Ruth bent over my own body, and wrenching occasional past evenings in the condo. It is a choice between the past and her frazzled expression. I am beginning to realize that of the causes of her cardiac arrest, beside whatever other contributing cause, my coma was certainly one of them. I'm not sure what I can do about it. I am telling you, this stuff about free will is just another illusion. We have free will to do what we are allowed to do. That's it. Anyway, as far as I am concerned, if it weren't for those moments of joyful yesterdays, I swear I would go crazy. Have you ever seen a crazy ghost?

It's almost worth trying.

On the other hand, I also realize that whatever benefits I derive from the universal replays, Ruth doesn't benefit from them in any way. Maybe they are what keeps me reasonably sane, but they also make me feel like an invisible leech.

"Actually, John, you are doing quite well."

It is a rare occasion indeed when Friend contributes something of his own accord. I raise a mental eyebrow.

"You used to be quite bellicose. Not easy at all," he says softly.

"Me? Like when?"

"Oh, about three-four thousand years ago. Does it matter?"

"You are kidding, of course," I must have let out a nervous laugh. Who the devil would throw prehistoric errors in someone's face?

"Don't you remember Kurukshetra? The battlefield?"

I am sitting in the chariot, arguing. My Friend, his face shining, holds the reins. He controls four white horses with the ease of a seasoned expert. He is my true Friend and I am his real devotee. We are alone. My Friend is enlightening me. He seems to be all-knowing, as though he knew the past and the future. I think of him as the supreme teacher, which he denies. But I learn each moment I spend with him.

An instant later I see a field of armies. Thousands of them: warriors, horses, elephants with high, elaborate *howdahs* holding up to ten men each. Archers. The armies stretch to the horizon. I hate killing. I try to convey my sentiments to my Friend. He shakes his head.

"Not so," he says. "You are an instrument of *karma*. You carry out what must be. And never think that you kill them. That which is immortal cannot die. They represent no more than aspects of you that you've already outgrown."

"You mean those people are just things?"

"No, John, they are your negative thoughts."

"But how can I be the judge of that?"

"You are not at the stage when you could understand. But you must fulfill your destiny."

"To be a killer?"

"To cleanse yourself."

Apparently, after this lecture I went quite berserk. I seemed to be in a habit of diving headlong into whatever I was doing. They say I slew hundreds, single-handedly. I hated myself for many years. Nothing my Friend said seemed to help. I am glad that's behind me. In this respect, I haven't changed much. I do what has to be done with total commitment. In those days I really trusted my Friend. Perhaps he's working to regain this trust. As for destiny, I'm still not sure where that fits in.

Anyway, so much for free will.

"You still don't remember?" We are back in our respective hammocks.

The vision of charging elephants is rapidly fading. I obeyed my Friend's instructions, but, somehow, I still have reservations. After thousands of years!

"Why is it so difficult to take another's life?" I can't help asking.

Actually, I do remember something similar. *Bhagavad Gita*—an excerpt from *Mahabharata*, the Hindu epic—is highly regarded for its great literary and philosophical value. Ruth was reading it only a few months ago. Strange how all things are interconnected. As though there really were no time. I remember because her reading had been interrupted by frequent 'ohs' and 'ahs', and one or two 'no-ways', followed by an elocutionary exclamation mark. She first read it in an edition filled with very learned explanations. Needless to say, the man who authored that particular edition carried the title of 'His Divine Grace', which, according to Ruth, in the light of the absence of even a modicum of humility, disqualified him outright. She almost didn't finish reading it. Then, purely by luck, she found a tiny pocket edition entitled *The Song Celestial*. Here the *Bhagavad Gita* had been translated directly from Sanskrit by Sir Edwin Arnold—according to Ruth, a poet of considerable measure himself.

"How else could he enchant me with every phrase?" she asked me some time later. And then she added, obviously alluding to the previous edition, "You wouldn't believe how much beauty the so-called experts can destroy by their facile elucidation."

I shake my ghostly head. I'm back with my Friend, swinging.

"Because we still associate the physical body with life itself." My Friend waits until I have finished my meandering thoughts.

"Struggle, always struggle..."

"Struggle to understand is essential. You must always strive to do better. That's what life is all about. No less and no more."

"But killing?" I forgot about the cathartic angle.

"Do you condemn a surgeon who amputates a leg to save the rest of the man?"

"Is that what killing is?"

"It depends on who is doing it. A surgeon with a lancet or a bandit with a rusty knife. But always remember. We are one."

"Struggle until we achieve sainthood..." I muse again, probably aloud.

"Saints are just states of consciousness. Saints cannot distinguish between individualization and the Whole."

"You mean they are complete? They have reached the end?"

"No one does that. As the scriptures say, 'I am a living god'. Since the potential is infinite—so must be the becoming."

"So Einstein was right? God doesn't play dice with the universe?"

"God gives you the dice and watches how you play with them."

I have to stew that over for a while. He keeps going back to what I can only call first principles. For me, it's like going back to square one. It's not easy to digest. Not that it matters so much this side of the great divide. Or at least not in the state of being.

"So the praying mantis simply does her job by eating her mate?"

No wonder Doris reminds me of one. She is not only vaguely reminiscent of a stick insect, which she most certainly is; but when reciting the Rosary, she often holds her arms in a prayer-like stance. On the other hand, *mantis* comes from the Greek word for prophet or fortune-teller. She might be the latter—the former she is not. At any rate, I would not like to be around her when she's hungry.

"Now a saint wouldn't think that," my Friend offers softly and promptly dissolves into thin air. Actually, I am not sure which is thinner—the air or my Friend.

When my cousins arrive at the General, I am already at Ruth's side. Brenda enters first at near-trot, followed by the measured steps of her mate. Evidently she hasn't been eaten yet. I wait patiently to hear what they have to say about my condition at the Lakeshore. I don't have to wait long. After a series of 'Darling', 'Darling', 'Darling', 'Darling'—I didn't count the exact number—they settle in two visitors' chairs which they pull up to be closer to the head of the bed. I brace myself. 'Here it comes,' I muse, with considerable trepidation. If I had lungs, I would hold my breath.

"We have just seen John," Brenda announces with unaccustomed gusto. "He looks quite fine, I think, don't you, Doris?" Brenda is full of beans, if not the remnants of such after an adequate digestive process. Still, I'm glad she's lying.

"He certainly does," Doris backs her up.

If I weren't already half-dead, I would be stunned. I have no idea what the two ladies are playing at. I would have thought that a little effort on their part would push Ruth over the edge, and the two of them would be that much closer to the inheritance they are obviously both counting on.

"You are so sweet to let me know. However, Nurse Joan called, at Dr. Morton's behest. I know of John's dubious condition. Thanks anyway." Ruth sounds, nonetheless, not at all depressed by the dismal news she'd already received.

"So you know?" Doris is, or at least sounds, aghast. As if she'd seen a ghost. (Sorry, I had to say that.) She is either a well-practiced liar—or a brilliant actress. I am more than prepared to bet my bottom dollar that somehow my cousins had already learned of Nurse Joan's telephone call. Of course, the offer is academic.

I realize I am blabbering, even if only to myself. Frankly, the relief I feel is overwhelming. I was really expecting Ruth to go over the edge if she learned, in her present condition, that her husband is falling apart at the seams.

"My dears," Ruth's tone is light as a feather, "you really mustn't worry. Once I learned about my own backsliding, I could expect nothing better from John. We are married, you know. We not only do, but also don't do, most things together."

How silly of me. Why didn't I think of that? But this still doesn't explain how Doris and Brenda learned about Nurse Joan's telephone call. Unless they went back after their coffee and asked Nurse Joan to call Ruth. I am toying with the idea of probing their mind. Then I decide to be generous. After all, Ruth was. As of today, I decide to be Mr. Nice Guy. No more sarcasm, no more backbiting. Not even towards my cousins. Provided they don't eat each other, of course.

Now this wasn't nice, either.

But, after all, I am an insect, aren't I?

**

16

I am a Leopard.

The savannah stretches as far as the eye can see. It has already turned yellow, with baked crust showing between scattered twigs. The air is shimmering with the heat waves rising from the parched earth. If rains don't come soon, my prey will die before I can hunt them down. I feel a great dryness in my throat. It's been five days since I've eaten. The larger herbivores, the giraffes or zebras, are long gone. The kudus, and gnu, have all but disappeared—moved to better pastures, I suspect. I cannot live on mice and gophers. They're not enough to sustain me. And they, too, are withered. My one hope lies in the impalas, though they're not easy to hunt down. Some can jump ten feet high and some thirty feet forward when sensing danger. That leaves the graceful gazelles; but they, too, must have moved on.

Only a month ago, the plains were brimming with food.

I am beginning to lose my strength, while the herbivores still get some moisture from the parched grass, and maybe even roots. They will be able to run better than I can. I am lucky I found some shade among these bushes. What's left is a single acacia between me and the distant horizon. It's cooler here than out in the open. Usually the long grass gives me sufficient cover. Now? Now even this lone tree is barely protection from the midday sun. I feel that everyone in the whole wide savannah is desperate to avoid me. They could be as hungry as I am.

I am trying to lick my paws, but my tongue has no saliva. Anyway, I must conserve it. Every drop. I look at myself. My fur is no longer as lustrous as it was. I definitely need some meat and,

maybe more so, some blood. There is no more water around. I
know, I looked. I would risk confrontation with elephants and lions
for a sip or two. But there just aren't any waterholes left. Perhaps
the climate is changing. My parents never had such problems. At
least, they never spoke of such. And this is the third year running.

For now, I must wait. As long as the sun is out, I don't have a
chance. I would dehydrate in seconds. It takes water to move my
weight at great speed. And my weight is all muscle. Anyway, I
prefer to hunt after dark. It's a lot safer. There are two-legged
animals that are dangerous to us. To all other animals. They kill
from a distance, even when not hungry. I can smell hunger, even
my own. They? They just kill for fun. My mother told me they are
either very primitive or very degenerate.

"Stay well hidden till after dark," she'd warned me. So long
ago...

Yet, I remember her message well. She was a grand old lady.
Hopefully, still is. Father died by venturing out of the trees in
daytime. He was a great male too. And so kind. I'm lucky. He gave
me my spots, which make me nearly invisible in the dry season.
Sort of brownish. A good defensive colour. Even in daylight, if I
keep still enough. Not that I have many enemies.

I keep myself alive by eating insects and rodents. I need
something larger, something even larger than myself. I can hide it
afterwards in these bushes, lest some lazy lion should try to steal it.
I don't trust lions. I don't trust anyone much. I prefer to be alone.
There used to be a waterhole not far from here. Some dumb
ungulates are bound to come by, still looking for it. They should be
easy prey. Only they are not coming. I might have to go out and
look for them. After dark, if I still have my strength.

How do those flies have the energy to keep flying? Buzzz...
buzzz...

Here they come!

There is dust on the horizon. It's coming my way. They're
moving pretty fast, considering the heat. There must be a great
number of them. I need only one. Just one to stay alive. I must
remain perfectly still. I even half close my eyes lest they reflect the
light of the setting sun. It's a bit early for hunting, but in these
conditions beggars can't be choosers. And I'm no beggar.

They come as a herd of thousands. I must wait till they are past me and attack one of them from the rear. Experience has taught me that's the best way. Their horns are no defense against my speed and power. They can jump well over my head, but... what goes up, must come down. Anyway, they only pronk to six or seven feet, not like the impalas. Pronking is like leaping, only it's straight up. I won't get distracted again. There are always stragglers. Serves them right. I've got to eat, don't I?

When I leap up in the air, on stiff legs, my back arched, I can see an ocean of red-brown stripes moving like a broad river. The leaders know where the water is. Frankly, I am a little tired. I was running around too much. Just for fun, and to find some tasty morsels. That's what we do. We have fun and we eat. Isn't life wonderful? I'll wait till most of my friends pass by me, and then join them. I need a little rest. Once I catch my breath, I'll be able to pronk as high as that bush over there. I might even nibble on it. I'll have to leave the herd for a moment, but it will be worth it.

I am within twenty feet of the straggler. I stretch, pull my legs below me, and leap. I cover the distance in three bounds. My teeth sink into her neck even as she pronks. We come down together with a thud. The rest of the herd didn't even notice.

He came at me out of nowhere. The moment I am caught in the vice of his teeth, I leave my body. There is no point remaining. I don't fight lost causes. Frankly, I didn't feel a thing. No pain. Just a tugging and then silence. I hope he'll enjoy the body I'd been using. Now, perhaps, I, too, will have a chance to wear spots. They are rather impressive. And, oh, he's so powerful…

"What do you think?" My Friend's eyes shine as if he'd been taking part in the hunt. I wonder if he was the hunter or the prey. Perhaps both. After all, I was.

"Both," he replies, smiling. "Weren't you?" As if he didn't know.

"Was that the purpose of the hunt? To teach me that my consciousness resides in both, the hungry and the prey? Is that really possible?"

"Are you asking me whether it is possible to be omnipresent or to be in two places at the same time?"

"You know exactly what I mean. But I haven't thought of the omnipresence angle. I must say, you're a great teacher."

"I am not. I only show you what you already know. Don't you remember being the incipient universe? The thought of omnipresence never entered your mind."

"That was different. There were no life forms then…"

My Friend stares at me with surprise in his liquid eyes. There is growing disbelief in them, but he remains silent. I can sense a question forming in his mind, 'Is this what you really think?'

"You are not talking about omnipresence right now, are you? You are saying that there is no time. That all these things, events, animals and human hunters alike are coexistent, aren't you?"

There is that smile on his face that a parent reserves for his child who just got the right answer. If he is my mirror, then he reflects a great deal more than I'd initially suspected. He is so down to earth, so patient and gentle, I find it hard to believe that he is the same Friend who drove my chariot in Kurukshetra. There, or then, he was almost godly. Commanding, telling rather than asking.

"Omnipresent means not only in all space but, by definition, in all time. Ask Einstein."

For a moment I am toying with the idea. I'm thinking of using the universal replay to shuttle back in time and ask the master. To ask Albert Einstein about the space-time continuum. Perhaps *he* would be able to explain it to me.

Instead, I replay the African event, in which I took part as both—leopard (or I could have been cheetah, I can't be sure) and that beautiful, straggler antelope. Being able to pronk, to jump some seven feet straight up, did not save it from the sleek bundle of muscle that wanted to live. The gazelle is probably the most graceful animal that Africa ever spawned. Or is beauty always just in the eyes of the beholder? As a leopard, it didn't register with me. Just hunger. Insatiable hunger. Instinct for self-preservation? Preservation of what, a transient body? There must be a different kind of consciousness ensuing from the body itself. I think Ruth called it the animal soul. We all have it. We humans, I keep reminding myself. There is so much to learn. We also kill to preserve our decrepit bodies. We are animals, only neither as fast nor as powerful as the leopard; nor nearly as beautiful as the antelope. I wonder what's our excuse for killing. It certainly isn't just to stay alive.

Those antelopes really are beautiful. Imagine, a whole river of beauty moving along a grassy desert. Too numerous to admire them individually. There are still vast herds of them in the southern part of the continent. Their function? I have no idea. To trim the grass? Recycle the nutrients? Keep a starving leopard from dying?

We all have a purpose. And only those incarnations are not wasted which fulfill that purpose. Unless we assume that there is only one incarnation—set on continuous.

She seems to me to be perfectly all right. Not sick at all. She doesn't even look pale—well, no more so than usual. Evidently the news of my impending disintegration did not have an adverse effect on her morale. She is smiling as Nurse Brown pats her pillow and draws the curtain to give the TV a better contrast. I see her look at the *TV Times*. There is a program on art today, and Ruth wouldn't want to miss it. I am glad she's keeping abreast of her favourite subject. Nurse Brown did the rest.

It's Sister Wendy Beckett's program, again. Her popularity is boosted by a second wind. Ruth loves her. Just out of curiosity, I peek into the Sister's mind, also. That's right, Beckett's mind that is thousands of kilometers away. Actually, in England. I can do that now.

I snoop around the nooks and caverns of her memories.

Born in South Africa, she enjoys dual vocations—God and Art. Both capitalized. Her vocations were nurtured by her school teachers, the Sisters of Notre Dame. Wendy began her novitiate in England. When the Order sent her to St. Anne's College in Oxford, she continued to live in the convent, maintaining a strict rule of silence. Things change. Now she's one of the great speakers on the

subject of Arts. Again, with a capital A. Mostly painting and
sculpture.

Even now, her fame continues to spread, far and wide, on both
sides of the Atlantic. When not lecturing, she continues to live in
seclusion, in a trailer, on the grounds of the Carmelite monastery at
Quindenham. In silence and solitude. And, I suspect, with her heart
filled with immortal works of art. And God, of course.

I strongly suspect that her god is the god of beauty. People
worship many gods. Mostly religious ones—those they'd created in
their own image. It must be easier to serve a god that reminds you
of yourself. Perhaps bigger, more powerful—well, yes, and
immortal. But still from the same metaphysical gene pool.

Sister Wendy loves her god dearly. She offered him her life,
her silence, her loneliness. And she still carries one of the most
beautiful, warm smiles I've ever seen. And I don't mean just
through Ruth's eyes. I've seen her programs, too. I saw her series
on *Impressionist Masterpieces* and the *American Masters*. I also
listened to her interview with Bill Moyers. I wonder if she's a saint.
By whatever definition.

I am tempted to stay and watch the program, again; but
suddenly I realize that Wendy and her programs are all firmly
etched in my mind. They'll probably stay there forever.

I am about to leave Ruth and Wendy when the telephone
rings.

"Mrs. Clarkson? I have a call for you from Florida. I'll put
you through." The operator must have been checking whether Ruth
was awake, I suppose.

"Ruth, is this really you?" It's her mother, sounding nervous.
She must have gone through the usual hospital pre-recorded run-
around. For such-and-such press this, or that, or the other. Then
wait and wait and...

"Yes, Mother, of course it's me. How are you all?"

"Oh, darling, I've only just heard. Brenda called me. She said
you are hospitalized."

"I'm perfectly all right, Mother, I..."

"I told you many times to take better care of yourself, dear,
didn't I?"

"Yes, Mother, you did, and I do. They are sending me home tomorrow. This was just a check-up, just as you told me to have one."

"Really? Brenda said there's something wrong with your ticker…" Mother's voice is already more relaxed. Good ol' Ruth.

"I'm all right, really…"

"And John? How is John? Is he all right, too?"

"We don't know yet, Mother. They are doing all they can. The doctor said John needs time to repair his body. He was a bit exhausted…"

"I told him, too. I told him to take better care of himself. Remember, dear?"

"Yes, Mother. How are John's parents?"

Ruth switches on the TV and cuts the sound. The screen comes to life, together with the smiling face of Wendy Beckett. Behind her are walls filled with paintings. She'll talk about them. Ruth already knows what the nun is going to say, but she loves looking at her, all the same. Sister Wendy has the gift of inspiring people.

"I told you, dear, I'm perfectly all right. It's you I'm worried about."

"No, Mother. I mean how are John's parents, Jane and George?"

"They went to the beach, dear. Don't worry, George is a good swimmer."

This is likely to go on for another ten minutes. I find it interesting that I can hear both voices with equal ease. Perhaps I am beginning to learn how to operate on both sides of the border. My Friend will be pleased. Assured that Ruth is coping well, even with Mother, I make myself scarce.

My Friend and I already talked about saints. They, he assured me, have powers beyond ordinary humans. Such as Father Pio. Wasn't he the one who is said to have had the power to bilocate? I had heard stories about that. He must have been in some sort of religious or self-induced coma. Actually, this is strictly Ruth's department.

To reduce my overt ignorance about odd phenomena, I visit her in our condo the moment I leave the hospital, transferring some months into the past. On the third attempt I get the right evening. I feel I need some ammunition to balance the odds in our chats with Friend. Continually advertising my ignorance does not do much for my ego. No life, no body, and now—no brains, so to speak.

We shall see, my Friend. We shall see...

I realize, belatedly, that I was referring to the future over which I have no influence. In other words, what I am going to discuss with Friend, I already know. Or knew, if you prefer. My being here, now, with Ruth, confirms this thesis. What really happened is that I forgot. Whenever Ruth begins to expound on her favourite subject, which bears little interest for me, I switch off—rather, I used to switch off—my attention. This time I am determined to listen closely.

Ruth is sitting in her usual curled-up position on her end of the sofa, her legs tucked under a pillow on which rests a sizeable tome entitled simply *Saints*. I am farther down the settee, taking advantage of the reading lamp at the other end. I am trying to read some construction site inspection reports. I always lag behind with those.

I rev fast forward until Ruth comes to Father Pio. I recall she shared his story with me. I just didn't remember what the story was. At least, not the details.

"In this day and age, when the sacerdotal fraternity's image suffers a great many scandals, it is joyful indeed to find a Roman Catholic priest whose sainthood no one questions," Ruth says, with obvious pleasure. Actually, he wasn't a priest, only a monk. Not that I'm that sure what the difference is.

I cannot deviate from what happened on that evening, but I can, in the now, place my attention on Ruth.

"Yes, dear." I observe myself smiling my usual non-committal response.

"He was only canonized in June 2002, by Pope John Paul II, but the evidence for his sainthood was overwhelming."

I see myself nodding. "Are you listening, darling?"

"Of course, darling." I nod more vigorously.

I was hoping she wouldn't ask me to repeat her words. Peeking into my own thoughts, I note that I felt, then, like a schoolboy who might have to stay after school.

"It's really interesting," Ruth continues. I wish she would get to those phenomena. "You know, of course, about his stigmata. That's general knowledge. But for me, what made him unique was his inexplicable gift of bilocation. There were dozens of people who swore that they each saw him in two places, far apart, at the same time. Makes you wonder…"

I love when Ruth delves into the mysterious. Her eyes grow dreamy, her smile becomes mysterious. On occasion, I may not have paid adequate attention to what she was saying, but I certainly kept my eyes on her. As a matter of fact, my subconscious recorded every syllable she uttered. Now, today, in moments such as these, I am prepared to say, 'to hell with the universe,' and go back into my body. The only problem is, I don't know if I can do that.

I have what I came for. The dope on Father Pio. I'll tackle this subject with my Friend. I watch Ruth for a while longer and split.

I find him where I left him. Where else? If he always follows me wherever I go, and he claims he does, then how come he's already here when I return? Well, almost always. I am about to open my mouth to talk about Father Pio when he beats me to it.

"Father Pio did not bilocate," he says. "He is or—as people in the physical world would say—was, omnipresent. As are you. He just changed his point of attention."

"You mean he was already there? I mean here and there, I mean…"

"Of course. No one can travel faster than light." My Friend is grinning as if he had just cracked the joke of the century. Then his face grows serious. "We already discussed this. He is as omnipresent as you were when you shared your consciousness simultaneously with the leopard and the antelope."

"So… we really are all one?"

It seems much easier to say it than to accept it as an immutable law of all realities. Also, I find that this truth must be continuously rediscovered. It's so simple, yet, at the same time, strangely elusive.

My Friend gives an impression of falling asleep. "You are doing all right, John. You are doing quite all right..." I hear him as though from a great distance. I am going to miss him. And then I realize that he hasn't moved an inch. It is my attention that has shifted.

My efforts with Ruth came to naught. I feel frustrated. I feel the need to show progress in my understanding. An idea strikes me. "And what about St. Francis of Assisi? Didn't he talk to the birds?" I have no idea why I said it. I suppose I am trying to catch him at something. Anything.

"Don't be silly, John. St. Francis didn't talk to the birds. He *was* the birds..." And, even as I hear his voice whispering in my mind, he melts into... whatever mirror ghosts melt into. Once more, I am alone.

It seems that there is more to understanding reality than spending an evening or two with someone who shows interest in metaphysics. It is life itself I must learn to understand. Out of the blue, I see an image of an ancient man in a long robe, his white beard flowing down to his chest. He smiles at me with kind, understanding eyes.

"The unexamined life is not worth living," he says, his voice unexpectedly young. The image dissolves into the blue sky.

Easy for you to say, I smile sadly. The problem is that my Friend's definition of life is not limited to my present incarnation. It deals with *the* incarnation. Just one. And even then it seems to have no beginning and offers no promise of an eventual conclusion. I am back to square one. I am that I am, I whisper. I am the *alpha* and the *omega*. The beginning and the end. And yet I am neither. I just am.

They unwrapped the rest of my face. I don't look that bad. My nose is still a bit askew, and part of my right eyebrow is missing. My face shows a permanent look of vaguely cynical surprise. Perhaps it's fitting. Since I left my body, I *am*, more or less, in a state of permanent surprise. But I don't think I turned cynical. Just the opposite. While I do not seem to have crossed any new ground, I am certainly committed to examining my past. Perhaps this is what Socrates meant in his momentary appearance on the screen of my mind. I bet my Friend was instrumental in that vision. Didn't he say he was my memory? A sort of subconscious storage of my past?

Back to my face. After three months and some days, Dr. Morton sees fit to expose my mishap to the world at large.

Ruth is coming out of the General tomorrow. If she sees me like this, it will send her over the edge, again. Let's face it. I was never a pretty face. Nothing tall, dark and handsome about me. Well, I am reasonably tall, not that it does me much good lying down. As for the dark, my hair is mousy, turning grey at the temples. My features, even before the accident, were more suited to a rugby field than to a conference room filled with CEOs, let alone with the prejudices of High Society. There were two things Ruth pointed out in my favour. The first was my high forehead.

"What is it that you're hiding in that great brain of yours?" she would ask on occasion.

And the other—my eyes. Sort of. A pale blue, bordering on steely-grey, now that I remember, in an almost permanent squint as though examining something. Which was what I was doing most of the time. Examining drawings. Presentation materials, construction documents... Masses and masses of drawings. And the rest of the time I had to read.

"It's not your eyes I love so much," Ruth said, returning my squint. "It's what's in them..."

Mostly permanent tiredness. I have a pair of glasses, but I hate using them. What's wrong with squinting, anyway? Frankly, I don't care what Ruth finds acceptable about my appearance, as long as she finds something. Anything. Now that my state of being is stretching on and on, I am again beginning to feel the dread of losing her. I find it strange that, although time doesn't exist, watching my past is registering in my awareness as lasting forever. It no longer progresses at the rate of twenty-four hours per day but seems to stretch into infinity. It is as though today would never end. An unnerving prospect. Perhaps this is why we invented time. To chop reality into little pieces, little segments, short enough for us to swallow. Or, perhaps, just to remain sane? The incipient universe I saw, or I was—the endless galaxies, the solar system, the planets and the moons—are all no farther away than all my other states of awareness. I am a tree, a leopard, an antelope and even a paltry insect, all rolled into one. I am also Ruth's husband. No less, though seemingly a lot more. I am all those things, yet I am none of them. I am nothing. No-thing. As I am finally beginning to accept, I just am.

Today I follow Ruth home. She walks fast, treating the distance as physical exercise. She has always done that, but today she takes a slightly longer route. She walks by a Catholic Church we used to go to at Christmas and Easter. Traditions. To my surprise, she goes inside. I really hadn't expect her to go there to pray. Surely, not for my recovery? On the other hand...

Just inside the lobby, there used to linger two or three men, or women, catching some respite from inclement weather. Today the weather is fine, but their habit apparently persists. Evidently, the parish priest allows the destitute to stay a while, provided, I suspect, that they don't take over the church as their permanent address. Some parishioners are afraid of beggars. Perhaps the faithful become aware of what they perceive as injustice in the world. This time there is only one elderly woman.

Ruth reaches inside her purse and pulls out a crumpled piece of paper. I watch as she pushes it into the woman's hand. It is a ten-dollar note. Wrapped inside it is the Rosary my mother had given her. The old woman hardly reacts. Perhaps she's given up on movement. On life. I wonder if she would have accepted the Rosary if it hadn't been wrapped in the paper bill.

My thoughts return to my previous musings.

There is a difference, I think. I love Ruth. I rejoice in my other states of being, previously of temporary becoming, but Ruth I love. We really are one. Inseparable.

***

Part Three

`

BECOMING

"Nothing is, everything is becoming."

Heraclitus of Ephesus (540-480 BC)

17

I am an Elephant

I remember it all. I am a state of being. I can do no wrong. On the other hand, I can also do nothing right, either. Is this why people in heaven are so saintly? They can do no wrong? Perhaps I'm in heaven, after all.

Soon I shall be in a state of growth. When I'm no longer nothing, I shall be in a state of becoming. Ergo, for now I am still no-thing. That's why no one can see me, hear me, or pay any attention to me. That's sort of funny. They don't pay any attention to God, either. Not that I do. Did. Anyway, you can't really pay attention to nothing—with or without a capital N. When I am something, I am creative. I contribute to the universe. I am in the process of evolution.

I should say, when I *will* be.

I know there is a reason why I am here, in this limbo-like mode of being. I develop a perspective of spatiotemporal omniscience. If I do come out of this alive, shall I remember it all? According to my Friend, I already forgot more than I ever imagined I knew. Does this make sense?

Questions. My Friend's specialty, although of late—if one can use such an expression in a reality where time doesn't exist—he does open up a lot more. Perhaps until just now he didn't think I could understand any of it. Understand the truth about how the universes are structured.

My Friend thinks that if it hadn't been for the Greeks, we would still be living in caves. Metaphorically speaking, of course. He drops hints, daily, about Lydia, a chunk of land dividing the Mediterranean Sea from the Black Sea. What makes it harder to keep up with him is that he's really referring to Turkey, not Greece at all.

"It is the cradle," he keeps repeating to himself. "The cradle of philosophy."

As an architect, my interests lie in buildings, in architecture, ancient or otherwise, that might inspire my own designs—not in philosophical connotations. I have heard of Troy, Sardis, Ephesus and Miletus, but hardly for the same reasons. Troy of Homeric fame, where Trojan Wars raged in the famous or infamous Iliad; Sardis, with its celebrated Gymnasium we all copied in third year of architectural studies; Miletus, with its magnificent theatre, thereafter copied for centuries by the later Romans; and Ephesus, where the Romans left their stamp by continuing the game of one-upmanship over their predecessors, the Greeks, with the Celsus Library, the Temple of Hadrian, and a scattering of other ruins. As for philosophy, this, once again, is Ruth's domain.

"None are equal to Ephesus, but..." he must have peeked at my thoughts, "long before the Roman era," he muses aloud. He tends to do that lately, as though he had all but given up hoping that I might, on my own, catch up on my own knowledge. "The city laid claim to Heraclitus, who was the first man to give meaning to the word *Logos*."

As I was saying, it is Ruth's department. I nod, saying nothing.

"He saw that opposites are necessary for becoming, but that, in essence, they are unified in a system of balanced exchanges."

"I don't really follow."

I didn't. I wish he would talk turkey. After all, that's where Ephesus now is—Turkey, though not as yet in the European Community. Anyway, isn't 'now' all that matters?

"Heraclitus equated becoming with life. He said that nothing is. That everything is becoming."

"Was he right?" I am slowly drawn into my Friend's philosophical rambling.

"Are you?"

"Am I right?"

"No. Do you exist?"

This stumps me. We have touched on this subject before. If all is becoming, then I don't exist. But I am, and Heraclitus claims that nothing is except for...

"That's not what he meant. He said that no-thing is. Being exists only in potential form. Your wife would say that heaven is a field of infinite potential. Like the unconscious. It is, but it's not becoming. Once you are a thing, an entity, you become individualized."

I must have looked pretty dumb.

"In order to enter the state of becoming, you must become individualized. Essentially, you remain part of the Whole, or One, but are no longer fully aware of this fact."

My first reaction is to tell him not to tell me what my wife thinks. Luckily, I stop myself in time, though not early enough to stop thoughts supplied by my ego. We humans, even in our ghostly form, carry enormous baggage. Our pride and possessiveness colour not just what we say, but even what we think. I assume that most of us seldom think before we open our mouths. Parenthetically, my Friend is right about Ruth's definition of heaven. She had used those precise words.

"It's like saying that God doesn't exist," I counter triumphantly, once I have calmed down my injured ego. I always had reservations about a long-bearded man overseeing our dos and don'ts.

"Not at all. What he said is that God is not a thing. Neither thing, nor being, nor, as you say, a long-bearded man. With or without a capital M. It also implies that the only way you can experience God is through His and Her creation."

"His and Her...?"

"I think of God as androgynous. Hermaphroditic, if you prefer. The potential of opposites accelerates the process of becoming. I also find them complementary."

"How does God come into all this?" Friend is beginning to give me a headache.

"You brought It up."

I must remember to keep my mouth shut. Since I left school, I have always preferred God to be an It. It seemed more politically correct. Still, for a guy from a long-forgotten town in Ionia, Heraclitus sure impressed my Friend. I'll have to check whether Ruth came across him in her own research. His philosophy surely borders on metaphysics. As for Logos, even Christians borrowed from him. Must have been quite a guy. Or... or he had a very good Friend.

"Hee, hee," reaches me from the other hammock.

I ignore that. I never asked him to listen to my thoughts.

"Sorry..."

I have to smile. Peeping or not, my Friend is nice. Always was. I mean, really nice.

I begin to realize that it all comes down to memory. If all reincarnations happen at once, then in order to separate them we must arrange them in a sequential order. To be able to do so, we need near-perfect memory. I mean, one reaching to the beginning of time.

I am no longer a tree, but my legs are trunk-like. I have a sense of enormous stability. Also of power and confidence. No one is likely to get in my way. Not even the so-called king of the jungle. If lion is a king, then I am an emperor. A king of kings. I need peace and quiet. I need it in order to organize my memories. That's my job. I must remember. Bring things into the present. Into the Now. After all, thoughts not only create but also maintain physical reality.

I have all the equipment necessary to protect my need for peace. Enormous size, stability, even thick skin. Neither fang nor claw, nor even a pesky gnat can bother me. I'm as close to impregnable as nature can make anything that walks on earth. But most of all, I am endowed with a brain that exceeds any other memory storage in history. Even the behemoths of the past didn't come near me. I don't mean the relatively small hippopotamuses Job refers to in his visions, but the monsters of sixty million years ago. The dinosaurs. Look at their heads. Tiny, especially when compared to their body. Can you imagine? Forty-five meters long and seventy-seven tons. I feel like adding, '...and deeper in debt'.

Sorry. Just a little jingle I heard in my other becoming. "You load sixteen tons, what do you get? Another day older and deeper in debt." It's about a man who couldn't die because he owed his soul to the company store. Merle Travis wrote that. It's a little like the other me, like John, only he's still trying to work out what his soul is.

As for the dinosaurs, can you imagine feeding their children? You'd need good eyesight just to spot them. They were not stupid, mind you. They served the process of becoming for some hundred-sixty million years. That's a lot longer than humans have done to date. On the other hand, they almost single-handedly (actually, they used four legs and a tiny brain) stopped the progress of evolution. That's right. I remember them well. Not in my present form, of course, but I do remember them. I remember the jingle, too.

Let me tell you. I remember practically everything. On Earth, that is. Everything that ever happened on the planet Earth.

I can't take credit for it all. Evolution endowed me with a brain unequalled before me or since, while granting me quite unparalleled freedom. As I already suggested, I don't have to run from any predators, and I can find nourishment everywhere. Yet, to achieve my purpose, I must conserve my energy. I am even equipped with a long trunk that enables me to find food, with equal facility, above my head or at my feet. I don't have to search it out. I can spend most of my time just remembering.

The development of my grey matter may be similar to that of humans, but let's face it—my brain weighs over five kilograms. It may not sound like much, but an adult human can boast only a quarter of mine, between 1,300 and 1,400 grams. If a human attempted to carry my brain on his or her shoulders, their neck would snap like a twig. There are, however, many factors that contribute to my ability to recall and retain masses of memories. One might be due to the fact that I don't prattle *ad nauseam*. If only humans learned to keep quiet, they would recall a million times as many facts and figures, not to mention patterns and even emotions. That's right, even with their tiny brain. What's even more important, they would remember things that matter. However, no species ever made so much noise as humans do. Never. Never in the annals of history. And I don't mean just subliminal chatter, either.

I feel a stirring on my left. Next, I perceive a smile. I hear a question invading my defenses.

"How do I know all this? I've got the brain for it," I answer. I didn't even open my mouth.

"Hee, hee, hee," my Friend is evidently having fun. Ghosts really do have a sense of humour. My mirror never did. If anything, it used to be rather depressing.

Seriously, elephants have a great deal to remember. We've been around for a long while. At least sixty million years, and no sign of extinction. Nature is well organized. When a particular species is done serving its purpose, it is allowed to disappear. To become extinct. Humans who attempt to preserve some used-up models are just titillating their ego. They think they are doing a good deed. There is neither rhyme nor reason for that. Life is not the body, life is what's in the body. I should know. I stepped out of my previous, human body, and looked at it. Pretty useless. I can live with it, but it's not much. What I find harder to reconcile with my human sense of morality is that some species seem to live exclusively to serve as food for other, larger species. Like anchovies. It seems unfair.

"We are all one," I hear from a great distance. "And anyway, you are mistaken. You are thinking of whales and large sea creatures. Not so. Humans also eat them, as do birds. And they are the most formidable fertilizer. Not many species can claim to be doing that much good."

That's all I need. An expert on agriculture.

I am back to now, but I did enjoy being an elephant. The strange thing is that I didn't lose my human identity—just enlarged it to include the elephant's. A new experience.

"We are all one," I hear Friend reasserting his dictum, this time a lot closer.

"I'm beginning to believe you," I whisper, confidentially, as if sharing a secret.

"I know. It is the beginning of becoming."

Ruth stands by the door, squints, blinks, and starts laughing. I am not impressed. This is not the way to greet your husband, not even one in a coma. And especially not when you first see his lacerated face. Didn't they tell her that people in a coma often hear things? And I don't mean just as ghosts. Physically hear things. Some sort of latent, subliminal awareness. She ought to know better. It just isn't nice.

A nurse comes in and reaches out for Ruth's arm.

"Are you all right, Mrs. Clarkson?"

There is real concern on Nurse Joan's face. Even to me, Ruth's laughter sounds hysterical. She leads Ruth to the nearest chair. My dear wife is making a visible effort to calm down. Eventually, she succeeds.

"I'm so sorry, Nurse Joan. Really…"

"Is something wrong?"

As I peek at Nurse Joan's thoughts, she is scanning the roster of psychiatrists who are on call today.

"You'll never believe it, Nurse, but John, my husband, looked like this the day after I met him."

"I beg your pardon, Mrs. Clarkson?"

By now Ruth has managed to contain herself. She wipes tears from her eyes, tries as hard to wipe the smile from her face, and leans back on the metal chair.

"My husband, when he was young and handsome," here comes that giggle again, "was a rugby player. He had a match the day after I met him. He was carried away from the field on a stretcher. His nose was broken, his eyebrow seemed torn away. I'll never forget the way he looked. Till the end of the rugby season, his teammates kidded him that he ought to be more careful when he's alone with me."

A short burst of laugher ends the story. The nurse is gradually relaxing. No need for the straitjacket. Not this time, she thinks. Cheeky girl. By now Ruth is her usual, self-composed self.

"Will he be all right, Nurse?"

"Oh, I am sure they can fix his nose, Mrs. Clarkson. The eyebrow? Don't you think it gives him a certain *je ne sais quoi?*"

"Un je ne sais quoi de mélancolie?"

This time they both laugh. I'd never been accused of having a hint of melancholy in my facial expression. Nevertheless, it does appear that my lacerated face was just the tonic Ruth needed. It also means that she's not terribly worried about my appearance. That's something from days gone by that I didn't even remember. The broken nose brought memories of a joyful past. So much so that Ruth couldn't help laughing—as if it had happened just yesterday. It does say something about the concept of time.

The nurse sits on the other chair and lowers her voice.

"Oh, Mrs. Clarkson. I'm so happy you didn't see your husband when they first brought him. His face was red and blue, mostly blue, his hair mottled with gooey blood, his right eyelid refused to shut on its own accord. It's amazing, Mrs. Clarkson, but actually, strange though it may seem, even as he lies here in a comatose condition, his body is actively making its repairs. Believe me, Mrs. Clarkson, to us, to all of us, right now your husband looks positively beautiful."

Nurse Joan delivers this report sounding conspiratorial. Now that she knows Ruth better, she must have had the need to share this optical burden with my wife.

"I know, Nurse Joan. He always was. Even when they carried him off the field..."

Dear Ruth is still in a different time, a different place. She may not be an elephant, but she does enjoy a wonderful memory. And, what is probably more important, the things she remembers are wonderful. Perhaps that's the secret: to see beauty in everything—then you remember them. People, things, events...

When I was young and... and beautiful? Dear Ruth. Dear, beautiful Ruth.

I am trying to run through my memories. I soon realize it's an exercise in futility. I search for them in the past. To remember, one must invoke them in the present. But there is more to Ruth's secret. As I mentioned, she remembers all things as beautiful. All things, all events, all emotions. I can only imagine that those not beautiful she discards from her memory. This not only serves to fill her life with enchantment; but, evidently, it is the greatest affirmation of her faith in benevolence that she claims to have lost. I know—I peeked. It seems that true faith cannot be lost. It is ingrained in millions of stages of becoming. If only the good survives, the good and the beautiful, then evil and ugliness have no substance. It also affirms the singularity of incarnation. If I'm whisked off the wrong path the instant before I die, then surely, I, the single incarnation, continue. One life, one incarnation, one universe—now. And, what is more important, I retain memory only of that which is good and beautiful. As Ruth does.

Is this why I am here? Has my life taken a wrong turn and I needed to be whisked out of my body? This will take some more searching. A lot more.

Ruth is different. She always was. "All memories are wonderful," she once told me. "Otherwise evolution wouldn't make sense."

I go back to the knoll and dig into my past.

"There you go again…" my Friend sounds desperate. Funny how we both revert to speech when we are alone.

"I know, I know. I'm to bring my past into the present."

His smile confirms that I am right.

Ruth is about to leave my bedside when Doris pokes her head around the door. She withdraws immediately, and her brown superstructure is replaced by Brenda's blond curls. Today she, too, has her hair pinned up. A marked improvement. Then there is a knock.

"May we come in?" Doris asks innocently.

I see Ruth's expression before she turns to face my cousins with a warm smile. It was a picture of stoic containment mixed with a silent prayer.

"Of course you can. Come in, Doris. And Brenda, of course. I am sorry, I was about to leave. Catching up after my hospital holiday," she says, her arm reaching for her coat. "I do hope you'll forgive me."

She doesn't escape. Each woman embraces her in turn, with kisses planted just outside both her ears.

"I really must go…" she repeats, in a vain attempt to extricate herself from the show of affection. She returns the embrace with her left arm, her right holding on tightly to her coat, like a drowning man—sorry, woman—grasping at a floating log.

"We just want to know—how is your mother? And John's parents? We called them, you know? We felt they should have been notified." Doris spelled out all the essentials.

"You never know…" Brenda says, only to get a dirty look from Doris, and one of surprise from Ruth.

"I wasn't about to depart permanently, dear cousin. But, I suppose one never knows." Ruth's smile could have melted the polar ice cap.

"I only meant…" Brenda starts. This time she's interrupted by Doris. "My cousin means that we were both terribly worried about you. And about John, of course. We said the Rosary daily, you know. One must do what one can to help," she finishes sadly, her face indicating appropriate concern.

Rosary daily? They must have been reciting it at home. They certainly didn't visit me daily for some time.

"That's very kind of you. When we both recover, ah… fully, we'll have you both over to celebrate."

If ghosts could laugh aloud, I would bring the house down. What I saw in Ruth's mind, *without* peeking, was a depth of despair. For a moment she was actually hoping that neither of us would survive. I wonder that no one could see and hear her thoughts. They were screaming out for help.

"That will not be necessary, Ruth. We are doing this for our cousin out of our hearts, not in the hope of a reward."

What a gloriously hurt expression! My dear cousin Doris really is an excellent actress. I suppose she was too ugly to get any parts. Sorry, after all, there's the beholder and all that. Pity Brenda couldn't match her. Not that she didn't try, but her facial expressions come a second or two after Doris's, which gives them a sort of instant replay or *déjà vu* feeling.

As Ruth's left arm disappears into the sleeve of her coat, Brenda volunteers a suggestion.

"You will stay to say the Rosary with us, won't you, Ruth? We would like you to take the lead."

Ruth cringes, though I'm sure I'm the only one who notices. Poor Ruth. She never really liked the Rosary. Then her mother brought it up after my accident. In fact, her mother gave her a string of beads with an oversized cross hanging on the end, to make sure she had one. 'It will make you feel better,' she'd said at the time. It didn't. And now she's being placed in the position of having to refuse to pray for her husband's recovery.

"Oh, dear. How very nice. I'm afraid I left mine at home." I can see that she's desperately searching for a way out. "And I really must go, my dears. Lecture tomorrow, you understand?"

"Didn't Dr. McKinley tell you to take a week off from work?"

"Oh... that was before they diagnosed arrhythmia. I'm all right now."

Among a million or two other things, this is what I love most about my wife. She can think on her feet. No matter what you throw at her, she'll come out unscathed. Well, almost. Actually, it is I who can't take it any more. Surely, sooner or later Ruth will slip. She's not at the top of her form. Can't be after her stint at the General.

Before the dear cousins can throw the next wrench at her, Ruth covers the five steps to the door and shuts it firmly behind her. I can see her outside, taking a deep breath, then almost running down the corridor. For a moment or two, silence surrounds my body. Then the floodgates open again.

I scram.

I follow Ruth with my thoughts. She thinks that it's so much easier to get up and go to work than to get up, glance at me and go, and return to an empty home. 'This time I was lucky,' she thinks. 'This time Doris and Brenda really helped.'

I have to smile. Everything and everybody have their purpose, I muse. Even praying mantises and scorpions.

Just out of curiosity, I slip back into my room.

"Well, I never..." Doris is the first to recover. "I believe she doesn't like us. Of course, John is our cousin, not hers." She looks down on my prostrate body. "And he's such a nice man..."

"Good riddance. We are better off praying on our own, dear."
Brenda touches Doris's elbow and points to the two chairs. "Shall
we?"

Like two puppets whose strings are pulled simultaneously,
they both reach into their handbags and pull out their Rosaries.
Doris lifts hers up and, grasping it firmly in her right hand, makes a
large sign of the cross. She slowly touches her forehead, chest, left
and right shoulders. Brenda follows suit.

"You lead?" Brenda asks redundantly.

"In the name of the Father, and the Son, and the Holy Ghost,"
Doris intones with a firm voice. She's done this before. She likes
leading. It's in her nature. I recall that leading means that she is the
one who recites the articles of faith, the Creed, and then follows up
with the first part of the Hail Mary. Brenda would supply the
second part of each Angelic Greeting. The Holy Mary part.

"I believe in God, the Father Almighty, Creator of Heaven and
Earth…"

I wonder what sort of god they believe in. It can't be a good,
benevolent god. Not a generous one, either. I wonder how many of
my cousins' dreams have been fulfilled. I doubt they accept that we
all, not only must but do, create our own realities. Our futures. *Be
careful and purify, attune, and expand your thoughts about Me…* I
doubt they have ever read Rumi. Of course, if it hadn't been for
Ruth, I wouldn't have, either.

It's always back to Ruth…

Time I split. I don't like competition. With all those Ghosts…
Holy or otherwise. I must admit, it's been a while since I prayed.
Certainly not since I became a ghost. It seems silly. I don't mean
silly for living people—they pray mostly out of fear, perhaps even
fear of death. For me it would be a bit abortive. Not only am I
probably more dead than alive, but also, I'm not quite sure which
side I would really want to make permanent. Not that being 'alive'
is ever permanent. On the one side, there is Ruth. On the other, I
have the universe virtually at my feet. What am I supposed to pray
for?

There is one other thing that I recall from my experience of
being alive. I mean BP. Before the pothole. I had been really busy
looking down the tip of my nose. Except at Ruth, of course. Some

people spend their lives navel-gazing. What it really means is that they equate the whole universe with their own tiny sphere of operations. Their own little world. What I now find even more surprising is that there was a time when I found this *modus vivendi* quite satisfying.

Yet, since I began gallivanting through time and space as if neither existed, I have experienced two emotions that were rare, or even completely absent, while I was alive. The first is the experience of 'now', of today, that is filled with constant awe. Not by the wildest stretch of imagination would I have been able to conceive of the beauty, the size, the scope that the universe holds in its gentle embrace. And the second is even stranger to me. I am progressively filled with an emotion that is hard to describe. The nearest I can come to is a feeling of gratitude. The problem is, I don't know whom to thank.

***

18

I am Human

I t's not as easy as I thought. It seems that I have some four
million years to examine—a mere instant in terms of eternity,
but a goodly stretch of the fabric of time, all the same. On the
other hand, in a way, it all happened today. It's still happening. I
am still trying to decide what makes a human—human. If we
belong to the species of the apes, in what way do we differ from
monkeys? We are humanoids. I wonder what makes human
humanoids so different from non-human humanoids. Are we better
at performing tricks? Do we merely excel in our machinations? In
rising to the top of the food chain? Or do we just specialize in
destroying the competition, all other species, for our pleasure,
amusement, to sate our exaggerated gluttonous needs? We
advanced from herbivores, through carnivores, to omnivores.
Whatever our innate debauchery commands, we eat. We devour
without giving thought to our need or even hunger. We sate our
hunger beyond what is good for our health. We also neglect our
bodies. We abuse them beyond rational explanation.

Why are we destroying our own species? Have we outlived
our purpose?

I'd ask my Friend, but I'm sure he'd come up with his usual
'What do you think?'

Well, I think we are on the top of the heap. Unfortunately, it is
becoming more and more a heap of garbage, a heap of redundancy,
a heap of our own waste, our excrement. We are the only species
that lives in its own offal. We surround our cities with it. We try to
export it to what we refer to as the Developing Countries, to what
we call with considerable derision as the Third World, forgetting
that that world is populated by the same species, by humans. We

dump our excesses into the oceans. Lately, we've begun sending it into outer space.

Is this what defines us as human?

I'm glad my Friend is around and attentive.

It can't be just our ability to make gadgets. We are good at that. But do we evolve at the same rate at which we evolve our gadgets? We discard them at the same rate as we create them. Alan Greenspan, the illustrious Chairman of the USA Federal Reserve for many years, had called it creative destruction. We build in obsolescence with which we pollute our planet. The soil, the water and the air. We are thorough. We have taken our first steps to become universal polluters. We have launched more than ten thousand satellites into orbit, most of them already obsolete. Is this what evolution is all about? Yet at the same time, our physical evolution progresses at snail's pace. I know that my body doesn't learn. Not really. I can teach it a few new tricks, like a reasonably intelligent monkey; but, essentially, it doesn't learn. It is not becoming more resistant to outside influences. In fact, it degenerates. Fast.

Should I care?

What do you...

Why should I care? When what my body has to offer no longer satisfies my ingrained needs, I shall be whisked away and placed in another species. I'm sure Mother Nature will come up with one.

Don't you wonder who exactly does the 'whisking'?

I bet my Friend knows and won't tell me, right?

Silence.

It happened before with the chimpanzee. Once, they were on the top of the heap. Maybe not in size and power, but they were the smart ones. In some ways, still are. They used their wits to survive. But they didn't go far enough. Now we, humans, use them for laboratory experiments. It didn't work out—the whisking. As with us. Perhaps we ought to wipe the slate clean and try again. When I say we, I don't mean we, humans. We've done harm enough. We came close to wiping the slate clean with the H-bombs. Thousands of them. On both sides of the Pacific Ocean. And the Atlantic. As I said, we're thorough. No species on earth has ever been that stupid.

That irresponsible. Maybe the chimpanzees were right in choosing to remain in the jungle. Perhaps that is where our future lies. After all, they still share 98% of our genes. Genes unscathed by our folly. I can't see the future, but I can dream, can't I? I see a green earth, blue sparkling waters, clear air that pushes the horizon away to infinity.

Well? Aren't you going to say something?

What went wrong? We did go wrong, didn't we?

What do you think?

Was it our greed? Our self-absorption? We define humans by an affiliation to a genus and a species of *Homo sapiens*. Homo in Latin means 'man'. Sapient means 'wise'. A Wise Man? We, humans, are equivalent to wisdom? This is not entirely accurate, is it? Wisdom is a perfect amalgam of two precious attributes of knowledge and love. We missed substantially on the latter. Yes, we definitely should get a fresh start. God knows, we messed up.

Be careful then, My servants, and purify, attune, and expand your thoughts about Me, for they are My House.

"Friend? Is that you?"

As so often lately, I am all alone.

It is hot. Very hot. I can hardly leave the shade of the foliage above me. I shouldn't have left my cave. It was much cooler there. But my children have to eat. It's always about food—nothing else matters. Food and safety. Survival. It's all right for others. Their kids drop on the ground and walk. Almost immediately. I have to feed mine till they learn to walk. I wish I were a lion or a cheetah. I wouldn't be afraid of anybody. Or even a gnu. At least I could run fast. Escape the fangs and the claws. Now, I have to hide. I have to use all my wits to survive. And to feed my family. My mate doesn't help much. He's always busy inventing some new weapon to fight off the cats. They are the worst. The cats. They are big and strong and fast and silent. I can hardly hear them when they come up on me. It takes a large group of men with long sticks to scare them away. Alone we don't have a chance. Sometimes I think that men actually enjoy it. The fight, I mean. They like making noise, swinging their clubs and getting the better of a hyena. Big deal. If I had time, I would wrestle the ugly dog to death myself. Only I can't take the risk. Who would feed my children?

"You've really reached far back, John. It must be three or four million of your years. Your toes hardly give you forward propulsion. They let you walk upright, though. Did you enjoy being..."

"What toes?" I'm a bit annoyed. I think I did well by bringing such a distant past forward.

"You can always do it again. I want to make sure you know what it takes to create a biped."

Only then do I realize that my cousins still spent most of their time on all fours. I decide to listen.

"What enabled you to stand on your hind legs was the structure of your foot. There is a reason for everything, sometimes a very simple one. Your new toes are designed to propel you forward. Only then did you become bipedal. Your cousins already do so when demonstrating something or showing off. But they can't keep it up. They lose their balance."

"My cousins?"

"Yes, John. The chimpanzees. Have you forgotten that you share ninety-eight percent of their genes? Actually, you both have a common ancestor—your differences are minimal."

"Are you calling me an ape?"

"Well, a hominid. You are an ape that walks on two feet. You're on the way to becoming human. In the purely physical sense, of course."

"And the toes sent me on my way?"

I'm only slightly mollified. Surprising, since recently I've been an elephant, a leopard, and even an insect. Somehow being called a monkey, even a tailless one, sounds different. Less gratifying.

"They were a contributing factor. Some eight million years ago—again, your time—Africa was covered with a lush forest. You needed arms and legs with similar anatomy to swing amongst the branches. You lived, in your present form, up in the trees. That's how you survived. Otherwise you would have been eaten up to extinction."

"And it took evolution another four-and-a-half million years to come up with a forward propelling toe?"

"There is no time, John. You should know that by now. And anyway, the toes and the upright position liberated your forelegs, your arms, to get busy on becoming more creative. You chose to use them for creating gadgets. Apparently, you never stopped."

I must have looked at him in amazement. "Gadgets?"

"You know... clubs, sharpened sticks—good for fishing, by the way—and spears. They saved many a life of your family members."

So it's always about survival... I gather the forest has withered. Where I was, actually still am, it's dry, very dry and bloody hot.

"Over fifty degrees Celsius. You need some help to survive in such heat. Everybody's hungry."

So I'm an ape that walks upright. I have two sets of toes that enable me to do so. And when chimpanzees want to show off, they do the same, without the aid of my evolutionarily advanced toes. Doesn't say much for evolution.

"And yet it was enough," my Friend smiles from ear to ear. I'm telling you, he looks like a monkey. "You must realize, John, that evolution operates on the principle of 'if it ain't broke, don't fix it'."

"Which accounts for its staggering pace of advancement."

"You adapted—other species became extinct. Like the Neanderthal man. What would you do differently?"

"I would experiment. Progress is worth the risk."

"Welcome to the human race. The difference between all other species of animals and *Homo sapiens* is that the human wants to fix things, even if they ain't broke. No other animal does that."

"That's it? That's the sole difference?"

There is a shimmering of air, and I am back in the hammock. My Friend is already waiting for me. I keep repeating, I have no idea how he does it. I note, with a degree of pleasure, that my arms, legs or most parts of my body are no longer covered with brown, rumpled hair. On the other hand, I don't really have arms or legs... Never mind.

"Pretty much. Anyway, just check for yourself. Don't forget the brain in the body you visited in Africa, or the brain of *Australopithecus afarensis*, that was endowed with hardly more than four hundred grams of grey matter. Not much to work with. And you needed every milligram of it to survive."

"Hey! Did you know that I was in a female body?" It only just comes to me. Strange that it hadn't made a bigger impression at the time. I mean, it didn't register as something special or different.

My Friend shakes his head in a gesture of desperation.

"I know, I know. I'm all those bodies, all the time, everywhere, and right now I am also dead." I really do keep forgetting.

"Are you? Then you make it well worth while dying."

"You mean I'm learning…"

"…like never before. Coma is not such a bad thing, John. If you accept the reality of universal benevolence, then coma must be counted among the greatest blessings."

That's probably the strangest thing my Friend has said to date. I file it for later reflection.

"I suppose humans are also the only species that reflects on its past. We even invented paleontology," I muse aloud. I feel obliged to defend my species.

Frankly, I am really quite enchanted by all the things I am learning. Somehow, I don't want to admit it out loud. Not that he doesn't know. Yet I'm a little afraid that if I do admit it to myself, with conviction, I'll wake up. And somehow, all this will come to an end.

My Friend remains unusually silent.

I must be getting tired. I never realized that even ghosts can soak up information at such a high rate that absorption seems to slow down. Perhaps this is only because I'm so new at this game. After all, some three months is not much compared to infinity. On top of that I don't eat, I don't drink, and I don't sleep. I decide to rest my invisible grey cells, my quasi-neurons, or whatever it is that ghosts use to store their memories in.

For some reason, my attention drifts to my office. I am past caring if such a visit would invoke any emotions of longing in me. I'm becoming ambivalent about almost everything. Whatever will be — will be. Frankly, I am losing faith in the powers of self-determination. It's not like being alive. And speaking of being alive — whatever happened to my imagination? As an architect I used it all the time. It was the primary tool at my disposal. Now?

I regard the BCD drafting room with a touch of melancholy. It's been a while. As my gaze travels over the various computer screens, I picture my assistants as my prehistoric predecessors. In an instant, they all become hirsute, shaggy, and the whole place stinks to high heaven. They are no longer sitting on their stools but seem crouching, with their hind legs drawn beneath their slightly less hairy asses. They all seem to be poking the computer screens with their fingers, emitting the most extraneous noises.

"At least their speech hasn't changed much," I muse, hoping my Friend is listening.

Just as I am about to blink the absurd image away, my secretary wanders in, her tail neatly tucked under her arm, the tip stirring her coffee. Other than that, Gracie hasn't changed at all. She looks as nice as ever.

Could it be that for centuries at a time, perhaps millennia, or even for eons, we remain very much what we truly are? Maybe inner evolution is even slower than the physiological one. After all, what's the rush?

I blink that image away also. It could be just my genetic pride, but I'm glad we're not monkeys anymore.

Every second day, Ruth spends a good part of her evening, a very minimum of half-an-hour, on the telephone. Her mother and both my parents take turns listening to her repeating the same news about her own and my condition.

"You quite sure you're all right, dear?"

This is the fourth time the question is repeated. First it was her mother, then my dad, then my mother, and now her mother again.

"You must tell me how *you* are, Mother. You haven't said a word about the weather."

Now this is truly staggering. Since the trio began spending their winters in West Palm Beach, the weather absorbed the beginning, the middle and the end of every conversation. Invariably, there was also some minor exchange of news about the temperature of the water in the swimming pool, sometimes even in the Atlantic; a word or two about the Easterlies blowing with untiring conviction ('It's so lovely, it never gets too hot...'); and finally about the diet. This included the price of fresh fruit, the local wines ('Much prefer the Californian, don't you think so, George?' or 'And they simply do not have our variety of cheese, you know...'), and an occasional lobster ('All the way from Maine, you know, dear, although I'm quite partial to stone crabs...'). Today there has been no mention of any of them.

"We? How *we* are? But darling, you know how we are. We are always all right, aren't we, Jane? You tell her, George. We are always all right. Go on, George, I don't think she believes me."

"It is just as Clara (or Jane) says. We are all right, Pet. We always are." The only male voice states the obvious with the authority becoming the only male voice.

"You see, I told you, Ruthie. You must believe me when I tell you."

This is when I decide that watching Ruth is better enjoyed in silence. There is one moniker she hates beyond all others. Ruthie. Ruthie dilutes the meaning of her name, its wonderful origins. Ruth, in Hebrew, means friendship. If I can define my relationship with Ruth with a word other than 'love', friendship would be at the top of the list. She once told me that one of her favourite saints said that friendship is the highest degree of love. Or it could have been Ralph Waldo Emerson. He, too, was big on friendship. At least, Ruth had said so.

"And Aristotle—you know how he defined a friend? A single soul dwelling in two bodies. I like that," she'd said, her eyes assuming the misty quality they always had on such occasions. "A single soul in two bodies," she had repeated dreamily. "Is this what we are, darling?"

If ghosts could cry, I would shed a tear at this memory. It strikes me as being so very close to the truth. Dear Ruth. My friend.

My Friend would be a good ape. Even monkey. He has absolutely no difficulty swinging on a tree. Two trees, and he does this without even touching them. As do I. Perhaps we still gravitate towards trees through some atavistic compulsion? I wouldn't be surprised. After all, he says, I am all things at all times. So I cannot exclude a monkey. On the other hand, as I review the human species, I am less and less enchanted.

I learned a new trick. I found that if I keep very quiet (by that I mean that I still my mind), don't move (in fact pretend that I am dead), then I can actually reach into my Friend's mind and pick at the tons of stored information. I do so with a clear conscience, as I know for a fact that he enters my own mind at will. The only problem is that it is up to me to sort the stuff out chronologically. Not easy, but—here we go.

For a while we, as a species, had been doing OK. Then things went seriously wrong. I was also mistaken in assuming that my own regression into the body of an *Australopithecus afarensis* was the oldest. Far from it. Paleontologists came up with another unpronounceable name, the *Ardipithicus ramidus*, whose bones are said to reach back some five million years. I refuse to regress myself to examine him. The *ardi-ramidus*. Or her, of course. Anyway, it's academic. I hate bones. Once, construction on my building site was delayed by six months because during excavation they had found some supposedly human bones, sacred to the First Nations. To this day I have no idea how they knew they were sacred. The delay cost me a small fortune. None of this says much for the biblical six thousand years or so that Fundamentalists still hold on to. Still, my own *Austro-afarensis*, (if I am allowed, once more, to simplify my name to something resembling a word I can pronounce), which dates back between 2.7 and 4 million years into the murky past, wasn't bad, either.

Apparently, we, humans, went through at least ten different species, the last of which the scientists now call not just *Homo sapiens,* but *Homo sapiens sapiens.* Like-wise-wise. To me it sounds presumptuous, to say the least. We, the Hss, have been around for some 200,000 years. *Homo sapiens*, the species to which we all belonged until very recently, is now regarded as the

link between *Homo erectus* and *Homo sapiens sapiens*. I note that
the previous affiliation has nothing to do with his sexual prowess.
Just vertical—but only a little smart? The *Homo neanderthalensis*
got lost somewhere in the translation. He is now regarded as a
completely different species. No matter. We are here, aren't we?

At least, you are.

I always thought that evolution worked on an upward spiral,
going ever better and higher. Not so. Evolution is a direct result of
mutations. When things don't work, nature makes what I suspect
must be a deliberate mistake. A mutation occurs. If the result is
better, it continues to evolve. If not, then it dies off, and another
mutation occurs. As with the single incarnation. To cut the story
short, we are the result of a number of mistakes, not the least of
which is present-day man.

Ouch!

I only wish it weren't true, but I seriously doubt if my Friend
would retain memories that are false. I even doubt if it were
possible. The lies would dissipate into ethers, like our unsuccessful
predecessors. At least, once they were killed off. Forgotten?

So where, or really when, did we go wrong?

Enter a dozen great mystics. They all tried hard to show us the
folly of our ways. They even offered their lives, to save ours. We
didn't listen. We still don't. We are too busy talking. Making noise.
And I don't mean just the heavy metal rock bands. I mean the noise
in our heads.

There are, it seems, only two ways to regard ourselves. We
can assume that we are at the top of the pecking order and continue
to grow fatter and fatter. If we choose this route, then the US of A,
Western Europe and some parts of Canada are doing the right
thing. According to my Friend's files (I don't have any dates, but
they feel very 'now'), more than 50% of my cousins of the *Homo
sapiens* species in the Western world are obese. Two thirds of
those—in turn—are morbidly obese. Talk of degeneration!

I'm so glad ghosts don't eat.

The second way is to assume that we are not our morbid
bodies but some sort of energy that manifests through the infinite
variety of life-forms—human, animal, birds, fish, plants, and the

rest of the lower kingdom, including the microorganisms and sub-microscopic life. In a way, hopefully, that would be me.

Now if I am a typical example of Hss (that's Homo, etc), then we are also in dire straits. Until the pothole was instrumental in not only flinging my body out of my car but flinging me out of my body, I never spent more than five minutes at a time pondering such grave matters. And I wish I hadn't used the word 'grave'. I have Ruth to consider.

How about you?

By 'you' I mean all of you who, God willing, will one day read my own, or is it your own, mind (good luck) to edify yourselves with knowledge that I whisked out of my Friend specifically and out of the universe in general. Once again, good luck.

For now, bear with me.

In the previous century (just one century, not millennium), starting with the Boxer Rebellion against Russia, Britain, France, Japan and the USA, and finishing with Kosovo's liberation war, we, the people, members of Homo (not very sapient), in approximately 110 wars—call them armed conflicts or genocides, if you will—murdered between 160,000,000 and 195,000,000 people. These numbers are very conservative. Not bad for a single century, is it?

Now I am not passing judgment on anyone. For all I know, a good percentage of people who were murdered in the name of whatever we'd believed in (at the time), were really nasty folks. I don't want to know. The fact remains that, as best as I can see, this last century has made all previous centuries apt to be compared to skirmishes between naughty kids having a bad day in kindergarten. It seems that we, the people, have come of age. It also seems to me that it is time to give the chimpanzees another chance.

Yet amongst those countless wanton murders, I note—equally as countless—the unnoticed, unnamed, forgotten acts of kindness, bravery—indeed, heroism—and even great, unconditional love. We, humans, are indeed a very strange species.

And there is more.

It is hard to accept that the vast majority of *Homo sapiens sapiens* will never realize their full potential. They'll never sense, experience, come to know what they really are—innocent babies and kind old ladies alike. They will remain semi-intelligent apes, who will continue to create gods reflecting their own limitations, never allowing themselves to peek, no matter how briefly, into the infinite depth of their own consciousness.

Again Ruth shimmers before my eyes. She's reading aloud:

"...and His name shall be called Wonderful, Counsellor, The mighty God, The everlasting Father, The Prince of peace... Do you think, darling, that people will ever understand that this is what must happen within their own hearts?"

If they are lucky, I muse. If they are lucky enough to hit a really deep pothole.

She's staring at the TV with unseeing eyes. It's a news program. There is not much to see, these days. A few dozen deaths in the Middle East, a few local murders, a rape or two, a half-dozen armed robberies, and the rest are just white-collar crimes. A billion or two usurped, here and there... Small fry. Money is a liquid asset. It flows.

Money you can replace. Life is tougher, they say, to replace. I wouldn't know.

Ruth switches off the TV and picks up a book. It's on art, of course. Her personal escape. It used to be religion. That part of her psyche is fading; it belongs to her past. Today is what matters. And today, though it happens rarely, she seems depressed. I suppose I am at the root of it all. But how can anyone expect me to come back after what I can see in my Friend's mind?

The minute hand on her wristwatch moves about a quarter circle. She's lying on the sofa, sleeping. I can just see rapid eye movement. She's dreaming. I wonder if I can enter her dreams. Would this also be cheating? After all, I am her husband. In a way, we always shared our dreams.

I can't resist...

I think her dream is therapeutic. Apparently, I am back and take her for a spin around the moon. Dreams are a strange reality.

For a while I cannot locate her precise thoughts. They seem so far away. A moment of dread touches me and in the same instant disappears. I thought she had died. I thought I'd lost her. I haven't. Dear Ruth. She's all right. She's only dreaming.

So very, very far away...

I tack onto her coattails. I float with her through space that is not space. It's a dream. My God! We are together. Inseparable. Can one do that in a dream? Become one? She chose me to dream about. We are floating effortlessly. Even as I did, once or twice. I never examined my past dreams. They are similar to being in a coma. Only coma is much deeper. More of your consciousness is withdrawn from your body. Almost all of it. This? This is like... it's like a dream. It's beautiful, but there is no grandeur.

We are one, yet she still feels so far away.

And then a realization strikes me so hard I almost wake her up. It is not Ruth that is so far, far away. It is I.

***

19

I am God

There has to be more to life than this. I still feel empty. I don't have that many options. My parents taught me to rely only on myself. To have faith that within me lies the potential to achieve anything. They taught me to reject all limitations. A little like what the Bible teaches. At least, the way Ruth reads it. To look for help outside my own capabilities is to admit my own inadequacy. Yet I still do so. Perhaps not outside myself, but I do rely on my position and my relative prestige. That's what gives me power. You need power to get things done. It is also what makes me feel good. Powerful. At least it did until now. I cannot do so anymore. I shall draw out of myself the truth of my being, and then live by its commands. Live? That's still to be determined.

"Who am I?"

There is only silence. There is no one who can answer my question.

I glance into my future. A few thousand years into the future, just before the pothole. I know exactly who I am. John H. Clarkson, FRAIC, Senior Partner of the leading architectural firm, BCD. Lots of people have heard about me. I hold a good position, reasonable wealth, and a decent name. I have my favourite table at the Ritz, a seasonal box at *Place des Arts* and a number of social benefits that go with my station in life. I am defined by that elusive, pompous, overused, relatively meaningless word—successful.

But that is my distant future. Has much changed?

I transfer back.

Now I am much richer. People bow low before me. They offer me obeisance. I am more powerful and more dissatisfied. I am also a seeker.

Now, to achieve my aim, I must reject the luxury of my present station. I've grown too comfortable, too complacent in my present way of life. I've learned to rely on physical things, on sensual indulgences, to sate my needs. Who am I to be so proud? Am I not a mere foundling?

I must go out into the wilderness of my mind and search for my true self. In utter solitude I must commune with my true self. The real 'I am'. This hunger to discover my inner nature has consumed me since my youth. I thought I'd find it by achieving fame and glory. And riches. Material wealth. For a while they gave me comfort, satisfaction. But only for a while. My inner hunger persisted.

Frankly, I am afraid. If I am to succeed, I have to throw off my belief in my residual limitations. I must assume that there is no one higher than I. Not even the Pharaoh. Pharaoh the Sun. What of the rest of the universe? What of the stars that shimmer above me as I stare at them during my sleepless nights?

"Who am I?"

I asked the stars this question many a time. They stretch out over me in an endless ocean, from horizon to horizon. To the outer limits of the endless desert. 'Look within,' I hear a small voice. A tiny whisper. I don't know where it comes from.

Look within, Moses.

I've been hearing such whispers for years. They must live in my imagination. Somewhere within me there is a place outside of time, even outside of thought, where I shall discover the true nature of my being. So far I have served my ego. It is a great state of consciousness. It represents all I have already achieved. But as such, it also represents only my past. Doubts still plague me. Who am I to decide to discard all my achievements, even my ego, that I might lead my thoughts out of the land of limitation?

"Who am I to defer my ego so as to free my thoughts from materiality?"

Look within...

The stars again. The stars are talking. Or am I growing weary? And deranged? Perhaps I've been working too hard.

Look within...

I am plagued by thoughts that rebel against my inner hunger. They persecute me. They suck the life out of my veins. Rebellion seethes within me. My body, my ego, my pride, all demand their rights.

"I am..."

...that I am. And thou shalt have no other gods before me.

I must have made some sort of noise out of the ordinary, because my Friend is hovering just over my head. He seems quite comfortable suspended, horizontally about two feet above my own body. I can hardly see the stars through his outer contours. He's almost solid. Almost real. Yet he hovers as light as air but inches above me.

"What happened?" he asks me, his voice filled with concern.

"Can you not read my thoughts?" I almost bark. I feel deeply shaken. Shaken, squeezed, expurgated, as if someone had run me through an old-fashioned mangle. I also feel as though half of me were missing.

"Not when you are communing with your true self," my Friend says slowly. There is a new colour, a new tone to his words. If I didn't know better, I would say: a smidgen of respect.

"With my what?"

"With that within you that is beyond all limitations. It is also beyond the reach of thought."

"Thoughts have limitations?"

"Thoughts are the executive power of your will. They create reality except the one that is limitless above all others."

"And how do we experience those... those other realities?" I am pushing while the pushing is good.

"Direct perception," he says. Now there is a trace of jealousy in his voice. "It originates from your source, from where you really are. Your true self. Your 'I am that I am'. You must have stumbled upon a sudden realization."

I let that sink in. And then the images that swept me come back as fragments of memories. "So I was..." I have no idea what I was.

"You were Moses. As in the Exodus minus the symbolism. It must have been tough."

Is my Friend feeling sorry for me? Surely, ghosts, especially those that are mirrors, don't feel.

"Don't you?" I see that he has amply regained his power to read my mind. "I feel what you feel. I hurt when you hurt. Only I cannot follow you when you enter the mirror and emerge on the other side."

"It sounds like black magic."

I hear my own nervous laugh. It's not funny.

Actually, I suspect I already know what he means. On the other hand, I wonder what the rest of the Moses story means when stripped from the veils of symbolism. My Friend smiles. Suddenly, his mind is an open book to me. It is as though he and I were overlapping, melding into one.

"People in the desert are your thoughts." His words resonate within me. "It feels like the desert because you have no idea, as yet, where you are going. You are lost. You are walking in circles. Crossing the Red Sea represents overcoming your deepest emotions. The colour red stands for emotions, and crossing the sea represents a great change of consciousness. Only if you cross it, of course. Once firmly committed to giving up your ego, no past can catch up with you. Ego is a function of time. Later, Moses' inability to enter the Promised Land is the sad part. Promised Land is, of course, your destination. The state of Liberation. The state wherein your consciousness is no longer hampered by any preconceived ideas. Your, or his, inability to enter the Promised Land says that you are still deferring to a power outside yourself, to your old concept of god. Mostly out of fear. Few men dare to accept that they are gods. Anyway, these were the traditional symbols in those days. They were common knowledge."

"It's that simple?"

"The Torah had been written for simple people, conducting simple lives. In fact, for simple minds. Only later did the learned men engulf it with mysteries that don't exist in higher realities. On the other hand, that is why the scriptures survived this many years. People, particularly the doctors—theologians of various religions—didn't quite know what to twist beyond all recognition."

I find myself at my condo. I must have had the need to escape the reality my Friend was unfolding before me. Just as Moses did, in his time. I couldn't quite absorb all that he was telling me. Somehow I couldn't go where my Friend couldn't follow.

There are fresh flowers on the coffee table. Daffodils. I can smell them just by looking at them. Judging by the light, it must be late afternoon. Ruth is alone, curled up on the settee. The CD is playing Mozart's Requiem. She must have been listening for a while. The *Confutatis* is almost over. Next is the *Lacrimosa*, perhaps our favourite. With the full choir. The *Lacrimosa* and the *Sanctus*. Sometimes we prefer the *Sanctus* because it is more joyful. People say that Mozart can lift you up to heaven. Not us. He brings heaven down to us. We remain in heaven long after the disk is finished. I know it by heart. We always play it when in need of inner relaxation. Or detachment.

Or is it our hunger for exultation?

Ruth is reading. I listen in on her thoughts. I virtually lost all my reservations. I don't feel I'm peeking any more. I am concerned for her. I also miss her. No matter what wonders lie before me on the other side, I still miss her. Anyway, she's reading somebody else's thoughts. The poem is called *Exodus*. How appropriate, I think—I just went through the Mosaic struggles, and now this.

> He said Lo and behold, I give you Promised Land!
> As we listened, enchanted we bent low, elated.
> And hence we continue to stoop, ever hoping,
> to give thanks to Elohim, for this glorious right—
>   each and every morning, each and every night....
>
> And for two-score years, we circled blowing sands;

our feet bleeding, lost in endless desert,
holding on, stubborn, to promise that was given.
Praying, giving thanks, straining our sight—
    each and every morning, each and every night...

And we went on, wandering, from station to station,
hungry and thirsty, in search of Promised Land...
Never suspecting in our relentless plight,
that it can only be found in depth of our heart—
    each and every morning, each and every night.

So I am not alone. There are others—in other realities, other universes—that gained a grain of understanding of the same events. Even if bent to suit a poetic expression. On the other hand, isn't the whole Bible just a wonderful poem? Like the *Bhagavad Gita*, or the *Suras*. I remember the Sufis. They claim the Koran has seven levels of understanding.

I listen to the music and share her thoughts. Then she closes her eyes and just listens. I keep looking, keep listening. I love her face. I love everything about her. *Benedictus... Agnus Dei, Lux aeterna*. It is as though time had stopped in its ceaseless journey.

There is nothing one can say after that. If heaven there be, I'm sure Mozart earned its citizenship. Notwithstanding his youthful peccadilloes. They say that you cannot see the face of God and live. I wouldn't know. But there is no such law about hearing Him. And then, sharing Him with others. As Mozart did. Thanks, Amadeus. You truly are Beloved of the Gods.

M y Friend is looking at me as though filing away whatever he can read in my eyes, or draw out of my mind. His eyes wide, attention rapt, as I would be if I had discovered something new. Of course, I do so daily. Most things are new to me, though my Friend denies that. He insists that I am only reliving my past. Yet he looks as though he noticed something important. I can't resist posing him a question. It seems as absurd as it sounds.

"Am I god?"
"What do you think?"

"No one is god. God is not a thing. Or a someone. It is a force, an idea."

"You sure that's all god is?"

I have to stop and think. Moses had come to a conclusion. He'd said I am that I am. I am that that is within me. My infinite potential. And the becoming, all rolled into one.

"Love?" I ask. I must have sounded timid. "God is all…" I correct myself lamely.

"Isn't that pantheism?" My Friend is smiling. "Spinoza postulates that to define God is to deny God. Any definition implies limitation. 'Define' comes from Latin *definire*, to limit."

"How do you know all these things?" I am impressed.

"Because you do," he answers immediately. I forgot. Surely, he couldn't make up such things. Such statements. I must have been a clever cookie in one of my previous bodies. A know-it-all. I hope I wasn't obnoxious.

"No. God is not all things." I return to our previous discussion. "God is all. It is all I can think of and everything I cannot think of; other than the past, perhaps. That rests in materiality. God is a living god. In us. All of us."

"Just how many of us are there, John? Are there as many gods as there are people?"

"No, my Friend. There is but one God. Moses said it best. I AM." I think I got it right this time.

"Or I and my father are one…" my Friend murmurs.

For some reason I am almost sorry I've reached this conclusion. To what or to whom can I defer now? Am I not all alone? And then I perceive a glimmer of hope. The only condition in which I am not alone is in the state of continuous becoming. Don't the scriptures say, I am a living god? Which is more than I can say for myself right now.

"So I cannot just, you know, continue as I am?"

"Gallivanting through the past, pretending that you are creating it?"

"Doesn't sound right when you put it that way."

For some reason, there is a peculiar silence that seems to fill the immensity of the universe. Past universes…

"But don't all people create their own worlds?"

"Have you read Genesis, John?"

"Just the beginning. It, ah, seemed too long... I stopped when God fashioned me from clay."

"That's just symbolism. But you read far enough. Looking back, what is the very first sentence in that marvellous symbolic treatment of the creative act?"

I roll back my recorder. Actually, what I really do is read my Friend's mind. The two are becoming synonymous. It is getting easier every time I do it. It's like reaching into my own memory, which, according to him, it is. We humans tend to externalize many of our attributes.

"*In the beginning God created the heavens and the earth...* Is that what you mean?"

"The word 'God' is translated from the Hebrew *Elohim*. There are many versions of the original translation, but the one in most common use, the King James Version, uses the word roughly two thousand one hundred and sixty-five times. And each time it is translated wrong!" This is the first time my Friend is showing a smidgen of emotion. He sounds as though he cannot believe his own words.

"So what does this, ah, *Elohim* mean?"

"It means gods. Not god, John, but gods. Plural. In the beginning gods created heaven and earth. Each his own I AM, so to speak. I am and there is none other—within your own universe, that is. Within your own universe thou shalt not tolerate other gods before you. Greater than you are." He sounds the way I imagine Moses would sound.

Again silence stretches from one end of my universe to the other. It sounds as though in my own world, in the reality I create, I am to play second fiddle to nobody. It also means that there is no one to pass the buck to. Not so good.

"So, in a way, they were right..."

"If you accept that the scriptures are always directed at a single person, then yes. In this sense they were right. But in such a case, no one should dare to interpret the scriptures for anyone else."

"Doesn't say much for all the religions," I comment dryly.

My Friend doesn't say anything. I have never heard him criticize anyone—or anything, for that matter. For once he doesn't even comment on, or correct, my thinking.

So I am god. In my tiny-infinite universe, I am the sole representative of the infinite potential that apparently manifests through me. Only now, for whatever reason, I am stuck in this half-life, waiting to make a decision. What strange complex beings we are. I have to decide if I want to be a god. Do I have a choice?

"What do you think, John?"

And then I am alone again. Not even Ruth is here to share my worlds without end. Ruth, my Eve. My soul. My friend.

I suffer from an acute shock. That's right—ghosts, too, can be shocked. Or at least this ghost can. To me, the accident happened today; yesterday, at best. As my Friend says, all things exist contemporaneously. It is up to us to arrange them in a logical order. I already said that, but it bears repeating. Although I am now well aware that time really does not intrinsically exist, things or events pertaining to my physical body are still anchored in time. There must be some sort of connection between my body and me. I am still compelled to visit it, periodically, if only to regard it from outside. Ruth once said that there is a silver cord that connects the inner and the outer bodies. Well, I haven't seen any cords, but I do feel a tenuous connection. Whatever it may be, it can't be easy to break.

For now, the incipient universe and the accident are as close to me, or as far, as my attention span. This is why it came to me as such a shock when I learned, or realized, that my body has been in a coma a full four months. How did I know? The old folks are coming back from Florida. In fact, they are in Montreal already. I bet they'll visit my room any moment now.

Any moment...

This will kill Ruth—I hope only figuratively, although I wouldn't be that sure about it. Mother can be fairly taxing, and Clara is no mean second fiddle. Once they get hold of their Rosaries again, Doris and Brenda will go wild. With Ruth—these last few months—picking her visits carefully, they held the centre stage. Perhaps Ruth could get another attack and stay in the hospital for a while? Perhaps they could move her to the Lakeshore?

I see them all this very evening. Of course, to me, all evenings are these very evenings. No matter. Jane, George and Clara, all look disgustingly healthy. I'm so glad I wasn't there when Ruth met them. All the preliminaries of 'But how is he really, darling?' are out of the way.

As usual, father is relaxed, giving the gathering a sense of sanity. Mother and Clara both came in with handkerchiefs poised in their hands. They must have forgotten that, in the hospital, paper tissues are free. Not much else is. Except waiting. They still don't charge for waiting. For wasting your time, your becoming?

It makes me laugh.

They all feel guilty! All three of them are now making a concentrated effort to look at least a bit haggard, which isn't easy with their beautifully suntanned faces. They must have spent lots of time outdoors.

Ruth arranged for Dr. Morton to be present at the family reunion. We are lucky. It's a small room; and with our parents, Ruth, the doctor and Nurse Joan, there is standing room only. If my body had any cognizance, it would feel as though it were partaking in hospital rounds attended by a bunch of very ignorant interns.

"Thank you, doctor," Ruth says, "I thought it would be quicker this way."

I swear Dr. Morton winked at her. The son of a... actually, this is what Ruth wanted. To get it over with quickly. It cannot be nice, sharing your decrepit husband with a bunch of people. Even family.

"I understand, Mrs. Clarkson. We all have families."

At this surely innocuous assurance, Nurse Joan's cheeks assume an attractive rosy hue. A nice contrast with her pristine white getup. 'Not yet, dear doctor, but you'll have one, soon enough.' I swear to you, those were her precise thoughts. I wonder if she's pregnant already. I hold back from peeking involuntarily.

They all shake hands, Mother holding onto doctor's longer than necessary. Her other hand reaches for her eyes. She looks like a tiny Pavarotti accepting congratulations after a rendering of *Nessun Dorma*. The hankie hanging from her left hand must be two feet long.

"Are you sure John's all right, doctor?"

"As sure as we can be, Mrs. Clarkson. As sure as we can be..." He looks in near despair at Nurse Joan. She knows what to do. Gently but firmly, she takes Mother by the elbow and leads her to the chair at the head of the bed. Only then does Mother look at my body. I mean, at me. Body sounds like a corpse... which may not be that far from the truth.

"But what happened to his nose? Please, Doctor, did he fall out of the bed? How could you..."

"No, Mrs. Clarkson. Your son was involved in an accident."

Ruth begins to study the non-existent pattern on the ceiling. With two Mrs. Clarksons around, at least she can keep a low profile.

"An accident? You mean he fell out..."

"No, Mrs. Clarkson. A car accident. He's resting now."

"So we must keep quiet," Mother whispers confidentially. She seems to have advanced substantially over the last four months. The beginnings of dementia, no doubt. She has access only to her less recent memories. Poor Mother. Dear, dear, poor Mother. If only I could help.

And then another idea forces itself into my resisting mind. It states, quite categorically, that had I a body, I would be covered in cold sweat. 'Is she a god also? Is Mother a god even as we all are?'

The next instant I know that I am looking at her body, not at her... whatever it is that I am. Dear Mother. Why can't we get rid of our bodies when they no longer serve us? If what we really are has little, or even nothing, to do with the envelope that we temporarily inhabit, why are we so attached to it? It doesn't feel fair. I could ask my Friend, but I know what his answer would be. I have to work out some things on my own. Perhaps we all must. We can't always rely on priesthood to lead us astray.

Sorry, I didn't mean that. I am sure there are many priests who let us make our own mistakes.

Poor Mother.

Unless... unless dementia is a process of reviewing older memories rather as I am doing now, whilst in a coma?

By now Mother seems quite content on the chair, right next to my body's head. She is looking at me, probably conducting a silent conversation with me, so as not to wake me up. Only four or five months ago, we all played bridge. Ruth refused 'to waste time', but Mother, Clara and Dad contracted me for a few rubbers. Mother did make a few mistakes, but so did everyone else. Anyway, we didn't take bridge that seriously. We played a quarter a point. I mean a hundred points, of course. One could still lose ten dollars over the span of an evening. I was doing my best to lose to my mother. Unless she was my partner. Then I just bid my best. On one hand we actually bid and made a small slam in no trumps. Not bad for a mother-and-son team. Even Ruth came by to watch.

I switch my attention to the present.

Dr. Morton is giving Dad and Clara a brief outline of progress, or lack of it, since the last time they saw me. At least they seem in good mental shape. Dad is five years older than Mother, but does lots of exercise. Father always managed to keep himself in excellent shape. Mostly, he walks a lot. Miles each day.

"*Mens sana in corpore sano,* my boy," he'd tell me. Healthy mind in a healthy body. "You should exercise more, too," he'd admonish with a good-natured smile. He knew I was busy. Dad still cuts a fine figure of a man. He is almost my height, keeps his back straight. His hair, the purest white, just like Mother's, gives him a very distinguished look. The old-fashioned type. Elegant. Not at all like his son. Poor me. Not just in a coma, but not even distinguished.

"She loves you for what you are, not for what you look like," Dad once told me, after I had complained that I looked like his unsuccessful butler. He was referring to Ruth, of course. The next moment he felt embarrassed. "I don't mean that you do not strike a fine figure of a man..." He got lost in his attempts to extricate himself. He was a kind, gentle soul. Still is.

So we are all gods, I muse, floating just under the ceiling. Wouldn't it be fun if they could see me? Perhaps if I made some funny noises...

We all create our universes and rule over them with our will, imagination and, according to my Friend, our thoughts. *Be careful then... and purify, attune, and expand your thoughts...* This strange quotation keeps coming back to me. If we are to be careful, then we must be held responsible for our lot. We, and no one else. Imagine. Responsible for the whole universe. Perhaps we really are gods.

It strikes me that our unmanifested universe, our future, lies all coiled up, like the goddess Kundalini, like the countless dimensions of endless universes the theoretical physicists talk about, in our unconscious. We scan its infinite possibilities, unbounded ideas lying dormant within, always imbued with a predilection, with a tendency, towards fulfillment. This inexhaustible fount resting in our unconscious is characterized not only by infinite patience but, apparently, by infinite creative potential.

To those who are still dormant, our unconscious is generous. It sustains us for millions of years on the chance that one of Its progeny, Its beloved children, creations, will live up to his or her potential. Yes, infinite, or near infinite, immortal potential.

But It is also a jealous Source. It guards Its secrets dearly. Yet when a worthy individualization of Itself comes forth, It showers it with gifts beyond human understanding. It might be a gift of music, or painting, or sculpture, or an inexplicable gift of healing... there are so many gifts, all waiting, patiently, to be accepted.

Waiting to be accepted.

If this enigmatic Source resides anywhere, then surely it must be within our unconscious. Its Son, the Conscious Mind, is alone empowered with all judgment, all discrimination—with the responsibility of being the best I AM that it can be. And the wondrous aspect of our individualized unconscious is that it is indivisibly connected to the Universal Unconscious spanning beyond all time and space. We are truly inseparable. In fact, if we could only imbue this concept with real meaning, we would realize that we are always One.

Aren't we lucky?

"I assure you that we are doing all we can, Mr. and Mrs. Clarkson. Really, rest assured…"

"We know, Doctor, we know. There is only so much you can do. We know."

Father does his best to cheer up the good doctor. I told you, Dad is like that. It must have rubbed off on Ruth. His kindness. Dear Ruth. She is happy to stand by the door and wait for Mother and Clara and Dad to finish. Actually, Mother was already quite happy going single-handedly through a box of tissues. She must have dropped her handkerchief. Clara helped her a lot—with the box, I mean.

Nurse Joan brushes against Dr. Morton and surreptitiously points to her watch. The doctor must go. He excuses himself.

"Are you going already, Doctor? And what about John?" Mother wants to know.

***

20

I am Me

My Friend seems preoccupied. While he looks self-absorbed, there is a fuzzy feeling in my own head. The two could be connected. Evidently, there is something preying on his mind, as if he were a real person. Ghosts don't usually show their emotions unless their mirroring qualities require such from them. Not that I'm an expert on ghosts, but my Friend taught me a lot. Or, possibly, I am imagining all this and making the whole thing up. I, too, have been preoccupied lately. I feel as if I were about to make a decision that might prove irrevocable. I want to make sure it won't be something I will live to regret. That is to say, if I were alive, of course.

You know what I mean?

Anyway, at other times, I am beginning to wonder if any of this really matters. It seems to me that if everything has cause and effect, then, sooner or later, all will come to pass, anyway. And, secondly, I also wonder, again, if I really have a will of my own. A Free Will that has been proclaimed and affirmed by the Church over the ages. I'm referring to the Catholic Church, the stable force of my youth. There are moments when I am sure that I am being guided along a predetermined path to... I don't know where. If the universe is infinite, then that gives the powers that be quite a range of options. Perhaps that is why people invented heaven and hell. Destinations so esoteric, so inaccessible, that no man, woman or child could possibly get there on their own.

"Before the accident, your memories, the sum-total of your becoming, had been stored in your subconscious. Now, as you must have noticed, you are gaining access to your unconscious mind."

This comes out of nowhere. My Friend is not in the habit of making dogmatic statements. He usually stimulates me to look for answers myself.

"Is this what you are? My unconscious?" Other than confessing to being my mirror, my Friend has never expounded on any particular function. My probing has led me nowhere.

"I can only externalize your mind for as long as you are not fully aware of this fact."

"Like with god?"

My Friend looks at me with what I can only describe as admiration mixed with sadness. I have no idea why he ventured into this subject on his own. As I said, normally he doesn't originate discussions. At least, not discussions about himself.

"Yes. Like with god. The human species is the first to externalize their state of consciousness. Or god, for that matter."

"You are not suggesting that, ah, other animals also believe in god, surely."

"No, they don't. My point precisely."

"But why?"

I didn't know whether to laugh or shrug my non-existent shoulders. I can't resist thinking, 'Surely, you're joking!' before remembering that he reads my mind like yesterday's newspaper. Do ghosts joke? My mirror did after a night out with the boys. Only then it wasn't funny.

My Friend waits until I settle down. Mentally, I mean.

"Why? What is it about *Homo sapiens*? They imagine that they are not only superior to all other beings, but that they alone have the affinity to recognize that god manifests through them, and through them alone? Have you ever seen the joy in the eyes of a Dolphin? The worry in the gaze of a Chimpanzee mother? The anger in a Lion's growl? The pensive cogitation in an Elephant's stride? Must I go on?"

"I'm sorry. I thought we were created as a reflection..."

"Of what!" I've never seen my Friend so excited. The next instant he reverts to his old stoic self. "What do you think, John?"

"I think we agreed that there is only one incarnation, so to speak. That I am simultaneously in all that ever was. But you can't blame me, my Friend. It is not a concept that is easy to accept, let alone understand fully."

My Friend's eyes show concern akin to those of a mother. Human or chimpanzee. If he is my mirror, do I look that worried?

"When you feel lost, John, always go back to the first principle. Remember? *A lamp am I to you that perceive me. A mirror am I to you that know me.* I live in your heart, John. Not just in your eyes or ears. Or even your mind. You will always know when you are right."

There is a vague yet growing unease in me. I still don't understand it, but I detect an undefined, tenuous finality in the way my Friend talks. His words sound suspiciously like a goodbye. Or am I just hearing things? Surely, he and I are inseparable? We always have been. Well, for the last four months or so. But there is no time. Aren't four months as good as an eternity?

I feel a strange tugging. Something is pulling at me. Like a thread attached to all my non-existent nerve endings. It doesn't hurt, but it is quite irresistible. Like an itch you cannot reach.

I am looking at a white ceiling. I don't move, but with my peripheral vision I see the tops of pale green walls. Why do they paint walls pale green? Such a dull colour. Not like the colours in nature, or among the stars... the intergalactic clouds... why am I thinking like that? Why can't I move?

Where am I?

"Remember, you are never alone. Never." I hear the words from a great distance.

"I don't feel lost, my Friend. At least, not with you around."

Even as I murmur these words, I feel that I am more lost than I've been since I was born. "You are my Friend, aren't you?"

"You still doubt it?"

"No, I don't doubt it. I don't doubt it at all. But why do I feel such disquiet?"

"You've had a long rest. Isn't it time you contributed to the universe?"

"You mean, you are sending me away? Back to my body?"

There is a suggestion of laughter without much merriment.

"John, I cannot send you anywhere. You are god, remember? If you don't believe me, then listen to your prophets. Ye are gods, and all of you are children of the most High..."

"*But ye shall die like men, and fall like one of the princes,*" I add with some trepidation. Suddenly I can quote the psalms at random. I feel an inexplicable connection to the storehouse of knowledge within me. Or... or I am still reading his mind?

"No, John. That is precisely the difference. Gods don't die like men. Men do. Gods don't die at all. It depends on whom you equate yourself with. It's your choice. It is always your choice."

"You have drifted a long way from home, John. It is time to go back." Again I register just a smidgen of sadness. I hope my destination is not pointing down and uncomfortably hot.

"From heaven?" I murmur hopefully.

"That's funny, John. Heaven is a state of consciousness. It is always waiting for you, wherever or whenever you are."

If I could breathe, this would be the time to take a deep breath.

"You really mean it?"

"Great mystics have always taught that heaven is within you and without you. Admittedly, the Christian theologians got it all muddled up. Not that others have done much better. They state, quite unequivocally and clearly, that god, the father, is in heaven. So far so good. They also all seem to agree that god is omnipresent. It follows that heaven is omnipresent also, lest god would have to step out of his abode and contradict them. Their limited consciousness couldn't reconcile the two. They are too firmly anchored in dualistic reality. They forgot that their true nature is, temporarily, in this world, but it is not of this world."

I feel almost sorry for the learned theologians. I am also glad that I never attempted to explain such a thing to anyone. I wonder if Ruth has it right. I suspect that Ruth has most things right.

"Now it follows, that since one can only encompass the infinite with one's consciousness, that must also be the place where god abides, got it?"

I nod. It still depended on what God is.

"Spinoza was right, John. We have already discussed this."

"So whatever I accept as God is my God?"

"*I am the servant of My servant's image of Me.* Remember? Jalaludin Rumi is also right."

"*… your thoughts are My House.* Yes, I do remember. It is a strange axiom to live by. In a way, I must virtually create my own god…"

And then it strikes me that my Friend refers to Rumi in the present. How come, I ask him.

"Because he is. The world is."

"Yes… but…"

"John, Rumi is. Don't you remember? Gods are immortal."

I see a man carried high on people's shoulders. It is my funeral. My heart is filled with joy. Members of five different faiths follow my bier. I feel I'm not worthy of such an honour. No one is. Yet this is the first Sebul Arus. The Night of Union. We are one.
I am glad my life wasn't wasted.

"I r-r-remem-mber…" I practically whimper. The vision feels as if it were taking place right now... right here.

So now you know. Ghosts stammer. Anyway, I am back. The present of the past is submerged in the present of the Now. We are discussing the images of gods we are all creating in order to give us, to give ourselves, a purpose in life.

"Isn't this what all people and all religions always did? Create gods in their own image? One can hardly compare the god of the Old Testament to the god of the New, can one?"

His voice sounds farther and farther away. Also his contours are losing their definition. He is becoming more transparent.

"So they didn't stray so far from the truth, after all."

"I am the truth."

I finally understand that heaven is such an exalted state that I cannot hope to embrace it with my mind. Perhaps with my consciousness? A state of raised consciousness. Such as Moses found on the top of Mount Sinai. It seems to lie beyond words, beyond sensual appreciation. Yet, at the same time, it means different things to different people, regardless of in whose image they are created.

"Never forget, John. You are the sole creator of your reality. Surely, you know that now." This wasn't a question. "Remember, John. All realities you've visited emerged from your mind. Mind is the creator. It is that which brings the potential into the manifestation. All realities already exist. Those you already brought out, and those you will bring out throughout eternity."

I am completely immobilized. I cannot see. Somebody put great weights on my eyes. My arms are held in a vise of iron. My whole body is clamped in a satanic straitjacket. What the devil is going on? I can hear voices. Dimly. They sound familiar.

"...hail Mary full of grace, the lord is with thee, blessed art thou among..."

It is very monotonous. It goes on and on.

My God! I'm inside my body!

Let me out!

I mustn't panic. I feel I can't breathe, yet a tube supplies my lungs with air. Of course. I've seen it from the outside. I also recognize the voices. It's the Praying Mantis. My cousin, Doris. Doris the stick. How nice of her to come. She's not such a bad sort. Not really. Perhaps a little boring.

"...holy Mary mother of god..."

That's the Scorpion. She seems set on automatic. They both are. I remember when she tried to help me when I got her baggage out of the car, the day she arrived from England. She must have thought I was her personal porter. She loaded me up with three bags. She nearly broke my arm. Funny how some memories linger on.

"...pray for us sinners..."

Yea, you do that, cousin. I wonder why so many people are so obsessed with being sinners. And why do they equate mumbling repetitive words with praying? Wouldn't they be better off admiring the beauty of creation? It's all around us. In every tree, every flower, in a single blade of grass. We are surrounded with beauty. I wonder why I cannot hear Ruth. Then I remember. She's avoiding my two wonderful cousins like the plague. I must speak to her about that. They really aren't so bad. Especially if you like insects. I remember. Insects aren't so bad, either.

Only I can't see. I am stuck in this...

It is coming to me. This time I take it more calmly. I am stuck in my own body. The weights on my eyes are my eyelids. Is this some sort of nightmare?

Friend?

I am alone. Alone with those people.

"...and in the hour of our death..."

You don't die, stupid. No one dies. You are all immortal. You are gods. You...

Are we all immortal? *All* of us? Don't you have to come alive before you can live forever? *Friend?*

What's the use... I know that even my lips aren't moving. I can sense three people present. Don't ask me how. I just can. There is Doris, Brenda and—I strain my olfactory equipment—I haven't used it for a while. It's Francine. Nurse Francine. She's watching me. Isn't that what Dr. Morton had told her to do?

I must try to blink. Just for the hell of it, to see if she'll notice. I'm beginning to relax. Then I tighten my muscles as hard as I can. It seems a completely abortive effort. I can't even move my eyes under my eyelids.

I am... I'm in a coma.

I am in a coma!

This is ridiculous. The memories inside and outside the body are completely different. Most of the time. I remember being an insect, but I forgot that my body was in a coma. Well, now you know. So what are you gonna do about it? You think I am faking? You try remembering that you're decrepit when you can cross eons of time and millions of light-years in less than a blink of an eye.

I try screaming. You know? With closed mouth, through my teeth. Even I can't hear myself. If only I could see myself from without. I mean, to regard my body from outside, the way I used to. I could see if anything moves. Apparently not. I can be in or out but not both. I don't see why. I seem to have done it before. Some cat in Africa and... a goat? A gazelle. A beautiful gazelle. Perhaps I can learn. Didn't others succeed? Anyway, didn't my Friend say that I am omnipresent?

Amigo! Now is your chance to prove it!

I hope he can hear me. I'm screaming as loud as I can. My
Friend must have taken a day off. Didn't he say he's always with
me? Surely, he wouldn't have said that just to cheer me up? After
all, he's my mirror, and I wouldn't say a thing like that to a mirror.
I mean... I have no idea what I am talking about. Silently. Not in
jest. I mean, it's not as if it were funny.

I can't move!

Silence. Within and without. As in heaven. Except for the Hail
Marys. I hope we don't have to pray in heaven. I mean with God
being right there, couldn't we just talk to Him? Very funny. I'm
just kidding. Only myself. Nobody else can hear me. Hey, don't
they put such people away? People who talk to themselves?

Only if they expect an answer...

That's his voice. I swear I could hear him. Right here, in my
head. This is awful. It's enough to make a grown man cry.

"Zees ees Nurse Francine. Ee asked me to call eem."

I like her voice. She's not at all monotonous. Not like buzzing
insects. Hey, they stopped, too. Francine sounds like a breath of
spring. I know, I've seen her, but her image is not clear. That's
right. I'd seen her on the other side. From the other side. I wonder
if she's cute in real life. Her accent is.

Real life? You must be kidding!

"Docteur Morton? Eet ees Francine. Meester Clarkson just
cried. No, not loud. I mean a tear came out of ees eye."

This is no fun. I can't hear what Dr. Morton is saying.

"Yes, of course, Docteur. Eet ees steel zere. No, I weel not
wipe eet away. No, of course not."

I can't believe what I am hearing. I have my suspicions. My
Friend really is still around. Thanks, Friend. You know something?
Gratitude is a wonderful feeling. It makes you feel good all over.

Suddenly I open my eyes. I can move my arms and legs. I'm
free again. Or dead. I wish I could be sure.

I am home. For a fraction of an eternity I missed my hammock. I
smile to the pines, to the buds about to burst forth with new life
on the maples; the snow is almost gone. It tries hard to hold on to

the deep furrows dividing the fields. A warm, gentle gust brushes my non-existent cheeks. Funny, how I can still feel it. There is a breath of spring in the air.

I am happy again.

My mind wanders in that lazy, relaxed way it does when suspended between the two pines. I wonder who came first—my Friend or myself. If he did, then what was he reflecting before he met me? After all, in the beginning I was nothing. Not a thing. He couldn't reflect the whole universe, could he? Frankly, I don't think I'll ever know who or what he really is. I'm just very glad I met him, face to face.

There are so many things I still want to ask him. Important things. Some important only to me. As for instance, I'm still trying hard to reconcile the concept that the Brazilian tribe of bow-wielding primitives, Einstein and Dubya Bush coexist in the same instant of eternity. And if they do... why. Why do they exist at all? I try to visualize Bush with a bow and arrow. Bush slinking in bushes. On the other hand, I'm awfully glad Albert was around. Still is, according to Friend. I like his parallel lines—those meeting in infinity. Remember? So many questions... Or if I decide to stay here, will my partners be all right without me? I don't want them weighing on my conscience for eternity. Ever assuming I have a choice, of course.

"You always have a choice."

Friend?

So he's still around, it's just that I can't see him. I hear him in my head, as clear as a bell. What he just said sounds suspiciously like free will; so, for now, I choose to ignore it. He probably means that I have a choice within my sphere of operations.

"Hi, Friend. I meant to ask you before, will my partners at BCD cope financially without me?"

I feel a stirring within me. "Weren't you always?"

"Yes, but I am worried about them."

"That's very kind. But you know that money is liquid. It flows wherever it is most needed. Think of it as a manifestation of universal benevolence. Not something invented by the Wall Street traders."

"You're kidding. Money—benevolence? I thought it's the root of all evil."

"There is no evil—or, at least, it is not real. Money is what enables one to pursue that which one should pursue. To pursue the purpose for which one is born. No, money is not evil even in the human sense of the word. What is harmful, however, is unearned money. Such as inherited or derived from commodities that are unearned."

I must have looked at him with surprise in my eyes.

"Such as crude oil or gold or raw diamonds," he explains. "Not when you earned the money and bought the stock, only..."

Momentarily my Friend hesitates. I sense that he is discussing matters he's never discussed before. He resumes with renewed confidence.

"In countries where crude had been found, the incentive for men to work, to be creative, has been enormously undermined. Men have a tendency to be intrinsically lazy. Basically, if we do things right, life is too easy. We can blame the generosity of the universe for that, I suppose. Men often think they should live by their wits, not by their inherent talent. That is why we are here. In dualistic reality. To learn to do better. To make the reality of becoming a better place than we found it. If you don't have sufficient funds, then you are most certainly doing the wrong thing with your life."

"An awful lot of people are not doing the right thing..."

"Precisely."

"But why?"

"Mostly lack of courage. They fear pursuing their dream. It's the fear of the unknown. But also insufficient faith in the omnipresent benevolence, as well as a misplaced sense of duty. Whoever is fulfilling his or her purpose is always enabled to do so. Perhaps not always in the way they expect."

"So we don't have to worry about money?"

"You don't have to worry."

"But money gives you freedom, independence."

"You have money. Do you have freedom, independence?"

"That's unfair." I think that was his sense of humour. "What about the communists?"

"Communists had the right idea at the wrong time in their development."

"You don't say!"

"Look, John. Jesus never had a penny. He never worked for money, either. Yet he fed thousands of people at a time. Sai Baba never had a job. He built state-of-the-art hospitals. Doesn't that tell you something?"

"If we can manufacture reality, then we can manufacture the reality of wealth, is that it?"

"Close enough. If communists could have pulled fish and bread out of thin air to feed thousands, or in their case millions of people, then they would have had the right system for living."

"You mean this can really be done?"

"It's a lot easier than creating a universe."

"So capitalism is also all wrong?"

"It is not a question of right or wrong. You must step beyond duality. For the United States, at their present stage of development, capitalism is probably the best solution to give equal opportunity for their citizens to evolve. It teaches responsibility, courage and faith in one's own potential. There are many good things about it."

"But it's not the real thing?"

I always thought that the success of capitalism is directly proportional to the amount of greed generated. Of course, there are as many 'advanced' people among the capitalists as there were, once, among the communists. About one in ten thousand.

"Look, John. How often did you spend hours burning the midnight oil, poring over your designs, plans, just so that you could get some money for it?"

"Don't be silly. I work because I love my work. You know that!"

"And money flows to you as a by-product of your work. Almost like a fringe benefit. As I can see it, your main reward is the opportunity to be creative, am I right?"

Isn't he always? There is one other thing. He is right that, on closer examination, I already knew the answers he's just supplied me. I remember reading Adam Smith, a Scotsman, who apparently had the right idea at the beginning of the 18th century. He wrote that: 'The natural effort of every individual to better his own condition... is alone, and without assistance... capable of carrying on the society to wealth of a nation.' No crude, no gold—just man's effort. I wonder whose friend Smith was. Or rather, who was Smith's Friend?

But why is it so difficult to face oneself in the mirror? What is it that we are ashamed of? Is it because we could do, or be, so much more than we are?

It is becoming abundantly clear that my Friend has been right from the very beginning. For some reason, we all seem to have a distorted view of ourselves. Every one of us. We also believe that we need guidance, help, advice to keep us on the straight and narrow. But why? If we are gods, isn't the truth within us—there for the asking?

"You are the truth." Again his voice reaches me from afar. These are precious moments.

Hadn't somebody already said that? Someone we are supposed to emulate? I strongly suspect he was not referring to our physical bodies.

I know it's coming. I know now that the closer I get to my physical body, the harder it will be to contact my Friend. Oh, he'll be there, all right, I know that now; but unless I learn to still my mind—I mean, to really relax—it will be of no use. It would be like people praying and expecting god or some saints to hear them and then do things on their behalf. It seems when people pray, they always talk but seldom, if ever, listen.

Once more, I'm observing my two visitors from the outside. You know what I mean. Funny how they talk in whispers in my room. Except when praying. It's as though they were afraid to wake me up. Isn't this precisely what they want?

Well, not my cousins, perhaps.

My mind wanders back to my previous meandering. I gaze at the two ladies dispassionately. I think everyone is given all the chances they deserve. We all get the guidance, help and advice we need, if only we learn to listen. I had all the opportunities anyone could hope for. I even stayed in a coma for more than four months. No one can expect any more. I got as lucky as one can get.

"Thanks, Friend. Even if you don't answer, I want you to know that I am grateful. Really grateful."

I don't see him anymore. Strange how quickly I began taking him for granted. I just opened my eyes, and there he was. It helps to be in a coma. I look down at my body. Such repose. If only I could achieve such a detached state when in it. Actually, for the moment I was in it, I felt stifled.

They are going now. Filing out as from a church crypt. Silently, with long faces. I wish they would smile more. I am not dead.

"I am not dead yet," I call after them.

I'm back at the knoll. It's lonely, here, this time of the year. Lonely and sleepy. It's all right when my Friend is here, but on my own, well, it's a bit lonesome. Nature is still asleep. I wish...

I am surrounded by trees with gloriously rich, green leaves that seem to have sprung overnight. Or at least since I was here last. Or seconds ago. Take your pick. Stretching in all directions is equally as green a prairie, speckled with wild flowers. Cone-flowers are most abundant, with black-eyed susans blooming just beneath them. Rattlesnake masters rise mysteriously between masses of yarrow, showing off their fern-like leaves. As rich a tapestry as even Ruth could imagine. I wish she could see it. Even as I stare at the new surroundings, a gust of wind moves the field in gentle waves of multihued living colour.

I wonder what god created this wondrous reality. I know this must be a springtime from my past. Although only the shooting stars can bloom in early summer, yet all other flowers are also spread before me, as though by magic. Divine benevolence? I have no idea what season this is. I cannot rev fast forward into the future. But spring is spring, by any other name, at any other time—though, I assume, all seasons are contemporaneous in heaven.

I also wish my Friend could see it. Perhaps he does. Perhaps he's now looking through my eyes. Aren't we one?

"What's mine is yours," I whisper. I sense a smile inside me. It is like smiling at myself, only on the inside.

I am glad I can share this with my Friend. After all, no one gave me as much as he did. He opened my eyes, my ears; he showed me the universe and the diversity of creation. Yet all this diversity is indivisible from the whole. He was my guide, my guardian angel, and as his name spells it out so eloquently, my Friend. Two souls in a single body.

That's why I shall have to go back. I must give my Friend a chance to witness becoming. To be a living god, not just one waiting in abeyance watching his past. No matter how glorious. The question is when. Visiting inner universes takes place outside the confines of time. Theoretically, I can spend eons out here before going back. Earthside, only seconds would pass. On the other hand, it does not seem to work like that. There is that silver cord Ruth talked about that keeps me connected to my body. And my body is aging, or, at the very least, it is subject to increasing bedsores. There may also be consequences arising from stagnation in cardiovascular circulation. Dr. Morton as good as said it a month ago. And here, the rate at which I can absorb knowledge seems affected by my partial presence in the physical body.

No matter, I'm sure it will all work out. Some day. Here, there is still so much to learn.

I can now see, for instance, how the idea of a guardian angel crept into the various religions. Someone may have begun speaking after falling into a coma. They called them visions, in those days. They didn't have the vocabulary to explain more of their true nature. I think Rumi and the *Baghavad Gita* came closest, but only if translated by a poet, not an expert on religion. I am sure Ruth knows of many other sources. That's why I need her so much. I need her in my becoming. Rumi understood fully the reality that lay beyond duality. Beyond the doing right and the doing wrong.

What a wonderful person he must have been. I'm sure Ruth would have loved him, even as I do. Isn't love what makes us one?

***

21

Armageddon

People got it all wrong. We all did. About Armageddon. I can't regress to there, as such a place doesn't exist. It's an imaginary place, and we make battle there. A place where battles have been fought many times throughout history. Battles on the hills of Megiddo.

Megiddo means, simply, a place of God. Hills, in the Bible, always symbolize raised states of consciousness. We fight there a spiritual battle, which my Friend tried so hard to illustrate for me in Kurukshetra. Arjuna never killed anybody. He destroyed his weaknesses—some very close to his heart. Like 'members of his own family'. We fight such battles daily. Not surprising, considering we're immortal yet continue taking part in becoming. Those of us who do not recognize our own spiritual nature do not fight there. Those who are still not awakened are recycled on the Wheel of Awa Gawan. The Wheel is set on automatic. For the rest of us, some battles are tougher than others. Some are as good as final. Those last are fought when the victor moves on to realities which we can neither dream of nor imagine.

Some say, there is an infinite number of realities. An infinite number of universes. Our scientists are also beginning to think so. Saint Paul claimed to have met someone suspended in third heaven. He wasn't sure. Whatever the truth, sooner or later we are faced with two choices. To stay or to go. Only those of us must decide who are given a choice. You will know when it happens to you. Mine happened today. Now. I have been struggling for the last few months. First, I had to find out what I am fighting for. In our human bodies, we are quite ignorant. Few of us know how to use our brain. I know that I didn't. Mostly, I still don't.

I always thought that a day would come when I'd achieve an illustrious state, such as attained by saints or great prophets, and thereafter I would move on, bodily or otherwise, through the Pearly Gates, to abide, ever after, in a state of inexplicable bliss. Doing what, precisely? Well, actually, nothing much. Just being, I suppose?

Just being. Basking in the sublime light of the Almighty. For ever and ever and ever and...

How sad.

The preachers are right about one thing. Whatever it is that we shall be doing will continue for ever and ever. And ever. Except that there is no time. My Friend taught me that. As of now, I finally believe him.

As I see my body resting peacefully, lacking nothing, basking in the meticulous care of the Lakeshore Hospital medical staff, nothing seems farther from the truth. A static existence is as close to non-being as anything man can imagine.

As in heaven?

This is not part of the plan. Or, to put it bluntly for the advocates of various religions, if God wanted to do nothing forever, He would not have created man. He wouldn't have individualized His consciousness.

Or else, we can put it the way my Friend taught me: God is a living God.

And this brings me to Armageddon.

Many great battles have been described in many great Scriptures. Always wrapped in a veil of symbolism, lest the great truth be trampled under our feet. Neither cast ye your pearls before swine, remember? After a near-eternity of rubbing imaginary shoulders with my Friend, I can quote various scriptures with the best of them. I can even take a stab at attempting to explain some of them, although my explanation might well apply only to me.

Pearls are nuggets of wisdom. Wisdom is a perfect blend of knowledge and love. They, these two nuggets, have their being, they live, in our mind—purify, attune, and expand our thoughts or, to put it more mundanely, we ought to be careful what we wish for. Believe me, there are great herds of swine just waiting to pounce on our pearls and smear them with their insatiable taste for death.

There are no restrictions on how we use our knowledge. There are consequences, but no restrictions.

And that's the problem with my Friend. He opened my eyes to the knowledge within me and left me to make my own decisions. It's my personal Armageddon.

I am certainly not a preacher, nor do I ever intend to be one. But I'll share with you my own experience. I still don't know what will happen. The future is as inaccessible to me as it is to you. This, however, is the only decision I can make that will affect my future.

As I've already mentioned, it's not the dying that's the problem—it's the coming alive. If only people got preoccupied half as much with life as they are with death, the world would be a very different place. It seems that many decisions we make, on earth, are motivated by our fear of death. As if such a thing were real.

Thank you, Friend, for opening my eyes.

My body has now been lying inert for about four months. Until now, I had not been aware that it was up to me whether I shall return to it or not. Gods have their privileges. I can reject this particular physical enclosure and wait to be whisked into, hopefully, a body with a straight nose, better shaped eyebrows, and a physique that did not suffer from years of relative neglect. The absence of a half-dozen bedsores would be an added bonus. To take advantage of the second alternative, I'd have to sever my silver cord. Yes, it is up to me. Never forget, we are gods.

Think about it.

My other option is to remain here, indefinitely. Having been freed from the obvious restrictions that a physical body places on me, I have the universe at my disposal. Perhaps this is why evolution progresses at such a slow pace. People who 'die' might well choose to remain in Limbo, in a state of suspended animation, for as long as they possibly can. I am sure that the more advanced they are, the greater their past, the less is their need to enrich it still further. Frankly, I can't complain about my own. I have touched the verges of infinity, and there is enough for me here to spend the next few eons this side of the Great Divide. I am sure that, prior to their last return, the great mystics, such as Lao Tzu, Buddha, Jesus,

Moses, Rumi and a few dozen others, didn't have to return to their physical form at all. Infinity was theirs to explore, virtually forever.

Yet they did.

We have written records of such. "Greater love hath no man than this, that a man lay down his life for his friends." I always thought this referred to dying. But this is not what all the various scriptures are about. All of them deal only with life. When a man lays down his life for another, he is not leaving his body. He is giving up life eternal, for a spell, to join his friends. Hopefully, to tell them about the real life, the real freedom. To tell them about the glorious state of Being.

To remind them that they are gods.

I think Ruth knows that. I think she will not even blame me if I choose not to lay down my life and wake up. No one can possibly imagine how great is the sacrifice of those who willingly return to physical life. To becoming. Some call them *Bodhisattvas*. Imagine. You're immortal. Almighty. Yes, you are god beyond any limitations imposed on you by time or space. Now you must decide if you are capable of giving this up. It's not like those who already have cut their silver cord through some sort of physical abrasion. Like a bullet or a deadly disease. They earned their stay in Bardo or wherever they'll experience the moment of infinity. By some fluke of fate, I was given a choice.

I wish I hadn't been.

Yet... I miss Ruth. I miss her badly. Is she my angel? Or is she the devil that tempts me with the joys of sensual pleasures? Believe me, Ruth, darling, even your physical beauty would not balance the scales. You are competing with gods...

Dear Ruth... beautiful as you are.

Two green-coated men I'd never seen before enter my room together with Nurse Joan. They roll in a stretcher on wheels, similar to the one on which they brought me here a few million years ago. The three of them effortlessly transfer my unresisting body onto the stretcher and wheel me out of my cubicle, carting all the paraphernalia with them.

I follow them with interest.

The dull, pale-green and cream corridor takes us to the oversized elevator, then to the third floor. The sign on the door says Radiology. Magnetic resonance imaging. That's what MRI stands for. I know, I've designed hospitals. Three of them.

I think they had used the machine on me before. It is the most accurate diagnostic technique available to assess the presence of tumours, developmental and vascular anomalies, such as aneurysms, stroke, disease of the pituitary gland... there are a number of other disorders. I peek into Nurse Joan's mind. Nurse Joan carries quite a little library in her pretty head.

They get hold of the sheet I'm lying on.

"On three," she commands, "one and two and three..."

I know the routine. On 'three' they lift my body and transfer it onto the long table. For a moment a number of plastic tubes are left dangling behind my body like vines in a tropical rainforest. Why not? I bet my body feels like a vegetable.

"I hope he doesn't suffer from claustrophobia," one man says. Nobody laughs.

I take another peek into Joan's mind. I know how to install MRI equipment, not how it works.

...unlike conventional x-ray, I ignore that, ...and CT scans, MRI does not depend on radiation. Good, I have no desire to develop a radioactive head. I have problems enough. ...radio waves are directed at protons, in a strong magnetic field...

Ouch. I don't trust scientists playing with protons or any other particles. Not in my head.

All my digging into her mind does not reveal why they are digging into my brain. Since Dr. Morton already admitted to Ruth that they have no idea what coma is, I wonder if they have any idea what they are looking for.

"What, no straps and bolsters?"

It's the joker again. This time Nurse Joan gives the man a dirty look. She doesn't really appreciate others' joking about her patients. Even those in a coma. She knows that some comatose patients can actually hear what is being said.

"No, Gaston. But you might put one on your mouth," she murmurs.

The guy actually blushes. It could be either embarrassment or anger. I don't bother to peek. Why should I care? He's probably new here.

As the table begins to slide my body into position, everybody leaves the room. From my inimitable vantage point, I see Joan and a technician outside the glass partition. Moments later they return, move my body minimally and do the same exercise again. A whole sequence. They are really thorough, these guys. In the meantime I have learned that Dr. Morton is not just a physician but a trained radiologist. I suppose all specialists must be physicians first and foremost. Bully for me. It seems I am getting the big guns. Actually, he was with me from the start. Nurse Joan also specializes in radiology.

Later they push my trolley to another room. Again, I peek into her mind.

...computed tomography... detects bleeding, brain damage, skull fractures, leaking aneurysms, blood clots...

So that's what CT scans are all about. I thought they'd already done it all. Can there be latent bleedings? What I really want to know is whether my body can wake up without agreement on my part. Do I have anything to say in all this? According to my Friend, I cannot affect anything in the 'real' world. But what about 'disaffect'. What about not playing the game? I peek again.

...numerous x-ray beams and a set of electronic x-ray detectors rotate around... measuring the amount of radiation being absorbed...

You crazy? You want my whole body to absorb radiation? Why don't you just drop an A-bomb on me and be done with it. Or I could pop in to Hiroshima or Nagasaki on the day the Yanks dropped their little toys. This is a hospital, for God's sake.

Of course, I wouldn't take my body with me. I'm not nuts.

I don't want to know any more. Whatever they are doing is a great argument for not returning to my radioactive body. I wonder if they asked Ruth's permission to do those CAT scans. They sound positively dangerous to my health.

It takes me a little while to accept that I cannot really boast about my health. Even before the pothole, I was, according to the local experts, in a bit of a mess. I also wonder why, all of a sudden,

I feel so possessive about my decrepit body. It's not as if it were doing me much good, is it?

The faster I get out of here, the better I'll like it. I wish I could talk to my Friend.

I am the only one swinging on my hammock. Actually, I'm not even swinging. I just lie there, stretched out, feeling sorry for myself. I vaguely recall stretching out before, my arms reaching over thousands of light-years. Or was it millions?

I really am lonely. Man is not meant to be alone. Isn't that why God created Eve? I know, she's just a symbol for Adam's soul, for his subconscious, but still, she must have helped Adam a lot.

I am beginning to philosophize. Presumptuous of me. Regardless of what Friend claimed, I don't know enough to share any pearls of wisdom. Not of my own knowledge. This is still only the first day of the rest of infinity. I lie back and start to amuse myself by changing the colour of the leaves. The reason I can do this is because the knoll is not real. It's an illusion. I go through four seasons in quick succession. You won't believe how beautiful maples are at this time of year. In autumn, I mean. I know it's spring out there, in the other world, but here I am king. I am the master of my domain. Two pines, three firs and half a dozen maple trees. I adjust the colour of the sky to enhance the contrast of the red and gold foliage. Then I pass the sunrays diagonally through the crowns. I'm in heaven. You can do the same if you close your eyes and relax. Just imagine. Sometimes it works.

I am fooling myself. None of this is real. I cannot do anything that will leave a mark even on the present. I create illusions, visions of the past, like a magician, with a sleight of hand.

I shut out the imagery. I cannot avoid it any longer. Napoleon had his Waterloo, I have my Armageddon. Only I cannot lose my battle. I must make the right choice, no matter what the cost.

I wonder what makes people go back to physical reality. What really pushes them over the edge? All my life I've worked like a slave. I know I enjoyed my work, but even so. Here I can get some rest. Have I not earned it?

And the firm. I set them up with a name associated with the best architectural designs in town. All they need do is maintain it. Surely, I shall have to retire sometime. How about a few years earlier? Frankly, all three of us have made enough money to live comfortably for the rest of our lives. As things are, I didn't even have time to spend any of that money. Too busy. Always too busy. Not that anyone held a whip over my head, but still. Haven't I done enough?

My parents are well set up with Clara in their duplex. They are comfortable. With winters in Florida they don't even have to put up with the Canadian climate. As neither do I, out here. In my private kingdom. If only Ruth were here. Even for a while. Perhaps we could then go back together... also, just for a little while? To say goodbye?

I change the trees back to the winter appearance I found them in, when I first got here. I imagine my Friend swinging on the other hammock, between the two slim pines. I see his image, but it's not him. It's just an image of a ghost. He lives only in my mind. He's not real. At least, not outside my mind. Nothing seems real anymore. Not even here. Not without him. He gave me an impression of life, of reality. Alone I am empty. Without substance.

I transfer to the Lakeshore. Ruth will be here any moment now. That's a joke—I am talking as if I were alive already. I'm talking about time. As the door swings open, I float just below the ceiling,

She's not looking very well. Tired? Her eyes look tired. Must be work. She is filling the gap I left behind with work. I shouldn't wonder she took on some more lectures. If I conk out, she could join the Carmelite Nuns. Or would she just meet someone with a nice country cottage? Somehow I don't like to dwell on this idea. On the other hand, she and Sister Wendy would make a hell of a team. Sorry, Sister, I mean a heavenly team. She'd also have to visit Clara and my parents on her own. She didn't bargain for that. On the other hand, I did not dig that hole in the tarmac. Bloody City. I wouldn't hire a single one of them in my office. Not one...

I don't have an office.

I don't have Ruth.

I am as good as dead.

And with a bit of bad luck, I'm radioactive. They should keep Ruth away from my body. She, too, might get contaminated. How lovely she looks...

I'm in charge. I am going in and out of my physical body at will. It's funny, in a way. I can also use dual presence. I am both in and out of the body. I forget that, wherever I am, I still cannot affect the reality of other people. I think I know why. Essentially, I'm still outside the confines of time. My in-and-out fluctuations last nanoseconds at most. At the longest.

While inside my physical body, I examine it in detail. What an astonishing miracle it is. No wonder it took millions of years to develop. It is constantly regenerating itself. Not just after a disease or an accident, but continuously. It is a wonder of engineering.

Each part has a prescribed function, working autonomously, yet it is also connected by an array of systems to other parts as well as to other systems. By yet another miracle, they seem to be coordinated. And there are many of them. The nervous and endocrine systems integrate various functions by means of trillions of electrochemical impulses per second. They not only coordinate the working of various body organs but also integrate them with a multitude of systems, all working in perfect harmony with each other. Musculoskeletal, circulatory or cardiovascular, immune, reproductive, integumentary, gastrointestinal, respiratory, urinary... which in turn have subsystems, all seemingly self-supporting, self-rectifying, self-maintaining. Just our immune system alone consists of the white blood cells, the thymus, lymph channels that integrate their function with the lymphatic system. The system also has an army of mechanisms to protect us from foreign invasion. Antibodies, cytokines and many others stand at the vanguard of our defense system. I'm glad I've been a physician in a number of my previous embodiments, or all this would be more like black magic to me. Believe me, our physical body already is truly magical. No wonder it takes years to get a medical diploma.

I am amazed at my own knowledge. My own mind reads like a medical journal. Nevertheless—we really are miracles of engineering.

Then there are what I can only call the sub-physical systems which the Hindus write about. I sense that within this sub-physical system are six chakras, wheel-like vortices, rising from the base of my spine to the top of my head. The seventh seems independent of my body, spinning over the top of my head. When I enter my body, these chakras show great activity, as though they were intermediaries at the nexus of metaphysical and biophysical energy. Ruth would love to see this.

It seems that there is so much more to 'me' than meets the external, physical eye. The same is true of my body as of the macro-universe. We are pinpoints of awareness, striving, often in vain, to get to know the universes in which we experience our becoming. Both micro and macro universes. And my Friend is right. As usual. These universes already exist. All we can hope for is to get to know them a little better. And, incredible though it may sound, both these universes are on the first day of the rest of the eternity of evolution.

I spend the rest of my presence examining my body in still greater detail. Each organ, each system, each cell hides wonders for me. I enter them, experience them by direct perception, then move on to my neighbour, a kidney or a liver, then float upstream through my cardiovascular system to my heart. In my brain I spend a fragment of eternity, yet it seems not enough. I linger on. It's good to have one's being outside time. I wonder if I'll retain any of this knowledge after I return to my body.

There, I said it. Not if but *after* I return to my body. My need for becoming has won. It wasn't my desire for Ruth. Not even my love for her. It is the need for becoming. It is like desire for life itself.

I am slowly regaining control of my body. When awake, we relegate the control of most of the physical functions to our subconscious, to knowledge inherent in every cell. Now, I must still take part in all this at the conscious level, which for now remains infinite. I am god. I cannot delegate. As I once said, the buck stops with me. I make adjustments. Millions of them. Billions. I really have neglected my body. I do them all on the verge of time. At that elusive divide where time and no time meet in seeming harmony. This is where saints perform their miracles. As I said, for a little while I am still god.

I go in and out of my coma. I remain motionless. I still have work to do. But I reach the stage of dual consciousness. I am ghost and I am body. Overlapping.

I continue to study, check and adjust every part of my anatomy. Then I examine my chakras. They are new to me. They take an extended study. Suddenly, like lightning from up above, I see it. It was not an act of my will that kept me in a coma these many months. It was Ruth. I told you she studies the inner workings of metaphysics.

Ruth, for reasons known only to herself, was convinced that I could not survive that car accident. Somehow she read it in the facial expressions or things left unsaid among the medical staff of the Lakeshore. When she was told that my body was in a coma, she was determined to keep me in the coma for as long as she possibly could. And all along I thought it was me. Perhaps Ruth and I really are one?

It was she who refused to let me go.

I rev back to the time Dr. Morton wanted Ruth to give her permission to disconnect my IV. It all comes back to me. She looks older, somehow. More mature? Determined? Nurse Joan doesn't appear her usual, controlled self. It's as if she were sharing a secret that she was not allowed to tell.

Only Ruth seems in perfect control. Cool. Unapproachable.

Dr. Morton is standing by the door, seemingly ready to escape. He looks worried, uncomfortable. Nervous? I dive into his mind again. I must search deep. It is just as I thought. My body was as good as dead. Somehow, Dr. Morton, an experienced physician though he is, does not have the courage to tell Ruth that I already am a vegetable. That to all intents and purposes, my brain waves are undetectable. Almost. They are, he thinks, inconsequential. I was so angry, so busy criticizing what I thought he might say, that I missed the whole truth. Ghosts, too, can make mistakes. We may be gods, but only in potential. We're not perfect.

Somehow Ruth refuses to accept it.

Since that day, Ruth must have worked on me at some psychic level. My decrepit body, slowly, very slowly, did the rest. Lately, the good doctor has begun to have hope mixed in equal measure with incredulity. Apparently I am almost unique in the annals of medical history. The nurses have begun to whisper among themselves about me

"It's Lazarus, I tell you. No kidding. The second Lazarus in history!"

The second Lazarus. I heard this in their minds before. I thought they were just kidding. I never imagined that they really meant it. I thought they were referring to a common garden-variety of coma—that all coma patients are virtually dead.

I'll show them!

I am straddling the two worlds. Fascinated by both, master of none. Without my Friend near me, without seeing his smiling face, some of the wind spills out of my sails. If Ruth were here, I'm sure this would change. With her we would have a few billions of years of sightseeing before us. We would forsake the future, but with her next to me, eternal present wouldn't be so bad. In fact, it would be a little like the religious concept of heaven. Eternal bliss. It would also be, as Italians say, *dolce far niente*. Sweet doing nothing. Carefree idleness. It may be heaven to some. To me it's just stagnation. I am a living god.

I have won my Armageddon. Or lost it, depending on your point of view. Theoretically, I should give Ruth a chance to join me here. But it must be her choice. I am willing to give up my holiday and start living again. To take on responsibilities, solve problems, add my twopence's worth to the advancement of humanity. Even if it only means designing the best architecture I possibly can. No matter what the effort. Regardless of rewards.

I am prepared to start becoming. Now.

***

22

Ruth and I

I've been doing it every night for the last seven nights. I think I am beginning to get somewhere. I cannot affect Ruth's brain waves, but there is some rapport with her subliminal mind, somewhere between alpha and delta waves. Remember, this is not at all like going back and reliving what we already have. This is crossing new ground altogether.

At first she didn't recognize me. So much has happened since my accident that apparently the memories, which I'd incorporated in my non-physical body, do not form part of my heritage. Not really, or at least even I lose touch with them. They are buried too deep. I mean, she thinks of me in terms that I thought of my Friend when I first saw him. Perhaps I was more shallow when she knew me, before that accident. Since then, however, I have become a true reflection of all that I ever was. Or at least, of what I experienced BP. That's Before the Pothole. There is still a barrier of knowledge between my Friend and me, but by now I am used to him. As for the remaining differences, well, I am still not that which, or who, he already is. I suspect that he is not just that which was, but that which is, and this means that he incorporates that which will be in a potential form. And such mental venture is still completely outside my capability. I suspect that it is more than just mental.

Back to Ruth. For now, I am a stranger to her.

The reasons I started my experiments were the problems she was having with my partners in my architectural practice. So far they treated my absence as a protracted holiday. Illness at worst. But there are no guarantees of recovery for people in a state of coma. They had to take legal steps. They offered Ruth the option of dissolving the partnership. It was intended to relieve her of carrying legal liability for work done by BCD Architects before my accident. In architecture, the liability is joint and several. This means that, should such be determined by a Court of Law, every partner can be held liable for total damages.

There was another problem. A physician must prove he's done the best he could. If a patient dies, he's not liable. Architects cannot merely guarantee the best intent; they must guarantee the result. If a building collapses, we are guilty—no matter how hard we tried to assure its structural integrity.

Hence my partners' offer.

If Ruth accepted the dissolution of our partnership, she would be left without a breadwinner. There are still many receivable accounts. The condo is paid up, and she is making a decent income on her own. She would be comfortable enough, but still, she deserves better. If I were to die, she, as the estate, might have possible legal problems. On the other hand, in case of death, we already have a dissolution clause in our contract; the liability would be null and void. Also, she would pick up a handsome insurance I carried, with her name on the top as the sole beneficiary. In the meantime, with me in a coma, she remains between the devil and the deep blue sea.

To cut the story short, the estate—Ruth—could be held liable for any mishaps that might happen in the office. We carry Liability Insurance, of course, but sometimes this might not prove to be enough.

During the last few nights, I have managed to develop a tentative rapport with Ruth while she's asleep. By the first morning, I sense that she treats our nocturnal *tête à têtes* as dreams. Dreams with someone she knows but cannot quite place as me in her memories. Exactly as I did initially with my Friend. Hence the problem. I cannot really be sure what's best for her. Why? Because she herself simply doesn't know.

Who could blame her?

This brings me to two possibilities. I must bring Ruth over to my side, or get back to hers. Or let her fall for that other guy—hopefully the guy she hasn't met yet. For all I know, I may be running out of time. I hate that. Anyway, I will not allow her to pay for my mistakes, if any. I decide to examine the first option. We had a discussion about suicide some time ago. In those days we were both avid readers of science fiction. Robert Heinlein, John Wyndham, Isaac Asimov, Stanislaw Lem, Arthur C. Clarke—there were dozens of them. Each was a superb writer with a flamboyant and unbridled imagination. Each, at one time or another, attempted to analyze the problem of immortality. Or at least of dying. In my early thirties, my bookshelves were full of their alternate universes. Those, and many other writers, have widened our view of the human equation. Anyway, we were trying to figure out if suicide could be acceptable under certain circumstances. We had both been brought up in the Roman Catholic faith, which didn't make our task any easier. I chanced upon that relevant day.

"You know, darling, we all commit suicide, don't we?" Ruth asks, but her tone does not really pose a question. It is a statement of fact. I choose to take it literally.

"Do we, honey? You're not serious?"

We are sitting on our tiny terrace, overlooking the distant Adirondacks. Through field glasses, of course. But even then, the naked-eye view is fantastic, the Scotch is great, and Ruth is by my side. Let me tell you, reliving is virtually as much fun as the original experience. And just looking at Ruth is reason enough to be here. Ruth still prefers sipping a deep red Merlot from Argentina to any cocktail or hard liquor, no matter how diluted. I'd left all my work in the office. I needed a break. To hell with work. I have a wife. Anyway, it's Friday. Ruth deserves me, I tell myself in all humility.

"It might take a while," Ruth continues. As usual, she ignores my casual remarks.

There is something festering in that beautiful head of hers that is not immediately apparent. This is why I am here, why I regressed in time to hear this very discussion in the here and now. I really am here, again, but only as an observer. As you already know, no matter how hard I try, I cannot change anything. Not even my own heartbeat. Of late, I have managed to maintain dual consciousness. I am completely within my body of some years ago, and I am also an external observer.

Now that I am here, I have a perfect recollection that on this evening, way back in the non-existent time, we'd been discussing the question of suicide. I forget why the subject came up, but it had something to do with all those sci-fi books we had both been reading.

"Do you intend to explain your thesis?" Again she manages to lose me somewhere along the way. On my rare evenings off, my mind tends to wander.

"Look, John," she leans over to me. "From the ancient Socrates through the Christian martyrs to Kamikaze pilots to the present-day Moslem suicide bombers, history is peppered with the glorification of the act of taking or, at the very least, risking your own life. Regardless of their beliefs, they all shared a single unifying factor." Ruth raises her glass triumphantly.

"I'll drink to that," I agree.

"Don't joke, darling, this is serious."

"Of course, sorry, darling."

I am not quite sure if the suicide, the unifying factor, or her Merlot is serious. However, I never argue with Ruth when she says she is serious, regardless of the cause. It might prove detrimental to my health.

We both take a sip.

"Socrates protected his beliefs. Buddha ate tainted rice so as not to offend his host. Kamikaze pilots, the Christians and the Moslems are promised first-class tickets to Paradise. No questions asked. It's not easy to get past Saint Peter, you know."

"Nor to satisfy seventy-two virgins," I murmur.

Luckily Ruth didn't hear me. I am sure she'll get to the point in her own good time. She seems distracted. I follow her eyes. She's studying the cumulus formations towards the west. They are convoluted as though trying to climb atop each other. It might rain tomorrow. No matter. We live tonight. Now.

"Such beauty," she whispers, after a moment of silence. Then she shakes her head.

"Are we not masters of our bodies?" I muse aloud, encouraging her to continue.

"That's beside the point. Anyway, it's an empirical argument that we cannot solve by didactic discussion."

Pity. I am sure my Friend would have a great deal to say on the subject if he didn't just ask what I think about it myself. Just as he began to open up, he—well, he more or less disappeared.

"You see, darling, it is all a question of cause and effect. All that the martyrs, the great philosophers, teachers or even mystics needed was to find a cause greater than themselves. This is why it's so terribly important to have a good cause. Otherwise we'd give up our lives for nothing. We'd waste the most precious gift."

"But you said that we all commit suicide, remember?"

"I'm getting to that."

I take a deeper swig of my Scotch. I feel that I am going to need it. Ruth has set sail for the seven metaphysical seas. *It was a dark and stormy night...*

"The whole question of suicide is overrated. As you so aptly observed, I already said that we all commit suicide. Slowly, painstakingly, but we do. Each time we eat too much, we don't exercise enough, let alone smoke or drink to excess," she raises her glass, "we commit suicide. We don't do so in a quick and efficient manner the way suicide experts would, but, nevertheless, we slowly and persistently kill our bodies. Our whole life is a protracted, and frankly extremely inefficiently executed, act of suicide."

"Cheers," I raise my Scotch and clink her wine glass.

"Here's mud in your eye, as Dad would say..."

"...or poison in your stomach." She's only half-smiling.

"It's good for my heart," I whimper weakly. Again, she ignores me.

I never took time to think this out, but it seems to me that quite a few people would be much better off dead. They would stop accumulating negative *karma*. But I am sure that Ruth would not stop there. It may sound far-fetched that people would willingly give up their life, or lives, for some extra saturated fat or even for a bottle of hooch. As for smoking, I know she's right. I smoked for some twenty years, until Ruth convinced me that there are better things to do with my lungs. Like oxygenating my brain. Lots of people still don't know that.

"Yet..." I encourage gently. She doesn't need much coaxing.

"I think we are just animals. We serve our bodies first and foremost," she says slowly, pointing to the bedroom with her head.

If only she knew what bodies I have inhabited since that day on the balcony...

"But what if we are not *just* animals?" Tempting as her nodding is, I want to pursue this just a little further. She can't resist.

"Well, darling, if you must..."

E ven as I observe myself lifting my glass, the balcony, the view, even Ruth, is covered by a haze of diffused light. I hear quite different voices. They sound familiar, yet they are reaching me from a great distance.

"There's no contraction of the pupil. You must have imagined it, Nurse Francine."

"I swear to you, Docteur Morton, I deed see heem bleenk. Just once, but I deed. Really."

Nurse Francine's voice is becoming almost tearful. If I understand her correctly, she saw my body blink its eyes. I have a vague memory of registering the colour of the ceiling, and... yes, and the top of the walls. I've seen them many times, but that was different. They were all pale. I seem to recall that all colours 'earthside', or observed through human eyes, are pale and insipid, as though seen through a haze. Compared to where I am now. We, ghosts, seem to register a much wider spectrum. Anyway, for now, Nurse Francine is in the doldrums. Poor girl. No one will believe her.

"Keep a close look, Nurse Francine. Report to me even the slightest movement, OK?"

Dr. Morton's voice is conciliatory. He found no evidence to confirm Nurse Francine's observations, but he doesn't want to discourage her, either. I'll have to keep trying. I gave them a tear and now a blink. What do they expect from me, a miracle?

I feel a great relaxation coming over me. As if I'd just run a marathon and was finally allowed to sit down. A funny feeling altogether. The next instant I am sipping Scotch. Again.

"...masters of our domain?" Ruth's voice is not at all like Nurse Francine's. She sounds confident of her facts. "It's up to us." She also sounds as though she'd just concluded her argument. I could roll back the 'tape', but this is not really why I am here. I wanted to recall if Ruth was firmly tied to Roman Catholic doctrine. Apparently she had evolved somewhat from her overseers.

And anyway, I just love listening to her voice. I must have thought that it was time to contribute to what appeared to be a slightly one-sided discussion.

"Alas, thou shalt not kill," I say softly. It sounds appropriate. After all, my body is here all the time. My old body. The young and handsome one. In those days I held that killing others and killing ourselves are both killing. That was long before I knew that we are all immortal.

"They are our bodies," she insists.

I wonder what arguments Ruth had been advancing when my attention shifted momentarily to the Lakeshore. I am trying to make sense of her words. I think it was something about aliens invading our bodies. Body Snatchers? Wasn't there such a film some time ago? I could rewind, again, but I got what I came for. She believes the question of suicide is vastly overrated. Probably to protect the tax base for the political oligarchies. The more citizens there are, the more taxes they can grab. Right now she is talking about kicking out whoever inhabits our bodies without her expressed permission.

"Not even invaders, no matter what their intentions?"

I must have caught her off-guard. Usually this is the sort of question she would ask. She looks at me as though seeing me for the first time.

"Shouldn't we first decide who we are before making a decision?"

I have a feeling that I have bitten off more than I could swallow. We both concentrate on our respective drinks. By now, the sun is kissing the very tops of the skyscrapers southwest of us. They look like a procession of men in luminous hats, retreating into the darkening distance. Perhaps into the future?

I love our terrace. We've spent countless evenings here suspended over the city.

"What now of suicide?" she asks.

She sounds studiously indifferent. A minute ago, she was passionate about the subject. To my utter amazement, she now seems completely willing to drop it. I can see that her eyes are drifting more and more towards the bedroom. It is abundantly clear that regardless of her feelings pertaining to the previous subject matter, she is determined to live to the full until she dies. I am not prepared to miss my chance. We get up without another word. I, the present I, know I cannot stay any longer. It just wouldn't be decent. Just as we turn indoors, Ruth leans her body against mine and looks into my eyes.

"Would we really kick the alien out and send him on his way? Would anyone really be proud of such an ungrateful act?"

Ruth's gaze makes me feel acutely uncomfortable. It's this dual awareness. A second longer and I would stay the night. "Well," she repeats, "would you?"

Frankly, I have no idea what she's talking about. I let the John of the joyful past take care of her question. To this day I have no idea what my answer was. I must have been blinking at Nurse Francine at the time. As I feel my attention withdrawing from her nearness, I am torn between two worlds. *Come with me,* I whisper. *Please, Ruth, come with me. Won't you come with me?*

And I am gone. Alone again in my own, wondrous, infinite universe with no one to share it with. No one at all. Not even my Friend. Nor even Ruth.

I have no choice. I shall do the reverse. Instead of giving up my life to gain heaven, I shall give up heaven to be with Ruth. I have to come back. I know I'd already decided that; but, don't forget, I have my being only in the present. Each moment of now is my total reality. My personal heaven still has boundaries, and Ruth defines them. I also have obligations. There is my office, the liability that Ruth might have to bear, the designs that remain unfinished, my parents. One day I must arrange all these in a sequential order. When there is time. Real, Earth time. One second following the other. It may be dull and primitive, but I know of no better way of becoming. One foot in front of the other. Like *Australopithecus afarensis* with his four-hundred-grams brain, and forward-propelling toes. Frankly, I don't feel much smarter. Perhaps intelligence is not related to brain only. Perhaps brain is a function of the mind, not the other way around.

"You got it, John!"

Guess what. I am swinging between two pines, looking at my own smiling face across the knoll. No body, just the face. And not quite my own, but much more like my mirror than when I first met him. Seems like millions of years ago. Billions? Even as I look, his facial features waver, then turn into a haze.

"We were always one, John. We always will be. It cannot be otherwise." You won't believe how good this assertion makes me feel. It makes me feel immortal.

"Thank you, my Friend," I really mean it.

"I know," he confirms. We both laugh.

I don't see him anymore. But he remains as real as if he were still swinging on his invisible hammock. I think he really will remain with me forever. No matter how long that takes.

It takes some preparations. I feel it must be a physical, emotional and psychological shock. I did it all on my own. Not counting on my Friend, though I am sure he is in on it. Although he remains invisible to my invisible eyes, he makes his presence known in all sorts of ways.

In the end, it turned out to be quite easy. Ruth is in the habit of kissing me goodbye after seeing me at the Lakeshore. Regular as clockwork. Just a gentle peck on my lips, as we did each night just before going to sleep. I guess she found some sort of continuity in this small gesture; as if not everything had changed. Except that I am already asleep and she comes in the morning.

OK, morning and night. Usually.

As you know, she comes early to avoid my dear cousins. They saunter in later with their Rosaries. My parents and Ruth's mother come two or three times a week, mostly after the evening rush hour. Just to say hello, I suppose. A one-sided hello.

Anyway, as Ruth leans over and kisses me, I bite her lip. I practised getting into my body, as I would into any other, and concentrating all my attention on the single motion of moving my teeth. I must have done it a thousand times before I had any results. It took just about as much effort as climbing Mount Everest carrying full gear, as I did some weeks ago. I know. I'd done it in a sherpa's body—I wanted to experience the real thing.

Anyway, Ruth sprang up, practically jumped in the air, and promptly collapsed on the floor. Nobody was present. Even Nurse Francine had stepped out for a minute to give Ruth a semblance of privacy. Poor Ruth. I nipped her lips just gently, but she'll have a nasty bump on the back of her head when she comes to.

In the meantime...

For less than a millionth of a second, Ruth enters a comatose state. Transient, ephemeral, but that is all I need. In that fragment of eternity, I take her for a ride through the universe. Earth-time, we must have spent a month there. Or it could have been years. Who can tell?

"Who are you?" is her first question.

"You really don't recognize me?"

Perhaps ghosts have a different perception of recognition. After all, a ghost is, in a way, the sum total of his or her memories. Since the accident, I saw Ruth daily. She saw only my static body.

"John? My John? You've changed."

For some reason she's no longer in shock. Come to think of it, nor had I been after my accident. Translation into a higher reality seems natural. The other way around is either automatic or is a pain in the you-know-what. For now, I sense serious doubt in her voice—yet it is the sound of my voice that convinces her. Rather funny when you consider that ghosts don't make any noise. It was my voice she heard in her mind. She wanted it to be me.

"I love you, darling..."

Poor girl. She attempts to cuddle up to me, and ends up behind me. Ghosts have no physical substance, no matter how strong the love between them. We can meld, but we cannot touch, so to speak.

"Oh! Oh, what happened?"

For the next few earth-hours I do my best to explain to her what has taken place. Then I tell her, briefly, of my own exploits, a word or two about the universal laws.

"There is the good part and the bad part." I am coming to the conclusion in my own ghostly expertise. "In your present condition you cannot affect physical reality. The good part is that it cannot affect you. Watch."

I embrace her with my consciousness as though we were a single entity and place my attention on the moon. In the same instant we are gazing at the beautiful crescent of the earth below us. It is blue and green and has white puffs of cotton emerging from the bright east and diving into the darkness in the west. I knew what would happen. Ruth is so completely overcome by the beauty of the image before us that she forgets to be scared out of her wits.

"That's the E-e-earth?"

I let the idea of the Earth suspended in nothing sink in. There is little point telling her that the image before or below her is the product of her own mind stimulated by my own. She sees unadulterated beauty in everything. Her next words are filled with even greater surprise.

"John, this really is you." No longer a question.

"You mean before you were attempting to cuddle up to a strange man?"

"I was testing you. I knew I would recognize your body."

How silly of me! Did any man ever understand how a woman thinks? Momentarily, I wonder how many men's bodies she'd tested in my 'absence', just to make sure… I dismiss the thought as soon as it has formed at the periphery of my awareness. I smile my acceptance. In a way, I feel as if I were her Friend. Her guide in the universe. For now. I'm sure that, once fully awakened on this side, she would know a great deal more about the universe than I do.

"Shall we?" I ask gently. She has lots to absorb.

Have you ever seen the Crab Nebula? On Hubble photographs it is full of colour. Well, you ain't seen nothing yet. We become brush strokes painted by an Old Master. Ruth and I become the various colours, we intermingle with others, we crisscross the Nebula as a child would a sandbox. Only the grains of sand are coalescing stars, in various stages of formation. The angular momentum is only just beginning to affect them. I spin our image and we see the Nebula as a mature galaxy—as we shall see it thousands of years from now on Earth—then back to the Super

Nova it once was. Whatever happens at any moment in time, we see in the eternal now.

"Is any of this real?"

Her eyes are as bright as the nearest stars. I think I am falling in love all over again. In her presence, the universe has become a brighter place. And warmer. It is different, no longer static. By the time light from the nebula reaches Earth, no doubt the astronomers will wonder what had happened. My Friend said that I cannot affect physical reality, but I am sure she does. Somehow. Or it could be that her reality is a mite different from mine.

We move on. We do all the things ghosts in love do. At least I think they would do, given a chance.

We fly through the centers of enormous suns—unscathed. We embody our awareness, each individually, in a different planet, and chase each other around another star. You'll never believe how fast some stars are spinning. Must be lots of rotations per second, earth-time. The only way the tiny planets can stop from falling into the blue-white furnace is by developing fantastic centrifugal forces. Again, Earth-time, their year must last mere minutes.

"Do you realize the universe is infinite?" I whisper when we're one again.

"Infinity of this?" She reaches out with her consciousness to embrace countless light-years. "Are there no limitations?"

"We are gods, darling. You are my goddess, you always were."

This is becoming too much for her. I can feel her attention fragmenting. It's not easy when you first realize that you are god. Or goddess. Trust me. It tends to be overwhelming. Once more I embrace her with my consciousness as I am sure my Friend must have done for me many a time. Perhaps he still does.

I hear a gentle chuckle.

I bring Ruth back and let her rest on the rings of Saturn. She seems to be taking it all in her stride. Not at all how I did when I first came over. Perhaps she knows more, or is more open-minded.

Or perhaps she really is a goddess.

And then it hits me like lightning from the infinite abyss of space. What I saw on this trip was different because Ruth, by her very presence, influenced the creative process. Ruth was not in a coma. Unconscious, but still very much alive. She could no more be passive than I could be active. It wasn't just Ruth I desired. It was the life force that embodied her. It was the force of becoming. In some strange way, she was my life. My future. I long not just to return to her, to my wife, my love—it was to life itself.

***

23

One

" She just collapsed, Docteur. I couldn't tell you why. She just deed." Nurse Francine is flustered. Even though she's speaking on the phone, she is waving her arms, illustrating just how quickly Ruth collapsed. It's not a bad performance, considering she wasn't even present at the actual event. She only stepped out for a moment, but she doesn't have to admit it, does she? And now Mrs. Clarkson is lying, on her back, at her feet. Nurse Francine is holding a cell phone in her left hand; her right is taking Ruth's pulse.

"I shall be there presently, Nurse. Don't do anything till I come."

"Yes, Docteur. I mean, no, Docteur..." Her voice trails off.

I no longer have any qualms about peeking into human brains. Minds, actually. Frankly, usually they have little to hide. If they knew what I was up to, they might be ashamed before me, but it would pass. A thought flashes through my mind. *I am the one before whom you have been ashamed.* I wonder where the quotation came from. It's transient, like everything else. Thoughts are like wind. You cannot grasp them, though sometimes they come back with a taciturn yet stubborn regularity.

Nurse Francine is very pretty but not particularly bright. Not yet—she's very young. Late teens? Let's see: four years of High School, two at CEGEP, plus four years to become a nurse... Maybe she's just a student nurse? She's trying, though. I suspect she'll grow. 'Eet could be bad,' she murmurs to herself so quietly it's almost like thinking aloud. 'First zee tears, zen zee bleenk, and now zees. Per'aps I am not meant to be a nurse. Per'aps...'

Just kidding. She doesn't think with a French accent at all. And, surely, we all experience doubts, at times. She's doing all right.

I'm still in my room when Ruth comes to. Somehow, when the three of us are together, it's different when running over old territory. This is as close as I can get to becoming. This is now. Strange that. I have the universe at my disposal and I long for the new. For the creative act. Ruth is creative with every breath she takes. With thoughts she generates each time she looks at my body. I know, peeking is like spying, but it's all I have. And anyway, the line of demarcation I always drew between her and my own psychic territory is becoming hazy. After the trip we took through the wonders of the universe, it is all but erased.

What keeps us apart, of course, is her physical consciousness. Personality. Our physical bodies keep us firmly anchored in dualistic reality. After all, it is a creation of our conscious mind, even if we draw on the information stored in our subconscious. I think this overpowering attraction is what is referred to as the instinct for self-preservation. It refers solely to our physical envelope. The rest of us—the real I AM—is indestructible. The real I AM cannot be injured, hurt, harmed in any way, and certainly it cannot be destroyed. I know that now. I have no doubts left. I have my being outside the confines of time and space.

I am *that* I am. I am the *other* I am.

The door swings open and a young resident shuffles in. Under thirty, stooping, like a bad impersonation of an old man. He looks awful. Hair disheveled, complexion pale, eyes bleary. He appears to keep them open by a conscious act of his exhausted will. Another day, another sleepless night? I read him like a used book. He has no defenses left. He's been on duty for the last 52 hours. He's also beginning to lose count. That's what his mind tells me. Second time this week and it's only Thursday. He slept less than five hours in the last two days. Who said that time doesn't exist?

I am hovering out of the way. Ruth is back in her body; I manage to stay out of mine. Mere seconds have passed since she fell down. Or it could have been minutes. I have no sense of time.

Collapsed, as Nurse Francine called it. Like a house of cards.
Scanning back through my many embodiments, I discover that I've
been a physician twenty-eight times. Or, at least, I stopped
counting after twenty-eight. It's amazing how much you can learn
from a bunch of recalcitrant physicians. My various specializations
include cardiology, neurology, obstetrics—I was a woman
then—an impressive array of Ph.D.s in different aspects of
neuroscience, and various subspecialties of surgical disciplines.
Not that Egyptian surgical operations at the time of the Pharaohs
could really be called science. Too much religion mixed in. I've
been a proper busybody at least since the day of Hippocrates. A bit
longer. According to my Friend, I must have been Hippocrates. I
never realized I was so smart.

Anyway, I'd learned, long ago, how to induce coma without
drugs. The ancients used the state of coma to do exactly what Ruth
and I have done. Well, almost. To induce visions. Greek mythology
attests to that. The Egyptians did so before them. In India, they still
do it. Some Christians had been reasonably successful at it, but
their ability has all but died out. When learned doctors of science
took over, they decided that whatever they couldn't touch, feel,
hear, taste or smell—didn't exist. That's progress.

I'd learned another thing. Earthside, Ruth and I had always
complained that the medical professionals don't know very much.
That, at best, they only alleviate symptoms without getting at the
real cause of the disease. Well, bully for them. Now I know that the
body heals itself. Mostly. As you already know, recently I had
occasion to slip into my body a number of times. I don't know what
they put in my IV, but I felt no pain whatsoever. Removing
symptoms is just fine with me. They must be doing something
right.

Oh, yes. And I am healing. Or my body is. It's well-equipped
for it.

I may have mentioned this before but, as of now, having melded
beyond the matrix of time and space, Ruth and I truly are one. In
a way, I also act as her mirror, only with my face. Ruth finds
herself in me. She faints, enters a coma. No, not because she saw

my face in the mirror. I am not that ugly. I repeat, I act as her Friend. Just act as one. Her real Friend is the sum total of her memories, since the beginning of time.

Actually, I am beginning to suspect, strongly, there is only one 'real' Friend. A single entity embracing the history of the universe. Not just humanity and our evolution, but all the universes. One Friend, one incarnation, in the here and now.

Nevertheless, for now, Ruth needs a personal Friend. As I did. In time she will learn to recognize her own features; they will displace mine. Actually, the mirror will show the totality that she is—which means, it will include me. That's exactly why I couldn't recognize my Friend. He was, he is, so much more than I am right now. For now, we see only aspects of ourselves in all realities.

"I see only the you I choose to see, not the you that you really are. I can meet the real you only by direct perception. I must become you. To do that I must die. I must die as a personality. We must merge." I try to explain. She seems to catch on much faster than I did when I first met Friend.

"We always were one, darling, weren't we?"

She's the most loving person I know, yet this is not quite the same. Not by a long shot.

"The same is true of every other person. The truths we perceive are always subjective. Only the whole is objective." It strikes me that Ruth had made an exhaustive study of the Bible. "This is what Saint Paul meant when he said 'I die daily.' He was willing to give up his personality to become an indivisible part of the whole. Of being one."

"Give up his individuality?" Ruth sounds skeptical.

"No, darling. Individuality is what makes us indivisible from the whole. *Individuus*, in Latin, means indivisible. What we must get rid of is our limiting personality. It is what keeps us apart."

Things change. Until the pothole, Ruth was always the teacher. Me? I was just a very inept student. On the other hand, according to my Friend, her knowledge is my knowledge. It is only a question of placing my attention on the right thing.

Ruth smiles. "*For there is no respect of persons with God*," she quotes from memory. "Romans, I think."

She's still externalizing god. It takes a while. It took me a few billion years.

"Yes, darling. The only way to become one is to stop being one of many."

I never sounded so clever in my life.

I close my eyes. Just for an indivisible fraction of eternity, we roam the universe together. Again. As one. It really is strange that in my reality all is 'now'. I find it harder to separate the various worlds. There are billions of them, yet there is only one. I in you, you in me, we in infinity. It's all thanks to Friend. I wonder if I'll ever see him again.

I hear a vague stirring within me. It is he.

How often must I remind you? You and I are one. And now, so is Ruth.

His words in my head are as clear as though he spoke them to my face. I remember his other admonitions: 'I am the source of all your knowledge, and all your experience translates into incredible power.' I feel his words surge through me as though creating yet another universe. Isn't this what *Logos* is? Worlds without end. Didn't someone say that?

"And I?" I ask. "What is my function in the universe?"

His voice becomes stronger.

"You are the becoming, the present yet to come. You are what makes me alive. Your life is my life. Your becoming is my growth. And now, my Friend," this is the first time he calls me *his* Friend, "I must leave. Always remember, there is nothing that your mind cannot create. Your will is the most powerful creative force in the universe. The future is yours. But always know that you and I are one. Never forget your past. You can always call on me. Only don't expect to see me. But you'll know that I am here. By your side. Always."

And he is gone. I am glad he didn't say goodbye. Not even so long. After all, there is no time. Not really.

R uth's eyes are wide open. I see the remnants of whirling galaxies slowly dying down. It's not easy coming back to the bland walls, the pale greens, insipid wishy-washy colours intended to relax patients. I rather think they bore them to death. Even the hygienic smell of antiseptic comes as a shock. For a moment, there, she was god. Not god the creator, but god the sustainer. The god of being. Hindus would call her Vishnu, the Preserver. It will take her a while to accept that she still is.

"Well, Nurse Francine, don't just stand there. Help Mrs. Clarkson get up."

The resident is really tired. When exhausted, he turns snappy. We all do. Who can blame them, after 52 hours?

Ruth is back on the chair. The fires in her eyes are all but gone.

"What happened, Mrs. Clarkson?" The resident wants to know. "I am Doctor Binder, I am here to help you." He wraps his fingers around her wrist and takes her pulse.

"Eet eez normal, Docteur Binder. I checked," Nurse Francine says. He checks it, anyway.

"What happened? I wish you would tell me. One minute I was bending over my husband, the next I was lying on the floor..."

Even as she talks, the index finger of her right hand drifts slowly to her lips. There is a little tender spot there that attracts her attention. I must have bitten myself when I fell, she rationalizes.

"And how are you feeling right now, Mrs. Clarkson?"

"Oh, I'm fine, Doctor. I'm perfectly all right. Thank you."

But she isn't. Something is missing. Something intangible yet more real than anything she'd ever witnessed in her life. I am elated. She remembers!

Dr. Binder turns to Nurse Francine.

"Let Mrs. Clarkson rest for a while, and then she may go." Dr. Binder turns to Ruth again. "You are sure you're quite all right?"

I am reading his mind: 'Nurses always over-react. They don't want to take responsibility. God, I'm tired,' he glances at his watch. 'Another six hours and then...'

I follow him outside. I also want to make sure Ruth's all right. After all, for an instant there, I took her life in my hands. Dr. Binder leans against the corridor wall and takes a few seconds' rest. He's not thinking about Ruth anymore. I find it amazing that whoever administers this hospital empowers men that exhausted to be in charge of saving other peoples' lives. It's like the blind leading the blind.

"Physician, heal thyself," I whisper. He doesn't hear me, of course, but opens his eyes and staggers down the corridor. I turn back.

I watch Ruth intently. She hasn't moved yet. I suspect that her memories are drifting away. Like the memory of a dream. Human mind, our conditioning, cannot accept true reality. Didn't someone once say that man cannot see the face of God and live? True reality is too wonderful to be retained in this world of temporal becoming. My God, shall I also forget all my experiences?

All my swathing, bandages and some tubes are removed. My lungs appear to be supplying my body with sufficient oxygen to keep my brain going. For what it's worth, Dr. Morton starts me, my body, on a series of intensive massages. I love massages. What a pity I have to get into a coma to enjoy them. And I don't. I simply do not feel a thing. Not yet. It is Dr. Morton's theory that I shall, in due course. He's a smart fellow, Dr. Morton. The last battery of MRIs and CTs proved that there is no physiological damage in my brain. Not anymore. By some means he doesn't quite understand, I seem to have mended myself. He's close to the truth, though the IV and the artificial lung played their part.

Dr. Morton accepts the boon wherever he can find it. He's not proud. Not unless some junior staff member is present.

He reminds me of me at the beginning of the 16th century, in Spain. I watched my body burned at the stake. I was Jewish then, and I had to practice my 'art' in secret. The Church didn't approve of laymen taking science into their own hands. Particularly if you were a Jew.

How time flies on earth. It seems like only yesterday.

But the best part is the masseuse. I'm glad she does her therapy when Ruth is away. She massages me everywhere. That's right, everywhere. It's supposed to restore circulation. Believe me, if I weren't in a coma, my circulation would rise all by itself. Everywhere.

I find it amazing that such a small girl—woman, to be politically correct—can turn me from side to side on her own. She must have been doing this for some time. I watch, admiring the economy of motion she exhibits with every move. Her hands are really strong, experienced. Maximum effect with minimum effort. She's a very smart girl. Her name, by the way, is, I am sorry to say... Brenda.

Brenda the non-scorpion. More like an angel.

With no disrespect to Ruth, let me tell you—if Brenda the Angel does not restore my circulation, nothing will. Nothing and nobody. I am a ghost, and I am turning hot under my collar. And I don't even have a collar.

I know what the problem is. According to the conversation I hear between Dr. Morton and his assistant, the haggard Dr. Binder, I should be coming out of my comatose condition any time now. They've also taken lots of EEG scans, and my brain waves indicate a pattern that is not exactly comatose.

"Frankly, Dr. Binder, I've never seen anything like it. It is more reminiscent of a graph indicating a forthcoming earthquake than anything that goes on in a human head. There, did you see that?"

He is pointing to some scans done over the last few days.

"Look, and here it is again. What do you make of it?"

The pattern, as best as I can see it, shows a momentary activity, followed by near absence of any waves. Then it returns to normal pattern. Normal for a person in a coma, that is. There is nothing normal about it. It is still almost in the delta range. Just below 2 to 3 cycles per second. Any slower and I would be brain-dead. Some of my architectural clients accused me of just that years ago. At last, they would be vindicated.

Dr. Binder is in a better mood today. Frankly, he looks like a different person. Two inches taller, clean, smart, hair well combed. He's almost smiling. Since I last saw him, he must have had a good night's sleep. Either that, or he's trying hard to impress a member of the senior staff, Dr. Morton. He is holding some EEG printouts, his forehead creased in concentration. He scratches his head.

"Correct me if I am wrong, Dr. Morton, but I saw something very similar last year. It was Dr. Yun's patient. I don't remember his name, but it turned out the patient had been a drug addict. Not the ordinary sort, though. He was experimenting with LSD. Without supervision. A dangerous hobby, I would say."

I jump to Dr. Morton's mind. This guy seems to know everything. He could apply to be somebody's Friend. I scan his 'library':

Originally synthesized in Switzerland in 1938, lysergic acid diethylamide, LSD, became a psychedelic drug of preference for people searching for hallucinogenic visions. ...later picked up by North American press when an American researcher, Timothy Leary...'

Who cares? I interrupt myself.

...Leary, somewhat lacking in discipline, experimented with the drug on himself. Since, during the Cold War, Pentagon was keenly interested in using it for interrogation and mind control.

It's like speed-reading a computer printout. The stuff goes on and on. The CIA also dipped their fingers in it... but CIA dip their fingers in almost everything. I don't care about the rest. What amused me a lot is that Dr. Morton thinks he's only vaguely familiar with the drug!

"So what do you make of it?" He looks at Dr. Binder with new interest.

"Well, even the famous Aldous Huxley, of *Brave New World* fame, spoke highly of drug-induced visions in his..."

"I believe it was *Doors of Perception,* Doctor Binder, and the drug was mescaline derived from peyote, the divine cactus, of Castaneda fame..." Dr. Morton allows himself a slight snigger, "not LSD, if I remember correctly."

"W-w-well, Sir, it does alter reality," Dr. Binder is near stammering.

"And just how does this help us in waking up our Mr. Clarkson, Dr. Binder?"

"Ah, well, not really. At least not that I know of…"

Suddenly Dr. Binder shrivels to the previous height he bore so bravely a day or two ago. His smile dissolves into a frazzled expression. Then he squares his shoulders and appears to change his mind.

"Well, Sir. If he's not coming back, then I wonder what's holding him back?"

Dr. Morton raises an eyebrow. He has thought of the conundrum himself, but wouldn't dream of admitting it, out loud, in front of a junior member of the staff. He had to maintain his authority. It was expected of him.

"Well, if you think of something, let me know."

With that Dr. Morton gives Dr. Binder a belated smile, spins on his heel and leaves. As I may have mentioned before, Dr. Morton's mind is filled to overflowing with seemingly completely useless bits of information. And now Dr. Binder appears to be joining the ranks. Much ado about nothing.

It is becoming abundantly clear that if I don't die quickly, I am in great danger of staying alive. Of joining the ranks of the living, walking, becoming. Of joining Ruth. This single last notion makes it all worthwhile. To give up the world and gain the pearl… There is a beautiful parable about that somewhere.

There are also my parents. Someone should look after them. And, of course, my office. I really like my work. At least, I used to like it. For some reason in all these months, I dropped into my office only once. It is like taking a sabbatical. I never did that before. The next moment I find myself in my office, at Beaulieu, Clarkson and Drake Architects. Jacques is in the conference room, as usual, trying to calm down a client who, also as usual, wants to know why there is a delay in construction. I read Jacques' mind. There is a construction strike on. It started two months ago.

"Why can't you get a court order, Jacques? Isn't that what one can do?"

"On what grounds, Mr. Harrison?"

"That's what I pay you for, Jacques. To come up with ideas, don't I?"

"Architectural ideas, Mr..."

If I know Harrison, this argument will go on for quite a while. Harrison is well known for being perennially late with paying his bills, especially to professional consultants. Long after we had to pay our income tax installments on our receivables.

I shrug and blend into a wall.

Frank is doing my job. His sleeves rolled up, he goes from station to station, sits down on a round stool, makes a comment or two, and moves to the next one. For a while, I follow him. Each comment he makes is spot on. It is—was—my project, but I couldn't do it better myself. Good old Frank. They are both good men, Jacques and Frank, though getting a bit long in the tooth for such a daily grind. Yet they do their best. They are still growing. Developing a new past.

I look down at the stools. They are relics from the good old days, when we'd used only drawing boards. A month before my accident, we had ordered small swivel chairs. Evidently they still haven't been delivered. They'll be more fitting for computer work. With me away, poor Frank has to oversee forty-two computer screens on top of doing his own work. It must be tough on him. And somehow, not fair.

My private office is empty. The door is closed. I slink in and look around. Nothing has been moved. They must assume that only the good die young. Not so young at that. I've spent twenty-two years in this room. It feels like home. I smile when I see my 2B pencils sharpened on my desk. Not the propelling ones. Those made of real wood with real lead inside—my only contact with the past. The rest is done on computers. Good old Gracie. I can see her arranging my desk in order. So many months ago. She'd been my secretary for the last eleven years. Honest, hardworking, punctilious. In a way, indispensable. I search Frank's mind, still doing his rounds. I find what I've been looking for. She said she'd come back when I do. A very loyal woman. Mother of two. I hope they are like her. Her children, I mean.

I am beginning to feel quite guilty.

I find myself back in my hospital room just as my two cousins come in. They, too, are loyal. Four months is a long time to recite a Rosary, even just twice a week. For quite a time they would do it daily. I try to visualize the expressions on their faces if I were to sit up while they're praying.

"A miracle!" Doris would scream.

"A miracle!" Brenda would echo.

They would be famous overnight.

They do that a lot, echoing each other. I suppose they do their best. Not everybody can be like Ruth. Or Gracie, for that matter. I wonder what they are going to do when they stop praying over my body. Find another hobby? Another corpse?

That wasn't nice. I feel guilty again.

Mother is resting after lunch. She's resting most days, most of the time. I learned from Ruth that the doctors can do nothing. What else is new? Dementia is a progressive disease. First you forget the immediate past. Like what you had for breakfast. Then, what you had for dinner last night. It's a disease that moves backwards. In a way, that's a blessing. You remember better and better your younger and younger days. Uncluttered by the exigencies of old age. Isn't nature clever? It cannot make you young, but it can replay your younger days for you. Still, it's not the same. I know. This is what I've been doing for the last four months. Believe me. It's not the same.

Mother will never recover. Anyway, no one can live forever. Not in the same body. Thank God. New bodies are so much more fun. Have you heard a baby cry? Of course you have. But wait till you hear him or her laugh.

"It's worth all the tears. All the sleepless nights," Mother had told me so many years ago; yet I hear her voice even now...

I don't dare probe Mother's mind. To me it's sacred. She lives in a world of her own. I hope she's happy there. I suspect her present state is a sort of introduction, a training ground for where I am now. Soon she will roam the universes in a state of being. Wonders upon wonders. Endless, inexhaustible wonders.

But for now, I know what she would really like. If she still remembers me, she would like me to stroke her grey hair and tell

her that everything will be all right. Always. And that I shall
always be with her. Forever.

Not so.

Quite accidentally, I see Mother's vision. Dad and Ruth are
stretching out on the grassy hill, sloping gently downwards towards
Beaver Lake, atop Mount Royal. Dad's a little tired today. He
overdid it yesterday in the garden—lately, his hobby and his
passion. I see all this in my mother's mind. Not peeking—it is
there, in the open, for all to see. As if she wanted to share it.

Mother sits up.

"Come, John, take me around the lake."

We often do that. Occasionally Mother likes to have me all to
herself. She anchors her arm in my elbow and with a lively step
takes off towards the water's edge. Within a hundred yards her
pace slows down, and she hangs more heavily on my arm. It's
always like that. Mother is an eternal optimist. She still thinks she
can circle the lake at a good pace. Her bad knee says otherwise.

"Now tell me all about it," she says, looking up at my face.

There is nothing special that she doesn't already know. I think
what she needs is the stroll, the nearness to her son. As in the old
days, when we all lived together. I tell her about my work, my
commitments, what Ruth and I did since the last time we met. I
don't think she listens much. She just wants to hear my voice. As I
said, to have it all to herself. Yes, this, too, is as in the old days.

I can sense Ruth and Dad following us with their eyes.

"I think we ought to get back," I suggest. We stop and sit on a
bench for just a minute or two.

Her eyes drift towards three ducklings breaking the mirror of
the lake. She sighs deeply.

Poor Dad. He really finds it difficult to cope. He'll be eighty-
five this year. He and Clara somehow make it work. Clara still
drives the car—she's much younger—while Dad carries the
groceries. Mother can vacuum-clean if you make sure she doesn't
do the same room twice. They share the main meal downstairs.
They cook it together. Once a week a woman comes and cleans the
whole house. Just once a week. She also does the laundry and some
ironing. It takes her all day.

They should have a live-in helping them. I'll have to arrange it the moment I get back. Help for Mother and Dad and Clara. Thank God they agreed to live in the same house. Clara's upstairs, my parents below. Duplexes are convenient that way. They swapped last year. Mother couldn't negotiate the stairs anymore. I should help them more. I should help them much more.

I feel guilty again.

Ruth is alone. I want to share my thoughts with her. About my parents, her mother, even about my office. I want to tell her how faithful Gracie is. How very loyal. And about Frank doing such a splendid job. And even about my cousins coming to pray over my body when no one is there to notice. Just the two of them. They can't be all bad, can they, darling? Of course, she can't hear me. If only Doris would eat a little more and Brenda stopped pretending all the time that she's a teenager, they would be all right. Well, they wouldn't be so bad.

You've got it. I feel guilty again.

I am the one before whom you have been ashamed.

Friend? Are you there? I know that he said those words. Yet, I am all alone. In the whole wide universe I am all alone. I am not really one with Ruth. Not yet.

***

24

Now

I had it all wrong. I let my body rest for another imperceptible timeless moment. A timeless fragment of the eternal Now. I know that only Now truly exists. My Friend didn't tell me, not in so many words, but I know. I also know that only being is real—becoming but an elusive dream. Each incarnation, each embodiment is an illusion. Yet it is in our dreams that we create reality. We invoke ideas that we add, subliminally, to the reality of being. When we awaken in our true state of true reality, we can visit all the places we've created. They live forever within our minds. In my latest fantasy I dreamt of Ruth. She became real to me. More real than any dream I'd ever had. More real than the twenty years she and I had spent together. Now she'll remain alive, forever, in my state of being. I made her immortal. In the reality of Now.

All along, during these last few months, I could have returned to my body and returned to Ruth. I may have concocted all sorts of stories, lame excuses, for tarrying; but truly, I just couldn't face losing my freedom. I am sensing a smidgen of an idea of what Yeshûa must have gone through to be reborn in a human body. To leave his home and join us in a prison of our physical limitations. You have glimpsed fragments of my inner kingdom. Can you imagine what he had to give up for us? He truly must have loved us. Still does, even now.

There is no one waiting for me at the knoll. It seems forlorn, deserted. Waiting for my next awakening? Even the pines look sad. For a moment I muse that if I stay here long enough, he, my Friend, just might look in on me. I fear it's too late. I am already becoming human. Once again I have forgotten that there is no time. Not here, not on this side of the Great Divide.

For the last time I transfer my attention to the Lakeshore. It is time for another dream to invade my soul. I can't keep Ruth waiting any longer. She's sitting at my bedside, all alone. Even my cousins drop in less often. I never thought I would miss them. Imagine, missing a stick insect and her scorpion consort, reciting the Rosary. What a farce. My sisters stopped calling from the States. The last time Elaine called was a month ago. Perhaps they think I'll remain a vegetable forever. As in a sci-fi movie: *The Eternal Flower*, or something. Only in my case I would be bound to shrivel to resemble an old cabbage. Can you imagine? *An Eternal Shrivelled Cabbage?* My body would look like that. From lack of use. Don't use it—loose it, I recall. I used to say that myself.

I would rather dream.

Now and then I escape into the outer limits of the universe, or the wilds of Africa, or sit and ponder about the glory of life on the top of Mount Everest. I sit and reflect on the eternal Now. There is something missing. Having experienced travelling with Ruth, even the same places we'd visited together do not hold the same enchantment for me. She's already there, but not in the totality of her being. She's there only as my creation. She must choose to be there of her own accord. I can go back in time and replay our joint spin; but, well, it feels like cheating.

"He should be responding by now, Nurse Joan. You sure you didn't detect any imminent signs of life?"

This is Dr. Binder. He really wants to show that he can do what his boss couldn't.

It really makes me laugh. In their dreams they all play games. That's really funny.

You don't have any idea, doctor, what life is. You want my corpse to get up and go? Well, get Jesus or Sai Baba. They can do

*it for you. They can create reality. What do you want from me? I
have a universe of my own. My home. My wondrous home.*

Dr. Morton comes in. He looks tired. I hope I am not the
reason for his dream going sour.

I begin reading his mind. He really is a lot smarter than he lets
on. If he would only sort it all out into a semblance of order, there
is an awful lot of knowledge there. Right now, his brain reminds
me of an intellectual pot-pourri, a hodgepodge. A neurological
jungle. Or better still, jumble. Perhaps he picks at it only at random,
if and when he needs it. That's what I do. Maybe that is how the
human brain works. Shove all the knowledge, or facts, you can get
into your brain, and then spend the rest of your life trying to
unscramble it. Some succeed; most apparently don't. We remain
stupid for a lifetime. By stupid I mean slow. Very slow.

He doesn't even have a filing system. No folders, no files, no
titled documents. Some of his knowledge is buried deep in the heart
of his cells. All over his body. Of course, mind uses all that's
available. Even the tips of your toes, Doctor. Never mind.

You'd make a lousy computer, Doctor!

Guess what. He doesn't hear me. He really would make a
lousy computer. Still, he's all I've got, unless I spend an eternity
scanning the whole universe. And believe me, it would take an
eternity. My own medical expertise is sadly outdated. Here goes
nothing... I'm arranging his knowledge on 'coma' as clearly as I
know how. I hope you can follow it.

"People in a coma may be able to hear and to understand what
is being said in their presence."

Well, I don't. Certainly not when my attention is elsewhere.
Anyway, I don't think he's referring to ghosts. Ha, ha. He's
definitely referring to 'real' people.

"There are several levels of coma. They define the patient's
increasing awareness of his surroundings. There is the Glasgow
Coma Scale level of cognitive functioning. The Glasgow Scale
defines the motor responses, eye-opening and verbal responses.
There are many subdivisions."

With the possible exception of my single wink, I do not
qualify on any of the levels.

"There is also the Rancho Los Amigos Scale..."—which I find equally as confusing. There is an awful lot of this stuff in his head, a hell of a lot more than he admitted to on day one.

Remember day one? Was I ignorant then! Not that I am doing so well now.

As for coming out of coma, Dr. Morton has an actual, real document filed in his brain. As far as I can see, he just crammed up on it recently on his computer. I wonder if he did it on my account. Good ol' Doc. I could learn all this from their various discussions, but this is much faster. I quote him verbatim:

> When coming out of coma, a patient may make incomprehensible noises and/or move one or both arms or legs in a random, uncoordinated, and repetitive movement. They may often try to pull any tubes out, have facial expressions, groan, cry or shout. They may also try to move and may resist people doing anything to them.

So there. Once I start acting like a congenital idiot, they'll assume that I am back to normal. Makes you wonder... At least for now, I have Angel Brenda doing her thing. I still can't feel anything, but I can watch, can't I? Her fingers go where no fingers have ever gone before. Except for Ruth's, of course. At least, I think they did. It seems like eons ago. The concept of Now can be most confusing—at least, until you enter the concept of time. There are so many time scales that you can get lost in microseconds flat. Read St. Thomas Aquinas, or Einstein, or any theoretical physicist. In fact, St. Thomas, as far back as nearly 800 years ago, argued the flexibility of time. He proposed *tempus*, the temporal or earthly time; *aevum*, time that defined mental processes; and *aeternitas*, time that concerned itself with the divine. I have my own theories. I could share them with you, but it would take years, your time, to explain. I'm sure you have better things to do with your dream.

Surely, I wouldn't forget the feel of Ruth's fingers, would I? Brenda's are like having a lap dance done to me all over. Not that I ever had a lap dance done to me.

But, as I was saying... never mind.

OK. I do feel a bit guilty. After all, if Ruth were here, I wouldn't watch. At least not Nurse Angel ministering to me. I mean Nurse Brenda. I'd watch Ruth. God, it may sound absurd after what I just told you, but I miss her something awful. She really is my life. My real life.

It's over. Nurse Brenda wraps various vials into a carry-on, wipes her hands on a towel soaked in a disinfectant, and leaves. I wonder why she's not wearing any gloves. Or washing her hands, for that matter. I would. My body's not that attractive any more. Assuming it ever was. I suppose she'll need a long soak in a hot bath, after touching me.

I am alone with my thoughts.

If I were alive in my physical body I would be feeling on top of the world. I shouldn't have thought of that...

I am sitting on top of Mount Everest, again. I'm not kidding. The sun is just rising, way down, between two peaks—golden-white and shimmering like angels' wings surrounding the god of light. It's amazing that I can stare directly into the sunlight and my eyes don't hurt. In fact, I can see through the sun. As if it were all made of transparent photons engaged in a feverish dance. Like a zillion Whirling Dervishes in a frenzy of joyful realization. I wonder if Rumi died and now has his being in the heart of a sun. Not a bad place to live in. The climate is reliable for eons at a time. Only... Rumi is immortal...

I miss Ruth...

I am sitting on top of the world and I miss Ruth. She would love it here. She would point out to me beauty where on my own I can't see any. If I could only take her for spins now and then. But I learned, way back when, that a coma cannot be induced more than once. People get too attached to the other side. Watch me. The true reality is an incredibly powerful magnet. All people would react like that, I shouldn't wonder. They start as saints—they end up in a lunatic asylum, spending the rest of their dream in never-never land. Neither here nor there. Neither being, nor becoming. Maybe that is what hell is all about? That's why I squeezed our jaunt in under a second. I wouldn't risk her precious mind. Or heart. Or body. God, how I miss that body.

"So ow are we today, Meester Clarkson?"

Nurse Francine is very proud of herself. She is taking full credit for all the physiotherapy I am getting. If it hadn't been for noticing the forlorn tear, and the single *bleenk*, sorry, blink, none of this would be happening. I am beginning to wonder if she thinks that I am faking the coma just to get the massage. I could peek into her mind, but I would rather keep fooling myself. As I said, since my Friend left, I feel lonely. I am creating my own little pseudo-reality. Sort of. In my mind. A two-dimensional reality.

Nurse Francine looks at my body as if I were in it. Last week she reverted to addressing me with the royal 'we'. 'How are *we*?' 'Did *we* sleep well?' We, we, we. Actually, that last is rather funny. 'We sleep?' 'Together?' I wonder if she fancies me. I know how I am, how I sleep; but if it weren't for Ruth, I wouldn't mind finding out how she is and sleeps. On her back? Tummy? Why do I have such idiotic thoughts? It must be the months and months without Ruth. Ages. I've never ever been unfaithful to Ruth. Nor could I ever be. It's my split personality that's playing tricks on me. Somehow my inert body is beginning to affect me.

Now Nurse Francine steps closer. She takes a quick look over her shoulder, making sure the door is closed, I presume, and puts her hand on my chest. After a moment or two, she slowly moves her palm downwards, never losing contact with my body. It's all done in slow motion. An inch or two at a time. As if the expectation were to be greater than the fulfillment.

I am straining to feel her hand. At the same time, I wonder why I care. I also wonder if this is a direct result of the thoughts I had about Ruth only moments ago. I don't tell you everything. What I mean is that I wonder if it was I who put the thought of touching my body in Nurse Francine's head. If I can blink and weep, perhaps I can communicate also. Just a bit? I will Nurse Francine to stop. She doesn't. Perhaps I am not yet as awake as I thought I was. I mean, I am not yet dreaming. Or perhaps Nurse Francine is missing someone as much as I am missing Ruth.

This is absurd.

You cannot serve two gods, a thought cuts across my mind like a searing arrow. Two gods? I don't see any gods. I don't serve any...

I am trying to have my cake and eat it, too. It cannot be done. I must remain in the world of being, or return to the dream of becoming.

"For you will either hate the one and love the other, or..."

This is Ruth's voice. Since I took her over to my side, she now has her being here. In my mind. At least in part. She took all her memories with her, including her studies of the Bible. But she is wrong. I don't serve god and mammon. So far I cannot even find a god I can serve.

But I know what she means. This is the only way she knows how to communicate with me. I must choose. Being or Becoming. I thought I'd already chosen. It seems that giving up life is not that easy. One never loses hope that one can have one's cake after all. But even then, I think Ruth is still wrong. I agree I cannot affect the physical side from here directly. I need a channel to do it through. Like a human being. Like a saint or a mystic.

Or—I don't even dare think it.

How come Ruth is always right?

It must all happen today. Now. Of course, now is also tomorrow and the day after. Procrastination. Now is now. Forever.

Again, I am losing contact with physical reality. I really have to choose quickly. Nurse Francine's ministrations didn't succeed. She did not raise Lazarus. She didn't even raise me. I am truly alone. No Friend, no gods to serve, not even my family visiting me. Apart from Ruth and the cousins. The other members of my family have pretty much given up on me. Not that I blame them. I could still hear Dr. Morton talking, the last time they were here. And that was two weeks ago. At least, I think it was about two weeks ago. It could have been last month, or... or yesterday. I'm truly lost in time. I can't really tell any more. I wonder if my mother understood any of what Dr. Morton was saying. I can hear him now. Again?

"There is no physiological reason why your son shouldn't wake up, Mrs. Clarkson. Apart from his brain waves, all his other vital signs are perfectly normal. And we did take a number of CT scans of his cranium, Mrs. Clarkson. There is absolutely no evidence of any injury. No blood clots, either. They would show up on other tests. No, Mrs. Clarkson. I suggest to you that your son will wake up when he chooses to, and not a second earlier."

I told you, Dr. Morton is a very smart man, although I don't think his latest diagnosis of my condition did Mother much good. And, by the way, this was the longest speech I ever heard Dr. Morton deliver. Even longer than the one Dr. McKinley gave when he was telling Ruth off for self-neglect.

"But is he all right, Doctor?" my mother continued, as though the doctor hadn't spoken.

Poor Mother. She's halfway over to my side, only without the fringe benefits. Clara came up behind her and led her to the nearest chair. They stayed a few more minutes and left. There was little point for them to stay. Not after Dr. Morton's protracted speech.

I could still die, of course. I could die instead of coming back. There is only one problem with that. I'm immortal. It seems that suicides don't help much, after all. Unless you have a really, really good reason. Not one from which only you are likely to benefit. After all, we are one.

I see Ruth bending over me. My Ruth. My soul. She speaks to me as though she were part of my inner self. I think she assumes that I am dying. I can see it in her eyes. I think she has decided that I don't want to come back. Can't blame her, after what Dr. Morton said. Again, I feel guilty.

I am tired of feeling guilty.

"When I was a child, I spake as a child, I understood as a child, I thought as a child: but when I became a man, I put away childish things. For now we see through a glass, darkly; but then face to face: now I know in part; but then shall I know even as also I am known."

She speaks softly, quoting from Paul's letter to the Corinthians. Poor Ruth. Her voice is just above a whisper.

"I am not dying, darling. I am falling asleep."

The words Ruth spoke no longer apply to me. The reverse must be true.

When I was a child, I spoke like a child, understood like a child, thought like a child. I was innocent, and knowledge had been given to me. But when I dream again, I shall put away childish things. Once again I shall see through glass, darkly, no longer face to face. Then I have known even as I was known. But when once more I become a man, I shall only be known in part, as in part only I shall know.

Unless a miracle happens.

I have a sense of impending doom. Of separation. I have been one, I shall become one of many. I feel that the facility with which I could contact my Friend is rapidly coming to an end. Not that he will be inaccessible to me, but that I will be, once again, too strongly anchored in time. I sense its convoluting tentacles already entwining the vestiges of my timeless mind.

"Goodbye, my Friend... so long..."

I know he can hear me. In a way it is like Ruth talking to her father. My Friend is still with me. I can hear him not so much in my head as in my heart.

If you want to enter my house, leave your personality outside. Personality dwells on Earth, and you cannot live in two houses at once. When you enter my house, you enter holy ground. The ground, the state of consciousness, that is whole.

He is always right. I already knew all he'd ever showed me. He truly was my light. Now? Now he's my mirror, if only I could see him as I did for the last few eons of eternity. But I do know that he's here. Within me. Within all of us.

Ruth and I are alone. Even nurses no longer keep a constant vigil. Gently, so as not to awaken my body, I slip into its constraining contours. I am both in and out, as I have been so often these last few days of earthly time. But no longer for just nanoseconds. It is a bizarre, almost suffocating feeling. The infinite universe contracts to a few trillion cells. A tiny, insignificant universe.

Friend, are you still there? Are you here?

It is time...

Ruth shimmers before my eyes. My physical eyes. She's smiling at me. It must be an image from the past. She is saying something. *"...so loved the world that he gave his only son, so that everyone who believes in him might not perish..."*

Dear Ruth. No one can perish. We are gods. Indivisible from the Whole. We are immortal...

Ruth is grasping at the vestiges of her faith. Desperately holding on to the faith that had given her strength over so many years. I imagine, in fact I am now sure, she thinks I am dying. I know why. I opened my eyes, but my pupils weren't moving. I really must look dead. Poor Ruth. It's so very easy to leave one's body. It is hard to come back. To give up life for a dream...

Coming back to life is the most unselfish act anyone can do for his friends. It's no longer just theory. Dying isn't painful. I nearly did over that pothole. It is coming alive that hurts. Leaving the whole universe of wonders beyond measure hurts. Life is the hardest thing to give up. Unless you completely forsake your ego. Only great saints can do that. Great saints and mystics. Not architects.

I hear the second-hand tick on Ruth's wristwatch. No human ear would detect so tiny a sound. For me it is like thunder.

Time starts again. My first act of becoming.

I close my eyes. I have to do it, for her. My world shrinks to insignificance. I see my Friend waving to me. It's time, he repeats. I hear his words from far, far away. I know he'll be there when I get back. When I return home. The next time with Ruth. Forever. I finally understand what John said in his Revelation: *Him that overcometh I shall make a pillar... he shall go no more out...* It's a long journey, but the rewards are great. I know that I must create my own heaven. A heaven where Ruth will reign with me forever.

"Hello, darling?" I say. It's a whisper. A hoarse whisper.

She thinks she's hearing my voice in her dream. She's right, of course. I repeat. Still no reaction. I reach out and touch her hand. Overwhelming surprise fills her eyes. Then tears come. Lots of tears.

"Now, is that any way to greet your husband?" I ask. My throat is dry, but I manage to speak.

I never got an answer to this question. Just as with my Friend. 'See you, Friend,' I repeat once more, and I open my eyes. I blink repeatedly. The mists clear slowly. Gradually, as though emerging from a past I had left far behind, the contours of her face become firmer. I can see Ruth's face with my physical eyes. This is not the face I saw on the other side, but I would recognize her in any reality. And now my eyes also fill with tears.

We are one.

I hear my Friend whispering in the depths of my mind. We are one. At last, I finally understand. I cannot see him outside of myself because we are one. Of course. It all happened before. And now Ruth, only I can see her. We are one only in part. I see her dimly, as through a glass, darkly... So that's what Paul meant!

I reach out to Ruth's mind. Did you hear that, darling? Did you hear my Friend speaking in my heart? She still cannot hear me. I repeat my Friend's words in my crackly voice.

"We are one," I say softly. My throat really hurts. It's a strange feeling. I experienced no pain for months and months. For countless eons? I know I'm back in the dream of duality. Buddha was right. It hurts.

I wish they would give me some water. I must tell Ruth all that I have learned. Quickly, before I forget.

If only I could remember it all, once I'm fully awake.

Once I start dreaming again.

***

EPILOGUE

So that's roughly what happened. I told you as much as I could remember, and what I couldn't, I made up. Don't get me wrong. What I made up is just as creative, and pretty much as real. After all, all reality has its being only in your mind. It cannot be otherwise. When we share our reality with another, it becomes objective, that's all, but no less and no more real. I hope you enjoyed my universe. I am sure you now suspect that there is an infinite number of universes. Such as yours and mine. An infinite number, with infinite numbers of configurations, dimensions and realities. That is as it should be. We are all unique. And, after all, isn't God infinite?

Some millions of years from now, we shall return to look at our universe, at our creation. Aristotle was right about friendship. A single soul dwelling in two bodies. Maybe this is also what Moses meant by *Elohim*. Didn't he use the expression YHWH? Like Yin Yang? Is this what is necessary for manifestation in a physical universe? We were always one, we just didn't know it. All people are equally part of us. They have their being in our unconscious. In a way, we live in theirs. We are one.

With the other side, it's a little different. Yod, Hé, Wau and Hé, the tetragrammaton YHWH, stands for the masculine and feminine principles of the universe. While in the physical universe they are split to create dualistic reality, up there, beyond, where I have been, where in the truest sense I still am, they are reunited. That is why I had to come back for Ruth. Don't get me wrong; she and I are gods in our own right. But together... well, you will have to find out for yourself.

For us, for Ruth and me, it wasn't all peaches and cream. Months passed before I returned to my office. Both my partners visited me at home, in an attempt to stimulate my interest in work. I believe they were successful. Not because I missed my office as such, but my 'visits' to the inner realm have filled me with such an abundance of ideas, of creative currents, that I longed for translating them into physical forms. I began scribbling on my pad, in my study, the old passions stirring within me. It was very much like work. Glorious, engaging, stimulating work. Each second counted. I had to fill it with ideas before it, the indomitable progression of time, turned it into the past. It takes tremendous effort to create something 'Earthside". Not at all like blinking one's eyes.

I'd also spent months doing physiotherapy, forcing my body to respond to the commands of my brain. We all take our neuro-network for granted, forgetting that a baby takes years learning to walk, run, and developing dexterity of their upper limbs. In a coma, certain parts of the brain assume they are no longer needed. They have to be reactivated, almost from scratch.

Ruth helped. She took time off from work to shorten my period of re-convalescence. After I told her as much as I could remember of my mental gymnastics 'on the other side', she startled me.

"Had you come back when you should have, you wouldn't have to go through all this now. This is your outwardly *karma*."

She always came up with statements such as this, only now I listened. Always. Also, there were compensations.

If it hadn't been for that single romp on the other side, together, we could never have been able to cross over again. Ruth retains sufficient memory of that event to strengthen her faith beyond a shadow of doubt. She likes to joke about it.

"I bet you a grain of mustard seed that we can do it again."

We did. Still do.

Only we do it in full consciousness, lying side by side on our marital bed. You should try it. Really. There are many things a lot worse than slipping into a coma. Especially if you have Ruth waiting for you Earthside.

Try it.

Try it now.

*****

Acknowledgments

As always, my thanks to my friends for their perceptive comments and to my wife, Bozena Happach, for refusing to just be, but of inspiring my life in the mode of constant becoming. As usual, my thanks go to Madeleine Witthoeft (and a host of friends) for their early reviews and preliminary proofreading. Special thanks go to Kate Jones, whose diligent editing as well as subsequent proofreading raised this effort of mine to acceptable literary standards.

In the body of this novel I borrowed, quite extensively, from a number of sources of inspiration: from the Prologue of my novel, *Gift of Gamman*, and from my essays on *Creativity*, *Genesis*, *Life*, and *Children of the Lesser God* [from my *Beyond Religion* collections].

Other quotations have been gleamed from my essay, *Who Am I* [*Beyond Religion III*, Inhousepress, 2002], which includes references from *Bhagavad-Gita* [The Bhadtivedanta Book Trust, Los Angeles, 1968, 1972] 7:8-11, 9:9, 10:8 and 20, 15:15; *The Gospel of John* 6:48, 8:12, 10:9, 11:25, 14:6; *The Nag Hammadi Library in English* [James M. Robinson, General Editor, HarperSanFrancisco, 1978]; The (First and Second) *Apocalypse of James*; Andrew Harvey's *Light upon Light, Inspirations from Rumi* [North Atlantic Books, Berkeley, California 1996], pg. 131, extract from *The Truth Is Within You;* Timothy Freke & Peter Gandy, *The Hermetica, The Lost Wisdom of the Pharaohs* [Judy Piatkus, London, 1998] pg. 37, *The Initiation of Hermes*; Apocryphal Acts of John; Mizra Khan, *Ansari*; and Exodus, 3:14. Information on *Coming Out of Coma*, Nabis' Brain Injury Information Line: http://www.abihelp.org. Data on *Wars and Genocides of the 20th Century* by Piero Scaruffi, also comes from Internet, http://scaruffi.com/politcs/massacre.html. My profound thanks to my publisher and all my other sources.

Sincerely,

Stan J.S. Law

INHOUSEPRESS, MONTREAL, CANADA
http://www.inhousepress.ca